PRAISE FOR

THE MOUNTAIN KING

"Superb. This crackerjack page-turner will keep readers up late."
—*Publishers Weekly* (starred review)

"Unsettling. De la Motte had me hooked from the very first page."
—Kyle Mills, *New York Times* bestselling author of *Code Red*

"A masterful thriller that succeeds on all levels: absorbing, deftly plotted, bone-chilling."
—Andrew Gross, *New York Times* bestselling author of *The Fifth Column*

"*The Mountain King* is Nordic crime fiction at its best: addictive, eerie and hauntingly atmospheric (fans of *The Girl with the Dragon Tattoo* will devour it). Leonore Asker, and the wonderfully named 'Department of Lost Souls,' are fascinating and unpredictable. This is the new series you need in your life. EXCEPTIONAL."
—Will Dean, bestselling author of *The Last Thing to Burn*

"The twisty, spine-tingling mystery that unfolds is creepy and sinister, laced with a touch of dark Scandinavian folklore."
—Willy Williams, *firstCLUE*

ALSO BY ANDERS DE LA MOTTE

THE
MOUNTAIN KING

A NOVEL

THE ASKER SERIES · PART I

Anders de la Motte

Translated by Alex Fleming

EMILY BESTLER BOOKS

ATRIA

NEW YORK   LONDON   TORONTO   SYDNEY   NEW DELHI

An Imprint of Simon & Schuster, LLC
1230 Avenue of the Americas
New York, NY 10020

First Emily Bestler Books/Atria Paperback edition December 2024

EMILY BESTLER BOOKS/ATRIA PAPERBACK and colophon are trademarks of Simon & Schuster, LLC

Simon & Schuster: Celebrating 100 Years of Publishing in 2024

For information about special discounts for bulk purchases, please contact Simon & Schuster Special Sales at 1-866-506-1949 or business@simonandschuster.com.

The Simon & Schuster Speakers Bureau can bring authors to your live event. For more information or to book an event, contact the Simon & Schuster Speakers Bureau at 1-866-248-3049 or visit our website at www.simonspeakers.com.

Interior design by Esther Paradelo

Manufactured in the United States of America

1 3 5 7 9 10 8 6 4 2

Library of Congress Control Number: 2023944592

ISBN 978-1-6680-3081-3
ISBN 978-1-6680-3082-0 (pbk)
ISBN 978-1-6680-3083-7 (ebook)

THE MOUNTAIN KING

One spring evening when he was eight years old he ran away.

One second he was playing with some older kids in the forest, the next he was gone.

All the locals desperately searched for him through the darkness, rain, and cold. Called his name time and again, their ever-hoarser voices echoing between the spruce crowns. But it was as though the earth had swallowed him up.

Then, just after dawn, when all hope was fading, he was found in a crevice in a rock face, burning up with fever and soaked to the skin.

He neither cried nor laughed at being rescued, just stared blankly into space. Couldn't speak of what had happened to him. Didn't recognize his own parents.

Or at least that was how it was told to him.

He doesn't actually remember any of it, other than in the way one remembers an old fairy tale. A story you hear so often it almost feels real.

But only almost.

Events after the incident, however, feel all the clearer for it.

The scratchy hospital sheets, people in white with compassionate smiles and soft-spoken voices. The intense headaches, the fever dreams from which he would wake drenched with sweat, his heart pounding. Dreams of dark, damp places deep in the mountain; of steel doors and chains, icy terror and searing pain. It would take several weeks before his meningitis cleared and he was allowed to go home.

He felt like a stranger. Needed his mother's help to find his own bedroom. Asked her at least a hundred times if he really lived there, after all.

It was only much later that he realized how it was all connected. The reason why he couldn't remember any of his childhood before that night. Why his head was filled with twisted thoughts and dark desires.

He was a changeling.

Someone who had taken the place of the little boy who ran away.

A creature born of pain and fever dreams who outwardly resembled a human, but who in actual fact was a monster.

This is how his story begins.

FRIDAY

SMILLA

"There it is!"

He runs ahead of her through the thickets, and Smilla struggles to keep up. They have walked at least a mile from the almost impassable logging road where they parked the car. The forest around them is filled with funereal blue conifers, interrupted now and then by deciduous saplings in shimmering October golds. Here and there sprawling brambles with blood-red stems that latch onto clothes and stab the skin.

"Wait!" she cries.

The steep uphill slope and blanket of leaves make the ground slippery underfoot. She loses her footing, lands on her knees. The camera strap tugs at her neck. Her system camera is heavy, but it takes far and away the best photos in weak light.

She scrambles back to her feet. Brushes the wet leaves from her knees. He has already disappeared into the thicket.

What was it he saw?

"MM!" she calls out. It's what he wants her to call him, though he has such a beautiful name. Malik Mansur. As soft as his eyes.

Officially he isn't actually her boyfriend anymore. They broke up back at the start of summer, not that either of them lets on about that. Both tiptoe around the fact that she'll be going back to Paris soon.

In summer, after she ended things, he got jealous, angry, wrote nasty messages. But now things are back to how they used to be. In most ways, at least.

MM has matured in these four months, grown more manly, exciting.

Even a little dangerous.

The sex is better, too. Much better.

Perhaps he has been seeing someone else?

She has seen small hints of it, but hasn't wanted to ask.

It's easier that way.

"Smilla!" His voice comes from inside the thickets.

She continues upward. Is more careful where she sets her feet.

The ground levels off at the top of the peak. There must be a hundred and fifty feet of rock beneath them, perhaps even more.

"Smilla!"

MM pops up right in front of her, his face glowing in that way she likes.

"There it is!"

The construction he is pointing at is so low and overgrown it's almost invisible.

Like a grim concrete kiosk, only with wire cages where the windows should be. The cages are filled with densely packed rocks. They remind her of the garden walls at her summer house in Falsterbo. She raises her camera, reels off a few shots.

"Gabions," says MM, patting one of the cages. "This bunker is the upper air inlet for the base, just like he said." His voice is both tense and excited.

He pulls her around the side of the building.

In their time apart he has become even more obsessed with urban exploration. That probably has something to do with a university module that he is taking. The Architecture of Decay. Either way, he can't stop talking about it—or his amazing teacher, Martin Hill.

Perhaps that's where MM met this new friend he keeps talking about—though on that question he is much cagier.

Around the back of the concrete bunker the bedrock cleaves up through the earth. Forms giant outcrops with moss-dappled backs. Through the camera lens they look almost alive. Hunkering, waiting.

She shudders, thinks of how far they are from the car. How hard it would be to get back there if anything were to happen.

She pats her jacket pocket. Her phone is there, just where she left it. But it isn't on.

MM made sure they both turned their phones off together, all the way back at the gas station. He had promised his friend that they would.

Because this whole explore is super-secret, he said. *Unique*.

"Here, look!" MM points at the back wall of the bunker. A piece of the wall is jutting out, revealing a sliver of darkness in the opening.

"The door's open, just like he promised."

Smilla tries to share his excitement.

And yet she can't shake her unease.

"What did you say your friend's name was?" she asks.

"Who, Berg?"

"Berg? Is that actually his name?"

He shrugs.

"And you've only known each other a few months," she goes on, "but he just happened to give you this incredible tip about the tunnel? The cave rain?"

MM doesn't hear the question, either that or he just ignores it. He's too busy inspecting the door. A blast door made of concrete, must be more than a foot thick. Almost melts into the wall.

The opening is narrow, and for a moment she hopes it will be too small for them to pass.

But as usual MM won't be deterred. He pulls off his backpack and squeezes in.

"Come on, there's space for you, too!"

She hesitates for a second or two.

Her computer at home is full of photos from other expeditions. Closed factories, abandoned houses, forgotten places just like this.

But no cave rain. That only occurs in a handful of underground sites, where the conditions are so special that the humidity forms visible droplets of moisture in the air. She would dearly love to get a shot of some cave rain, he knows that. Still, she hesitates.

They aren't rookie urban explorers; they have phones, flashlights, and spare batteries to hand. Even so, something about this place—the forest, the elevation, the hunkering outcrops and heavy concrete door—makes her ill at ease.

And then that friend. Berg.

A perfectly normal Swedish surname.

Yet the word's meanings all chime in her head.

Berg. Hill, mountain. Rock.

She glances back at the outcrops. They remind her of trolls from an old book of folktales. Primeval mountain creatures. Evil.

"Just get in!"

MM reaches out to her through the opening. His voice is impatient now, the face looming in the darkness tense.

Still, she hesitates. Wants above all to turn around and head back to the car. Turn on her phone and call someone—her mom, dad, sister, anyone—just to hear another voice. Tell them where she is. That she wants to go home, now—right now.

But then MM's face lights up. He cracks that smile that she has missed for so long, the one that always makes her melt.

"Come on, Smilla," he says softly.

She resists for another second.

Then takes his hand and lets him pull her through the gap in the door.

The space inside is small. Walls, floor, ceiling, everything in gray concrete.

On the inside of the concrete door sits a large handwheel in a rusty brown metal, to operate the lock mechanism. Something about the handwheel and lock bothers her, amplifies her unease.

MM doesn't seem to notice.

"See?" he says excitedly, sweeping his flashlight around the walls. "No graffiti. That means basically no one can have been here. The bottom entrance is sealed—this is the only way in."

Smilla gives a steely nod.

From a hole in the middle of the floor rises the frame of a gray caged ladder.

She shines her flashlight down the hole.

A damp waft of air hits her from below. Brings with it scents of water, stone, metal. The bedrock's breath. She came across the expression once on an urban exploration forum somewhere, and at the time she found the thought beautiful. As if the mountain itself were a living being. But now, as the smell hits her from the depths, that prospect feels less appealing. A few feet below, her flashlight lights up a similar room with another hole in the floor, through which the ladder leads farther into the darkness.

"Come on."

MM hangs his flashlight from a strap around his neck, takes hold of the top rung, and starts climbing down.

She pauses again. Glances back at the door. There's something about that giant handwheel that she just can't put her finger on. Something that deepens her anxiety.

But MM will soon be down in the next room, and she can't let him go on alone.

She steps onto the ladder and follows him.

The rungs are cold and coarse, the metal speckled brown where the rust has eaten through its galvanized surface.

Her heart is beating ever faster.

MM hardly stops to look around the second room, just shines the flashlight around and then moves on. Rock walls now, no concrete. A little bigger than the bunker, but still completely bare. MM is already on his way down the ladder again, through the next hole in the floor and deeper into the darkness.

The mountain is silent; the only sounds to be heard are those of their movements and panting breath.

A third room, slightly bigger still. Nothing in here causes MM to stop, either. The bedrock's breath is getting all the sharper. Her camera smacks into the ladder, and she has to slide it around to her back.

"MM, hold up!"

He stops short, just a few feet below her.

"What is it?"

"Nothing, can we just take a breather? We're going so fast! Hardly have a chance to look around."

"But we're almost in the tunnel now. I can see the bottom."

He doesn't wait for a reply, just keeps on descending.

She has no choice but to follow him.

The caged ladder ends halfway between ceiling and floor in the fourth room, forcing them to carefully lower themselves down the final feet.

"They've sawn off the ladder," says MM while helping her down. "Must be to stop people from getting into the tunnel."

Smilla exhales deeply. They won't get any farther, which comes as both a relief and a disappointment. She looks around. The fourth room is perhaps three times the size of the original bunker, and the jagged bedrock walls are dripping with moisture.

"Look."

MM shines his flashlight at the hole in the floor through which the ladder should have continued.

Two shiny rails that she didn't initially notice rise up a little way out of the hole. It takes Smilla a second or two to realize what they are: another ladder, a much newer one, made of aluminium.

Her unease is back.

"Wait!" she says again, but MM is already on his way down.

Is out of sight before she even reaches the ladder.

"MM, wait!" But he doesn't listen.

The bedrock's breath is now so intense and so moist that she has to wipe it off her skin with the back of her hand.

"Wow!" he calls out. "Hurry, you've got to see this."

The aluminium ladder is perhaps fifteen feet long, and ends in a puddle of water on a floor of sharp crushed rock.

This space is bigger than the others. Stones and rusty, twisted metal lie strewn around the floor. At the end of the space is a doorway that leads to a passage through which the bedrock's wet breath courses, hitting her on its way up through the hole in the ceiling.

MM is already through the passage. She can see his flashlight flitting around on the other side. His voice echoes excitedly:

"Come on, Smilla, hurry."

The passage slopes down steeply, and with the gradient and rock floor she almost stumbles into the next space.

She gasps. All of a sudden it is as though her hesitancy and anxiety are no more.

"Well?" he says with another one of those smiles that she loves.

"It's incredible," she gushes.

The train tunnel that they had expected to find is in fact an enormous, oblong cave. It must be almost three hundred feet long, and ends in a massive stone gateway that looms on the edge of their flashlight beams.

The ceiling is at least thirty feet high. The walls are a mixture of concrete and raw bedrock, with slender rivulets of water weaving their way down. The floor is a shallow pool, its surface broken by railway tracks that rise a few inches out of the water at the end where Smilla and MM are standing, but disappear toward the gateway where the water is deeper.

Here and there, stones that have probably fallen from the ceiling and walls peer out from over the surface of the black pool. Along the right-hand side of the cave runs a loading bay with two rusty-brown steel doors leading off it. But it is neither the doors, the railway tracks, nor the gateway that have caught her attention—but the air.

The updraft from the passage through which they came is so strong that it sends cold, damp air whirling around the cave, forming small, but fully visible, droplets of water in the beams from their flashlights.

"Cave rain," Smilla says in awe.

"Told you," MM replies with a smirk. "Berg keeps his promises." Smilla puts her flashlight down on a ledge and starts taking photos.

"Shine your flashlight there," she tells MM. "Get up on the loading bay."

She takes photos, instructs him on where to point the flashlights.

After a while he tires of playing photographer's assistant and starts inspecting the metal doors by the loading bay.

Smilla goes on taking photos. The light is weak, and she has to do some maneuvering with her flashlight and adjust her camera settings to get the images to come out the way she wants them.

She plans to enlarge them, maybe hang one on her bedroom wall in Paris.

A choked sound cuts her off.

It sounds like a cry.

She looks around for MM, but he isn't there.

Only now does she notice that the left-hand steel door on the loading bay is open.

"MM?" Her voice echoes through the cave. "Malik?"

No reply. She shudders, not only from the cold.

The unease from before is back, twice as intense this time.

She stares at the open door, the darkness lurking just beyond the threshold.

And suddenly she realizes what it was that bothered her back up in the bunker.

The concrete door that they had crept through had a large hand-wheel on the inside.

But on the outside its surface was completely smooth.

Which means that whoever had opened it did so from the inside. Just a crack, just wide enough for someone to get inside. Like bait.

And that name.

Berg. Hill, mountain. Rock.

The flight impulse comes from nowhere, like an icy jolt to her body. Is magnified by the compact darkness there beyond the steel door, makes her heart start to pound.

She should get out of here, now.

Run back to the ladders and climb toward the light, as fast as she can.

Part of her wants nothing more.

But another, more pragmatic part tells her that MM could be hurt. That he could be lying there, just inside the door, in need of her help. That every second she spends wavering could be crucial.

"MM!" she cries again.

The echo hovers unanswered in the cave for a few seconds, then falls flat.

She takes out her phone and turns it on, which is obviously stupid. A reflex that costs her precious seconds, only to confirm that she has no signal down here in the belly of the mountain.

She takes a deep breath, puts her phone away, and collects herself.

Then slowly makes her way toward the dark doorway.

A faint smell wafts through the doors. A musty smell, one she didn't pick up on before. As though the bedrock's breath has shifted. Become thicker, more raw.

The smell scares her. Makes her even more sure.

This is a monstrous place.

An evil place.

But she has no choice but to go on.

Into the darkness.

MONDAY

ASKER

Leo Asker wakes up with a creeping feeling in her bones. A sort of premonition, a warning, that something is about to hit her.

Something big, for which she has had no chance to prepare.

It may have something to do with the new case.

A young couple missing since Friday, vanished without the slightest trace.

But she has run similar investigations before without this kind of doomsday feeling.

Even after one hundred push-ups and as many sit-ups on her bedroom floor, the feeling refuses to subside. If anything it is reinforced by the gray weather and darkness outside.

It's still October, and the trees in the park bear their autumn hues. Normally she likes this time of year.

Fresh air, geese flying in Vs against a bright blue sky.

But the chill and damp mists on offer this morning echo the feeling in her gut, a warning of what is to come.

Winter in Skåne is a mix of gales and biting rains that feel as though they cut through the soul. She hates winter, hates the cold.

Has already had enough of it to last a lifetime.

One must steel oneself, as Prepper Per used to say. *Discomfort and pain are just laziness leaving the body.*

That he should come to mind on a day like this is no surprise. Doomsday feelings were always Per's thing. His lifeblood.

The house isn't hers; she's housesitting for a family who are abroad. Lives in the guestroom. One of the guestrooms.

It's an old, flashy pad; the renovation alone cost millions.

Copper roofing, balconies, herringbone floors and moldings.

Panoramic windows with lake views.

Asker is rarely here. She comes home late, goes out early. It's how she prefers things.

She takes a scalding-hot steam shower, puts on some jeans, a shirt, and a blazer. Then downs an espresso over the marble worktop in the enormous kitchen while pulling up Smilla Holst's Instagram account.

Still no updates to either her or her boyfriend's accounts. Only that selfie from Friday, the last sign of either of them.

It was Smilla's family who raised the alarm on Saturday night, when she hadn't picked up the phone in over twenty-four hours. A police investigation was opened almost immediately, which is unusual when it comes to missing people.

But all of Malmö knows who the Holst family are. The sort of wealth they represent. The power.

Despite the coffee, the sense of foreboding clings on. Gradually turns to a pounding headache. She knocks back two aspirin, then locks up and sets the alarm. Puts on her headphones, pulls up the hood on her jacket, and lets the music clear her mind of Prepper Per and everything else he brings.

"Hello, Leo!" exclaims the dog-walking grandpa as she passes him on her way to the train. "Monday again! New week, new opportunities!"

Asker doesn't hear him, but reads the words on his lips. One of the many random talents she has Prepper Per to thank for. Though in this case lip-reading isn't any great feat. The man has only about four stock greetings, and this one is number three.

Asker forces a polite smile and a wave, doesn't stop to chat even though he does, just points at her wrist as if to say she's in a hurry. The grandpa is a widower, lives in the former gatekeeper's lodge at the end of the drive, which makes him her closest neighbor.

He's the sort of man who doesn't know how to appreciate solitude, instead fights it tooth and nail through idle chitchat with strangers.

It's seven a.m. when she reaches the station. Sunrise is still a while away, and the platform is half-empty. The mist dampens the squeal of the train's brakes.

As soon as she steps onto the train and pulls down her hood she catches a whiff of cigarette smoke.

The source of the stink: a long-haired man in a leather jacket and ripped jeans. He is unshaven, has hoops in his ears, leather wristbands, and a tattoo that coils its way up his neck. Legs spread so wide you would think he had cacti growing in his crotch.

Besides the fact that he's brazenly puffing away, the man is obviously drunk. Either he started unusually early, or—more likely—is on his way home after some overnight escapades at one of the more remote stations on the regional train line.

In front of the man stands a female train conductor aged around twenty, to whom he is loudly proclaiming that he'll smoke his bloody cigarette wherever the fuck he wants.

The other passengers are staring out of the windows or at their phones, pretending not to notice, since obviously they don't want to get involved. A Swedish national sport.

Asker turns off her music, tilts her head to one side, and scans the man from head to toe. He's around fifty, about six feet in height, 190 pounds—ten of which are excess. He's confident, used to a bit of boorishness being enough to get him what he wants. Thinks he's a prizefighter but definitely doesn't move like one.

"The train can't move until you put it out!" the conductor says, trying to keep her voice steady. The man detects her fear, savors it.

"Blow me," he sneers, blowing smoke in her face.

Asker sighs. Pulls her headphones down and walks over.

"Put that out." She shows her police badge.

The man's eyes narrow. She can see the cogs turning in his skull, read the inferences in his eyes as he sizes her up.

Police, early thirties, blonde. Short hair, unusually tall and broad-shouldered for a woman. Different-colored eyes—one blue, the other green. The condition is known as heterochromia, but of course this dude doesn't know that. Besides, he's too busy checking out her figure. She sees him add up his surface findings, pair them with his over-inflated ego and drunkenness, and arrive at the expected conclusion.

"Hey sweetcheeks!" He flashes a nicotine-yellow grin. "If only all cops looked like you." The man pats one of his thighs in invitation.

"But here's the thing, love, old Jocke's been round the block a few times, so if he's going to have to put out his fag, then you might as well call for backup right now. Or else you can just sit pretty till he's done." He lifts his cigarette to take another drag. Winks at her as he does.

It isn't the underestimation that annoys her most, or Jocke's stale view of women, but the fact that he talks about himself in the third person.

Besides, she has a headache, which lowers her already-low threshold for assholery.

Without the slightest warning, she bats Jocke's cigarette away. Grabs one of his ringed ears and gives it a good pinch.

His body reacts to the pain long before his brain, instinctively doing all it can to relieve it. Before Third-Person Jocke even knows it, he's up out of his seat and staggering through the carriage, bent forward with one of his wrists locked behind his back.

"What the fu . . ." is all he can splutter before his legs are kicked out from under him and he nosedives onto the rainy platform in a humiliating bellyflop.

A few of the sleepy passengers fumble around with the cameras on their phones, but it's too late.

Out on the platform Jocke scrambles to his feet. His face is purple, his fists clenched. Asker stands in the door and studies him.

He has two options: he can either try to restore his wounded pride through violence, or swallow his frustration and pretend this infuriating incident never happened.

She raises her eyebrows in a *well?* to hurry along his decision.

Jocke is still hesitating. He clenches and opens his fists, his jaw, too. Tries to stare himself to a decision, but now that his self-confidence has taken a beating, her two-toned eyes make him even more unsure. She can see the questions in his face.

What is she; who is she; and how can he deal with her?

Before Jocke can make up his mind, the doors glide shut and the train pulls softly away. He plucks up his courage, runs up and bangs on the window. Shouts something idiotic to save a shred of self-esteem, before he and the platform disappear into the gray haze.

Asker takes a seat and puts her headphones back on.

The cellphones around her lower in disappointment.

"Thanks," mumbles the conductor, who gets a nod in response.

The young woman looks as though she wants to say something more.

But Asker has already put on her music and turned away.

ASKER

Malmö was first built on a sandbank, sandwiched between marsh and sea. Its situation was practical rather than strategic, having to do with the herring fishery and the commerce that that brought with it.

In the seventeenth century, when Skåne changed hands from Denmark to Sweden, Malmö became a border city. It was severed from the surrounding wetlands by bastions and a long moat that fed out into the sea, transforming the city into a fortified island that was almost impossible to capture.

Two hundred years later the city started to grow in earnest. The fortifications were torn down, and the moat was turned into a canal.

The small lakes and wetlands that had once surrounded the city were drained and rebuilt as new city districts. Rörsjöstaden, where the police headquarters are situated, is one such district.

The headquarters lie at the intersection of Exercisgatan and Drottninggatan, with a view over the spot where the canal turns northwest on its way back to sea.

In recent years the site has been further bolstered with a detention center, district court, and outposts for the Prosecution and Economic Crimes authorities respectively, forming one enormous justice center. Perhaps it is because the ground it stands on was once marsh and seafloor that the cold and damp occasionally seep their way through the building's heavy doors and airlock insulation. Especially on days like this, when the wind kicks up off the sea.

The Serious Crime Command is located on the sixth and top floor of police HQ, with a view over rooftops and water. Glass walls, big-screen displays, soft lighting. Dark carpets that absorb the sounds of the phone signals pulsating through the air. No expense spared; even the coffee machine in the airy kitchen is first-rate.

Asker has worked at Serious Crime for almost four years now, which is less time than most, but she has already progressed to head of section. In a matter of years she expects to be running the entire command. Not all of her colleagues relish this thought.

She stands at the front of the state-of-the-art incident room. Unlike the rest of the department, this room has no windows onto the outside world, but a glass wall that overlooks the large internal atrium running straight down through the center of the building.

Before her sit fifteen of her police colleagues in rows. Several are new faces, loaned in from other departments, which surprises her a little.

At one minute to nine the department chief enters and takes a seat on the back row. Vesna Rodic is between forty and fifty, round of build and a head shorter than Asker. Normally Rodic isn't the sort of manager to get involved in investigations like these, which is one of the things Asker likes about her.

Asker prepares to start the presentation, stands up tall and clears her throat.

"Good morning, everyone! For those of you who are new, I'm Detective Inspector Asker and I'm head of section here at Serious Crime. Today's case involves two missing people, which we are treating as a suspected kidnapping."

She clicks the remote control, which brings up the selfie of the two missing youngsters on the giant screen behind her.

"The people we are looking for are Smilla Holst and Malik Mansur. They were reported missing by Smilla's parents on Saturday night, and the last sign of them was a social media post from Friday morning, which means they have now been missing around three days."

She lists the known facts, mostly for the new arrivals.

"Both of their phones have been switched off since Friday, but we are of course keeping an eye on them in case they are turned on again. We have requested all saved operator data, but as most of you know that process tends to be . . ."

Short pause.

". . . challenging," she adds with a caustic smile. "Based on previous experience I would expect us not to have a response until toward the end of the week."

She waits for the collective groan.

Next image, only Smilla this time. She is beautiful: pale skin, curly blond hair, blue eyes. On her nose a few lingering freckles that will surely be gone in a few years. The sort of unspoiled beauty that only exists between seventeen and twenty.

"Smilla Holst, nineteen years of age," Asker goes on. "Graduated from high school in spring, now studying in Paris. Currently home for reading week. Smilla is registered at her parents' address in Limhamn. She's conscientious, ambitious, and has good grades. Her parents claim they have a very good relationship, and that there's no reason why she would cut contact voluntarily."

"Which is exactly what everyone says when they don't want to admit they're bad parents who don't keep track of their kids."

The man who has interrupted Asker is Johan Eskilsson, who for some inexplicable reason goes by the name Eskil and not Johan.

He is a year or two older than her, and half an inch shorter, which annoys him, since he's the sort of man who would get annoyed by such things.

As always, Eskil's hair is neatly trimmed and his face freshly shaven, and he smells of both aftershave and the hand cream he bought at his favorite influencer's recommendation. The same cool cat who inspired his haircut, shirt, tie knot, thumb ring, and watch—and perhaps even the privately leased sports car that Eskil drives between home and Pilates classes.

Eskil the Detective—as he calls himself on Tinder—is a very good cop. At least in his own humble opinion.

He has plenty of other opinions, too. One of them being that he should be head of section and not Asker.

Asker ignores Eskil's comment and clicks up another slide.

It shows a young man with curly dark hair, pronounced features, and velvet eyes. He, too, looks almost impossibly handsome.

"Malik Mansur, known as MM, twenty-one years of age. Lives in an apartment in Värnhem, is a second-year architecture student at Lund University. He is also described by his parents as conscientious—"

"Well . . . ," Eskil scoffs, to the approval of the colleagues around him. He is unusually chipper this morning. Has placed himself right at the front, surrounded by his usual stooges. Some of the more bro-ish colleagues who would rather have a leader with balls. In the literal, not metaphorical sense.

"What Eskil here is so keen to point out is that Mansur has a few hits in our databases," says Asker. "A summary fine relating to a minor drug offense from a few years ago, and some intelligence notes from the summer about him being a passenger in a car used by a hardened Malmö criminal."

"Exactly." Eskil nods smugly. "And if you ask me that's the connection we should be focusing on."

Asker has had enough.

"But I didn't ask you, Eskil," she says. "And until I do, I would appreciate it if you could spare us your invaluable insights."

She fixes her two-tone gaze on him. He looks around shiftily for backup, but his yes-men and the rest of the room avoid eye contact. Know just as well as Asker does that his balls are more physical than metaphorical.

"Well excuse me," he mutters.

Asker changes the slide again. The same one she started with.

"This selfie, posted on Smilla's Instagram account on Friday morning, is, as mentioned, our last trace of the two of them, and also the closest we can come to an actual description."

The young people are standing cheek-to-cheek, gazing happily into the camera. The clothes that are visible look practical: turtlenecks and waterproof jackets—his black, hers turquoise. Around Smilla's neck hangs a camera strap, and behind them the hood of Malik's black car is visible.

Off on new adventures reads the caption, followed by *#newadventures* and *#love*.

"Smilla and Malik have been together a few years," Asker goes on. "Met at a mutual friend's party. According to her sister they broke up over the summer, just before Smilla moved to Paris to study, but they stayed in touch. Judging by this picture their relationship was back on."

She clicks again. Brings up images of two humorless-looking men who appear to be father and son.

"Smilla's father, Tomas Holst, who you see on the left here, is CEO of Arkadia Holdings. Arkadia was founded by Smilla's grandfather Eric Holst, on the right, who is still its principal owner and chairman of the board. The reason why I mention this . . ."

She gives Eskil a stern look so that he won't try to interrupt her with yet another inane comment, but fortunately he seems to have learned his lesson.

". . . is that the Holst clan is one of the richest and best-known families in Malmö. They are the primary sponsors of pretty much every sports club. So we can't rule out this disappearance having some sort of ransom motive, though I'd like to note that as it stands we have received no ransom demands. We should therefore take care not to wed ourselves to any particular theories."

Eskil whispers something to the woman beside him and both share a smirk, but whatever he says it's nothing he wants to air publicly.

"In conclusion, we have sent out descriptions to every radio car under our jurisdiction and have also issued a notice for Malik Mansur's car, which you can also see in the picture. A black Golf GTI, personalized license place with the letters MM."

Asker concludes the briefing by assigning tasks: to hold more detailed interviews with family members, request bank details, try to trace friends and classmates.

Once she has finished, she looks at Vesna Rodic to see if her manager has anything to add, but gets only a brief shake of the head in response.

"Then let's get going. Call me as soon as you have anything to report."

She thanks them for their time and heads toward her office. Eskil and his yes-men stay put, whispering excitedly over his phone screen. Something about their body language and self-satisfied smiles concerns her, amplifies the sense of foreboding that lingers on in her gut. As though something is afoot, a threat she hasn't conceived of.

Asker gets a cup of coffee, sits down at her desk, and pulls up Smilla's Instagram account on her computer screen. Malik has an account, too, of course, but like his other social media accounts, it hasn't been updated in a long time.

Smilla, however, is particularly active.

The last six months or so are full of images from Paris: sights, university auditoriums, the odd nightclub. Smilla is constantly surrounded by people, and the comments fields are brimming with emojis and joie de vivre. All the way up to the image from Friday morning.

After which they vanish. Two well-mannered Gen-Zers who grew up with phones in their hands. Silence. It doesn't bode well.

Asker massages her temples. The headache and doomsday feeling still won't pass.

Her phone starts to buzz.

Would you mind popping into my office.

She opens the top drawer of her desk, where she keeps her painkillers. Washes two down with coffee before she gets up and leaves the room.

Vesna Rodic's office is twice the size of Asker's, in a corner of the building. Her walls are full of diplomas, award flags, and group photos. If you start at one corner and work your way to the other, you can chart her entire policing career. Every rung on the ladder so far.

Rodic has headed up Serious Crime for five years, and is ambitious, well liked, and capable. In recent months a rumor has started circulating that she is on her way to a promotion.

"Hi, Leo," she says in her usual low-key way. "Shut the door and take a seat."

"Is this about Eskil?" Asker asks while sitting down. "You know what he's like, he and his clique need to be kept on a short lead. He's a follower, not a leader. Only problem is he doesn't see that himself."

Rodic shakes her head wearily.

"You know what I've told you about bulldozing people in public. That's not how you get respect."

"Isn't it?" Asker raises an eyebrow. "There must be fifty male managers in this building who beg to differ. *Strong leaders who rule with an iron fist.*"

She emphasizes the last statement with ironic air quotes, which Prepper Per would no doubt have hated.

Her boss sighs.

"We've been through this a thousand times, Leo. You're a good detective. Very good, even. But if you're going to progress in your career—sit in this chair, for example . . ."

She pauses, gives Asker a meaningful look.

". . . then you need to get better at dealing with people who don't have your capabilities, which essentially means the rest of us mere mortals."

Rodic leans in over her desk.

"And sometimes you need to know when to just swim with the tide and not make waves. Which brings me to the real reason for this conversation: the Smilla Holst case."

"Yes?"

"Where are we? What do we know?"

Asker shrugs.

"You were at the briefing. It's early days, still a lot of question marks. Some phone traffic would definitely help things along, but as usual it's slow progress there. In the meantime we're working the case. Trying to piece it all together."

"Is it a kidnapping, do you think?"

"Are you asking me what my gut feeling is?"

"Yes."

Asker pauses as if to gather her thoughts, which she doesn't actually need to do.

"Kidnappers usually want to get their hands on the money as soon as possible. The longer they drag things out, the greater the risk of being caught. Or getting cold feet or just starting to feel sorry for the hostage. We've already gone three days without any demands. So I'm dubious."

"OK, so if it's not a kidnapping then. What's happened?"

"I don't know yet. But I think it's important that we keep all our doors open."

"The parents, what are they saying?"

"We've only spoken by phone. I have a meeting with them in an hour."

"Your impression?"

Asker pulls a face.

"The father is serious and to the point. Wants facts, answers, results, preferably yesterday."

"And the mother?"

"She's more cautious and emotional. Used to keeping in the background."

Rodic fidgets uncomfortably.

Asker waits. There's more, she can tell. Something important that this entire conversation has been dancing around so far.

"The commissioner called," says Rodic.

"He did?" Asker sits up straighter in her chair.

"Apparently the Holst family's lawyer has been in touch. Was pulling a bunch of strings."

Something about the word *lawyer*, combined with Rodic's body language, makes Asker immediately twig.

"Lissander and Partners," Rodic confirms. "Your parents' firm."

"My mother and stepfather's," Asker corrects her.

"Right, yes. In any case, your mother has been in touch with the commissioner. Apparently they're old friends. She wanted to make sure we've allocated every possible resource."

"Hence all the new faces at the briefing," Asker remarks. "Isabel usually gets what she wants."

"Yes . . ." Rodic fidgets again, briefly. "Isabel will also be present at the meeting with the family later today, so it's best that I take it."

"Why?" Asker loves this question. Can repeat it endlessly.

"To avoid a needless conflict of interests."

"Are you kicking me off my own case?"

"Formally speaking this is my case, as you know," Rodic says dryly. "I'm in charge of all preliminary investigations until the prosecutor steps in. And my assessment is that from now on I should handle all contact with the family."

Asker's instinct is to go on asking questions, as that's the way she works, but she checks herself. Rodic's body language says that there's something more she wants to get off her chest.

"One more thing."

Rodic takes a deep breath.

"The commissioner has decided to ask the National Operations Department for assistance. They're sending someone down from Stockholm tomorrow. A familiar face, in fact."

Another pause. Awkward, tense.

Far too tense.

Suddenly Asker realizes. The sense of foreboding that has been hanging over her all morning—the whispers after the briefing, the headaches, her boss's comments on not making waves—all of it falls into place, as the danger that she sensed suddenly comes into view. A gleaming, dazzling threat that's steaming straight toward her as she stands in the middle of the tunnel. A doomsday train that not even Prepper Per would have been able to prepare her for.

"Jonas Hellman," Asker says. Reads the response in her manager's face long before it reaches her mouth.

Damn it!

THE MOUNTAIN KING

Not long after he was discharged from the hospital he received an unexpected gift.

His stepfather was a gruff man, and the two normally avoided each other as much as possible. But on that early summer evening he came up to him in the garden behind their desolate house.

"Here," he said, holding up a glass jar.

Inside it fluttered a butterfly.

Its wings were rust-red, with small blue dots running along the white outer edge.

"A mourning cloak," his stepfather went on. "I used to catch butterflies as a kid," he added, with a voice that sounded almost soft.

He smiled in response, or at least he thinks he did. Something about the whole situation—not just the beautiful butterfly inside the glass, but also this unexpected confidence from the otherwise so morose man—pleased him.

"Here, I'll show you how to take care of it."

To his delight, his stepfather took him down into his basement workshop. A place that was normally off-limits.

On the walls hung tools in arrow-straight rows. The air smelled of paint, glue, and white spirit. But beneath these scents lay something else, too. A dull, damp tinge that felt strangely familiar. Basement; rock; earth.

In the middle of the room stood a workbench with a model landscape. Small houses and figures made of plastic—some of them already painted, others on the way. A miniature world slowly coming to life that captured his imagination. Intrigued, he reached out to touch the landscape, wanting to experience it with his fingers and not just with his eyes.

"That's no toy!" his stepfather grumbled, which made him pull his hand back in fear.

"Here, look." His stepfather took down a hammer and a sharp awl from the wall and then punched six small holes into the lid of the jar.

"There, now the butterfly will get some air," the man said. He then explained to him that he should drop sugar water through the holes.

"You can keep it for one week," he said. "But after that you have to open the lid. Without hope nothing survives long."

He did just as his stepfather said. At least to begin with.

Kept the butterfly jar in his room, fed it. Could sit there for hours just gazing at it. Enjoying its colors, its details, its movements.

The sound of the paper-thin wings beating against the glass.

But he also enjoyed the power.

The dominion over that beautiful, living creature so desperately trying to escape. He wanted to see more, get even closer. Feel what the butterfly felt.

After a week he should have opened the lid and set the butterfly free. But he couldn't bring himself to do it.

The butterfly was his now. His property, one he would never relinquish.

After twelve days the Camberwell beauty lay motionless at the bottom of the jar.

Its wings shiny with the sugar water that it had stopped drinking the moment it lost hope.

Even in death it was extraordinarily beautiful.

And still his.

SMILLA

Smilla wakes up mid-breath.

Her head is pounding, her mouth tastes of metal, and the nausea rises in her throat. Her abdomen is tight from needing to pee.

She tries to open her eyes to orient herself. Realizes after a second or two that they are already open.

But everything is dark. So dark that she can't even see her own hands, not even when she holds them up in front of her face.

"Hello!" she utters, though it's barely more than a whisper.

"Hello!" she tries again, a little louder. No reply. Just black silence.

Her heart starts to pound. Thunders against her eardrums, makes it impossible to think.

To breathe.

As though her rib cage is constricting with every breath. Stifling her from within.

She swallows, clamps her eyes shut. Slowly counts down from ten, just as she has learned. Takes deep breaths, one at a time, so that her brain gets the right mix of oxygen and carbon dioxide.

Three . . .

Two.

One.

The trick works. Her pulse slows, and the panic eases enough for her head to clear.

Where is she? How did she end up here?

Not long ago she and MM were in a cave. And then . . .

Then?

She remembers a scream, a dark doorway, a foul smell.

Fear.

Beyond that only muddled images.

And darkness.

One arm feels tight, her fingers brush against a Band-Aid on the inside of her elbow.

Has she been drugged? If so, how long?

And where is she?

Her pulse starts to race again.

She redoes her countdown.

Three . . .

Two.

One.

She has to try to compose herself.

Back in spring, she and her older sister attended "hostage school," as they jokingly called it. The course was a Christmas present from Grandfather Eric. Both she and Helena had found it more than a little absurd. Over the top in some way.

But since no one ever refuses Grandfather Eric, they spent three days at a center out in the middle of nowhere. Told their boyfriends they were off on a spa weekend and turned the course into a secret in-joke that had given them plenty of laughs.

Now Smilla does all she can to try to remember what she learned.

First and foremost, she has to find out where she is.

Her hands cautiously grope around. She is lying on a bed, with a soft mattress and cushion underneath her and a scratchy blanket over her legs. At the head and to the right of the bed stand smooth concrete walls. On the other sides—empty space and darkness. She throws her legs over the edge and sits up.

The air is cool, but not cold. It smells like the deeper metro stations.

But she recognizes something else. The way her calls of hello just disappeared, swallowed up by a dull background hum that is almost audible if she listens very closely. And then the darkness, that oh so compact darkness that only exists in certain, special places.

Her heart starts to pound again.

She's underground.

Deep down inside the mountain.

Imprisoned.

The scream that she has tried to hold in ever since she woke up finally slips out. Hangs there in the air for a few short, piercing seconds, before being consumed by the darkness.

TUESDAY

ASKER

It is only five a.m., but Asker is already wide awake and dressed. She rarely sleeps more than four or five hours, even less when her mind is racing.

The grounds around the house are cloaked in darkness. Just a few points of light from the golf course on the other side of the lake. Yesterday's mist is gone, replaced by a light autumn drizzle.

She has set out the contents of the gray backpack on her bed.

All the objects are grouped in the right order: the flashlight, thin nylon rope, first-aid kit, and multi-tool for getting out.

The passport, credit card, wad of cash, and burner phone for getting away. Protein bars, underwear, socks, and a toiletry bag so she can stay on the move. She can see Prepper Per before her. Sees him tenderly ticking off the items.

Everything you need for a getaway, Leo. I've got it down to a T.
Two minutes, that's all it takes to disappear.

She has no idea why she perseveres with this ritual. Why she keeps the gray backpack in her wardrobe, regularly replaces the items with a limited lifespan.

Prepper Per has been out of her life a long time, but still the backpack remains. A constant reminder of what once was. As though, after all these years, she still hasn't quite managed to break free.

The coarse fabric is stained and full of patches. The stitches on the oldest are crooked, childish. With time they became all the straighter; more durable, more effective.

The last one she remembers well.

She was sixteen years old, about to go to high school.

Her and Per's last summer together, the summer that was almost her last.

Subconsciously she scratches her left forearm, then slowly packs up the contents again. Positions them all as he taught her. She can do it with her eyes closed.

Once she has finished, she returns the backpack to its spot at the back of the wardrobe and walks into the kitchen. Presses the espresso button on the hi-tech coffee machine.

Two minutes, and she could be gone forever.

Tempting, given what is to come.

She should have guessed it back when Hellman was transferred to Stockholm.

But she was so relieved to see the back of him that she made do. Assumed he was gone for good. That he would find other interests, never set foot in Skåne again.

Assumption is the mother of all fuckups, as Per would have said.

Then he would have forced her to do push-ups, scrub toilets, and take ice baths, or do some other unpleasant chore to atone for her mistake.

For Jonas Hellman was just that—a mistake.

It was Hellman who first recruited her to Serious Crime. Who taught her much of what she knows today.

Everyone likes Jonas Hellman.

He started flirting with her even before she got the job. It was exciting, she has to admit.

Even more exciting when he became her boss.

Hellman had an entire entourage of admirers at his constant beck and call. The few, the chosen, the special ones. And she was one of them.

The most special.

There was a time when she would have done almost anything for him. For six whole months they were completely wrapped up in each other. She still thinks about it from time to time. Maybe mostly about the sex.

Wild, unbridled, intoxicating.

Then, by chance, she bumped into him in town, with his wife and kids.

Of course she'd known they existed, but until that point she had somehow managed to block them out and pretended they weren't her problem.

They looked happy. A happy family that she was helping to destroy.

Self-discipline means never choosing the easy way out.

Another one of those small pearls of wisdom that Per loved to scatter.

Only in this case he was right.

So she ended things. Just like that, from one day to the next.

Ripped off that Band-Aid, sucked up all the discomfort and the pain, just as she had been taught. Stupidly believed that that would be enough. But the thing with people like Jonas—talented people who are used to success, to constant admiration and praise—is that, more often than not, they don't deal well with rejection.

Very badly, in fact.

She had known that long before Jonas came into her life.

She learned that truth in the hardest possible way.

She thinks of the backpack again.

Of Prepper Per.

Per Asker.

Her father.

The tattoo is on her inner forearm, extending from the inner crease of her elbow almost all the way down to her wrist. She had it done the day she turned eighteen, despite her mother's fierce protests.

But she needed to do it. Needed to remind herself of what she had been through. Of what it took to survive. One word, three syllables, ten letters, forever encased in her skin.

Enough to almost cover the pale, ragged scar beneath.

She follows the letters with her index finger. Reads the word aloud.

Resilience.

Jonas Hellman is going to come for her; she doesn't doubt that for one second.

And she has to be prepared.

ASKER

By around seven the rain has eased up. On the approach roads the traffic is at a slow crawl. The train is rammed with people all staring at their cellphones, and there isn't a seat to be found. The smells of perfume and aftershave mingle with those of paper-cup coffee and garlic breath. It all makes the autumn air feel that much fresher when the doors finally open at her stop.

Malik Mansur's apartment is a quick walk from the station.

His mother is waiting outside.

Forensics has already been there: have taken photos, scoured the place for bloodstains and other DNA. But Asker wants to form her own impressions.

Malik's mother, Hana, is around fifty. She is dressed in a suit with heavy makeup to hide the bags under her eyes. She speaks good Swedish, but with a clear accent.

"Malik loves Smilla very much," Hana says, without Asker having asked.

"He was born and raised here," she adds, as though that is somehow important. "A clever boy. Kind, good grades. He's going to be an architect."

Asker knows that Malik's mother is a dentist, and that his father retired early due to illness, both from Iraq. Malik is their only child.

"Loves Smilla very much," Hana repeats.

The apartment looks out over the churchyard of Sankt Pauli Kyrka. A caretaker on a ride-on mower is raking the paths and doesn't exactly appear to be in any rush. Little birds flap around behind the mower, nibbling at what the rake pulls up.

Asker looks around the living room. IKEA furniture, about as clean as you can expect of a student. On one wall hangs an enlarged photo of a derelict industrial building. Concrete, rusty steps, walls full of graffiti. Despite the decay there is something beautiful about the image.

"Smilla took the photo," says Hana. "She's good at photography. It was her birthday present to Malik. The lime factory in Limhamn. I think they went there together. Though maybe I shouldn't say that?"

She covers her mouth.

"Why not?"

"Because you're not allowed inside. What's the expression: out of limits?"

"Off-limits."

"Yes."

Hana appears to correct her inner lexicon.

"Does Malik often visit restricted sites?" Asker asks.

Hesitation, followed by a nod.

"Why?"

"He wants to be an architect. He's at university in Lund."

"Yes, you mentioned that. Do any of his courses have something to do with this pastime?"

"I don't know." She shrugs dejectedly, then lights up again, as though she has remembered something important.

"There's another one in the bedroom."

She leads the way, and eagerly shows Asker a photo hanging over the unmade bed. It is Smilla and Malik together.

He is wearing a tux, she a dress.

"Her graduation ball," Hana says proudly. "They looked so lovely."

She sobs, and for a brief moment Asker is afraid she's going to burst into tears. Instead she takes a deep breath, straightens her back.

"We don't understand it," she says. "None of this."

"Smilla broke up with Malik when she moved to Paris, didn't she?" Asker asks.

Hana nods.

"He was very sad."

"Angry?"

"Boys don't tell their mothers those things," Hana replies evasively. "But . . . yes, he was angry. I know that he wrote some stupid things to Smilla. But he regretted them and apologized. And when she came back everything was good again. See for yourself, she was staying here!"

Hana points at an open suitcase by one of the bedroom walls. Smilla's name on a luggage tag on the handle.

Her colleagues have already searched it, but Asker does the same anyway.

Underwear, T-shirts, a few nice tops, and a pair of jeans.

In a side pocket a jewelry box with a necklace.

"From Malik," says her mother. "He bought it for her just before she came home. He didn't have enough for it, had to borrow off me."

Asker holds up the necklace. A gold heart with the initials M and S. She takes a photo of it on her cellphone.

"We spoke to Smilla's parents a few times over the weekend," says Hana. "They were just as worried as we are. But since yesterday they stopped taking our calls. Do you know why?"

Asker avoids the question, or, rather, the answer. The Holst family's lawyer has probably advised against any further contact with the Mansurs, since they suspect Malik was involved in the disappearance. The lawyer in question also happens to be her own mother. But she can't say any of that.

Hana starts making the bed. She doesn't need to, of course, but the instinct to try to bring some kind of order to the inexplicable is hard to resist. Asker knows this from personal experience.

"Malik would never hurt Smilla," Hana mumbles while fiddling with the bedding. "Not on his life, never! He would rather die."

Asker doesn't know if the woman is talking to herself or to her.

But, judging by her comments, she seems to sense which way the wind is blowing.

"We're keeping our options open," says Asker, mostly because she feels she has to.

Hana turns away, puts her full focus on the bed.

Asker goes on looking around the room.

On the bedside table lies a well-thumbed book.

Forgotten Places and Their Stories.

The book contains images of roughly the same style as those on the walls, each accompanied by a few pages of text. In some places

Malik has folded down corners or made brief notes, as though that specific page was particularly interesting.

On the title page stands a handwritten inscription.

To my star student MM, with best regards, Martin Hill.

The name gives Asker a start.

She quickly turns to the author photo on the cover flap. Her heart has started beating a little harder. He is sixteen years older, and looks in much better health than she remembers him, but there's still no doubt about it. It's *her* Martin Hill.

What a strange coincidence.

THE MOUNTAIN KING

The summer when he was thirteen, a family moved into the house at the bottom of the hill. A young couple and their little baby.

He would mow their lawn. Sometimes they invited him in for something to eat or drink.

The parents seemed so happy. Their home was light and beautiful, filled with laughter and music, especially compared to the big, joyless house in which he lived.

Once he saw them dancing with each other. The window was part open, the sheer curtain within swaying faintly in the wind.

The father was wearing jeans and a T-shirt, the mother a white cotton dress with a light-blue pattern.

Their bodies close, their skin shiny with sweat. The man's hands on the woman's back, her hips. Farther in under her dress. She laughed, batted them away jokingly the first time. But not the second.

He stood rooted to the spot, unable to move.

His heart beat wildly in his chest, like butterfly wings on a glass jar, as he watched them through the window.

He stood there transfixed for several minutes, before he finally managed to break the spell and stumble back to the lawn and beyond, to the shelter of the forest. His body thrummed with excitement, desires he couldn't explain. Desires that tormented him. Sparked his fantasies.

Just like the butterfly in the glass jar, he wanted to see more.

Get closer. Feel what they felt.

The following week he returned. In the middle of the day, when he knew that no one would be home. The spare key was hanging on the back of a beam in the shed.

Once inside the house, he made straight for the spot in the living room where they had stood, his heart pounding.

Imagined that he was the father, moved his hands in the air just as the man had done. But the excitement soon faded.

So he sneaked upstairs, into their bedroom.

Carefully pulled out the drawers in their chest, opened their wardrobes. Handled the objects and garments that were their most private.

In her bedside table he found a packet of condoms.

Beneath them, underwear so small and transparent that it took him a long time to realize it belonged to an adult.

His heart pounded all the harder, his mouth was dry as a bone.

In the father's bedside table he found something even more unexpected.

A pistol.

He could tell from the smell of gun oil that the pistol was real. What's more, it was loaded. Why would someone keep a loaded gun by their bed?

His thoughts were rudely interrupted by the sound of a car coming up the drive. The staircase led straight to the front door, so he wouldn't be able to get out in time. But a quick glance through the window reassured him.

It wasn't their car arriving, but a pickup that he didn't recognize.

The driver, a thirty-something man in sunglasses, strode purposefully up to the front door.

He hid behind the curtain, held his breath.

The man with the sunglasses rang the doorbell impatiently. Once, twice.

Then moved on to banging on the door, calling out her name.

"Come out so I can talk to you!"

The door downstairs was locked, which was a relief.

The man called her name again, then started walking around the outside of the house.

Cautiously he followed him, watched from behind the upstairs curtains as the man tried to peer in through the windows below.

Soon the man was back at the front door. He took a step to one side and pulled down his zip. Stood and pissed on the beautiful roses right next to the front steps. Once he was done, the man did up his trousers, spat on the ground, and left.

He barely dared breathe until the pickup had driven away.

He thought about the pistol. Something told him it had something to do with the man in the pickup. That he had stumbled across a secret. That even happy people had something to hide. The thought made him giddy with excitement.

Made him want to take something with him.

A memento, a secret of his own.

He briefly considered stealing the pistol, but realized that that would be a bad idea. If he stole something big and important, they would know that someone had been here. Hide the spare key better, maybe even change the locks, and then he would never be able to come back. And he wanted to come back.

A pair of simple earrings on her dressing table caught his eye. If he took just one, she would think she had lost the other; that it had ended up on the floor, in the vacuum, down the drain. She would search for a while and then give up, since an earring was just an earring, after all.

He held it up to the light, then to his nose. Almost thought he could smell her. A perfect souvenir.

As he carefully returned everything he had touched to its rightful place, he thought about the pickup man. How he had marked his presence, like a dog. A message that said that he had been there. That that place was his territory now.

He should do the same. Leave something in exchange for the earring. He felt around in his back pockets, but couldn't find anything fitting.

But in one of his front pockets his fingers grazed against something small and hard.

A plastic figure from his stepfather's model railway, which he had found on the floor just a few days before.

The figure was three-quarters of an inch tall, unpainted and featureless. Invisible, imperceptible; suggestive of a person, without being one.

Just like himself.

He tucked the figure away at the bottom of an underwear drawer, where no one would find it. And if anyone did, they wouldn't realize its meaning. That it was proof of his conquest.

ASKER

Asker is sitting in her office with the door shut.

Yesterday's sense of foreboding is back with an almost over-whelming intensity, which is no surprise. The usual background drone that seeps in through the glass door to her office is rowdier, more boisterous today, punctuated every now and then by loud peals of laughter. The sounds of Jonas Hellman's triumphant return.

She has trembled at the thought of this moment. Gone through it a hundred times in her head, trying to find as painless an outcome as possible. But it's impossible. Nothing about this situation is painless.

Might as well rip off that Band-Aid.

Hellman is standing in the break room, a coffee cup bearing the National Operations Department's logo in his hands. Asker is 100 percent sure that she has never seen the mug in the cupboard before, which means he must have brought it with him. To show that he's in another league.

Hellman is already surrounded by an entourage of admirers.

The years in Stockholm haven't changed him all that much. A forty-something sprinkling of grays in his stubble, which only makes him more attractive.

Otherwise he looks just the same. Blazer, jeans, tailored shirt.

Blond, athletic, confident to the point of cocky.

The room's natural center of gravity.

Eskil is standing at Hellman's side, his face full of lapdog adoration. A fawning little copy who laughs too loudly at his master's jokes, his own leadership ambitions already thrown to one side.

Asker takes a deep breath and holds out her hand to Hellman.

"Hi, Jonas, good to see you!"

The chatter in the room fades abruptly, and every eye turns on her.

Hellman leaves her hanging just long enough for the situation to get awkward. Then gives her a smile.

"Asker, hi!" He shakes her hand. "I hear you're running the Holst investigation. I look forward to working together."

Relieved smiles, meaningful looks. He uses her surname as if to emphasize that she is simply one of the crowd. A well-planned performance.

High time to cut the crap. And she knows exactly how. The word that irritates him most.

"Why?" she asks, tilting her head to one side.

"Sorry?" That cocky smile falters.

"Why do you look forward to working together?"

Hellman stares at her. His entourage squirm awkwardly. The temperature in the room drops to freezing point.

After a few seconds Hellman manages to force out a strained little chuckle, as though it's all just a joke. His disciples follow his lead.

"Like I said, always nice to see you, Asker."

He goes on shaking her hand and smiling—at least with his mouth.

But his bright-blue eyes are ice-cold.

Half an hour later they are all gathered in the incident room. The place is teeming with officers: Rodic and Hellman up at the front, Asker on the front row, in the audience. The atmosphere is tense, expectant.

Just one minute before they are due to start, something unexpected happens. The door to the incident room opens slowly, almost deliberately so, and for some reason everyone in the room turns their head that way. Asker, too. As always whenever her mother steps into a room, everything seems to stand still.

Isabel Lissander is impeccably dressed, as per usual, in brands so expensive that they don't need to advertise themselves with logos or patterns. Her makeup is discreet, her hair perfect, the coloring so skillfully done that anyone would buy that she is still flaxen-haired despite being almost sixty. On her face that lawyer countenance that she has spent forty years honing. British monarch with a hint of great white.

She surveys the room, then takes a seat in the back row and gives a faint nod, upon which time seems to start ticking again.

Rodic clears her throat.

"Well, welcome everyone," she says. "I doubt Detective Superintendent Jonas Hellman here needs any introduction."

Rodic gestures at Hellman, who smugly stands up a little straighter.

"Those of you who haven't worked with Jonas before will certainly know *of* him," she goes on. "His results both in this department and at the national police homicide unit speak for themselves, and we are obviously very happy to have him here."

Asker doesn't say a word. It surprises her that Rodic is capable of such flattery. She knows exactly what kind of person Hellman is, and yet here she is singing his praises.

"Hello, everyone!" says Hellman. "It's great to be back, though obviously I wish the circumstances were better. I've already managed to read up on the case, and in my view we have a few clear lines of inquiry to focus on."

He gestures at someone to start the projector. His body language is so relaxed and self-assured that everyone simply has to listen.

"I've spoken to the Holst family, and according to them Malik Mansur became threatening after Smilla broke up with him in summer. They claim she was afraid of him."

His eyes linger briefly on the back row, and even without looking around Asker knows he is looking at her mother. Clearly they have already been in touch, which makes Asker's blood start to boil.

An image appears on the screen.

"This is backed up by these messages, which Mansur sent to Smilla in August and September."

Asker bites her lip. Hellman has already got his hands on the phone data that she has been waiting for. But he hasn't shared it with her. What's more, he has also found the time to speak to the Holst family, presumably at the meeting yesterday that Rodic insisted on taking in Asker's place.

"As you can see, the tone of many of these messages is threatening," Hellman goes on. "*You're going to regret this. No one does this to me. Karma's a bitch.*"

Hellman looks straight at Asker. One corner of his mouth twitches infuriatingly.

She knows why. The quotes could just as well be directed at her.

"On top of that, we have been able to confirm the link between Mansur and Ibbe Farakhad, a known Malmö criminal with a high capacity for violence. Among other things, Farakhad has a prior for kidnap. As I'm sure you all recall, we have an intelligence note that places Mansur in a car occasionally used by Farakhad. And on at least two occasions Mansur has called a phone that we know to have been used by Farakhad. Unfortunately we haven't found any text communications between the two of them, but that just means they're smart enough to use WhatsApp, Telegram, or any one of the other encrypted messenger services that we don't have access to."

Asker can't hold it in anymore.

"That or they haven't had any contact at all," she says. "Thugs swap phones and cars all the time. Mansur's connection could be with another gang member entirely."

Hellman summons one of his most charming smiles, as though he doesn't mind the interruption in the slightest.

"Of course. We're keeping every line of inquiry open. But as you'll find on the next slide, we have several pieces of circumstantial evidence."

He picks up a laser pointer and aims it at the screen.

"Both Smilla's and Mansur's phones were turned off at 11:03 a.m. on Friday. At that time they were in the vicinity of the Shell station in Gårdstånga, north of Lund. The gas station is a common meeting point and has a separate parking area. The E22 runs straight past it, as do a number of smaller roads in almost every direction. The fact that both phones were turned off simultaneously means it can't have been a case of low battery, technical fault, or something similar. The phones were turned off intentionally, and the only reasonable explanation is that this was done to ensure they couldn't be traced."

Next image. Visa and Mastercard logos. Transactions and payments. Yet more information that he seems to have turned up in no time, without sharing with anyone else.

"Mansur's credit card statements show that he has mounting debt, for which he is basically only paying off the minimum amounts,"

Hellman goes on. "Mansur's debts amount to almost ten thousand dollars. He is also running late on his monthly utility bills, which has led to several reminders from debt collectors."

He lowers the pointer.

"So, to summarize, we have a missing woman from one of Malmö's richest families, and a spurned, threatening, jealous former boyfriend with debt problems and contacts with the criminal underworld. Everything points to this being a case of aggravated kidnap, motivated by ransom. Four years to life by current sentencing guidelines."

"But Smilla and Malik were back together," Asker argues. "Smilla was staying at his place. He had even borrowed money from his mother to buy her a gold necklace."

She pauses briefly, just long enough to note that Hellman didn't know about the necklace. One point to her.

"Besides, we haven't seen any demand for ransom, even though it's been four days," she goes on, as composedly as she can. "Isn't it a little early to lock in on such a blinkered hypothesis as Mansur kidnapping his own girlfriend? I mean, how does he plan to get away once the ransom is paid?"

The room falls silent for a few seconds. She gets no nods of agreement, no one dares look her in the eye. Not even her own manager.

Instead everyone's eyes are locked on Jonas Hellman, who in turn takes a long look at the back row before turning back to her.

"Thank you for your input, Asker," he says with a cool smile. "It's always good to ask these questions and get some alternative perspectives."

He looks away again.

"Naturally we remain open to all lines of inquiry," he goes on. "After all, anything else would be misconduct."

SMILLA

Smilla is almost through the shock stage. The period when brain and body activate every crisis function.

She has worked her way through all of them.

Has cried, hyperventilated, called out for MM, for her mother and father.

Let out the worst of it until the pressure eased off her chest.

The tears burn on her lips; she licks them away. Rubs her eyes with the back of her hand.

Soon, very soon, her mind will clear; that's what she learned at hostage school. It will move on to the survival stage, start finding out more about where she is and the person who has, or the people who have, brought her here.

She remembers more about how she got here now. Remembers a corridor, rows of doors. One lone, red light.

An evil eye in the darkness that slowly drew her in.

She has foggier memories, too—of glass jars, dead butterflies, and small plastic figures. Of the bedrock's ever-mustier breath.

Perhaps that part is more dream than reality.

But her last memory, at least, is razor-sharp: the chilling realization that she isn't alone in the darkness.

She still can't shake that feeling.

That there is someone out there. Someone who can see her, who is watching her every move, sneaking into her room while she is deep asleep. Sitting on the edge of her bed, touching her. She doesn't know what makes her think that, but the thought makes her chest clench up once again in horror.

New tears burn at the corners of her eyes, but she blinks them away.

Purses her lips and swallows the sobs, one at a time.

She is almost through the shock stage, and she has no intention of going back.

ASKER

It takes a full hour after the briefing for Asker to be called into her boss's office. This gives her some time to think through Hellman's probable plan of attack.

Clearly his aim is to take the reins of the investigation and kick her out into the cold.

The phone and bank data he obtained via his own contacts and didn't share with her. The—mildly put—suggestive quotes that he had handpicked just for her. The barb that he wouldn't want to commit misconduct, when that was one of the things she had reported him for. He has made quick work of it, has evidently already managed to win the trust of not only Vesna Rodic, but of the Holst family and Isabel, too.

But in his haste he has also made missteps. Latched onto Malik all too soon, dismissed anything that points another way. Like the necklace he knew nothing about.

She also has one other trump card that Hellman has missed.

The signed book from Martin Hill, in which he calls Malik his star student. That could be worth exploring. The status of "star student" is definitely at odds with the image of petty thug that Hellman has been so keen to paint.

But first, yet another obligatory meeting with the headmistress. *Important to work together, don't make waves, what's best for the investigation,* blah blah blah.

However, Rodic surprises her. Instead of a long-winded slap on the wrist, her manager gets straight to the point.

"The commissioner's been in touch. On closer consideration he's decided that there's an unfortunate conflict of interest at play in the investigation."

"Oh is there?"

"Yes, since the family is represented by one of your relatives."

"You mean my mother."

"Uh, yes. In any case, the commissioner doesn't want there to be any circumstances that might distract us from the task at hand."

Asker laughs. "What does he think I'm about to do—leak details about the investigation? Isabel was just there at the briefing."

Rodic remains deadpan.

"No one's accusing you of anything, Leo. But the commissioner thinks it's an unfortunate situation. So he's decided that you should be temporarily reassigned."

Asker's smile is sharply extinguished. This twist is so surprisingly absurd that for once she is too thrown to question it.

"Do you remember Bengt Sandgren?" Rodic goes on, without waiting for a response. "He taught at the police college for a while. Years ago he wrote the first version of the 'Murder Bible.' He's chief down in the Resources Unit."

Asker knows of Sandgren, but has never heard of any Resources Unit. Besides, her brain is too busy trying to get a grip on what's going on.

"Anyway. Sadly Bengt suffered a heart attack a few days ago, which led to a bad fall. He's currently in the hospital—apparently it's still unclear which way it's going to go. Sad . . ."

Rodic inhales through her teeth, then goes on.

"Since Sandgren's department is without a manager, the commissioner wants you to step in there straightaway, until Sandgren's situation becomes clearer. A good opportunity for you to bulk up your CV with some managerial experience at a departmental level."

Asker's brain has now caught up; the pieces of the puzzle are falling into place. Her confusion turns to rage.

"And this *opportunity* . . . ," she says, adding air quotes to the last word, even though her voice is already dripping with disdain, ". . . it wouldn't happen to have anything to do with the fact that I once reported Jonas Hellman for misconduct, and have questioned his cocksure, hastily drawn conclusions in the Holst case?"

"Absolutely not!" Rodic holds up both hands defensively, which is definitely one gesture too far.

"This is temporary, the commissioner wanted to make that clear.

You are one of our most trusted colleagues, and this transfer is actually a promotion. You'll be heading up a department."

Asker takes a deep breath. Tries to buy herself some time to gather her thoughts.

"What sort of cases does the Resources Unit handle?" she asks with as much composure as possible.

Rodic squirms.

"I'm not familiar with their remit," she replies evasively. "But, as I said, the commissioner made it clear that this is a promotion."

Asker sits in silence for a few seconds. Now it's all crystal clear.

"So, just to be clear . . . ," she begins, a sourness to her voice that would be impossible to hide, even if she tried, ". . . this is purely a question of career development. A fantastic opportunity for me to manage a department that no one has heard of and that handles god knows what cases?"

Rodic's hands drop to her lap. For a brief second she actually looks tired.

"Just take the job, Leo," she says quietly. "Don't make waves and stop asking questions. For once in your fucking life."

THE MOUNTAIN KING

The visit to the young couple's house gave him a taste for blood. That same summer he took on more lawn mowing jobs, and quickly learned where people hid their spare keys—if they even bothered to lock up.

Soon he had several different houses that he explored in their owners' absence.

He unearthed their secrets, spent time in their most private spaces. Invisible.

From each place he would steal a little object and replace it with a small, white, faceless plastic figure.

He built up a collection of artifacts, which he hid under a floorboard in his room. When the silence settled over the big house at night, he would take them out and relive the feelings from each theft.

The excitement. The tension. The power.

But then autumn came. The lawn-mowing jobs dried up, and people shut themselves away in their homes. Shut him out.

He took comfort in his little collection, but soon that wasn't enough. He wanted more. Needed more.

As the days grew shorter and the darkness spread, another idea began to take hold.

One that was much more dangerous. But that held the promise of even greater rewards.

To enter a house while its owners were still at home.

The first time he did it was at a relative's house. One of his older stepsisters who lived in a cottage not far from his home.

He chose her for several reasons. First, because he knew the cottage well, and had an idea of when his stepsister would be alone. But also because he had always found her beautiful. She barely paid him any attention, treated him like one of the many kids who came and went in that big house, whose name was barely worth learning.

Perhaps it was that very arrogance that decided it?

He entered through the back door. Even though he had visited the cottage in secret before, it still felt different. As though the occupant's presence changed its energy. Charged the rooms with tension.

He forced himself to move slowly, so as not to make the slightest misstep in his eagerness to reach the bedroom. The door was ajar, and over the sound of his own pounding heart he could hear her breaths from within.

She was lying on the middle of the bed, had kicked off the duvet. Her nightshirt had crept up, revealing one bare leg and an exposed buttock. She was wearing no underwear.

The sight made his eyes swim. He stood there in the doorway and watched her with pulsing loins. Her heaving chest, the breaths slowly streaming from her half-open mouth.

She had no idea that he was there. That he was watching her in her most defenseless state.

His power over her was complete. Just like the butterfly in that jar. She was his.

He owned her.

ASKER

Back in her office, Asker sits silently with her eyes shut. Takes slow breaths to dissipate the worst of her anger. According to her watch, it takes five minutes and fourteen seconds for her mind to start to clear.

All of this is clearly Hellman's doing.

But he probably doesn't have enough weight in the force to have gone straight to the commissioner and have had her kicked off, especially not with their history. Someone else would have had to pull the strings. Someone with sufficient power, contacts, and authority. A blend of British monarch and great white.

Asker reaches for her cellphone. Her mother answers on the second ring.

"Isabel Lissander."

States her full name, even though she can see who's calling. Her voice is cold, businesslike.

Asker decides to skip the pleasantries.

"You had me kicked off the Holst investigation."

A statement, not a question.

Short silence.

"Kicked off? As I understand it you got a promotion. Managing a department is a step up, no?"

"Bullshit. I got kicked off the investigation because I disagreed with Jonas Hellman. Did you know I reported him for misconduct?"

Another silence. Her mother has honed her pauses to a fine art. Whets every little silence into a sharp, pointed weapon.

"Oh yes, I'm aware of your personal conflict," she says, unnaturally slowly.

"Conflict? He harassed me after I broke up with him."

Silence again. Asker tries to swallow her rage.

"The version that was presented to me was that the two of you had a brief affair some years ago, despite Hellman being a married man . . ."

A fourth, piercing pause that meets the chink in Asker's armor.

"Hellman maintains that when his conscience got the better of him and he ended your little affair, you reported him to HR," her mother goes on. "I've looked at their investigation. It indicated that, while Hellman did behave inappropriately, he wasn't guilty of any formal wrongdoing. The few witnesses who were prepared to go on the record supported his version of events over yours. Nevertheless, Hellman was transferred to the NOD in Stockholm. At his own request, to get his family away from you."

Asker's head is on the verge of exploding. She takes a deep breath, tries to contain herself.

"That's not what happened at all," she says with hard-fought composure. "Hellman harassed me both in and outside of work. He and his posse did everything they could to bully me out of the department . . ."

"So much the better that you aren't working on the same case, then," her mother interrupts. "Not least for poor Smilla Holst's sake. After all, it is *her* best interests that come first, no? And Jonas Hellman is a very skilled, highly qualified police officer . . ."

Another pause, which hits Asker right in her throat.

Asker wants to point out that there are in fact two people missing. That Hellman has already latched onto an unproven hypothesis, thereby risking both victims' lives. But her tongue is tied by her rage.

"You've got a new job," her mother summarizes measuredly. "A managerial position, far away from your would-be tormentor. I genuinely don't see what you're complaining about."

"So this isn't your petty-minded way of punishing me?" She shouldn't be opening this door, but her rage has got the better of her.

Isabel's voice goes ice-cold, which means she has hit the mark.

"I have no idea what you're talking about."

"Oh you don't? So it doesn't bother you in the slightest that I chose not to be a lawyer or work at your firm? News to me . . ."

Her turn to land an attack-pause. She isn't quite as proficient at it as her mother, but is still good enough to draw blood.

"I'm afraid I have to end our call now," her mother says curtly. "Take care, Leonore."

It is unclear who hangs up first.

Asker had hoped to be able to sneak out quietly, had waited for a moment when the corridor was empty. But of course they were lying in wait. As soon as she sets foot outside her office the corridor fills with people, with Eskil and his cohort the first on the scene.

Their master has returned from exile, and the mood is buoyant.

They lean against walls and doorposts. Laugh and chat loudly, pretending not to see her, all while gloatingly watching her Golgotha walk from out of the corners of their eyes.

Asker says nothing, just keeps her head up high and her eyes fixed firmly in front of her.

Waits while their eyes burn a hole in the back of her neck, as the sluggish elevator takes its own sweet time to arrive.

"Karma's a bitch!" Eskil hisses, just as the elevator doors shut behind her.

ASKER

Asker doesn't need to see her reflection in the elevator mirror to know that she looks like she has been fired. Everything from the cardboard box under her arm to the humiliation blazing in her face points that way. The camera in the ceiling takes in every last detail. Instinctively she turns her back to it.

She has already considered fighting this. Going straight to HR and the union, or simply quitting in sheer defiance. But she doesn't want to make any rash decisions, wants all the facts on the table first. The chance to see just how bad her situation is.

The journey down goes quickly. Thirty seconds or so, then the elevator dings.

"Level minus one," a voice announces with a hint of hesitation. As though wondering if Asker really meant to go here, or simply hit the button by mistake.

Until now Asker has assumed that the underground levels of police HQ housed only the garage, shooting range, and dark, silent archives.

But apparently they are also home to the Resources Unit. Which also happens to be essentially the only information the intranet had to offer on her destination. Nothing on the department's remit, or about who, besides Bengt Sandgren, works there.

The elevator doors slowly glide open.

She stands there for a second or two, trying to delay the inevitable for as long as she can. The surveillance camera's mute eye goes on staring at her.

Minus one.

That doesn't sound promising.

The corridor she enters appears to be straight out of the seventies. Fifty feet of gray vinyl flooring, a row of closed office doors along one side. On the wall opposite a few paintings, all of which are slightly skewed. Pale, sepia-toned John Bauer reproductions depicting trolls, elves, and other creatures from the unknown.

One of the paintings is even missing, its only remnants the hole left by a nail and a lighter rectangle in the bubbly fabric wallpaper. The air smells of stale coffee and basement. On the ceiling a fluorescent tube light flickers unrhythmically.

Asker takes a deep breath. The contrast between this place and the department she just left could hardly be greater.

"You must be Leo Asker," says a soft voice from obliquely behind her.

The man, who has appeared out of nowhere, is fifty or perhaps sixty years old. He belongs to that rare breed of people whose age is extremely hard to guess.

"Virgilsson," he introduces himself.

No first name or title.

He is short and stocky, dressed in a white shirt and a dark-blue knitted sweater vest. His head is planted almost directly on his shoulders, which, combined with his side parting and wide mouth, gives him more than a passing resemblance to a toad.

"The department's gatekeeper, one might say," he goes on. "Or its cicerone. This one is my own little sanctum."

He points at the door nearest the elevators, which is now slightly ajar, releasing a curlicue of classical music.

"Bengt Sandgren's office is right at the end, and I assume you'll want to base yourself there. Tragic story, by the way. Bengt was a good manager."

He pulls a sad little frown.

Asker finally finds her tongue.

"What sort of assignments does this department deal with?"

The man smiles cryptically.

"Oh, it's a bit of a mixed bag, one might say . . ."

He pretends not to notice the confused look on her face.

"We can get into that later, but first I thought I'd introduce you to our team."

He knocks on the second door, then opens it without waiting for a response. The woman at the desk jumps in fright, as though caught with her hand in the cookie jar. Behind her a grime-streaked window gives out onto a dim atrium.

"Gunilla, this is our new manager, Detective Inspector Asker," Virgilsson says briskly.

"Temporary manager," Asker adds.

"I s-see." The woman stands up and adjusts her glasses, then wipes her hand on her burled cardigan.

"Gunilla Rosén. But everyone calls me Rosen."

Her hair is graying, and it doesn't appear to match her actual age. She has shifty eyes and moves nervously, like a wounded bird. Her hand is warm and clammy.

"And what are your responsibilities, Gunilla?" Asker asks.

"I . . . uh . . . handle the administrative side of things. Database searches, filing, and I also register and allocate incoming cases."

"What sort of things do we see most of?"

"Oh, I couldn't quite say." Rosen fiddles with the sleeve of her cardigan, casts a furtive glance at Virgilsson as she does.

"We'll come to that," the little man says placatingly. "Shall we go on?"

He leads Asker back out into the corridor.

"Rosen is the department's rock," he whispers. "But one must be slightly careful with what one tells her. She's a little . . ."

He taps his index and middle finger against his thumb a few times.

"What do you mean by that?"

Instead of replying, Virgilsson knocks on the next door.

Pounds, rather.

"Zafer has trouble with his hearing," he explains after the second attempt.

The door is opened by a man in thick glasses. He is wearing a short-sleeved shirt with a pencil case in the chest pocket, and jeans held up by both a belt and braces.

"This is Detective Inspector Asker," Virgilsson says loudly and clearly.

The man stares at Asker, then nods in greeting without extending his hand. The top of his head is bald, with a ring of gray, straggly hair around the back and sides. Over his ears, by the temple tips of his glasses, sit two large hearing aids.

"Enok Zafer," he introduces himself, slightly too loudly.

"Enok deals with technical matters," says Virgilsson.

"I *assess technological resources*," Zafer corrects him testily. "I have a report due in on Friday."

Asker peers into the dim office behind him. It is double the size of Rosen's, is in fact two joined-up offices so jam-packed with shelves that you can barely see the windows. The shelves in turn are loaded with electronics. Small flashing LEDs are all over the place.

"Asker here is taking over from Bengt Sandgren," Virgilsson informs him. "Temporarily . . . ," he adds, before Asker can get a word in.

"Ah, right," Zafer replies, once again slightly too loudly. "That doesn't affect me so much, since officially I report directly to the director of technology, not Sandgren."

He looks over his shoulder.

"I really must get back to it. A report due in on Monday, you see."

"Friday," says Asker.

"Sorry?" Zafer holds his hand up to one of his ears.

"You said the report was due on Friday."

"Oh, yes." He turns and mumbles something in a language that Asker isn't able to identify before the door swings shut again.

"You can take all that about who he reports to with a pinch of salt," says Virgilsson. "It's an idea Zafer got into his head, and Bengt held off from setting him straight. Purely out of sympathy, I should think."

He leads Asker on along the corridor, which gives her a few seconds to contemplate her situation.

So far, her so-called promotion has put her at the head of a team consisting of a little toad-man, a jumpy woman cosplaying an old lady, and a half-deaf IT specialist with delusions of grandeur.

She doesn't have high hopes of what is to come.

They pause by a third door. On the wall beside it shines a red light with the text "Do not disturb."

"We'll try this one a little later," Virgilsson says with an apologetic turn of the hand. "In any case, this office belongs to Kent Atterbom, nicknamed Attila. I'm sure you'll have heard the name. And a fair few rumors, perhaps?"

Asker has indeed heard of Attila—every cop in Malmö has.

She thought he had been fired long ago. Should have been, certainly. But clearly he has managed to cling on here underground.

"I imagine you've heard that he was once the self-defense instructor for the riot squad, where his party trick was choking the cockiest young officers until they blacked out?" Virgilsson asks. "Or that he once almost beat a pumped-up, heavyweight boxer to death in a drunken brawl?"

"Something along those lines." Asker chews her lip.

So her fourth team member is a violent old bruiser. Hellman and his crew must really be in stitches.

Virgilsson pulls an amused face.

"Most of it is actually just rumor. But Attila keeps himself to himself. He and Sandgren never saw eye to eye. Some old to-do, I don't know all the details but . . ."

The little man checks himself abruptly, as though he has heard a sound from inside the closed office door.

"Swiftly moving on," he says quickly.

They pass another few closed doors.

"Long-term sick leave," Virgilsson remarks with a flick of the hand. "Nothing you need worry about, HR takes care of it all. It's unlikely we'll be seeing them again."

They walk past a little room with pigeonholes for mail, a photocopier, a printer, and a charging station holding two police radios. Above them is a metal key cabinet.

"Unfortunately for the time being we only have one car at our disposal," says Virgilsson. "An old workhorse that's on its last legs. Bengt was trying to resolve the matter, but I don't know how far he got with it. In any case, the key is here. You can book the car using the list on the back of the door. I'll have Rosen mark up a pigeonhole for your mail."

The little man leads her farther down the corridor, past a poky kitchen and another door or two, before stopping by an office at the very end of the corridor, just next to the storeroom.

"Final destination!" he says with a wry smile. Pulls out a large bunch of keys from a patinated retractable key chain that's clipped to his belt, and unlocks the door.

DETECTIVE SUPERINTENDENT BENGT SANDGREN, DEPARTMENT

CHIEF, reads an old-fashioned gold nameplate that is almost certainly a vestige of other, better days.

"You wondered what sort of cases we handle," says Virgilsson as he opens the door. "The answer is: anything that no one else wants."

Asker gasps. Almost every surface in Sandgren's office is strewn with files and papers, with the exception of his office chair and a shabby, old leather sofa that appears to have recently been slept on. The air is stale and reeks of dust and paper and, more faintly, of sweat, alcohol, and despair.

Virgilsson smiles.

"Welcome to the Department of Orphaned Cases and Lost Souls!"

THE MOUNTAIN KING

The autumn when he turned fifteen was in many ways transformative.

By this point he had a few dozen different houses that he would frequent, most of which by night, and his collection of souvenirs had grown in earnest.

He took good care of his collection, treasured every last object, savored the feelings they called forth from within him.

But lately he had started to suspect that someone was snooping around his room. Small signs, things that any other teenager would have overlooked. Drawers that hadn't been pushed back in all the way, piles of clothes that had moved a couple inches because someone had looked underneath them.

His stepfather kept mostly to his basement and model trains, and cared little for him or the other kids. And although his younger siblings were curious, they were also terrified of setting food on the steep, dark attic steps, since he had hammered it into them that the attic, where his room was, was haunted.

Which left only his mother. She had started taking more of an interest lately in what he was doing. Asked questions about school, what friends he had, girls, what he did in his spare time.

Every now and then he had overheard snippets of conversations between her and his stepfather. Realized that his transition from child to young adult was something that concerned her.

If she had already started snooping around his room, then it would only be a matter of time before she found his collection. Still, he couldn't part with his artifacts. He needed to know that his things were safe, that they were in a secure spot he alone could access. A place where he would never have to let them go.

But none of the hiding places he came up with were good enough.

In the end it was Uncle Johan who saved him.

Johan was one of the many strange relatives and friends his stepfather kept company with. Johan had a mustache and always smelled of a mix of oil and cigarettes.

But Johan had another smell, too, one that no one else seemed to pick up on. He smelled of sickness.

Of death.

It was his mother who suggested he spend the autumn half term with Uncle Johan. She probably wanted to make sure he got out of the house. Maybe even found a new male role model, new interests. In which case her plan failed miserably.

Johan never said more than five wheezing words at a time. Instead he alternated between chain-smoking and coughing, and in the car he would play his music so loud that they couldn't have held a conversation even if they'd wanted to.

They drove around inspecting the military sites that were dotted around the area. Barracks, mobilization depots, radar masts.

Johan would check that the fences were intact, that the warning signs were still in the right places, and that no trees had been blown down in the vicinity. All exactly as boring as it sounded.

But then, on the fourth day, they followed a rutted logging road through the spruce forests behind his own house. They parked right at the foot of the low mountain crest that he could see from his attic window.

"I rarely come here," said Johan as he pulled a massive flashlight out of the trunk and lit a cigarette. "Someone accidentally wiped this place from the register a few years ago. It's more or less forgotten. But I thought you might like it."

In the distance he could hear the hum of the fast train as it passed on the southern mainline. He had heard the sound a thousand times before, but on that particular day, in that particular place, it had a different ring to it. Awakened a strange expectancy.

Johan led them between two steep rock faces covered with huge camouflage nets. Almost without warning they found themselves in front of a crevice in the rock, one barred off by a wrought-iron gate with a rusty chain. A few feet beyond it loomed an enormous stone gateway.

Johan stopped abruptly, rested his hands on his knees, and started coughing and spluttering. Eventually he spat a thick gob straight out onto the ferns, then lit another cigarette, and started fiddling with the chain and padlock.

He stood there as though transfixed, unable to breathe or move. He recognized it. The bars, the chain, the stone door.

The smell of ruin, of damp and decay. It was as though someone had opened his head and stepped right inside his deepest, darkest fever dreams.

"This place is a little creepy," Johan wheezed. "You're not afraid of the dark, are you?"

He couldn't bring himself to reply. His heart was pounding, his mouth dry as sandpaper, and from somewhere nearby he thought he heard a sound.

A dull, vibrating tone that was beckoning to him.

Summoning him.

"This is our little secret," Johan crowed as they stepped into the darkness.

Into his dreams.

It was overwhelming—he couldn't put it any better.

Not even now, when he has long since grown up. As though the words still don't go far enough.

The very next night he stole the keys.

He had found a new home for his collection.

And for himself.

ASKER

Of all the things that Asker has seen in her first hour in the Resources Unit, the atrium outside her office windows is the most depressing. Even more so than Sandgren's dump of an office.

The atrium consists of 150 square feet of bare stone paving, which can't be reached as there is no door.

The murky rays that do manage to find their way in through the skylight all those floors above are, by the time they reach her office, so faint that they can hardly be called light. And the lights on in the offices on the floors above make the shadows down below even deeper.

If she stands right by the grime-gray window and looks directly upward, she can just make out the well-lit windows of the incident room in Serious Crime. Can even see the people moving about inside. Discussing her case.

Her fall from grace.

Asker steps away from the window and takes a seat in Sandgren's creaky office chair. The computer is old, and it takes several minutes of whirring before she can find her profile and log in. The keyboard is so shiny from wear that some of the letters have disappeared.

This role is an exercise in humiliation, a means of punishing her so cruel and so calculating that she almost has to take her hat off to Hellman.

He has exacted his revenge, and even though she saw the threat coming she found herself powerless to stop it. He has turned her own weapon against her—even her own family.

So what options does she have now?

Complaining to the commissioner is hardly in the cards. He has already told her, via Rodic, that this job is in fact a promotion. Which is also why she can't expect any help from the union, either. Besides, they never like to get involved in conflicts that stem from one colleague reporting another for misconduct.

She can apply for another job in the force, but that takes time, and something tells her that any application will be met with rejection, anyway.

The only remaining way out is for her to resign. Find another job, or suck it up and start working for Lissander and Partners. She does have a law degree that she isn't using, after all—something her mother never passes up on any opportunity to bemoan. But even if she resigns, she will still have a three-month notice period to serve. Three months in this place, with the added upshot of giving Hellman exactly what he wants: her out of the police force. And that she cannot allow.

She listlessly thumbs through the dusty folders on Sandgren's desk. A motley collection of old police reports, memos, and internal documents, mixed with what must be his own private interests. Bills, receipts, a catalogue of model railway accessories.

In the middle of one pile she happens across a book with a familiar title. *Forgotten Places and Their Stories.*

The same book she found on Malik Mansur's bedside table.

No signature from the author this time, but on the cover sits a handwritten Post-it note. The handwriting, which she assumes is Sandgren's, is sprawling.

Martin Hill, he has written.

Followed by a cellphone number.

Asker hasn't thought about Martin Hill in years, but suddenly in a matter of hours she has come across his book, signature, and now his phone number.

A more superstitious person would say it was a sign. That fate was trying to tell her something. Luckily she doesn't believe in that nonsense.

Besides, her original claim isn't true. She has thought about Martin quite a lot.

Wondered what became of him, if he ever found out what went down on her very last night on the Farm. And if so, why he never got in touch. Even so, she has resisted the urge to google him. Told herself he belonged to her past.

A door that must remain closed.

She flicks to the author photo again. Reads that Martin, besides being a best-selling author, is also a lecturer at the School of Architecture in Lund. The same program that Malik Mansur was studying. That would explain why he described Malik as his "star student."

But Sandgren has been in hospital since before Malik and Smilla disappeared, so his interest in Martin can't have been anything to do with the kidnapping.

She takes out her phone and googles Martin. Manages to find a recording of a lecture that's just a few months old.

Grown-up Martin Hill moves gracefully and confidently around the stage. Has the audience eating out of the palm of his hand right from the start. He talks about his book, mentions a handful of different forgotten places and tells the stories behind them, along with some pictures. One is about an eccentric millionaire who built his empire based on information he claimed to have been given by extraterrestrials, whom he thanked with a UFO monument.

Martin is charismatic and funny, just as she remembers him. Only older and better looking. She isn't alone in that observation: every now and then the camera pans out to the audience. The majority are women in their twenties and up, many with admiring faces and twinkling eyes.

But another one of the faces is familiar. She pauses the video, jumps back, and zooms in. Malik Mansur is in the front row, a big smile on his lips. He seems to be lapping up every word Martin says.

Is this the same person who is also planning to kidnap his ex-girlfriend?

Asker pulls the Post-it note off the book and moves it thoughtfully between her fingers. After some deliberation puts it back. It isn't her case anymore, so she has no reason to be contacting Martin with questions about Malik Mansur.

There comes a knock at her door.

Virgilsson pokes his head in.

"I'm popping out to meet one of our regulars. Just thought I'd see if you'd like to join? Get a little insight into what it is we deal with."

"Regulars?" she asks.

"I'll explain on the way," he says with yet another enigmatic smile.

Asker gets up and puts on her jacket. She stops in the doorway, goes back to the desk, and puts the book with the Post-it note in her pocket.

Martin Hill, she thinks again.

A ghost from her past.

SEVENTEEN YEARS EARLIER

She is fourteen, in eighth grade. Is standing by her locker in the long school corridor.

The steel door is dented, and even though she has turned the key as far as it will go the door doesn't budge.

She sighs, looks at the clock. Her math lesson starts in six minutes; running over to the caretaker's office will take four.

Add to that the time it will take her to explain that she needs to borrow a screwdriver yet again, and then run back and pry open the locker, and she'll be at least five minutes late. Even more if the caretaker isn't there.

She hates being late.

"Won't it open?"

It's the new kid. He has been assigned the locker next to hers, and so far they have only exchanged nods.

He is a head shorter than her, has light brown skin, and black, curly hair. A scrawny build, his clothes look a size too big. The skin around his eyes is ashen, and his lips a shade or two too pale, as though he isn't in good health.

The cool kids in tenth grade call him Darky Marty, and he pretends the nickname doesn't bother him. Laughs along in the hope that they'll leave him alone. Sometimes it helps. But not always.

"Your locker," he says again, pointing at the dented metal. "What happened?"

"The idiots in tenth grade like to punch it as they go past."

"Why?"

She shrugs. Can't be bothered to explain that, despite being two years younger, she's as tall and almost as strong as most of them, and much better at fighting, too. That just a few weeks ago she headbutted one of them in the schoolyard when he said something mean about her different-colored eyes, and that bashing her locker is their petty revenge.

"I've got a screwdriver if you need one?"

Without waiting for a reply, he starts rummaging around in his back-pack. A big bag made of coarse nylon that looks like it has been patched in several places, which reminds her of the one she keeps under her bed. Inside it she spots a flashlight and a few loose door handles.

"Here!" He hands her a chunky screwdriver.

It takes Leo only a few seconds to pry open the door and bang it vaguely flat again. She tests out the key a few times to make sure it's working again.

"Thanks," she says, returning the screwdriver.

"No problem!"

Leo's curiosity takes over.

"Why have you got . . . ?" She points at his backpack.

He closes the flap again quickly.

"It's a secret," he says with a smile. "At least until we know each other better."

He holds out his hand.

"I'm Martin Hill."

"Leo," she mumbles as they shake hands. "Leo Asker."

"Nice to meet you, Leo Asker," he says with a smile that isn't actually as annoying as she expected it to be.

ASKER

The Resources Unit's sole vehicle is, as Virgilsson so diplomatically put it, a faithful old workhorse. More accurately: a wreck.

The car is a dark Volvo that is at least ten years old and, if its spongy suspension and depressed seats are anything to go by, has seen a lot of use. The smell inside is a pungent mix of diverse bodily fluids and fried food. The wheel is shiny from wear, one of the buttons on the FM radio is missing, and the glove compartment has a tendency to sporadically pop open while the car is in motion.

Virgilsson is at the wheel. He is talkative. Prying.

"So you've come straight from Serious Crime. Were you working on the Holst kidnapping?"

Asker considers denying it, but what does it matter anyway.

"I was," she admits.

"Wow, so one second you're in the middle of all the buzz and the next you're here."

He smiles, not necessarily in a pleasant way.

"So where are we heading?" she asks, to change the subject.

"To Skurup," he replies. "To meet Madame Rind. As I said, she's one of our regulars. Our direct line to the spirit world."

"What?"

Virgilsson gives her a big grin.

"Madame Rind used to call the switchboard several times a week. Bombed us with tip-offs about every single case that was mentioned in the press. The authorities considered applying for a restraining order, but instead Sandgren suggested we pay her a visit once a week. He thought that would be easiest on everyone. And I agree."

Asker can hardly believe her ears.

"So you're telling me we're going to see a psychic?"

"She prefers the term *medium*," Virgilsson chuckles. "We take it in turns to go. There's a nice lunch place nearby. They do a great all-you-can-eat barbecue buffet in summer."

Asker shakes her head dubiously.

"Is this an ordinary Resources assignment?" she asks.

"Not really," says Virgilsson. "I'd say our assignments are anything but ordinary."

"What do you mean?"

He takes a deep breath before replying.

"In short, the Resources Unit takes on any cases that can't simply be written off, but that don't really fit anywhere else, either. Orphaned cases, as I like to call them."

Asker raises her eyebrows.

"Have you got any other examples?"

"Certainly. I've got an ongoing case with a farmer in Billesholm who, after every midsummer, finds strange patterns in one of his fields. Another with a woman in Flyinge who claims someone is kidnapping her cats and releasing them over in Vollsjö, twenty miles away."

"And we devote police time to this?" Asker asks.

"Yes, since at the end of the day both are recurring crimes."

Virgilsson goes quiet for a few seconds while maneuvering around a parked car.

"Besides, it's not as though we lost souls are likely to be entrusted with anything more pressing," he adds with a wry smile.

Asker is speechless. She has never previously considered where in the policing hierarchy those sorts of cases ended up.

Now she knows.

All the way down on level minus one.

In the Department of Orphaned Cases and Lost Souls.

And now she is its chief.

When they arrive in Skurup, the wind has picked up, and dark clouds are looming in the sky.

Madame Rind lives in an elongated cottage in the traditional Skåne style, with slanting walls and a sunken thatched roof. From its decayed eaves hangs a set of wind chimes that jangle ominously in the wind. At the clap of their car doors, a clamor of rooks takes off from the poplars behind the house, making loud warning cries.

In the front yard they are met by a senile pug with milky-white eyes, who cautiously sniffs around their legs.

"That's Garm. Apparently he can see into the spirit world," says Virgilsson with mock gravity. "But unfortunately in our dimension the little pooch is blind, so watch you don't step on him."

Slightly surprisingly, Madame Rind turns out to be a beautiful woman in her late thirties with straight, raven-black hair, alabaster skin, and heavy makeup. She is wearing a black shirt, black jeans, and boots, and her neck is swathed in silver jewelry that looks home-made.

Madame Rind squeezes Asker's hand and locks her eyes on hers for slightly too long. Her handshake is firm and rough. A tattoo twists out from under the cuff of her shirt and continues over the back of her hand. Her fingers are loaded with rings.

"Detective Inspector Asker," she says, almost as though she is tasting the name and title. "Welcome. Garm and I have been expecting you."

Asker and Virgilsson exchange glances, while Madame Rind leads them into the house. The ceilings are low, the walls painted in dusky colors. Large oil paintings of scenes from Nordic mythology, deer and stag horns dotted between them. The room smells of incense and old animal hides.

They sit down in a worn leather sofa suite, in the middle of which stands a coffee table and tea tray.

"So, Madame Rind. What do you have for us today?" Virgilsson asks with a wink.

"Drink your tea first," the woman commands.

Virgilsson obeys with a surreptitious smile, as though he likes to be ordered around.

The pug has jumped up onto his mistress's lap. Stares at Asker with his sightless eyes, his long tongue dangling from one side of his mouth.

"He likes you!" says Madame Rind. "Can feel your energy."

Asker sighs inwardly. If the old mutt could actually feel her energy, he would probably be hiding under the sofa by now.

"What a shame about poor Bengt," says Madame Rind. "The spirits were very upset that he hadn't understood their warnings."

"Hadn't understood?" asks Asker, mostly to have something to say.

"The spirits are never wrong," Madame Rind answers her gravely. "But sometimes their warnings can be difficult to interpret. One must be attentive. I am but a vessel, a mere medium for their messages."

Asker opens her mouth, but closes it quickly again.

This entire situation is so absurd that for once in her life she is at a loss for words. Both the strange woman and the blind dog go on staring at her unblinkingly.

"Well then, Madame, shall we get started?" Virgilsson prompts. He places his teacup on the saucer with a clink. Only now does Asker notice that the tabletop is full of letters, like a Ouija board.

"Yes, let's."

Madame Rind takes out a notepad and quickly rattles through a series of different cases that have been mentioned in the press, and what the spirits have to say about them. What color sweater the offender was wearing, why a certain crime was committed, where they should look for evidence. Even though her reports mostly consist of disjointed sentences, Virgilsson appears to be listening with rapt interest, and even jots down a few notes. He actually appears to be quite taken with Madame Rind.

Asker, on the other hand, has already zoned out. The only sound she hears is the clunk of her career hitting rock bottom.

She gazes through the window. The rooks have returned to their vantage points in the poplars. Through the dark clouds a plane emerges on its way to Malmö Airport. The desire to escape is overwhelming.

She thinks about the backpack under her bed. Two minutes, that's all it would take.

". . . and then finally that missing girl and her boyfriend," says Madame Rind.

Asker wakes up.

"The spirits are particularly concerned about that case."

Asker casts Virgilsson a furtive glance. The Holst case hasn't reached the media yet, so how could Madame Rind know about it?

The mystery turns out to have a perfectly banal explanation.

"The parents' cleaner was here yesterday for a consultation," says Madame Rind. "The family are devastated. Apparently they suspect the boyfriend."

"And what do the spirits have to say about that?" Asker asks dryly.

Madame Rind gives her a long look.

"They are concerned," she replies solemnly. "Very concerned. Garm, too, poor thing hasn't been able to sleep a wink. That only happens when something serious is at hand. When great evil is circling."

She strokes the pug's neck. The dog goes on staring at Asker. The room falls silent, save for the tick of the tall Mora clock in the corner.

"Well then, I think it's time we were moving on," Virgilsson says with exaggerated politesse. "Thank you for the tea, Madame Rind, and au revoir."

They pull out of the drive and head back toward town.

"So, what do you think?"

"I think it was a complete waste of time. Obviously people have a right to believe whatever they want, but it's not the police's job to validate their delusions."

"Perhaps not," says Virgilsson with a slight smile. "But you have to admit, the tea was good. And she is a handsome woman, Madame Rind, has a certain je ne sais quoi . . ."

He breaks off, gives one of his usual enigmatic smiles.

"Besides, I have a quick errand to run nearby," he adds. "A friend has a smokehouse five minutes from here. I thought I'd pick up a batch of smoked eel for some of our colleagues at HQ. Of course there'd be some for you, too, if you want."

Asker gives him the side-eye.

It took a few hours, but now she knows exactly what her so-called promotion entails.

HR nightmares, crackpots, meaningless investigations, and personal errands on police time.

Employees who sleep in the offices, with Martin Hill's book as bedtime reading. *Forgotten Places and Their Stories*.

The Resources Unit definitely fits that description.

A forgotten place filled with orphaned cases and lost souls. She wonders what Martin would have to say about it all.

For a few seconds she considers calling him, but quickly bats the thought out of her mind.

Surely Martin Hill is busy with more important things. Unlike her.

HILL

When it comes to getting past a fence, one of the many things that Martin Hill has learned is never, ever to climb.

When he was a child he didn't have all that much choice.

Back then he was far too sick and feeble to even dare try to climb. Would have to dismount his bike on even small uphill slopes to avoid losing his breath, since his heart struggled to pump the oxygen around his body.

Still, it was worth the effort. He never tired of seeking out buildings that no one had visited in years. Abandoned sites where nature was slowly reclaiming what mankind believed would be its forever.

Now, as an adult, he is healthy, fit, and agile. Still, a single rusty barb would be all it would take for an adventure to become fatal.

The risk of blood loss, even from a minor cut, is one that he cannot afford, to quote his cardiologist.

But even as a child he realized that it was often easier to walk along a fence instead of climbing over it. Search for the hole or natural channel that, in his experience, tends to crop up every fifteen hundred feet or so. Even more often if the building inside has been abandoned for a while.

Patience is important in urban exploration. The ability to keep calm, not panic or make stupid decisions.

Sofie, who is a few steps ahead of him in the thicket, knows this all too well. She is almost as experienced an urban explorer as he is. But today she is impatient.

In theory Hill has called it quits with this kind of illegal excursion. He is no longer the adventurous twenty-year-old he once was, but a thirty-something, well-known university lecturer and best-selling author. Neither his employer nor his publisher would be pleased if he were to get arrested for unlawful entry.

But every now and then he makes the exception, for Sofie. At least that's what he tells himself. In actual fact it's just as much for him, too.

He was the one who first got her interested in exploring abandoned buildings and sites. Who got her to see beauty in the decayed and abandoned.

In nature's reconquest.

She lives in The Hague now, with her husband and children, but spends a week or so in Malmö every other month for work. Each time they will spend a couple of nights together, and he will go along with her to a new abandoned place.

A place that she hopes will give her answers.

But every time it ends the same way.

She gets the plane back home to her family, her everyday life.

Leaves with equal parts disappointment and relief at what they didn't find.

As expected, a hole appears in the fence after just a thousand feet. Hill and Sofie help each other to climb through it.

The asphalt within is losing its struggle against nature. Potholes have left it punctured and cracked, with tufts of grass springing up all around, and in several spots the birch saplings have taken root and are on their way to forming thick trunks. The leaves shimmer in gold, are still clinging on ahead of the first autumn storms.

"See?" Sofie points at the factory building, in front of which stand four large containers. "Demolition starts next week, so this is our last chance."

Hill has been here before, seven or eight years ago, when the disused factory building was more or less open to the public. But since the authorities bought the plot, the building has been completely closed off. Every door obstructed with large concrete blocks, windows barricaded with thick sheets of steel.

Until now nature has had free rein. But a new round of tug-of-war is about to begin. As Malmö continues to expand, old, desolate industrial plots like this are to be turned into homes. Mankind will regain the upper hand, and in just a few weeks the abandoned building will be gone, every trace of those who once occupied it obliterated. Which is why they are here.

He stops for a moment to take in the beauty, as he usually does.

The contrast between the elements that have fought so hard to break down the building, and the crumbling concrete and rusty metal that continue to stubbornly resist them.

Sofie is already standing by the dented, shuttered doors. Is checking if they will budge, while also trying to shine her flashlight through the small, dirty windows.

"I see graffiti in there," she says. "On the far wall. It looks like Tor's."

She kicks the door.

"Shit!"

The sound echoes through the empty premises inside. Returns like a muted, ominous bass note.

Beside the large door there is another, smaller door that also appears to have been recently secured.

The surface of the door is flat, with only two holes where the lock and handle once sat.

Removing door handles is the absolute cheapest and easiest way to prevent access. And a pretty effective one, too. The angled latch bolt is still in there, but without a handle and matching spindle it can't be retracted.

Still, Hill has encountered this problem many a time before.

He rummages around in his backpack. Pulls out a door handle and a can of WD-40. Then a case containing a few rectangular sleeve adapters, which he threads onto the spindle until one of them fits the hole where the handle once sat.

He turns the handle. The latch slides back; the door squeaks but still refuses to open. A few sprays of WD-40 to the hinges persuade it to change its mind.

"You're a magician!" Sofie whispers as they step inside.

On the other side of the door, a large, desolate storeroom opens up before them. The air is raw and damp, smells of asphalt, dust, and waste oil. Here and there faint inklings of light creep in, and the wind makes the old tin roof creak.

At the far end of the hall, a metal staircase leads up to a mezzanine level.

Sofie is already on her way toward a large, concrete wall completely covered with colorful graffiti. Hill follows her lead. Even though he is wearing thick boots, he cautiously zigzags his way between shards of glass and boards with rusty nails.

At the bottom of the wall lie piles of rubbish: beer cans, half-rotten fast-food packaging, pallets stacked to make seats; even the remains of an improvised campfire.

"People have camped here!" says Sofie.

"Years ago, in any case," Hill agrees.

Sofie scans the wall of graffiti with her flashlight, carefully searching for familiar figures or symbols.

After a few minutes she groans in disappointment.

"Nothing?" Hill asks.

Sofie shakes her head.

"Tor might have been here, but the most recent stuff isn't his."

Tor is Sofie's little brother. A nice guy, but not without his issues. Fights with his parents and school, drugs, petty crime. For a while Sofie was even his guardian. She got him into an art class that he of course dropped out of after just a few months. Back to blazing up and spray-bombing train carriages and public walls.

Then just under a year ago he went missing. Didn't leave the slightest trace.

The police aren't doing much. Grown adults have the right to cut contact, and wayward minor druggies don't tend to live long, happy lives.

But Sofie keeps on searching. Tracks down different abandoned premises, like this one, where Tor might have stayed. Where he might have left some sign of life, a trace, a clue. Anything that might give hope, or at the very least—answers.

They walk on toward the mezzanine level, where they find that the staircase has been cut at around fifteen feet up. The lower half is lying on the floor, but it's too heavy to move, and there's no other way up.

Yet another trick to limit access.

Hill doesn't fancy the climb.

"The offices were really scuzzy, as I recall," he says, before Sofie can get any ideas into her head. "Mostly pigeon shit, mold, and old papers. But there is a basement."

He points at a steel door, which is also missing its lock and handles.

It takes Hill just a few minutes to get the door open.

The concrete staircase is crumbling; with all the rust, the steel reinforcements are peeking out on at least half of the steps. Forces them to point their headlamps right down and take very cautious steps.

The basement ceiling is low and supported by pillars, the darkness compact. The smell down here equal parts oil and mold.

Hill stops short, shines his flashlight around the room.

The floor is strewn with debris. Planks, machine parts, pallets with empty jute sacks. On a tripod on the far side of the room stands a large, rusty-brown oil tank. On its side more graffiti that has been part-consumed by the rust.

They stop by the tank. Shine their headlamps at the corner of the basement. Down here silence reigns completely; the only thing to be heard is the sound of their own breath.

And then something else. A faint, metallic click that is only audible if they really prick up their ears.

"Oi, Tin Man, I can hear your heart," Sofie whispers.

"Good thing, that," Hill whispers back. "At least you know I'm still alive."

She sniggers in spite of the serious atmosphere, which gladdens him. His artificial heart valve isn't actually made of tin, but of carbon fibers.

He got it in his late teens, as soon as the doctors felt that his body had stopped growing. It is the reason why he will have to take blood thinners for the rest of his life, and avoid at all costs any cuts or risk of internal bleeding.

Hill has long since grown used to the faint clicking sound in his chest, which is made when the valve opens and closes. Has taught his brain to filter it out as background noise.

But sometimes, in really quiet places like this, when the acoustics lend a hand, other people can actually hear it, too.

"Tell me what that detective wanted again," Sofie says as they carefully move through the basement.

"Bengt Sandgren?" Hill replies. "Not so much, really. He'd read my book, asked a few questions about urban exploration in general. I explained to him that it isn't really as far-out as it sounds. That it mostly boils down to the same sort of curiosity that almost everyone has as a child, which some people take with them into adulthood."

"And then?"

"We chatted for a while, mostly about sites from my book. He asked me what other places urban explorers tended to visit. I mentioned a few spots and gave him a few tips of websites. But I also explained that most people don't advertise the sites they visit, that sometimes they want to keep certain places off the beaten track. He thanked me for the help, and it was only as we were hanging up that he asked me if I knew Tor."

"And what did you say?"

Normally Hill doesn't like being cross-examined about questions he has already answered. He often complains that he isn't one of Sofie's defendants. But this time he lets it go.

"That you and I dated for a while, and that the three of us had been on some explores together," he replies. "But that that was a long time ago. Sandgren ended the call before I could ask him any questions."

"Do you think he was investigating Tor's case?"

"Don't know. All I could get out of him was that he was working on a case that had something to do with UE, but clearly he either couldn't or didn't want to say much about it."

"And this was a week ago?"

"Exactly. Like I told you, I tried to call him back to fish around a little more, a day or so later. But his phone was turned off and he hasn't got back to me since."

Sofie stops short. Appears to be mulling something over. The cross-examination seems to have ended, which is a relief.

"OK," she says. "I've got a meeting with some old colleagues from the Prosecution Authority in a few days. I can do some digging into who this Bengt Sandgren is and what he does."

They walk on around the big oil tank. Behind it, in the space between tank and wall, lies an old mattress with damp stains, some more empty cans, a few blankets and odd pieces of clothing.

On the wall above it is a piece of graffiti. A woman's face consisting of a single line, where one of the eyes is red. Beneath it a tag that both of them recognize.

"Tor," Sofie gasps. "He's been here!"

She starts feverishly rummaging through the clothes.

Hill steps back, leans against the tank, and shines his flashlight in her direction.

This isn't the first time that they have found one of Tor's pieces in an abandoned building. And given the fact that this place has been completely shut up since last year, it's hardly a fresh trail.

Sofie comes to the same realization, and after a while her movements go from eager to resigned. There are no leads, nothing to suggest where Tor went or what happened to him.

Hill looks around, his flashlight illuminates an object just a few feet away. Curious, he steps closer.

On the side of the rusty oil tank Tor has painted another one of his tags. Above it, balanced on top of a projecting pipe, stands a small white plastic figurine, about three-quarters of an inch in height.

Hill picks it up. The figure lacks facial features entirely, but still clearly represents a man. He stands wide-legged, his hands half-outstretched in front of him.

Despite his size, there is something eerie about him.

Hill has stumbled across far stranger things in old buildings over the years, and has always resisted the temptation to take something with him. Has strictly stuck by the urban exploration code of leaving only footprints and taking only photos.

But today he makes an exception and, without saying a word to Sofie, slips the figure into his pocket.

In the heat of the moment he doesn't quite know why.

Nor does he later, when he pulls the figure out again and places it on the base of the desk lamp in his study.

The closest he can come to an explanation is a hunch that that faceless little figure is much more important than it looks.

That its presence down in the dark basement means something.

Something he doesn't quite understand.

Something that concerns him.

WEDNESDAY

ASKER

Asker begins her second working day in Resources at seven a.m. By then she has already fit in a tough session in the police gym. Imagined that the sandbags were Jonas Hellman and her mother. Beat the shit out of them both, until the lactic acid made it impossible for her to lift either her arms or her legs. It helped, at least a little.

On the way out of the changing room she sees a sinewy older man with gray, closely cropped hair. She has noticed him in the gym before, but doesn't know his name or department.

The man gives her a curt nod of greeting. Maintains eye contact a second or two too long.

"Can I help you with something?" she asks, perhaps because she is still in a bad mood.

The man studies her silently for a few seconds.

"You're Asker, aren't you?" he says eventually.

"Yes, and?"

"I saw you with the punching bags earlier. Impressive."

"Thanks," she replies, still trying to figure out what this conversation is about. But before she can, the man nods goodbye.

"Have a nice day, Asker."

The bleak corridor on minus one is silent and empty, which doesn't surprise her. The Department of Orphaned Cases and Lost Souls is hardly bustling with industrious worker bees, as was crystal clear from yesterday's tour. A nervous, possibly loose-talking bird-woman, a deaf, delusional technician, and a strange, secretive little sweater-vest man with an obscure background—this is her team so far, and she hardly expects there to be any dramatic improvements in terms of personnel. On the other hand, no one appears to be demanding anything of either the department or her.

Her first assignment, to try to find a cup of coffee worth drinking, also proves harder than expected. The tiny kitchen boasts only an instant coffee machine that looks like it dates back to the heady days of the 1980s. Although right next to it there is an old but trustworthy coffee brewer, the cupboard above it, where the coffee and filters appear to be kept, is locked.

Despondently she presses the button for a cup of instant coffee. Waits while the antiquated machine huffs and puffs out a spurt of brown water, before heading to Bengt Sandgren's office.

The mess inside is just as depressing as it was the day before.

She has tried to come up with a strategy—a plan for the future, a goal to work toward—but unfortunately it still hasn't materialized. She needs more information on the extent of Hellman and her mother's scheming. Which means she must reluctantly bide her time.

She decides to focus on a short-term goal instead. Whatever the future holds, she will have to spend at least a few weeks down here. So tidying up Sandgren's chaotic office is a useful, achievable goal that could offer her at least a pinch of satisfaction.

Asker takes a sip of the coffee, which tastes exactly as vile as expected, then gets to work.

She starts by clearing some of the shelves on the bookshelf and transferring the many piles of loose papers and case files from the desk, windowsill, and essentially any other flat surface to them. Then she removes the pillow and blanket from the sofa and carries the old coffee cups and plates to the dishwasher in the kitchen. Ends by throwing away the two fossilized plants that were hidden behind the piles on the windowsill.

She stands in the doorway and takes stock of her work.

Perhaps not exactly good, but a clear improvement at least.

She picks up and puts on the desk the cardboard box that had been waiting in the corner, containing her own, tidily arranged things. Then sits down on Sandgren's creaky chair and opens the desk drawers.

The top drawer contains a small tray with the same mix of coins, odd keys, paperclips, rubber bands, and broken pens that sooner or later amass in every desk. The next one holds even more assorted case files, which surprises her just as little as the half-empty bottles of liquor to be found in the bottom drawer.

A cough makes her look up.

Virgilsson is standing in the doorway. Asker hasn't heard the elevator doors open, which suggests he was here before her. Or that there is a way of reaching the department that she isn't aware of.

"Good morning," he says with one of his strange smiles. "Have you seen the *Sydsvenskan* headline?"

He lays a newspaper in front of her.

MILLIONAIRE'S CHILD IN SUSPECTED KIDNAP

She quickly skims the lede.

Daughter of known Malmö entrepreneur missing since Friday. Police are silent—source claims NOD have been called in from Stockholm for backup.

"It would appear that someone in the building has leaked to the press. They can't be too happy about that up in Serious Crime."

Virgilsson pulls a malicious smile, and Asker realizes what he is getting at. He has drawn the same conclusion that everyone up in Serious Crime will draw: that the article is her petty way of taking revenge at being kicked off the investigation.

Virgilsson hovers in the doorway, as though waiting for her to say something, confess or deny it, which obviously she doesn't do.

After a moment's silence, he shrugs.

"Anyway, Hellman's called a press conference because of all the chatter in the press. Half past nine in the press room?" Virgilsson raises his eyebrows insinuatingly.

Asker shakes her head.

"As you know, my responsibilities have changed. The Holst case is Hellman's problem. Besides . . ."

She taps the newspaper.

". . . after this I can't set foot in the press conference. Everyone will assume I'm the leak. Which I'm not," she adds, completely unnecessarily. "Leaking a suspected kidnap to the press puts the victim in danger. Just like holding a press conference. It's utter stupidity!"

Asker shuts her mouth. She and Virgilsson don't know each other. The little toad is indecipherable to the point of creepy, and she has no reason at all to explain herself to him.

"Well," he says with a smirk, "I'm sure there are other people in the building who don't belong to the Jonas Hellman fan club, either. Rumor has it he's after Vesna Rodic's job as chief of Serious Crime."

Asker tries not to react, but it's impossible.

Virgilsson spots it.

"Oh yes, apparently he and his wife have been looking at houses on the coast," he adds smugly.

She regains control and turns away, feigning disinterest.

Virgilsson lingers in the doorway. Either he doesn't get the hint, or he simply ignores it.

"You've cleaned, I see," he says. Bengt was a little . . ." He sighs. "Disorganized, one might say."

"Do you know how he's doing?"

Asker isn't only asking out of politeness. She has been thinking about the note with Martin Hill's phone number, and is curious as to why Sandgren would have sought out his contact details.

"Still unreachable, according to the hospital. But they'll be in touch straightaway if and when he comes round."

"With you?" Asker raises her eyebrows. "Doesn't he have any family?"

Virgilsson shrugs.

"No one he kept in touch with in any case. Bengt had his weaknesses, as you may already have noticed." He nods meaningfully in the direction of the drawers, once again appears to be expecting a reaction.

Asker doesn't move a muscle. Sandgren's drinking is his business alone, and she doesn't know him. He certainly wouldn't be the only drunk in this building, and she has no interest in gossiping about it. Her silence provokes yet another cryptic smile.

"Whatever his shortcomings, Bengt was a good police officer, once upon a time," Virgilsson adds. "Loyal, reliable, engaged. Lately I'd had the impression he'd decided to pull up his socks again. The heart attack came at a most unfortunate time . . ."

"Do heart attacks ever come at a good time?"

Just like the encounter with the man in the gym a little while ago, she is increasingly certain that this whole discussion is actually about something else entirely. That this strange figure in the doorway is testing her, probing her for weaknesses, which she has neither the time nor interest for.

"I have a lot to get on with, if you don't mind . . . ," she says.

"Of course. I'll go put on the coffee. Let me know if you need help with anything."

Virgilsson turns and disappears into the corridor. But after just a few seconds he's back in the doorway.

"By the way," he says with yet another enigmatic smile. "Should you happen to want to watch the press conference a little on the sly, I know a way. Just let me know. In case you're as concerned about the case as the spirit world appears to be."

He disappears.

Asker stands up, takes the lid off the box she brought down with her from Serious Crime. So getting her out of there wasn't just about revenge. Hellman is after Rodic's job, which is why he wants to solve the Holst case single-handedly. Make some powerful friends among Malmö's elite.

A good plan—if he can pull it off, at least.

Her copy of the case file is at the top of the box.

Instead of picking it up, Asker stands there with a frown.

One of Prepper Per's favorite exercises, ever since she was a child, was to move, hide, or replace something in her room without warning. Afterward he would cross-examine her as to what had changed and what that could mean, and—naturally—dole out a suitable punishment if she failed.

She closes her eyes. Rewinds her brain to when she was packing up her things yesterday afternoon. The box was sitting on her desk up in Serious Crime, the lid beside it. Her coffee mug, the Holst case file, a few other bits and pieces nearby.

She moves her hands in the air, visualizing what she saw when she packed up the objects. Then opens one eye and looks down into the box.

Everything is there. Everything seems to be in order.

Even so, she is certain.

Someone has been snooping around her stuff.

ASKER

Asker has spent two hours trying to get Bengt Sandgren's assignments in order. But having gone through all his papers, she can only throw up her hands in defeat. Everything is an utter mess, and there isn't the slightest logic or hint as to what Sandgren was actually working on. If he was working at all, that is.

Little by little, she is starting to suspect that *no one* at the Department of Lost Souls works—not on any police assignments, at least.

That the orphaned cases that trickle in remain orphaned, since no one else in the building asks or cares about them.

To make matters worse, she is increasingly sure that at least one of her new colleagues is spying on her. Her office door was locked when she came in this morning, so whoever it was who went through her papers has a key. Did the same person also leak details about the Holst investigation to the press?

Impossible to know, but from now on she intends to take all her papers home with her, regardless.

She tries to access Sandgren's computer account so that she can browse through his work emails and documents. Unfortunately she doesn't have the right permissions, so she calls a self-important guy in IT who tells her to complete a service order. He almost laughs out loud when she asks him how long it will take. The sort of conversation she never had to have back in Serious Crime.

She slams the phone down in irritation, gets up, and walks over to the grime-streaked window. Leans in so close that she can see the lights on in the incident room up in what was her old workplace.

She needn't worry about being seen. No one up there ever looks down; she knows as much from personal experience.

Something is going on up there. Every now and then she sees someone flash past the window, and suddenly she gets a glimpse of

Jonas Hellman. He is holding some papers in his hand, facing his audience, and from his body language he appears to be saying something important.

Asker takes a step back. On one of the overloaded bookshelves she has already spotted an old pair of binoculars. She grabs it, goes back to the window, and twists the focus onto Hellman.

He is still visible diagonally from the side.

She adjusts the focus more, tries to zoom in on his face and mouth. *The boyfriend's mates*, she catches him say, followed by *smoke them out*. Then a string of words that could be *press conference* before he disappears out of sight.

Asker waits there for a while with the binoculars fixed on the window, but he doesn't return. She looks at the clock. The press conference starts in fifteen minutes.

She puts the binoculars down on a pile of papers. Considers calling the IT guy again and threatening him with a beating if he doesn't help her. Instead she steps into the corridor.

Virgilsson's door is ajar. He is sitting at the computer, his reading glasses perched on the end of his nose. The screen is turned away from her, but based on his muscle movements she guesses he is playing solitaire.

She knocks and steps inside without waiting for a reply.

The room is immaculate, strangely furnished for a police office. On the floor lies a Persian rug, and from the radio on the windowsill she hears classical music playing at low volume. On the wall behind Virgilsson hangs an oil painting of sailboats that feels out of place to say the least.

The little man looks up and slowly takes off his reading glasses.

"Detective Inspector Asker," he says with a smile. "How may I be of service?"

"You mentioned something about the press conference. That you could arrange for me to be there . . ."

"A little on the sly," he finishes her sentence. "Oh yes, that's right."

He looks at the clock.

"We have just enough time."

"Great, thanks."

She is about to turn around.

"By the way, before we go," he adds. "Bengt's unexpected ill health has meant I have had to do rather a lot of overtime this week. It has to be certified by my line manager."

He slides over a clipboard with a time sheet and a pen.

Clearly he has predicted her request and prepared himself accordingly. Not only that—he wants her to know it.

The proverbial back-scratching.

She could say no, of course. Follow the press conference on her phone through one of the news sites. But it wouldn't be the same. She wants to see Hellman for real. Feel what he feels, nose around for weaknesses in his arrogant façade.

She takes the pen and signs the time sheet without a word.

"Thanks," says Virgilsson with yet another little smirk.

"Shall we go then?"

Instead of taking a left toward the elevators, he leads her down the corridor, past the kitchen. Stops at a steel door marked ELECTRICAL ROOM. *Danger! No Access.*

The warning doesn't appear to concern Virgilsson in the least. He pulls out the well-worn retractable key chain clipped to his belt. Finds the right key immediately.

The room inside is filled with humming electrical cabinets in various shapes and sizes. At the far end is another door that leads to a small utility tunnel with concrete floors and cable ladders along one wall. Despite the dim light, Virgilsson strides through without hesitation.

Roughly halfway through the tunnel they reach another steel door, which Virgilsson unlocks. They enter some sort of shaft with a galvanized spiral staircase leading both up and down. Probably some sort of emergency exit.

Virgilsson moves surprisingly swiftly, takes the stairs two at a time until they have climbed two floors up.

"Hurry," he whispers, holding open another door. "It's about to start."

They enter a dark ventilation room filled with whirring fans. Instead of continuing toward the clearly signposted exit, Virgilsson guides her through yet another steel door.

Another utility tunnel, this time for ventilation ducts. The ceilings are so low that they have to walk bent double.

"Here we are!" Virgilsson says quietly, while tentatively cracking open something that most resembles a metal hatch in the wall.

"Empty," he notes after peeking inside. "Perfect!"

He steps inside and moves out of the way to let her in.

Asker climbs through and stands up straight. The room they have entered is dark, and only fifteen to twenty square feet in size.

Along one wall, below a window with dark-tinted glass, stands a mixer table. Along the other, a rack of flashing sound equipment. Opposite the mixer table, a wooden door that is the room's real entrance.

Virgilsson makes sure the door is locked, then points at the window. It gives onto a large room where ten or so rows of seats stand before a podium and a long table rigged with microphones. In the front rows they can see the backs of seated observers, while in front of them a couple of TV teams are fiddling with their equipment.

Asker realizes that they are in the sound booth at the back of the press room.

"The sound technicians sit out there nowadays," Virgilsson whispers before she has a chance to ask. "Control everything remotely with an iPad. Hardly ever set foot in here anymore. The perfect place to see without being seen, no?"

Asker can't help but be impressed. She has worked in the Justice Center for years, but never even knew about any of the rooms that they have just come through.

How can Virgilsson find his way around them so well, and how did he get all those keys?

As usual, the little man doesn't offer any other response than one of his mysterious smiles.

"It's starting."

He points at the press room, where Hellman has just taken a seat at the table. To his right sits Eskil, to his left Vesna Rodic.

A few camera bulbs flash; the TV team appears to be rolling. Virgilsson turns a button on the mixer table, making the speakers in the booth pipe up.

"Welcome, everyone, to this short press briefing," Hellman says commandingly. "My name is Detective Superintendent Jonas Hellman of the National Operations Department. Beside me is Assistant

Commissioner Vesna Rodic, chief of the Serious Crime Command here in Malmö. The reason we have invited you here today is to comment on certain unsubstantiated information that has recently started circulating in the press."

He clicks a button, and on the large projector screen behind him appears an image of Smilla.

"We can confirm that Malmö Police and the National Operations Department are conducting a major kidnap investigation. The victim, as you see in this image, is Smilla Holst, nineteen years of age, who has been missing since Friday."

As Hellman talks, Asker stares at the image behind him. It is Smilla's graduation photo, an image evidently chosen with care. No mention of Malik so far.

"Smilla's latest known whereabouts are Gårdstånga on Friday morning, when she was most likely traveling in the following vehicle."

Hellman hands over to Eskil, who nasally starts reeling off a description of Malik's black Golf.

His blazer looks new. He has also found the time for a spray tan since she last saw him, perhaps even whitened his teeth. As though he was expecting to be in the press.

Eskil repeats the details, drawing out his seconds in the limelight.

"At the time of her disappearance, Smilla and her companion were wearing the clothes that you can see in this image," he goes on.

The Instagram post from Friday appears on the screen. Smilla and Malik in waterproof jackets and polo necks, leaning against his car. To Asker's surprise, Malik's face has been blurred. Clearly he is not considered a conceivable victim, but something else.

"We urge anyone who might have seen anything to contact the police hotline," Eskil concludes before handing back over to Hellman.

The latter leans forward.

"To conclude, I would like to address the person or people responsible for Smilla's disappearance," he says gravely while staring into the closest TV camera. "We have the entire judicial system's resources mobilized, and it is only a matter of time before we find you.

The very best thing you can do right now is to immediately return Smilla to her family."

He stares down the camera for another few seconds, then leans back and nods at Vesna Rodic. Appears to be giving her the order to go on, as though he's the one calling the shots.

"So now we'll open up for questions," Rodic says into a crackling microphone. "But in view of the confidential nature of this investigation, we will be very restrictive with what . . ." The microphone crackles again, then drops out completely.

Virgilsson taps Asker on the arm.

"The sound technician has stood up. He must be on the way over to fetch a new mic. If you want to make sure you aren't seen, then . . ." He points at the hatch in the wall through which they came.

Asker reluctantly tears her eyes from the podium. The three police officers at the table, the image of Smilla and the blurred Malik on the wall behind them.

"Idiots," she mumbles while climbing back out into the utility tunnel, before Virgilsson shuts the hatch behind them.

HILL

Martin Hill lives in an apartment in central Lund. From his bedroom window he can see the magnificent copper tower of the cathedral soaring above the rooftops.

The university is within walking distance, but as usual he prefers to cycle. Takes a detour to get the pace up, opens his jacket and loosens his tie to let the wind cool him down before he arrives.

Hill's father would have words for him if he could see him. Would tell him he could catch pneumonia, or any number of illnesses that he believes are caused by the cold.

His father, John, hates the cold, blames it on his Caribbean genes. He wears long johns from September to May. Every year he tries to convince Hill's mother, Ingrid, that they should move to warmer climes.

Hill, on the other hand, loves the cold. Loves to feel it biting at his skin while his heart pumps an even stream of warm blood through the body.

It reminds him that things haven't always been this way.

Once upon a time he was a sickly, anemic little dweeb who always got picked last in P.E., and had to push his social skills to the max to avoid the worst of the bullying.

Now that he's an adult, everything is different. An athletic man with light brown skin and dark eyes, he is well aware that the popularity of his lectures isn't only down to the fact that he happens to be a good teacher who works in an interesting field.

A number of older colleagues grumble behind his back. Call him a pretty boy, a semi-celeb, and other, even worse names.

But Hill doesn't care all that much what other people think. His days of fearing bullies are far behind him now.

He loves his job. Loves giving lectures.

He locks his bike on the rack, uses his pass at the staff entrance, and forces himself to take the stairs slowly so that his pulse has a chance to slow.

He hangs his jacket in his office, then throws his cycle bag over his shoulder and makes his way toward the auditorium. As usual he forgets to button up his shirt and tighten his tie.

The steep rows of benches are full, and also as usual he forgets to take attendance until someone reminds him.

He quickly works through the register all the way to the letter M. "MM, are you here?"

He looks at the front row expecting an "obviously" and a big smile.

Malik Mansur has never missed a single lecture so far. He usually even hangs around afterward to chat. Jokingly nags Hill about writing another book, offers him tips, shows him pictures of abandoned places. Drops hints that he knows a few really special sites that barely anyone else knows.

It was in one of these post-class chats that he introduced Hill to Mya, a quiet young woman with a shy yet determined gaze who had come to meet MM.

MM and Mya seem to be close friends. Look at each other the way people do when they share a secret.

That's probably why he feels an extra affinity for MM.

Sees something of himself in him. Something of someone else in her.

Someone whose friendship once meant a great deal to him.

"Malik Mansur, where are you?" Hill tries again.

Only now does he realize the atmosphere in the auditorium has changed.

He looks around, but is met only by an oppressive silence from the seats, and the sneaking suspicion that there is something that he has missed.

Once the lecture is over, he stops two students on their way out. "What's up with MM?"

The students exchange looks.

"He's missing, or something . . ."

"Missing?" Hill asks.

"Kind of. It's all online. Search Smilla Holst. We've got to go now, don't want to be late . . ."

He lets them go. Pulls his phone out of his blazer pocket and searches the name they gave him. Immediately lands on a news site.

Police urge kidnapper to release millionaire heiress without delay.

He skim-reads the text. Sees the accompanying image, which, although blurred, still clearly depicts his star student.

"Shit," he mumbles to himself.

ASKER

It takes Asker and Virgilsson almost ten minutes to weave their way back down the way they came. She tries to orient herself, to figure out the extent of this network of utility tunnels, passages, and fire escapes, but it's impossible. They could cover as much as the entire block.

She wants to ask, but Virgilsson, as on the way up, is keeping a few feet ahead of her. Has his key chain at the ready at every door, hurrying her along. He actually reminds her more than a little bit of the stressed white rabbit in *Alice in Wonderland*, only with a sweater vest and retractable key chain in the place of the waistcoat and pocket watch.

Back in the Resources Unit's grim corridor, Virgilsson shuts and locks the door to the electrical room carefully behind them. His shoulders sink, and he appears to relax.

"How about a cup of coffee?" he suggests.

When they step into the kitchen, there is already someone there.

A man with gray, closely cropped hair that emphasizes his sinewy body and face. Asker immediately recognizes him. It's the man from the gym.

"Well, would you look at that, here's Attila," says Virgilsson, slightly too enthusiastically.

The man doesn't reply, simply goes on pouring coffee slowly into a mug.

"This is our new department chief, Leo Asker," Virgilsson continues in that same excessive tone. "She'll be covering for Bengt until further notice."

"Yes, Asker and I have met before." Attila puts the coffee decanter down and turns around slowly.

Eyes them both from head to toe.

"Been on an excursion, I see." He gestures with his cup at Asker's trousers.

Asker looks down, realizes that she has construction dust on her knees. Virgilsson, too.

Attila takes a slow sip of coffee. He is wearing a flannel shirt with the sleeves rolled up and black cargo pants tucked into a pair of well-polished boots. His eyebrows are bushy, which, with his pointed nose, make him look a little hawkish. Despite his age, and his not particularly tall stature—at least not compared to certain other police officers—there is something threatening about him.

"What exactly are your responsibilities in this department?" Asker inquires. Virgilsson flinches, as though she has just done something outrageous.

Attila lowers his coffee cup and stares at Asker. Rounds his shoulders forward and lowers his chin an effective three-quarters of an inch.

This is clearly a tried-and-tested move: his eyes, head and shoulder movements, the way in which he almost imperceptibly turns his elbows out. All of which intended to scare the shit out of whoever he is talking to.

Normally it must do the trick nicely.

But Asker has played staring contests like this one since preschool. All she has to do is glare back and let her different-colored eyes take care of the rest. Coax out that uncertainty something unusual almost always brings out in people who are accustomed to the exact opposite.

She can see the effect come creeping onto Attila's stony face.

First the surprise when he notices that the look in her eyes is fluid, impossible to pin down. Then the disbelief when his own steely gaze flickers. And finally: the second when he realizes the unthinkable—that he is about to lose in one of his specialty sports.

Attila dives down into his coffee cup with something that sounds like a snarl.

When he comes back up for air, he takes a few resolute steps toward the door, which makes Virgilsson jump to one side in fear.

Attila stops in the doorway, stands there for a second or two, and then slowly turns around.

"You asked what I work on."

He runs his eyes over her again. Then gives a slow nod, as though he has come to some sort of decision.

"I handle the department's IT support," he says in a tone that is neither friendly nor unfriendly, before disappearing into the corridor.

Virgilsson stares at Asker, appears not to quite know what to believe.

"Did you want coffee?" She raises an eyebrow and holds up the pot.

Virgilsson can only nod silently.

SMILLA

Smilla has figured out how it works now. Has learned all the signals.

The rattle of the hatch at the base of the door, the red light that turns on, signaling that the food is ready. The number of steps it takes to get there.

The same with the latrine in the corner. She has even got used to the choking chemical smell that comes when she lifts the lid.

But she has learned other things, too.

That the food and drinks she is given probably contain drugs that make her sleep for long periods of time. That give her horrifying nightmares about figures moving in the darkness. Sitting on her bed and stroking her hair. Whispering things in her ear.

You're mine now, all mine.

She knows all of this now, and part of her is still paralyzed with fear. But another part goes on gathering knowledge.

For with knowledge comes power.

And with that—hope.

ASKER

Asker spends the afternoon trying to familiarize herself with her new workplace. This turns out to be something of a challenge. Virgilsson has slinked out on a case, Attila's door is shut, the do-not-disturb light shining in an angry rebuff. But she does find Zafer and Rosen in the latter's office, engaged in a heated conversation.

". . . needs it on Friday!" she hears Zafer say as she steps through the door.

"What's going on?" she asks.

Rosen jumps in fright, the same way she did the first time they met.

"No-nothing. Enok was just asking for some documents."

"Important statistics!" Zafer interjects, two volume levels too loud.

"Is this about your report?"

He shuts his mouth and looks around suspiciously.

"I'm not sure if it can be discussed so openly," he hisses out of one corner of his mouth, nodding obviously in Rosen's direction. "Classified information, etcetera, etcetera."

Rosen rolls her eyes.

"You'll get your stats, Enok. Just give me ten minutes."

The balding technician glares at her. Mutters something, turns on his heels, and leaves the room.

"Is he always like that?" Asker inquires of Rosen.

Rosen sighs wearily.

"He has his good days and bad days," she says. "I know there's a fine line between genius and insanity, but Enok mostly lands on the wrong side."

Asker gives a slow nod. She knows a few others who would fit that description.

As she does so, she notices that Rosen is observing her. That same fearful facial expression is still there, but beneath it she glimpses something else. Something easily overlooked. Intelligence, curiosity. Perhaps even cunning.

Asker goes back to Sandgren's depressing office. Scrolls through the news on her phone while trying to convince herself that she is working. But besides eavesdropping on the press conference and a few bizarre interactions with her oddities of colleagues, she has spent her workday literally pushing papers. She is still none the wiser about what Bengt Sandgren was working on, or what she is expected to do down here. If she is even expected to do anything at all, besides keep out of Jonas Hellman's way.

Nor does she know who went through her things. Virgilsson, possibly, but that suspicion is purely based on the fact that he appears to have keys to every door in the building. Enok Zafer is hardly a suspect; he has his hands way too full with his own papers to go rifling through hers.

Rosen, on the other hand, appears to be much more attentive than she appeared on first impression. Virgilsson also hinted something about her being a blabbermouth.

And then finally the mysterious Attila. There was something in the way he looked at her, both at the gym this morning and then later, in the kitchen.

Not to mention that sentence that bugs her even more when she replays the conversation in her head.

Asker and I have met before.

Not *already met*, or *met this morning*.

But *met before*. As though some time has passed since their meeting.

The office landline jangles with such an old-fashioned ring that it makes her jump.

"Hello?" she replies uncertainly, since this is neither her extension nor her office.

"Ah, hello . . ." The man on the line sounds hesitant. "I'm looking for Bengt Sandgren."

"I'm afraid he's unwell. Who am I speaking to?"

"Ah . . ." The man clears his throat. "My name is Kjell Lilja, and I'm president of the model railway club up here in Hässleholm."

"Right."

"Well, Sandgren and I have been in touch a few times. He asked me to call . . ."

Asker sighs. She has seen a model railway catalogue somewhere in all the mess; this conversation is clearly hobby-related.

"As I mentioned, Bengt Sandgren isn't here."

"Do you know when he'll be back?"

"I'm afraid not."

"And he hasn't said anything to you? About the investigation?"

"What investigation?"

"The one into the figures being put in our model."

"Figures?"

"Yes, the small plastic figures we use to create different layouts and scenes. Someone is inserting figures into our model."

Asker tries to recall if she has ever seen a model railway other than on TV. "Isn't that the point of a model railway? That there are figures in it?"

"Yes, of course," Lilja replies. "We have several thousand of them. Our model is huge, we've been working on it for over forty years." His voice swells with pride.

"We follow a very meticulous plan as to which layouts are to be built and which figures and objects should be included. Extremely few changes are made, and when they are, all members must agree to them."

His voice grows more serious.

"But someone is making a mockery of the whole thing, inserting figures that aren't part of the plan. Probably a lapsed member."

"And Bengt Sandgren was helping you to investigate the matter."

"Yes, exactly!"

Yesterday's headache has returned. Asker pinches the bridge of her nose.

"We discovered two new ones just over an hour ago," Lilja says breathlessly. "Sandgren asked me to call as soon as it happened again. Said it was of utmost importance."

"Uh-huh." Asker rubs one of her temples, hopes that her tone will convey her level of interest.

"I can email you a few photos," Lilja goes on. "If you don't have the time to drive up here and collect the figures this evening, that is. So that you can update the investigation straightaway."

Asker is this close to telling him to just forget it. To explaining that there is no investigation, that Bengt Sandgren was just pretending to conduct one because it probably—no, *definitely*—isn't a crime to insert plastic figurines into someone else's model railway. Instead she bites her tongue and gives him her email address, mostly out of pure politeness. Lilja seems to pick up on her lack of interest nonetheless.

"Will you look at the pictures straightaway?" he asks anxiously. "Sandgren seemed to think it was very urgent."

"Sure," she says to wrap up. "Thank you for calling."

She hangs up. Pulls on her jacket and rummages around in the pockets for some Tylenol. She keeps a blister pack of headache tablets in every jacket she owns, along with a penknife and a pocket first-aid kit.

Old habits that she just can't shake.

She swallows the pill without water.

Just as she turns off the office lights, she hears the *pling* of her inbox.

Obviously she should ignore it. Go home, put on her running shoes, and try to clear her mind. But her day is already ruined, so why not finish it off in style: with her very first orphaned case.

She sits back down at the desk and logs into the computer.

Lilja's email contains two images.

She opens the first. It depicts an enormous model railway layout that appears to extend across several large rooms. Stations, villages, farms; even mountains and forests. Asker has never seen anything like it, actually can't help but be transfixed. It must have taken thousands of hours to build it and required enormous amounts of patience and a great eye for detail.

The second image is taken much closer up, and it makes her stiffen. The image contains two figures, a man and a woman, standing in front of a car. They are huddled together, and the man has his arm extended, to all appearances holding a cellphone.

The figures and the car behind them are meticulously painted, down to the last detail. Hair color, facial features, the shade of their rain jackets, and the glimpse of their sweaters underneath. Even the two letters on the car's license plate.

Asker's heart is, for once, faster than her head. Manages to thrum a double beat before her brain cottons on. Realizes where she has seen that scene before.

What those small model figures actually represent.

Or, more accurately—whom.

The figures are an almost exact copy of Smilla Holst's last Instagram post.

THE MOUNTAIN KING

When, that winter, the cancer put an end to Uncle Johan's life, he played sad. Stood up by the coffin with his head bowed, surrounded by mourning relatives.

In reality he was struggling to keep himself from beaming.

No one but Johan had known about the mountain.

Now his secrets were completely safe.

Deep down in the endless darkness.

Perhaps that was why he grew reckless?

Started taking unnecessary risks that led him down even more dangerous paths?

It all started when his stepfather caught him red-handed, just a few days after the funeral. Thinking the house was empty, he had snuck downstairs to top up his stocks of small plastic figures.

But instead of telling him off for trespassing, his stepfather took his presence there as a sign of interest, and proudly showed him around his little model workshop. Explained how the houses and landscapes were built, how to paint and place the plastic figures to make them seem as alive as possible.

The next week his stepfather took him along to the enormous model railway that he and his friends were working on together.

"Over fifteen hundred square feet," his stepfather explained. "And it's going to be even bigger. We're adding to it all the time."

After that, his stepfather showed him the controls and switches that operated all the circuits, before getting caught up in a debate about gear trains with a couple of his friends.

But what captured his imagination were the layouts themselves. The villages, streets, fields, and forests. He found several of the houses that he had visited in secret, represented down to the smallest detail. Even his secret mountain was there, nestled in among the forest-topped peaks in the middle of the model.

But most fascinating of all were the thousands of painted figures. A couple parting on a platform, workers loading a freight train, a family throwing a birthday party in an apple orchard, kids playing in a playground, fire engines tearing off down the street, and people holidaying by a lake with real water.

The model was in fact an enormous fairy-tale landscape full of frozen, expectant moments. Miniature scenes that came to life for only the briefest of moments as a train passed. When that happened you could almost hear the sounds, the music, the voices. A perfect, flawless world.

He stood there as though spellbound. Turned his gaze to another little scene in the model and waited for the next train. Again and again, until his stepfather said it was time to go home.

It was then that he met her, just outside the door.

Marie.

Marie's father was commander of the regiment, and they lived in a big house right in the center of town. All the boys in school would gaze at Marie, not only because she was new in town and beautiful. There was something else about her, too, something magnetic. Something that was multiplied a hundredfold by their short meeting at the model railway club.

Marie and her father were on the way in; he and his stepfather on the way out.

Both men stopped and exchanged a few words while he stood there opposite her.

"Hi!" she said, and even though he tried to reply, all he could get out was a mumble. He couldn't tear his eyes off her. Her blond hair, her smooth skin, her beautiful clothes—everything just as perfect as the little figures in the model.

As they drove home, he had already decided that he had to visit her house. Make it his.

As soon as possible.

To think what might have become of him had he decided against it. Resisted the temptation.

How different might his story have been then?

ASKER

Asker sits in the light of her desk lamp. She has set out her materials from the Holst case on Sandgren's desk.

Kjell Lilja said that they had found the figures in the model railway just an hour or two before he called her, which wasn't long after the news sites started publishing the information and images from the press conference.

Far too little time to locate suitable plastic figurines, paint them in minute detail and wait for the paint to dry. Not to mention insert them in the model. So whoever made the figures can't have come across the image on any of the news sites, but on Smilla's Instagram account instead. She opens Instagram. Smilla has around five hundred followers, but her account is open, which means anyone can view her posts.

The selfie of her and Malik is from Friday morning. In other words plenty of time to make and insert the figures.

But why? What was the point?

There are also other things that niggled.

Lilja said that Sandgren wanted to be contacted immediately if more figures appeared. Even implied that Sandgren had driven all the way up to Hässleholm, over an hour away, to collect the figures that the club had already found.

None of that fits with what she has heard or observed about Sandgren thus far, which was why she hadn't initially taken Lilja seriously.

And even though she is now trying to reevaluate the case, besides the model railway catalogue there is nothing in Sandgren's office to support what Lilja has said.

These two Sandgrens simply don't stack up. And even though she is using his computer, she can't access his user profile without his log-in details.

But perhaps someone else in the department knows more about him?

She stands up and steps into the corridor. Almost everything is dark, but at the base of Rosen's door she spots a thin sliver of light. A faint murmur coming from inside.

Asker knocks and enters in one fell swoop. She is their chief, after all.

Rosen is sitting at her desk, holding the receiver of her landline in both hands, like a fragile object. She claps one of her hands to her mouth, stares at Asker with an expression wavering between startled and caught.

"I'll have to call you back, James . . . ," she says in surprisingly good English to the person on the end of the line, then hangs up.

Asker looks at her questioningly.

"M-my son-in-law," Rosen stammers. "They live in Australia. My daughter's sick . . ."

"And you don't want to make expensive international calls from your own phone," Asker fills in.

Rosen gulps nervously.

Asker lets her stew in her fear for a few seconds before changing the subject.

"Bengt Sandgren. What was he working on lately?"

"I d-don't really know." Rosen is a bad liar.

"No? I thought you were the department's rock."

The nervous little woman gulps again.

"He was working on something slightly sensitive, I think. He didn't really want to say what."

"But you were helping him?" A shot in the dark, but it hits the mark.

"Only the odd database search, that sort of thing."

"What kind of searches?"

Rosen squirms.

"What kind of searches?" Asker repeats.

"M-missing persons. Bengt asked me to . . ."

She trails off, looks over Asker's shoulder into the corridor, as though to make sure no one is eavesdropping.

"Bengt asked me to put together a list of missing persons with some kind of connection to Skåne. Background info, that sort of thing."

"Do you still have it?"

She nods.

"Yes, he asked me to update it every now and then."

"How long have you been doing that?"

Rosen shrugs.

"A few years. The last time he asked me to update it was about a month ago."

"So you've been compiling a secret register using information combed from cases that neither the department nor Sandgren were involved in?"

"Oh, no." Rosen throws her arms out to her sides. "Not a register, just a list. Bengt said there was no harm in it. He usually says . . ."

She pauses, bites her lip, as though hesitant to go on.

"Bengt usually says that no one has any idea what we're doing down here in Resources. That the bosses upstairs couldn't care less what we're working on or what rules we're following, so long as we keep a low profile and don't attract attention."

Asker raises her eyebrows at the claim.

At the same time, up until just a few days ago she'd had no idea that there was a department for lost souls or even a level minus one, even though she took the same elevator as them every day.

"So you were maintaining a secret list for Sandgren," she sums up, trying to get back to the point. "Did you email it to him?"

Rosen shakes her head.

"Bengt wants everything on paper. He doesn't like reading on a screen. Prefers to have it on paper in his hands."

Asker thinks for a second.

"I haven't seen any of these lists in his office. Every document on his desk is at least two years old. Do you think he took the list home?"

Rosen shrugs.

"Don't know. Bengt can be pretty secretive at times . . ."

"Could you print out the list again?"

"Certainly."

"Good, I'd like it on my desk first thing tomorrow."

"All right. Oh, and would you like me to add those two . . ." Rosen trails off, as though she has said too much.

Asker tilts her head to one side.

"You mean Smilla and Malik?"

"Is that what they're called?" Rosen tries, but the lie doesn't work this time, either. She already knows the full names of both of the missing people.

Asker sizes her up carefully. She can quite easily picture the nervous woman rummaging through her files.

"Yes, you can add them," she says. "Oh, and one more thing."

"Yes?" Rosen looks concerned.

"Did Bengt ever mention a Martin Hill?"

The woman shakes her head.

"No, why?"

"Nothing in particular," says Asker. "Just a name I came across in his files."

An old friend, she adds silently to herself.

SEVENTEEN YEARS EARLIER

It is a hot Saturday in early summer, and she is exhausted.

Her father has a visitor, an old military man from Norrland who is staying with them for a few days. They are reviewing the Farm's every defensive measure—the height of the fences, the quality of the barbed wire, the depth of the bunker, and the diameter of the tunnels. What things they must work on, prepare for. Within a matter of days they will be enemies.

That's how it is with Per. He can listen for a while, but at the end of the day no one ever knows better than him.

But until that inevitable fallout comes, he is occupied, at least, which gives her some time to herself.

She spends it cycling around, as usual. Stops outside her classmates' houses, watches them through her binoculars.

The sheep, as Per calls them.

The idiots, the ones who let themselves be duped.

The ones who haven't understood the Great Truth. The danger that awaits.

Today she is spying on Martin Hill.

Not for the first time, either. The Hill family live on a small redbrick terrace that gives onto a forest grove. The perfect spot to watch them from.

She knows that Martin's parents run a pub.

That his father's skin is a dark umber, his mother's a chalky white. That they work a lot. But she also knows that they are kind to their son.

Hug him often. Laugh together. Sing.

Her own mother has remarried, still lives in Malmö with her little sister, Camille. They see each other only one weekend a month. Stiff, uncomfortable hours devoid of hugs or songs.

But that isn't why she watches Hill's family, but because of his secret. The backpack of tools that he always carries with him.

Today she is in luck and arrives just as he is cycling off with his backpack on his back.

Following him is a piece of cake. He only looks around a few times, and she keeps in his blind spot, just as she has been taught.

He pedals slowly, seems to tire easily.

Gets off and walks on even the small slopes.

Gradually they travel farther and farther out into the forest, on increasingly small trails. Then he stops without warning, pushes his bike a little way through the bushes.

Through the binoculars she sees him looking at a map. After that he walks straight into the forest. She parks her bike and follows him.

Shadowing him through the forest is even easier than on the bike.

Martin doesn't care about finding the stealthiest, quietest route. About taking unmarked trails or avoiding clear obstacles. He trundles along, snapping twigs, gets caught in a thicket. Swears and coughs loudly.

All the things Per has taught her not to do, ever since she was little. For in the forest the one who is quietest always wins, as he likes to say.

No one has explained this to Martin. She could sneak right up behind his back and he wouldn't hear a thing.

The thought makes her smile.

The abandoned cabin appears among the trees, almost without warning. It's so overgrown with brushwood and moss that it's barely standing.

Stares straight out into the forest with gaping, empty window-eyes that were smashed years ago. Martin walks up to the cabin. Stands on his tiptoes to peek inside.

She watches him through her binoculars.

His body language has changed, more eager now. Excited.

It's obvious he wants to get inside. But he doesn't take the window, as she would have done. Instead he opts for the front door.

It's completely flat; the door handle was removed long ago.

Martin puts down his backpack, rummages around in it, and pulls out two different handles. Tests them in the door, makes a few small adjustments.

And hey presto, the door opens.

She can't help but be impressed. Martin may not be any outdoorsman, but he has definitely done this before. Has encountered enough doors without handles to know to bring his own.

Cautiously she moves closer. The cabin is small, and she can't get inside behind him without breaking cover.

So she finds a better lookout point, to try to see what he is doing in there. She sees him every now and then through one of the windows.

He is shining a flashlight, moving slowly. She makes out the occasional camera flash.

After about half an hour he comes back out again. Carefully shuts the door behind him and removes the door handle before putting on his backpack.

His trousers and sweater are flecked with dust and dirt.

He looks so incredibly happy, so content, that she simply has to find out what he was up to in the cabin.

She waits for him by the bikes. Makes herself completely visible so as not to shock him.

He gives a start when he sees her, but quickly composes himself.

"Leo Asker," he says, amused. Uses her full name in a way that, strangely enough, she likes.

"What are the odds?"

He adds a smile. His eyes are twinkling; he doesn't look as sickly as usual. Perhaps not quite as surprised as she expected, either.

"What were you doing in the cabin?" she asks with a twinge of irritation.

"Nothing."

"Nothing?"

He shrugs.

"Just looking around. Took a few pictures."

He can tell that she doesn't believe him, and an offended furrow appears on his brow.

"I didn't take anything, if that's what you're wondering. I'm not a bloody thief."

She tilts her head to one side.

"So you cycled all the way out here, plodded all the way through the forest, and broke into a cabin just to look around?"

"Yeah," he says. "Though it's much more than just looking."

He purses his lips and looks at her, as though trying to come to some sort of decision. Then seems to make up his mind.

"I think old buildings are cool, OK?"

"Cool?" she repeats ironically, even though she shouldn't.

"Yes . . . or maybe even . . ." He sighs, as though he can't be bothered to hold it in anymore. "Beautiful."

"*Beautiful?*" *She does it again. Can't help herself.*

He looks away, blushing, and suddenly she regrets her churlish tone.

She has uncovered his secret.

Or, rather—he has revealed it to her. Confided in her.

No one has ever done that before. Not like this.

A fragile gift, one that she must nurture.

She nods slowly. Forces an awkward smile.

"*Beautiful,*" *she says again, more softly this time.* "*I get it!*"

HILL

Hill has ended his working day by ticking off his daily dose of university admin. Normally he would meet up with a few friends for a quick drink, maybe a bite to eat. Call Sofie and suggest a film, maybe something more. She is in town for another week before heading back to The Hague, and he likes spending time with her.

Perhaps even more than that.

But the shock revelation about MM has sapped him of any desire for adventure. The news sites are being relatively tight-lipped, of course, but it's still pretty easy to read between the lines that the police consider MM the prime suspect in Smilla Holst's disappearance.

Hill has always thought himself a pretty good judge of character. It's a skill he has had ever since he was a sickly child with heart problems whose family flitted around the country. Never more than a few years in one place, always a new pub or restaurant to run, which for him meant new schools, new friends, and new tormentors.

So reading people and moods has always been his specialty. A survival strategy that has with time become his superpower.

His grandmother has another theory.

Nana Hill is from the Caribbean, and she practices the old religions. Makes offerings of rum and cigars to the saints and the spirits. Nana claims that his extraordinary people skills are all thanks to the fact that she wrung a black cock's neck with her bare hands by the light of the full moon. Or that she chopped a red cock's head off by the light of the new moon. The story has shifted somewhat over the years.

But this time the memory of Nana Hill doesn't bring a smile to his face.

For the first time in his life, he doubts himself. If someone as recently as this morning had asked him if MM was capable of kidnapping his own girlfriend, he would have laughed in their face. *MM is friendly, sociable, and talented*, he would have said. *A good kid.*

Has he really read him so wrong?

It is already dark outside when Hill leaves the campus.

On the streets there are only a few people around. The autumn wind sweeps the dead leaves into a dance between the buildings; the streetlights are lit, and the rain spatters draw ominous patterns on the ground.

He cycles down to the big supermarket opposite the train station and picks up what he needs for dinner. Despite being the son of publicans, he only has seven go-to dishes. Normally he prefers to eat out.

Tonight dish number four will have to do. Bangers and mash.

On the way back to the bike rack he spots a familiar figure.

It's MM's friend, Mya.

She is wearing a beanie hat, has turned up the collar on her green military jacket, and is staring down Järnvägsgatan as though waiting to be picked up. Puffs an e-cigarette as she waits.

He has to speak to her, find out if she knows anything.

"Hi!"

His greeting startles her.

"Sorry, I didn't mean to catch you by surprise," says Hill.

"No worries."

The young woman takes a drag on her e-cigarette. They have only met once or twice, but something about her feels very familiar.

She is fairly petite and slim, in her early twenties, with dark hair peeping out from under her beanie. Her eyes are framed by dark makeup, her gaze watchful and intelligent.

"Isn't it awful, all that with . . ." Hill's question hangs in the air, and he tries to conclude it with a hand gesture. "Malik."

"I don't know anything about the kidnap stuff, if that's what you're asking," she replies tersely.

"But I had the impression you two were close?" Hill attempts.

The young woman takes another drag, gives him a watchful look. Then shakes her head.

"We used to hang out sometimes. I don't know his girlfriend, so . . ."

She shrugs. Looks away, apparently done with the conversation.

"When did you last see each other?"

Another shrug.

"A week or so ago, maybe."

"Have you tried to reach him?"

She nods, takes another drag, lets out a puff of smoke.

"But when I call it goes straight to voicemail."

She glances down the street again. Exhales a cloud of fruity vape smoke.

"You do urban exploration, too, don't you?" he asks.

It isn't such a wild guess. She has already told him that she liked his book, she hangs out with MM, and besides that she has scratches and cement dust on her boots.

She waits for a few seconds before replying, then nods.

"Have you and MM been on expeditions together?"

"Yep."

"Where?" He doesn't really know why he asks. Perhaps he just wants to keep the conversation going.

Mya doesn't reply.

A dark van comes sweeping down the street, stops fifty feet away and flashes its lights. The engine hums quietly.

"My cousin," says Mya, nodding toward the car. "He's here to pick me up."

She quickly turns off the e-cigarette and slips it in her pocket, then makes to go. Stops short as she does.

"MM used to talk about you all the time," she says with a softer tone of voice and the hint of a smile. "He said you were the real deal. That you could be trusted. Is that true?"

"I hope so," Hill replies, trying to look as trustworthy as possible.

Mya opens her mouth as though to say something more, but as she does so the van beeps.

The sound startles her. For one brief moment she almost looks scared.

"See you!" she says quickly.

Hill watches her as she jogs lightly over to the van.

The rain is falling heavier now, draws sharp lines through the cones of light. The van's windshield wipers are already on. Even so, the driver doesn't come closer, but waits down the street.

And when Mya opens the door, the internal light doesn't come on. Something about the whole situation sparks Hill's concern.

He walks over to the edge of the pavement and tries to catch a glimpse of the driver as the van goes past. But all he can make out is a dark silhouette in the driver's seat.

Mya, on the other hand, is staring straight at him. Presses her palm to the window in a silent motion that could be a wave.

But afterward, when he thinks about her eyes, he has the impression that it was something else.

THURSDAY

ASKER

As usual, Asker wakes up long before her alarm goes off. She puts on her running gear and does her Thursday run, a headlamp lighting her way through the autumn darkness. She turns up the volume in her earphones to get her body going.

She exits the grounds, does a lap of the lake, and runs onto the golf course. Turns by the old oak that serves as her return point for a three-mile run. It's cold out, so she ups the pace to get it over with as soon as possible. Sprints the last stretch when she starts to lose the feeling in her fingers.

After a hot shower she compares her time with last week's, to make sure she's maintaining the same level.

That she hasn't declined, lost pace, aged.

Over breakfast she browses the news sites, but besides the images from yesterday's press conference nothing new has emerged. Nothing that has reached the press, at least.

She pulls up the image of the small figures again. They are almost eerily precise in their detail.

Of course, it could always be some moron who saw the picture on Instagram, got wind that Smilla and Malik were missing before the news broke, and then set to work on the figures and car.

All of a sudden it hits her.

She opens the Instagram selfie of the couple and zooms in. Yes, the black car is visible behind Malik and Smilla, and someone could feasibly be able to guess the model. The license plate, however, isn't visible at all.

And yet the little model car reads "MM" on the license plate, just like in reality.

She quickly scrolls through Malik's social media, but can't find any picture of his car.

In theory it would probably be possible to dig up the license and registration number from the Swedish Transport Authority's records.

But that would make things unnecessarily convoluted.

The simplest, most logical conclusion is that whoever painted those figures had met Malik Mansur, seen his car, and noted the personalized license plate. But this conclusion begs even more questions. Why create those figures, why insert them into the model railway, and why now?

The only way to get more answers is to head north.

Into the forests, toward the Shadowlands. The very thought makes her shudder.

There are four cars parked in the house's garage. Asker is allowed to use any of them, but always plumps for the electric car parked closest to the door. Not that she couldn't drive any of the muscle cars, or the big Range Rover parked farther in. Or the quad bike or motorbike, for that matter. Thanks to Prepper Per she can drive pretty much any vehicle going. Do makeshift repairs, too, in a pinch. But on Per's farm they had no electrics; they hadn't been invented back then. That might be why she prefers them.

Quiet, fast, modern.

With no ties to the past.

The journey takes an hour and twenty minutes. The scar under her tattoo itches, like it always does when she heads toward these parts.

North of Lund the landscape is undulating at first. Rolling fields and wind farms, dapples of deciduous forests around Ringsjön Lake.

Water; deep blue skies; blazing autumnal reds and yellows. As pretty as a picture.

Then, little by little, the conifers take over. Replace the autumnal hues with blues and greens, dusky shades that encroach ever more upon the road. Interrupted only now and then by dark glints of water or severe rocky outcrops.

The Primeval Boundary, as Prepper Per used to call the area. Only to then launch into a sermon on the solidity of the bedrock on the Fennoscandian Shield, while sneering contemptuously at the more porous, southerly rock types that were hardly worth dipping a shovel in. Only sheep got involved in that sort of nonsense.

But in his bunker deep down behind the primeval shield, Per Asker and his daughter would be safe. Secure.

At least from the rest of the world.

But in the end the real threat didn't come from the outside.

She runs her finger along her scar again. Digs her nails into the letters until her skin starts to throb.

ASKER

Hässleholm is both a railway hub and an old garrison town of just over twenty thousand inhabitants. It is situated almost exactly in the center of northern Skåne, equidistant from the Kattegat Sea to the west and Hanö Bay to the east, and just about twenty miles from the provincial border with Småland.

The model railway club is housed, suitably enough, in a converted tank factory. Steel gates, barbed wire fence, few to no windows.

Gray clouds have crept in over the horizon and will cover the entire sky before long.

Kjell Lilja is waiting outside the premises. He is slim with a curving back, and wears a pair of horn-rimmed spectacles that he is constantly poking back up to the bridge of his nose. A hairline approaching the Polar Circle.

She has googled him, found out that he will soon be fifty-five, and is a school headmaster who enjoys orienteering, baking shows, and—needless to say—model railways.

"Now, let's see . . ." Lilja fumbles with the keys, and then with the alarm. "It's rarely me who opens up," he says apologetically. "We normally meet in the evenings, and by then someone else has got in before me."

"How many people have keys and the alarm code?" Asker asks.

"Well . . ." Lilja scratches his neck. "I've tried to figure that out. We've had quite a bit of turnover with members, and it's all a little . . ." He searches for the right word, and eventually lands on "muddled."

"So you don't know?" Asker notes.

"Well, no. I'm relatively new here as club president, and security didn't use to be such a high priority. But all that is going to change. Our security firm is coming over a little later today. So then, step inside!"

He opens his arms in an inviting gesture.

Through the front door they enter a foyer with a ticket booth. A note on the glass states the opening hours and ticket prices.

"And you're open to visitors," Asker notes.

"Yes indeed, two weekends a month. And we also arrange model railway fairs and a few other things besides."

Lilja leads her farther in, past a few glass display cases containing old train signs and up to a steel double door. Once again he fumbles with his keys before managing to unlock the doors.

The room inside is big and almost pitch-black. All that is visible are small red LEDs that briefly call to mind Enok Zafer's office.

Lilja fiddles with a circuit cabinet, bringing the fluorescent light tubes in the ceiling to life, one row at a time.

Asker has already seen the model railway in photos, but even so it is hard not to be impressed by its size. Lilja appears to have noticed her reaction.

"Soon we'll have reached two thousand square feet," he says with a swoop of his hand. "We use a 1:87 scale, or HO as it's called in model railway circles."

He reels off a load of figures about the number of feet of tracks and how many trains can run at the same time. Asker hums encouragingly, but her attention is focused on the model. Before her, beyond a small, transparent plastic screen, stands Hässleholm railway station, complete with sidings and loading bays. Beyond the station building lies the town proper. Neon signs and windows gleam. Sixties cars line the streets.

Everywhere, on streets and platforms, in gardens and houses, appear small, colorfully painted figures, almost all in the process of doing something. Loading a train carriage, stepping off a bus, driving a car, mowing a lawn, gossiping with neighbors or waving their kids off to school. The idyllic, pastel-colored small-town life roughly as we see it in old newsreels. The illusion is so well executed that in some places it is almost possible to imagine what the figures are chatting about.

". . . middle of the sixties," Lilja recounts. "That's the era we generally keep to."

"Who decided that?" she asks.

"Oh, that decision was made long before my time," he chuckles.

"You see, the first tracks of the model were laid over forty years ago. Most of our original builders are no longer with us. But the plan is still in place. Our goal is to build all seven of the stations that existed in the municipality when rail traffic was at its height. We're working on station six in the next room."

He points toward a large doorway a little way off to the right, through which the model appears to continue.

"In there we have a winter scene. We try to vary our seasons a bit. But the majority of the layouts, as you see, are in summer."

He gestures at her to follow him along one side of the model.

In the middle of the layout rises a forest-topped peak that towers over the rest of the layout by almost three feet. Then flattens out toward the side that they are walking along. Becomes farms, fields, plains.

"I see the model contains far more than just trains."

Asker points at a few tanks. Lilja pushes a button by the plastic screen, which makes cannons boom from a speaker as small flashes of light spark in the mouths of the cannons.

"A little homage to our military connections," he says, pleased. "As you will have noted, the Swedish Armed Forces are our landlord. But you're quite right. Some of our members are more interested in driving the trains, while others place much more importance on the model-making itself. On creating a perfect world, down to the last detail."

He goes on ahead of her, follows the track into the room to the right. As promised, the layout now transforms into a wintry landscape. The figures are bundled up in hats and warm clothes. Some of them are skiing or ice-skating.

"The distance between the stations isn't true to scale, of course—that would have made the model far too big. But otherwise we try to keep everything as realistic as possible," Lilja goes on. "Like here, for example."

He presses another button, and a snowplow starts driving along one of the winter streets.

"The cars and movable figures are on small magnetic loops, which are fixed to the substrate and then painted over."

Asker can't help but admire the handiwork. Even the headlights on the snowplow are beaming, and the driver can be seen at the wheel. She can almost hear the sound of the blade scraping against the road.

"This way!" Lilja waves her on.

At the far end of the room the layout is still a work in progress. The railway tracks continue, but only a few of the buildings and other objects are in place, and the chipboard is as-yet unpainted. There are no hills or trees, which makes the layout feel flat and two-dimensional.

"The world's end, so to say," Lilja explains. "And here they are." He points at a car and two figures standing on the bare chipboard at the front of the layout.

Asker immediately recognizes them from the photo. Malik's black Golf and the two young lovers in front of it, frozen in a selfie pose.

Asker leans in and studies it as closely as she can. The hair colors, the clothes, the pose—everything is, if possible, even more realistic than she had grasped from the image that Lilja sent.

"How did you come across the figures?" she asks.

"A few other members and I came in yesterday afternoon to work on this new layout. We saw them pretty much straightaway. I think he wanted us to. Otherwise I don't suppose he would have put the figures exactly where we were working?"

"He?" Asker stands up straighter.

Lilja shrugs.

"The overwhelming majority of our members and visitors are men."

"When did you last work on this section of the model?"

Lilja appears to have anticipated the question.

"On Friday. We went home just after seven p.m., and the figures weren't there then, I'm certain of it. At the weekend we had an open house for the public, Saturday and Sunday from eleven to three. From what I gather there were quite a few visitors."

He makes an apologetic gesture.

"You see, as president I'm normally always present for the open weekends, but last weekend I was prevented from attending."

"So in theory any of the visitors could have put the figures there?" Asker asks.

"Yes, in theory," Lilja confirms. "But I'd still be inclined to think it was one of our members. Either active or former."

"What makes you say that?"

"Above all, the handiwork itself. Painting figures at as small a scale as 1:87 requires the right brushes, paints, tweezers, probably a workstation with a craft light and magnifier."

He pauses, like a teacher wanting to make sure his pupil is still following. She is.

"And if you look closely at the figures you'll find they're perfectly painted," he goes on more quietly. "Not the slightest smudging or streaks. This is someone who knows what he's doing. Someone with the requisite tools, skills, and patience. Someone who wants every last detail to be just right."

He nods in satisfaction at his own conclusion.

"Besides, as you know, this isn't the first time someone has inserted illicit figures into our model. Have you spoken to Sandgren?"

"I'm afraid Bengt Sandgren is in the hospital. And as it stands I don't have access to the materials from his investigation."

"Oh, I'm sorry, I had no idea." Lilja pulls a sad frown.

"Can we rewind a little," says Asker. "You mentioned you were pretty new as club president?"

"Yes, that's right. We moved here a few years ago when I was offered the post of headmaster. But I actually grew up not so far away. And since I've always been a model railway enthusiast it was only natural that I apply to join the club. A place for like-minded souls, so to say."

Lilja pushes his spectacles up his nose for what must be the fifth time.

"I started out as your average member," he goes on. "But quite soon it became evident that there was some simmering discontent with the previous president."

"What sort of discontent?"

"Well . . . ," Lilja says fidgetingly. "Ulf Krook had been at his post a long time, he was starting to get on in years. The members thought it was time for some fresh blood, so I was voted in at the AGM last December."

"How did Ulf take it?"

Lilja gives a self-conscious smile. But he's in full swing now, and can't help but go on.

"Not particularly well, if I'm honest. Ulf isn't an easy man to deal with, but his father was one of the club's founders. Ulf and some of his supporters felt that the presidency was his birthright, so to say."

"So there was a dispute?"

"Unfortunately, yes. We had quite a stormy AGM, where Ulf initially refused to step down. In the end the police had to be called. A regrettable turn of events."

Lilja grimaces, as though to convey how regrettable the situation was.

"Ulf's most loyal hangers-on threatened us with all manner of things. It made for a few tumultuous months, but things have settled down now."

"And where does Bengt Sandgren come into all of this?" Asker inquires.

"He called me shortly after I was elected president. Must have been around June. Sandgren explained that he was working on an important investigation and asked me to contact him immediately if we found any figures in the model that shouldn't be there."

"Which you did?"

Lilja nods.

"Just a few weeks later we found a figure in the model spraying graffiti. Hardly something that would have happened in the sixties. Everyone was convinced Ulf was behind it. But since Sandgren had expressly asked me to call him, I got in touch with him anyway. He came up the very same day, took photos, and removed both the figure and what he had been spraying. He used rubber gloves, took everything extremely seriously, which I certainly hadn't expected. But Sandgren explained that it wasn't the first time that something like that had happened."

"Do you know how many times it had happened before?"

"At least three, if I understood Sandgren correctly. Apparently he and Ulf Krook had been in touch about the matter. But I'm afraid I don't know any more than that. Ulf never mentioned anything about it. As I said, certain members are quite convinced that he's the one behind it all."

"And what do you think?"

Lilja scratches his neck again.

"I try to see the best in people. Though with Ulf let's just say that's a challenge. He's a difficult person. Still, conflict or not, that simply isn't the done thing. It's just not how we treat other model-makers. It goes against everything we stand for."

"What do you mean?" Asker asks.

"As I mentioned before, a model railway is about much more than the trains themselves. Look at this, for example."

He points at a building.

"We've built a school here. You can see the children playing in the playground. A few are playing hopscotch, others kicking a ball around. The caretaker is raking the leaves, the postman is cycling past, there's even a cat sitting up in one of the trees. A perfect little story that we tell together, part of a wider world that we are also building together. But whoever does this . . ."

He waves his hand in the direction of the figures of Smilla and Malik.

". . . doesn't care about collaboration, they just want to tell their own story."

He straightens up, as though he has finished speaking.

"Where can I find Ulf Krook?" Asker asks.

Lilja looks surprised. "Well, Ulf's been retired a long time, so I'd suppose he's at home. But . . ."

"But what?"

He lowers his voice. Pushes his spectacles up his nose.

"As I said, Ulf is rather peculiar. And he lives in quite an isolated place. I have to wait here for Daniel, our alarm technician. And Ulf and I are like oil and water, so . . ." Lilja fidgets again, as though these disjointed sentences are paining him.

"What are you saying?"

Lilja takes a deep breath.

"I'm saying that you perhaps shouldn't go there alone."

HILL

Martin Hill's office has a view overlooking a park with an outdoor gym. Often—especially in colder months—he will sit with a cup of coffee and watch the few people working out below. See them lifting, pressing, pulling, jumping. Will reluctantly admire the almost military discipline required to force themselves out in the nasty weather and torture themselves in that way.

He for one is far too lazy. For him, cycling offers just the right amount of exercise, and as luck would have it he has inherited his father's metabolism, which means he doesn't need to give much thought to what he eats or drinks.

Today there is one solitary person down there in the outdoor gym. Working through exercise after exercise with steely resolve, not missing a single rep.

Their tenacity makes him think of Leo Asker once again.

She has been on his mind quite a lot lately, ever since MM introduced him to Mya.

Mya is shorter and more petite than Leo was, and dark-haired besides. Still, they both have something in common. That combination of strength and vulnerability that he finds difficult to resist.

He hasn't seen Leo in many years, not since Christmas when he was sixteen.

Still, thoughts of her have been humming at the back of his head. Tormenting him.

Perhaps that's also why the whole kidnapping situation has hit him all the harder. It's almost personal.

Of course he has tried googling her, but without success. She isn't on social media, which given her past doesn't surprise him in the least. Prepper Per wouldn't even let her be in school photos, in case Big Brother was watching.

Still, Google had no trouble finding Leo's mother, stepfather, little sister, and brother-in-law. They all work together at Lissander and Partners, one of Malmö's most prestigious law firms.

The whole family is represented in professional studio headshots on its website.

Judging by the photo, Leo's little sister, Camille, is a softer version of the Leo he remembers.

Camille's husband, Fredric Gylling, looks like a typical lawyer. Side part, expensive suit and watch, and a cool smile intended to seem both trustworthy and serious. Roughly the same smile that Isabel's husband, Junot, has in his shot.

But Leo's mother, Isabel, conveys the most authority of them all.

Her gaze is firm, her mouth determined, her posture that of someone who is used to being listened to.

To being obeyed.

Hill has actually met Isabel once. The only lasting memory he has of their encounter was that Leo and her mother both seemed pretty much equally uncomfortable in each other's company.

Leo told him that she could have stayed with her mom and sister in Malmö after the divorce, but that back then Prepper Per was still relatively normal.

Leo loved him and looked up to him, so she chose her father. Her relationship with her mother never quite recovered after that.

Hill leans back in his chair. All it would take would be a phone call to the law firm. He could explain to them in a friendly tone that he and Leo are childhood friends, and ask for some sort of contact details. He would probably get them. He's good at instilling trust.

Still, he doesn't make the call.

Obviously he knows why. He's been struggling with the same dilemma for sixteen years. Has been on the verge of picking up the phone, just like now, more times than he can count.

But in the end the guilt always wins out.

Hill drains his coffee cup and turns on his computer. The day's to-do list is waiting, but he has no desire to work.

Instead he activates the student database and searches for Mya's name and address. As suspected, no one by the name of Mya is enrolled in his course.

But he has the impression he might have seen her at one or two of his lectures. The university entrances aren't locked, and from time to time it happens that people turn up who aren't enrolled. Normally urban explorers who are intrigued by him. Maybe she's one of them, or maybe she just went along with MM for fun.

He has replayed yesterday's conversation in his head several times. All the way from her first reply to that strange wave.

She was trying to play it cool, but she seemed anxious at the mention of MM's name. And he got the feeling that in a way she was almost asking him for help. Sending him some sort of subconscious signal, in roughly the same way that Leo had so many years before.

Back then he was too young to get it. Avoided stepping in.

Now he's older, wiser, and has more resources.

But how can he help Mya if he doesn't even know her surname?

Hill kicks his chair back in frustration.

The movement makes his desk shake, toppling the little white model figure on his desk lamp for what must be the tenth time. He picks it up and pops it in his pocket. Then looks out the window again.

The fitness freak down in the outdoor gym, clearly done for the day, is jogging off through the faint October drizzle.

Eventually disappears out of sight.

Leo Asker, Hill thinks again.

He has never met anyone like her.

SEVENTEEN YEARS EARLIER

"Fuckwits," Leo *mumbles to herself.*

She is standing in front of her locker, her gym bag slung over her shoulder, her hair still wet from the shower. The steel door is dented again, won't open.

Someone has scrawled something on it, too.

Written the word Freak *in marker pen with sloppy letters.*

There are only a few weeks left until the end of the year, and the cool kids in tenth grade are getting bolder. Have decided to push all the rules to the breaking point.

What could happen to them now? They're about to finish school.

Which makes them all the more unbearable. They are at the height of their popularity and power.

She turns to look for Martin. *Wants to ask him to borrow his screwdriver, as usual.*

But even though their breaks coincide, Martin isn't there.

She frowns, peers down the corridor.

There's a commotion over by the bathrooms. Violent movements, crude, adolescent voices.

*"Get the little n****r upside down!" she hears someone shout.*

She should keep out of it. Just a few more weeks, then they'll all be gone.

She clenches her jaw.

Stares at the words scrawled on her locker. A new burst of laughter rattles through the corridor.

She puts her gym bag down. Pulls out one of her wet sports socks and starts heading down the corridor.

One of the school doors has been propped open with a round rock, to let in the early summer air.

She picks up the rock and puts it in the sports sock. Twirls it in the air a few times to stretch it out and get a feel for its weight and equilibrium.

Once she has, the sock is three feet long, the rock down in its toe. She holds it behind her back and makes her way toward the bathrooms.

A circle of onlookers has gathered. Curious pupils from every year who are both amused by what's going on and relieved it isn't happening to them.

The cubicle is open, and two of the cool kids are holding Martin's head down in a flushing toilet.

A third kid, some knockoff beefsteak whose name she doesn't remember beyond the fact that it ends in Y, is standing to one side, giving orders.

"Push him all the way down so he gets nice and clean."

There are three of them, which means she will have to be fast. Decisive.

She steps inside the circle of onlookers. Y-name spots her and gives a big grin.

"Well well well, if it isn't the freak. If you're coming to help your little b—"

The sock whines in the air, quickly picks up momentum before the rock hits him in his crotch with a heavy thud. He groans, grabs his crown jewels, and drops to his knees.

The next kid lets go of Martin. Instinctively takes a step forward.

Makes it no farther before the whooshing rock strikes him somewhere between his chin and the tip of his nose.

He wails, claps his hands to his face, and stumbles away.

The third cool kid is still holding Martin's neck.

Goggles at his fallen leader and then at Leo, as though he can't see what's coming.

She swings the sock, makes a few loud spins. Tilts her head to one side and waits for him.

He lets go of Martin, scrambles out of the cubicle, and whimpers away, back to the wall in terror. She slows her spins, lowers her arm.

The guy on the floor, the one with the Y-name, is groaning in pain. His right-hand man has sunk down by the wall with his hands over his face. Blood and saliva seep out from between his fingers.

Around them stands a semicircle of speechless faces, all of whom seem unable to get their heads around what they have just witnessed.

ASKER

The rain patters against the windshield in irregular bursts and intensifies the grayish browns of the patches of land nestled in among the dense woodland. The deciduous forests have almost entirely disappeared. Only a few stubborn birches remain here and there, gleaming yellow-gold among the conifers. The roads are getting narrower, the blacktop rougher, the sky lower.

When Asker is halfway to her destination, her cellphone starts to ring. Her sister's number. As usual she ignores the call. Waits for the obligatory, long-winded text message that is guaranteed to follow.

Camille has only two reasons to be calling her. Either to (a) remind her of an upcoming birthday, or (b) invite her to the celebration of such an occasion. Neither of the two appeals to Leo in the slightest.

Ulf Krook's house is situated on a forest-topped peak just north of Hässleholm. A worn gravel track leads the way. A rusty sign announces that it is a private road, and that unwanted visitors would do best to keep away. The road is dotted with potholes that are filled with brown rainwater, forcing Asker to zigzag her way along. Above the car, the bluey-green conifers close in to form an ever-heavier ceiling.

Occasionally sideroads appear that lead deeper into the forest, and at the end of some of them she spots flashes of small, ramshackle cottages. A few crooked mailboxes suggest that some of them are probably inhabited.

As she pulls up to her destination, she sees an open swing gate drooping down toward a ditch at the side of the road. On the gatepost sits another sign that repeats the previous warning that this is private property and that entry is at one's own risk. For added emphasis someone appears to have shot bullet holes in the metal.

The yard in front of the house is a mud bath. The rain is kicking up a storm in the puddles, making the dark surface of the water thrum.

Along the left-hand side of the yard runs a large shed, the moss-laden roofing of which has partly fallen in. Along the right is a corrugated-metal car shelter filled with old wrecks of cars and rusty machines that haven't been moved in years.

The house stands in sharp contrast to the rest of the property. A stereotypical house of horrors, it's a shambolic, three-storey building in a cheerless, quasi-gothic style that Asker hasn't seen before, at least not in Sweden. The wooden façade is flecked with dirt and algae. Above it a steep roof that slopes at every imaginable angle.

The weathervane depicts a black cat. On the roof ridge beside it perch a pair of crows who stare curiously at Asker as she approaches. They immediately call to mind the flock of rooks outside Madame Rind's house.

Even though she has never been here before, something about the site feels familiar. Its remoteness and gloom, the hint of suspicion toward the outside world. The Shadowlands, as she used to call it. The place where nothing is as it seems.

Prepper Per's world.

Outside the front door stand five cars, none newer than ten years old.

A little farther away stands a dirty, dark van. She parks next to the cars, does up her jacket, and pulls up her collar to keep out the rain, then opens the car door. The electric car has snuck in so quietly that no one seems to have heard her coming.

A long, steep concrete staircase leads up to the front door. There is no doorbell, only a heavy metal knocker. The sound echoes faintly through the rooms inside, but no one opens.

Asker tries again, harder, but the result is the same.

She goes back down the steps and tries to peer through a window, but the house stands on such tall foundations that she can't see in. Besides, the upper windows are screened by heavy curtains.

The basement windows, however, are almost at waist height. She cups her hands against the glass. There is a grille on the inside of the window, but behind it she makes out a boiler room and, beyond that, something that looks like a workshop.

She continues around to the side of the house. Tries to dodge the water streaming down through the broken gutters. The lawn is a weed bed, the fruit trees beyond it contorted, bursting with long water spouts.

Just before the next corner, Asker sees a tall staircase made of cracked concrete leading up to a back door.

The crows up on the roof caw in warning.

Asker stops short, looks around cautiously.

Still no one to be seen. The only movements are those of the rain splashing against the ground.

The third basement window does indeed belong to what is a surprisingly neat workshop. A workbench with a craft light and magnifier, tools big and small in rows on the walls. Shelves of paint cans and brushes. Everything Lilja mentioned.

Below the window stands a table bearing a model house and a number of small plastic figures. Asker holds her phone up against the window, and is just snapping a string of photos when a sudden clap makes her start.

A gunshot.

She whips around, crouches down, and looks around her.

Yet another clap, and this time she's sure. It's a pistol or revolver of a fairly high caliber, and it's being fired nearby.

Asker squeezes into the corner between the back stairs and the wall of the house while instinctively feeling inside her jacket for her firearm. She realizes the truth of the situation long before her hand confirms it.

She came here straight from home, without picking up her firearm from HQ.

Prepper Per would have meted out many hours' hard labor to atone for that mistake. Wouldn't have cared about her excuse that this was hardly an official case, that she was just going to visit a model railway club and was hardly expecting to get shot at. Besides, how often does anyone actually expect to get shot at?

A third clap, followed by a fourth. The sound is slightly more muffled, a different gun than the first. Two marksmen, then.

However, she has heard neither the whistle of the bullets nor the sound of them hitting a fixed object. A fifth clap, followed by a sixth and a seventh. Then a cry, or perhaps rather a whoop for joy.

Asker cautiously stands up straight, wipes a drop of rain from the bridge of her nose.

The shots aren't being aimed at her. In all likelihood it's someone firing at targets.

Carefully she peers around the corner to the back of the house. What once was a garden continues all the way up to a barn. The sun has drained the deep red from the painted wood façade, and here and there on the dark roof she can see holes from missing tiles. A sliding door in the middle of the barn is open, and she can hear voices coming from inside.

Asker takes the garden path in that direction. Intentionally kicks her feet in the gravel a few times so that they will hear her over the rain.

Adds a "Hello!" as she is getting closer.

It's never a good idea to catch people by surprise when they have weapons in their hands.

The voices fall silent, and a ruddy man with a black leather jacket and goatee pokes his head out the door.

He is wearing a pair of big, round, metal welding goggles that, combined with his clothes, make him look like a steampunk character.

The man glares at her, then disappears back into the barn.

Asker slowly steps closer and stops in the doorway.

The barn must be fifty feet long. At the far end lies a huge pile of old straw bales, but beyond that it has been cleared of objects. The wooden walls, like the roof, have gaps in some spots, letting both the daylight and rainwater in. The air smells of damp and gunpowder.

In the middle of the barn stands a table on which lie three handguns, along with a few cartons of ammunition.

Over by the straw bales stand two life-sized cardboard silhouettes.

Goatee has positioned himself next to an elderly man, seems to say something to him that she can't catch.

"Well, who the fuck are you?" the elder of the two asks, raising his goggles onto his head. He is around seventy years old and has a burly build, his jeans held up by both a belt and suspenders. A black fleece jacket on top. His hair is combed back into a gray ponytail, and his wide face treads the line between unshaven and bearded. A pair of earplugs dangle from a string around his neck.

"I'm looking for Ulf Krook," says Asker.

"And who's asking?"

Asker shows them her police ID.

The men look at each other.

"Ooh, and a city pig at that," the elder one chuckles. "All alone out here in the woods."

The man, who is clearly Ulf Krook himself, hawks up a yellow gob, which he spits onto the ground.

"I hear you've been in touch with my colleague Bengt Sandgren about some model figures," says Asker.

"Sandgren, that old boozehound." Krook's mouth breaks into a malicious smile. Goatee smirks, too, as though it's what he's expected to do.

"What did you and Sandgren discuss?"

Ulf Krook snorts.

"Ask him! I don't feel like chatting to pigs just now. As you see, we're busy with shooting practice." He points at the guns on the table. "And before you ask, I've got a license to trade in firearms so everything's in order there. They're real guns, these, not those weedy nine-mils you pigs use."

He waves her off dismissively and starts fiddling with his earplugs and goggles, as if to say that the conversation is over.

Asker glances at the table. Two revolvers, one semiautomatic shotgun.

"I'd take my weedy nine-mil over those two cock-extenders any day," she says with a nonchalant sweep of the head.

"What?" Ulf Krook stiffens. "What's wrong with a .357, if I may?"

"I'd love to explain, if only I felt like it," she replies with feigned disinterest.

"The .357 is the best fucking gun that money can buy," says Krook, almost offended.

"If you say so." Asker shrugs.

"What the fuck would you know about guns, anyway? I'll bet you've never touched such fucking great gear in all your life." The old man gestures mockingly at both his crotch and the guns on the table. Goatee smirks along.

"How about we make a deal," Asker suggests. "If I can tell you which models you've got there on the table and explain why they're worse than my police firearm, you'll answer my questions."

She gives the old codger her heterochrome look.

Krook takes the bait.

"Deal!" he snarls, and takes a step to one side to block her view of the table. After a few seconds, Goatee gets the hint and goes and stands next to him.

"So then, dearie," the old man says mockingly, "show us what you've got."

"Well," says Asker, nodding at the table now obstructed by the men. "The .357 you're crowing about is a Ruger GP100. A half-decent revolver, bit of an all-rounder. Not good at anything in particular, but not bad, either."

She gives a caustic smile.

"And the other prick prosthesis is a Magnum .44, more accurately the Smith & Wesson Model 29. Loved by gun fetishists ever since Dirty Harry whispered homoerotically that it takes a real man to hold a Magnum."

Asker amps up the acidity in both her voice and her smile.

"I'd be willing to bet that in the last fifteen minutes at least one of you has waved that .44 around and yelled *do you feel lucky, punk*, or something like that, amirite?"

Goatee looks away self-consciously.

"The .44 is perfectly OK, too," Asker goes on. "But it's heavy, loud, and has a real kick of a recoil, just like the .357. In the time it takes to shoot and re-aim those handheld cannons, I can fire off three shots on my nine-mil firearm and have twelve left in the magazine, to the revolvers' five. Which means I don't have to count bullets like Dirty Harry. Besides, the nine-mil is lighter, takes up less space in my belt, and is faster to draw. All in all, an easy win."

Ulf Krook stares at her, his face bright red, his mouth half-open. Goatee looks more dogged.

"And the shotgun is a Remington 870," Asker adds. "The best-selling pump-action shotgun of all time. Or the wankmaster, as it's sometimes known, which probably refers to the owner as much as the loading movement itself. If I had to have a pump-action shotgun, I'd go for a Mossberg 590 instead. That holds twice as many cartridges and just looks much cooler."

She ends with a cool smile.

"How the fuck . . . ?" the elder man gasps.

Asker could tell him that for her entire exchange year in the USA she had a part-time job at a shooting range, but that she was also familiar with guns long before that. That she could also pick up any one of those guns, take it apart, put it back together, reload it, and even then still turn those cardboard figures over by the straw bales into confetti.

But she does none of that.

"General knowledge," she simply says with another shrug. "My turn to ask the questions."

THE MOUNTAIN KING

Three nights after he first saw her, he found himself standing in the garden behind Marie's house.

Almost all of the windows were dark; there was only the faint glow of a lamp up on the first floor. The air smelled of dew and freshly cut grass.

He hadn't bothered with all his usual safety measures. Had neither visited the house in daylight nor found access to a hidden spare key.

But he had no need for that anymore. By now he was so adept, so quiet, so careful that he was basically invisible.

His arrogance was only intensified when he found the back door unlocked. No one in the house was expecting anyone like him.

A nocturnal visitor, an intruder.

He stood quietly in the kitchen for a few minutes, going through his usual routine. Let his eyes adjust to the darkness and the sounds of the house wash over him, learning which were its natural sounds and which were made by its inhabitants.

As always, this ritual excited him. His fingers groped at the little faceless plastic figure he carried in his pocket.

The house was about to become his. In just a few minutes he would be standing in the darkness upstairs, watching over the people who lived there.

Observing them as they slept peacefully in their beds, wholly unaware of his presence. His power over them.

Whether or not some of them were in fact awake. No matter their age, profession, or status. There, in the darkness, all of them were his.

A muffled growl cut short his reverie.

The sound sent an icy jolt running down his spine, made his muscles freeze.

A dog. A large German shepherd whose presence he had entirely overlooked, and who was now slowly heading straight toward him. Even in the darkness he could make out its raised hackles and bared teeth.

"G-good dog . . . ," he whispered, but his terror-stricken voice only made the growl louder. It turned to a howl as the dog leapt straight at him.

He jumped to one side, heard the clap of its jaws right beside him.

His hip knocked against a side table. By sheer instinct he grabbed hold of the table and, with a strength that surprised even him, managed to hurl it at the dog.

A loud crash followed by the sound of broken china resounded through the room, mixed with the dog's wild barks.

He leapt at the back door, stumbled on a dog bowl that he should have noticed on the way in, but managed to catch his balance just in time.

Claws scraped against the stone floor behind him. The dog's bark gave way to another howl, but at the last second he managed to slip through the door and somehow got it shut again behind him before the dog came crashing into it.

Crouching, he ran through the garden, saw the rectangles of light on the lawn that meant that lamps were on up in the bedrooms. The shadows that flapped as the inhabitants ran to the windows. Heard the cries that meant he had been seen.

When he jumped over the low back fence, he noticed that one of his legs was stinging, but he didn't stop to look.

Not until he had cycled all the way home and the pain finally outweighed the adrenaline.

One of his trouser legs had a long tear and was flecked with blood. Perhaps the dog had managed to bite him after all—either that or he had cut himself while overturning the table. Luckily enough the cut wasn't deep, and he would be able to dress it on his own.

Still, the wound was clear proof.

He wasn't invisible, not at all. Nor invulnerable.

The tears welled up in him, and he stood in the darkness behind the garage and cried.

Didn't pull himself together until he heard the sound of sirens from down in the village.

ASKER

The kitchen inside the back door at the top of the cracked stairs is just as timeworn as the rest of Ulf Krook's home. Scuffed linoleum floors, dirty dishes, four spindle-backed chairs around a rickety table with a stained waxed tablecloth.

The rest of the house remains hidden behind a rough-hewn door. Still, it's as though something is seeping out through the cracks. Something old and unpleasant.

"Unusual house," she says.

"My grandfather designed and built it. He was a bit of a crackpot."

Ulf Krook slumps down heavily onto a chair.

Asker sits down opposite him.

Goatee gets out two odd mugs and pours coffee for Asker and the old guy, but not for himself. Doesn't sit at the table, either, but leans against the countertop and starts nibbling at a nail. He still hasn't said a peep, but his eyes suggest that he is listening intently.

Meanwhile, Asker's little master class has made Ulf Krook more talkative. Clearly the old guy intends to keep his promise.

"So that fuddy-duddy headmaster sent you here," he remarks. "I heard last Christmas they found a figure in the model spraying swear words on a wall. A right fucking laugh!"

He grins, which makes Goatee immediately do the same.

"Lilja's a sanctimonious jackass, I'll have you know. His father was a pastor in the Free Church. And he's this la-di-da school headmaster but he can't even keep a handle of his own son. A right little punk, that one."

The man's grin fades. His tone sharpens.

"I was club president for eighteen years before Lilja trounced in and started shit-stirring. My father was one of the founders—"

"Yes, he mentioned that," Asker interrupts. "Can we fast-forward a bit? When was the first time you noticed figures in the model that shouldn't have been there?"

Krook glares angrily, then blows his nose loudly in a grubby napkin.

"At least ten years ago," he mutters. "Maybe even fifteen. One of the members found a car in the model that was way too modern. I mean, the model's supposed to go up to the late sixties, but this car was newer. Eighties or nineties, with two figures outside it. We all thought it was a prank."

"Why?"

"Well . . ." The old man picks his ear with his little finger. "As I recall, the car was ugly. Different-colored doors, flecks of rust, or whatever. Besides, one of the guys outside the car was holding a crowbar. Two good-for-nothings and a piece of scrap metal in our perfect model, it reeked of April Fools' to me. But no one owned up to it."

"Have you got any pictures?"

Krook sniggers.

"Fuck no. We mostly just laughed at it. Threw the shit away."

"But then it happened again. When?"

He takes a glug of coffee.

"Don't remember exactly. A few years after the Volvo in any case. Another one of the members found a figure sticking his thumb up, hitchhiking. He was wearing headphones, that was the rub. Kids didn't run around with those on in the sixties."

He cups his hands to his ears.

"Fuck knows how someone managed to spot it, I mean, the figures are only about three-quarters of an inch tall and we've got thousands of them. But some of our members have eagle eyes when it comes to nitpicking."

"So a young male hitchhiker wearing headphones was the second figure you found?"

"Yep. Aren't you going to take notes?"

Asker ignores the question.

"No pictures from that time, either?"

"Nah." Krook shakes his head. "I never saw it myself. It came up at a meeting, as I recall. Just like the first time, no one put their hand up and owned up to it."

"And the third time?" she asks, since she remembers every detail of Lilja's account to the point that she could repeat it in her sleep.

Krook taps his finger impatiently on his coffee cup, and Goatee tops it up straightaway.

"The third time was a year or two ago," he says. "Whoever found it got their knickers in a twist and reported it to the police before they called me. Otherwise I'd have told them to leave it."

"Why?"

The old guy snorts again.

"Because I like to have as little to do with the authorities as possible."

The words echo familiarly in Asker's head. Prepper Per and Ulf Krook would have got on well, at least to begin with. Until they became mortal enemies, in any case.

"And thanks to that police report your friend Bengt Sandgren showed up," Krook goes on. "Stinking of booze, looking like he'd slept in a car. A real wreck."

He grins, picks his ear again with his little finger.

"But when he caught sight of the figures, he sharpened up. It was like someone turned on a fucking light bulb in his skull. He took loads of pictures. Packed the figures up so carefully you'd think they were the bullets from Prime Minister Palme's assassination."

"Did Sandgren say anything about why?"

The old man inspects his little fingernail.

"Nah. Just asked a shitload of nosy questions, just like you. After a while I got sick of it and told him to go fuck himself. Said that if he went on driving round these parts poking his nose into other people's business it could end badly." He wipes a little blob of earwax onto the tablecloth.

"What were the figures of?" Asker asks. "The ones that got Sandgren going?"

Krook pulls his lips back. His teeth are yellow and crooked, his canines exaggeratedly pointed, like a predator's.

"Why don't you ask him yourself?"

"Because Sandgren's in the hospital and can't be reached."

"I see." The old guy smacks his lips. "Rehab?"

He looks at Asker as though expecting a reply, which he doesn't get.

"The figures," she repeats. "What were they of?"

Ulf smirks again.

"Well, this time we're talking about a sick fucking sense of humor." He leans in. "There were two figures, and they'd been put in a forest. One was a blond woman running."

"Running? You mean like on a run?"

"No, no, not like that!"

The old man shakes his head.

"She was running like you do when you're being chased. By something you're fucking petrified of . . ."

He leans in even closer. His eyes are gleaming, his breath a mix of coffee and putrefaction. Goatee diagonally behind him has paused his nail-biting and appears to be listening keenly.

"Behind her in the forest there was a male figure," the old guy goes on. "It was clear that he was chasing her. That she was running for her life. But here's the really nasty bit."

He sucks in through his teeth, as though savoring each word. Doesn't want to miss the slightest little morsel.

"The woman was very well painted. Hair, clothes, face, even a red backpack on her back. Eight or nine colors, teensy brushstrokes and not a dot out of place, even though she was only three-quarters of an inch tall. A real pro job, must have taken ages to do."

He pauses, looks over his shoulder, as though to make sure Goatee is listening.

"But?" Asker says.

"The man following her was white," Ulf whispers. "Unpainted, no face. The other members thought it was a question of time. That whoever put them there was in too much of a hurry to paint more than one figure. Your friend Sandgren had the same thought. But if you ask me, they were wide of the mark."

"Why?"

Once again the old man pulls back his upper lip so that his canines are visible. His eyes glitter darkly, excitedly.

"Whoever put those figures in the forest wanted them exactly like that," he says in almost a whisper. "A good-looking young woman, so detailed that you could see the terror in her face. And then someone chasing her. Someone barely human. A monster."

THE MOUNTAIN KING

The day after the dog sniffed him out, everything was different. In school everyone was talking about the break-in at Marie's place. That it might have had something to do with her father's job, that the police were still inspecting the scene of the crime. That it was all thanks to the dog that nothing more serious happened.

Marie was the leading lady at school, constantly surrounded by a big group of students who soaked up every last word of her story.

Meanwhile he slunk around on the sidelines. Tried to keep as far from Marie and her admirers as possible. Perhaps she had managed to get a glimpse of him. Perhaps she would reach out and point at him, shout that he was the one she had seen running across the lawn.

And then they would all be on him.

Push him, punch him, kick him.

Call him names, drag him up to the headmaster's office until, humiliated, he confessed to his deeds.

He felt sick, both burning up and icy cold, but staying home from school was out of the question. His mother would immediately put two and two together.

So that evening he went along with his stepfather to the model railway club, even though he still felt unwell.

The chatter about the break-in refused to let up. All of the members were there, almost twenty men, but for once they weren't talking about the model. Several of them knew someone who claimed to have had an intruder in their home in the past year. They had never reported it, or even talked about it, since there were no clear signs of a break-in and nothing important had been taken. But now, after the incident at Marie's family's house, the witness testimonies came flooding in over the coffee table.

Testimonies of things that had been moved, of dirt trailed in over bedroom floors, or just a vague feeling that someone else had been in the room.

He felt all the sicker. The air in the kitchen was thick and hard to breathe, and he staggered out into the room that held the model. Supported himself on one of its edges, stared at the small houses and figures.

He had thought he was invisible. That that gave him the power to do almost anything he wanted. When in actual fact he was help-less.

At any point he could have been discovered, disgraced, spurned.

The room was spinning, as voices from the kitchen seeped out.

"Only a fucking perv sneaks around in other people's houses."

"If only I could get my hands on the psycho."

"Hang the fucker from a lamppost."

For one brief moment it was as though all of the hundreds of fig-ures in the model came to life.

"Monster," they hissed.

"Maniac!"

"Troll."

The room spun even faster. Ceiling and floor gradually swapped places.

He reached out to steady himself on one of the plastic screens around the model, but his hands refused to obey him.

Instead his knees buckled, and he fell headlong into darkness.

ASKER

It has stopped raining by the time Asker drives away from the down-at-heel house, but the sky is still hanging low above the treetops. The text message she'd expected from her sister covers half her phone screen. She swipes it away without reading it.

At one of the turnings in the forest a young woman is emptying a mailbox. She looks up as the car drives past, but makes no attempt to stop it. Presumably she lives in one of the cottages.

The woman stands there watching the car until the forest swallows her up.

For one brief moment Asker wonders if the woman was actually just a figment of her imagination. A brief glimpse of what she herself could have been, had things gone differently.

If she hadn't . . .

She ups the speed. Even with the heating and seat warmers on, the car feels cold and damp. The wheels send cascades of brown water shooting up out of the holes in the road. She knows these kinds of places, has them etched so deeply in her mind that she can't ever truly forget them.

Still, she won't let that stop her trying.

The phone rings when she is halfway back to Hässleholm. At first she thinks it's Camille, and is about to reject the call. At the last second she realizes it's someone else.

"Leo Asker," she says.

"Yes, hello, this is Madame Rind. We met yesterday. I'm afraid I'm calling with some bad news."

"Oh?"

"Garm died last night."

Asker doesn't quite know what to say.

"Oh, how sad," she manages.

"Indeed, but he had a long life. Nineteen years. He passed away in his sleep, in his favorite spot under the red maple tree in the garden. A nice place to cross over into the spirit world."

"Right."

"Anyway, he wanted me to tell you that you shouldn't worry."

"Garm? Your dead dog?" Asker's brain is feverishly fighting to make some sense of this conversation, but she's starting to suspect it's impossible.

"Yes, exactly. I dreamt about him last night. As I do every time that he dies. In the dream Garm tells me which form he will be reborn in, and where I should look for him."

"OK," says Asker, as that's the only word she can come up with.

This conversation must be about to break some kind of insanity record.

"He asked me to let you know which breed he intends to return as. Said that it was of utmost importance that you know. A question of life or death."

"And which breed is that?" Asker asks, as collectedly as she can.

"A papillon," says the woman. "Garm asked me to tell you to keep your eyes out for a papillon. So there, now you know. Have a good day, Leo Asker."

As soon as she hangs up, Asker bursts into laughter.

Hässleholm police station lies in the center of town. A grayish beige four-storey building with an angular glazed corner, not far from the railway station. Although Ulf Krook did give her more information about the figures, it's not hard to see why Lilja both suspects and fears him.

Since Krook is a creepy old man who despises the police, it follows that there is probably a colleague in the local force who has some experience of dealing with him and can tell her more.

Asker introduces herself to the receptionist and explains that she is looking for someone who is familiar with the conflict at the model railway club.

The woman gives her a long look, but asks no questions. After a few phone calls a door opens and a uniformed police officer of around her own age steps out. He is slender and athletic, just under six feet. Something about him feels familiar.

"Jakob Tell," he introduces himself. "Deputy chief of the police district. And you must be Asker?"

His eyes are bright blue and his smile is charming; his light, tousled, side-swept bangs are, too.

"We met a few years back at a crime scene," he goes on. "A drunken homicide at an apartment in Tyringe. I was duty sergeant."

"Of course," says Asker. She remembers him clearly now. "You had a cadet with you. A dark-haired kid who was a little green in the face. It was his first murder scene."

"Yusuf," he replies. "Good memory you've got. He works in Traffic now. Would you like a coffee?"

He swipes her in with his pass and shows her to a break room.

"I actually wanted to be a homicide detective once upon a time," he says over his shoulder while getting coffee for them both.

Asker waits for the continuation that usually follows. A whiny harangue about how hard it is to get hired on detective positions, peppered with the not-so-subtle insinuation that white men are filtered out in favor of women and minorities.

But apparently Tell isn't one of the whiners.

Instead he drops the subject.

"Here you go." He serves the coffee and sits down opposite her.

Unlike in Krook's filthy kitchen, Asker takes a sip.

"So, now I'm curious," says Tell. "Why is Serious Crime interested in our little model railway club?"

Asker takes a deep breath. The question is a good one—unlike her answer.

"I . . . ," she begins, then puts down her coffee cup. "I'm standing in for a colleague. My predecessor Bengt Sandgren left a few question marks lying around."

"Sandgren, didn't he write the 'Murder Bible'? He gave a lecture when I was at police college."

"The very same," Asker confirms. "Sandgren's in the hospital following a heart attack. We're not sure whether he'll pull through. He was working on an investigation that involved the club in some way."

"Ah, I see. And you have no idea what kind of investigation that was?"

"Something about illicit figures being added to the model—sound familiar?"

"Illicit figures? Afraid not . . ." Tell raises one corner of his mouth. "Is that even a crime?"

A good question, which she leaves unanswered.

"So you haven't been in touch with Sandgren?" she asks instead.

"No, though he might have spoken to one of my colleagues, of course. I can ask around."

"Thanks, I'd appreciate that."

Tell gives her a searching look.

"Apparently there was some trouble in the club when they changed president, is that true?" she goes on.

"You mean their infamous AGM, I suppose? Yes, that's right." He shakes his head. "I was there myself. Thirty old-timers bickering over a model railway. Brandishing their fists and calling one another nasty words like *rascal* and *rapscallion*."

Asker can't help but smirk.

"I spoke to the president, Kjell Lilja, earlier today," she says. "Do you know him?"

"Not personally. But he's sorted out a lot of the trouble at the school. My sister's a teacher there, she has only good things to say about him as headmaster."

"I understand that Lilja has a son who's a little disruptive."

Tell frowns.

"Yes, that's right. Oliver Lilja. Minor drug offenses, vehicle theft, driving without a license, a few other things besides. He's in a young offender institution right now."

He raises his coffee cup to his mouth. "Who told you that?"

"Ulf Krook," she replies.

"Ah . . ." Tell smiles again. "The old mountain troll himself. How did you get in touch with him?"

"I was having coffee in his kitchen less than an hour ago."

Tell almost chokes on his coffee.

"And he spoke to you? Normally Ulf tells the police to go to hell."

"Well." She shrugs. "I can be pretty persuasive."

"I'll be damned." Tell studies her with an amused yet impressed look. "Ulf Krook's record here is an ongoing adventure, but I'm sure you've already gathered that. Fights with his neighbors, the local authorities, the county administrative board, you name it. Plenty of people are afraid of him. But clearly not you."

Asker doesn't reply.

"Was he alone? No woman there?"

"Not that I could see. Why do you ask?"

Tell shakes his head.

"Ulf has had plenty of partners over the years. Been married four or five times. But it's been a while since anyone lived there permanently. Most only stick around a few years."

"And why should that matter?" Asker finds Tell's interest slightly unexpected.

He pulls a face, both apologetic and amused.

"It isn't, I was mostly just curious. It's not often that you meet someone who's been allowed to set foot on Ulf's property—even less in his inner sanctum. What was it like?"

"I only got as far as the kitchen. The rest of the house felt almost sealed off. And weird, to put it mildly."

"Was anyone else there?"

"A man in his thirties. A quiet type, with a cap and goatee," she says.

"Finn Olofsson," Tell says with a nod. "Ulf's stepson, or one of them at least. Like I said, Ulf has had plenty of different partners. He's got kids and stepkids over half the district. A whole little clan. Finn's a truck driver, he's got a few minors to his name. Lives just a couple miles from there, is kind of like Ulf's right-hand man."

"You certainly know a lot about these people."

Tell smiles.

"Well, that's what us community police are here for, isn't it? Besides, like I said, Ulf Krook in particular has attracted a lot of attention over the years."

"And yet he's still licensed to trade in firearms?"

"Indeed. He must have had that license forty years. Uses it as an excuse to stock up his gun cabinet with various mini cannons that he'd never be allowed to keep otherwise. We've tried to have the license revoked, but despite the many rumors, Ulf hasn't been convicted of anything more than a few speeding offenses and a misdemeanor for receiving stolen goods. And he gets an expensive lawyer from Kristianstad to take care of any appeals."

Tell gives a resigned gesture.

"Ulf is a wily old fox. He knows he can pretty much do whatever he wants up there in the forest. No one dares accuse him of anything, let alone stand as a witness. So long as he keeps to his den, we can't lay a finger on him."

"Those derelict cottages in the forest," Asker goes on. "I thought I saw a young woman there."

"Ulf rents them out sometimes. Mostly to various relatives or people he struggles to find accommodation for otherwise. Most of them keep a low profile and move on after a while, so it's impossible to keep track of them."

Tell falls silent, purses his lips, and studies her for a few seconds. His expression goes serious, as does his voice.

"It's a pleasure to chat with you, Asker, but isn't it about time you told me what this conversation is really about?"

ASKER

Asker is saved by her phone. Her sister's number again. Normally she would simply swipe it away, but right now she needs an excuse to weasel out of this conversation with Jakob Tell. Although he does seem smart and level-headed, she has no desire to reveal that she suspects the Holst kidnapping and the railway model are linked.

"I'm afraid I have to take this," she says with a grave expression. "But thank you for your help. Do get in touch if you come across anything else."

Tell doesn't exactly seem happy, but in any case he gives a curt nod.

Asker gets up and taps the answer button.

"Leo Asker," she says as formally as she can.

"It's Camille." Her sister sounds relieved, as though she hadn't expected her to answer.

"Oh, hi," Asker says while searching for the exit. "Just a second."

She finds the right door, steps into the parking lot, and gets into the car.

"Right, now I can talk."

"Well, uh . . . How are you?" Camille still sounds unsure.

"Fine, thanks. All good?"

"Oh yes. The girls are in school now, and Fredric is busy with . . ."

She trails off as she always does whenever she mentions her husband, as though the topic is full of land mines. Which it is.

"I just wanted to check if you're coming tonight?"

"Tonight?"

"To Junot's name day, I've texted you about it several times."

Asker groans inwardly.

"Are you still doing that?"

"Of course, it's a family tradition."

Junot Lissander is Isabel's husband. Camille, who grew up with them, calls him *Dad*. Family legend has it that little Camille felt so sorry for Junot, whose untraditional name didn't have a name day, that their mother introduced a sort of moving name day. A celebration that takes place whenever Isabel feels like it. Which apparently is today.

"Six p.m., at the office. There'll be champagne and canapés."

Asker searches for an excuse, is about to play the job card when Camille gets in first:

"You know how happy it will make him if you come."

Asker bites her lip. Fact is, she likes Junot. He's the most normal person in the whole family.

"The girls will be there, too, obviously," Camille adds, almost imploringly.

Asker closes her eyes for a few seconds.

"OK," she says," I'll come."

Her phone beeps.

"I've got to go, I've got a call on the other line."

Asker switches to the other call. It's Kjell Lilja.

"I just wanted to let you know that our security guy is currently changing our locks and upgrading the alarm system."

"Ah, good."

Short pause. The security update is just a pretext for this call, she can tell. Still, she has no intention of helping him out.

"So, did you get to speak to Ulf Krook?" he says.

"Oh yes."

"And what did he say about it all?"

"I'm afraid I'm not at liberty to discuss that. It's confidential to the investigation."

"Ah, of course, I understand." Lilja clears his throat self-consciously.

"I actually do have a question," she says. "The figure doing graffiti that you found a year ago. Ulf said something about him spraying a swear word."

"Yes, but that turned out to be a misunderstanding."

"How so?"

"Well, you see . . . The figure was actually spraying an abbreviation that we'd initially assumed was something obscene. But it wasn't. One of my pupils explained it to me . . ."

"What was the word?" she interrupts.

"Urbex. It stands for Urban exploration. It's when people explore abandoned buildings, often illegally, and—"

"Thank you, I've got it now." She starts winding up. "Call me if anything else comes up."

She ends the call. The turning toward the old tank factory appears a little way ahead. Her conversation with Lilja has given her an idea, and she turns off.

Outside the model railway club's premises stands a pickup bearing the name of a security firm.

She finds the alarm technician inside the building. A tall, bearded man with a friendly face. Asker shows him her police ID and introduces herself.

"Daniel Nygård," he replies, holding out a giant mitt. "I own the company."

"Ah, great," says Asker. "I wanted to ask you for a small favor. But it needs to stay between us."

"What did you have in mind?"

"I'd like you to install a hidden camera in this building. Without telling anyone."

Nygård makes a surprised grimace.

"Ah, I'm not sure," he says hesitantly. "I mean, the club is my client. Anyway, don't you police usually handle that stuff yourselves?"

"True, but our technical staff aren't available right now," she lies. "Look, I'm afraid I can't give you any details, but it's urgent, otherwise I wouldn't be asking."

Nygård scratches his beard thoughtfully.

"Like I said, I don't really feel comfortable about spying on my client . . . ," he mutters.

"You won't be the one tracking them, I will," she argues. "I'll take full responsibility if there are any complaints. You're acting on my request."

Nygård goes on scratching his beard, but she can see that he's on the way to giving in.

"It would really be a massive help if you could work with me on this," she adds with as soft a voice as she can muster.

Nygård sighs.

"OK, since it's the police asking then . . ."

"Great. And like I said, this is between you and me. I'll cover any costs, and you're not to mention this to Kjell Lilja or anyone else. Are we clear?"

Nygård nods thoughtfully.

"I've got a discreet little camera that can be fitted almost anywhere. Would you like online access to the feed?"

"That'd be perfect."

He nods again. "I'll get it done. Give me your cell number and I'll send you a link with instructions. Might as well set it up straightaway, before one of the members gets here."

She thanks him, then takes the chance to do another lap of the model before returning to the car.

There is something deeply fascinating about it, and not only because of its size. The model is a kind of picture postcard of a Sweden that no longer exists. Happy streets, where everyone is cheerful, sated, and safe.

Almost everyone, at least.

For in the midst of these cozy little scenes, someone else is telling a different, more sinister story.

The only question is: Who?

THE MOUNTAIN KING

When he woke up, he was at the hospital. The doctor explained that he had had some sort of epileptic fit. Was foaming at the mouth, his eyes so far back in his head that only the whites were visible. He also had a fever of 104 degrees.

It probably had something to do with the meningitis he had suffered as a child.

When they asked him how he felt, he replied—fine.

That he didn't remember anything of the last two days.

The last part was a lie. He remembered every single detail of his fever dreams. The same dreams he had had as a boy, only this time much more detailed.

Ruins, darkness, the mountain.

His mountain. His realm.

People calling for help from inside it—his classmates, neighbors, parents, the old men around the model railway. All banging their fists bloody against the stone walls in despair, without anyone to hear them.

No one except him.

They were in his world now.

A kingdom where he held the power.

And just like the last time he was in hospital, he came out of it changed. A new being, with new insights.

He had been thinking all too small.

There were far better spoils to be had than odds and ends, rubbish.

But he would have to adapt. Not act like a changeling, but adopt a new guise. Hide the monster deep within him, and pretend to be human.

A few days later, Marie came to school puffy-eyed from crying. Said that the night before their dog had eaten something poisonous and died on their back steps in great pain.

Instead of sticking to the sidelines, he walked right up to her. Stood up straight and said how sorry he was, that he had a dog who had died, too, a few years ago.

That he knew exactly how much it hurt. In return for his lie he was granted a grateful smile. The first step toward being accepted by the community.

At home he started being kinder to his younger siblings, offered to help out around the house, and, to his mother's surprise and delight, started participating in conversations at the dinner table.

Not long after that he was back at the model railway club. Asked interested questions, made an effort to smile and laugh in the right places at the old men's stories.

Later, when no one was looking, he bent over the plastic screen and swiped one of the small figures from the model.

Moved it from its original position over to Marie's house, where he placed it on its side just outside the back door.

The figure was a German Shepherd.

Every time he returned to the model railway over the years, he would always search for that particular figure.

His very first scene.

Would reminisce about how he had stuffed meatballs with tiny nails and rat poison, before poking them through the fence at the back of Marie's garden. How he had stepped back and watched while the dog gobbled them down, then cycled home with a new feeling in his chest, one ten times stronger than anything he had ever felt.

His power over life.

And over death.

ASKER

Asker gets back into the car and drives south, toward Malmö. Takes the same forest-lined highway that she drove along that morning. The rain clouds are retreating, the gray mist scattering, the sky getting higher.

So what does she know?

That the case involves a total of eight small figures, inserted at five time points over more than ten years.

Three times under the former president Ulf Krook's leadership:

The two petty crooks in the ugly Volvo, then the lone hitchhiker with the headphones. Then the woman being chased through the forest by the creepy, featureless man. Both Ulf Krook and his voiceless wingman, Finn Olofsson, seemed to enjoy that particular detail a little too much.

And then, both of Lilja's discoveries: the young man spraying the word *urbex* on the side of a building, and the latest addition: Smilla and MM in their frozen selfie moment.

How are they all linked? Are they even linked at all?

Bengt Sandgren seemed convinced of it, at least.

Something about the woman in the forest and her featureless pursuer had caught his attention. Made him personally go to collect both them and, later, the graffiti artist. Not to mention instruct Lilja to get in touch immediately if any new discoveries turned up.

But she has gone through Sandgren's office in minute detail. Besides a well-thumbed Märklin catalogue she hasn't found the slightest trace of the investigation, even less the commandeered figures. Did he lose interest? Sling everything in the nearest wastebasket and go back to his drinking?

That's plausible, of course.

Still, she isn't quite prepared to accept that theory.

At least not yet. Not so long as there are more questions to be asked. Such as where Martin Hill comes into the picture. Sandgren obtained his phone number, perhaps even contacted him.

Her thoughts are sharply interrupted by a familiar feeling. An anxiety that starts at the nape of her neck and spreads down her spine.

It is a feeling she lived with her entire childhood. One she honed, learned to trust blind. One that saved her life.

The feeling that something is wrong.

She looks in the rearview mirror. A little more than five hundred feet behind her is another vehicle. It has been there for a while without getting any closer, she has already noted.

And now her subconscious is raising the alarm.

She didn't overtake it, so it must have caught up with her. But the driver is keeping a distance, as though they don't want to get too close.

She studies the vehicle carefully in the rearview mirror. A dark van, of roughly the same model that stood in Ulf Krook's muddy yard. But she only saw that van at a distance, and the one tailing her is too far away for her to be sure that it's the same.

Asker slows down. The space between the two vehicles contracts for a few seconds, only to expand again.

This is all the proof she needs. The van is following her.

A little farther ahead she spots a small turnout and pulls in sharply, without indicating. Stays in the car while the van looms ever closer in the rearview mirror. It is missing its front license plate, she notes.

As the van approaches the turnout, it suddenly accelerates and zooms past at high speed, blue diesel smoke pouring out of the exhaust. The only glimpse she gets of the driver is of a cap and hooded jacket.

Asker pulls out behind the van and floors it. It takes the nifty electric car only a few seconds to catch up.

The van does have a back license plate, but it's covered in mud. Driving as close as she dares, she tries to get out her phone to take a photo. The paint work is dark brown, and the model is the same as the van in Ulf Krook's yard. But she needs a license number to be completely sure.

Without any warning the van brakes. Sends gray smoke whirling across the road from its tires, while its brake lights scream in red alert.

Asker turns sharply, and with only an inch to spare, manages to swerve around the obstruction. The car lurches, the tires screech against the asphalt, and it takes her a few frenzied wheel maneuvers to get the vehicle back under control. In the rearview mirror she sees the van turn off down a side road.

Asker swears loudly and brakes. Once the car has stopped, she puts it in reverse and floors it, traveling against traffic. Once she has picked up speed, she twists the wheel to swing the car 180 degrees and shifts it into drive, so she is still going against traffic, only now front-first.

She skids onto the side road. The van has already disappeared out of sight, so she accelerates even more. The road is narrow and winding, its every bend obscured by spruce trees or houses. Asker pushes the electric car to the max, taking each bend like a rally driver, and by the skin of her teeth manages to avoid a collision with an oncoming truck. She is rewarded with an angry toot.

Another sharp turn, followed by yet another, but the van is still nowhere to be seen.

Asker goes on pushing the pedal to the metal for another couple miles, but when she reaches a small residential area she takes her foot off the accelerator.

She should have caught up with the van by now, which means the driver must have tricked her. Turned off down some small forest track, or hidden around the back of a building while she zoomed past. That's what she would have done to shake a pursuer in a much faster car.

Shit!

Asker returns to the same highway, but the van is nowhere to be found.

She tries to gather her thoughts. The color, make, and model match, so she is almost certain that it was the same van she saw at Ulf Krook's house. The van was following her, that much was abundantly clear.

But why? And who was driving it?

ASKER

Back at the Department of Lost Souls everything is still. Every door to every office is shut, and the tube lights in the ceiling flicker idly.

Asker knocks on Rosen's door and opens it without waiting for a reply. Just like before, the woman looks caught in the act. Not particularly strange, given that she is knitting.

"I d-didn't realize you were in . . . ," she stammers while shoving her knitting away in a desk drawer. "Virgilsson said you were out on a case, and . . ."

Asker waves off her apologies.

"Have you got what I asked for?"

"Of course." Rosen pulls a few pieces of paper out of a different desk drawer and hands them to her. "The list that Bengt asked me to keep up to date. Missing people from the last fifteen years with some sort of connection to Skåne."

"What's it for?" she asks while Asker flicks through the documents.

"I was going to ask you the same thing."

Rosen shakes her head anxiously.

"I don't know any more than I've already told you. Bengt asked me to compile this list, that's all. He's very secretive about his work."

Her gaze flickers ever so slightly more than normal.

"But," Asker says. "There is something else, isn't there?"

Rosen moistens her lips.

"One of the names on the list is Julia Collin, the girl from Ängelholm who disappeared almost four years ago."

"And?" Asker tries not to sound impatient.

"She . . ." Rosen clears her throat, looks around as though to make sure that no one is listening. "Bengt was her godfather."

"Godfather?"

"Yes, or 'oddfather,' or whatever they're calling it nowadays. Bengt and her father were close friends. I know he took her disappearance very hard. He tried to help the family find her. It was one of the reasons for his . . ."

She licks her lips nervously.

". . . poor health. And also his redeployment here," she concludes.

Asker nods thoughtfully.

"Anything else?"

Rosen shakes her head a little too emphatically.

"No, that's honestly all I know. Bengt never told me anything. Nothing at all."

Asker takes the documents into Sandgren's office and shuts the door.

There are a total of twelve names on the list, and she skims through them quickly. None of them mean anything to her.

Fortunately, Rosen has been more thorough than expected. She has attached a summary of each case, all of them surprisingly concise and professional. Definitely to the same standard that Asker is used to getting up in Serious Crime.

She starts with Julia Collin's case.

Twenty years old at disappearance, lived with her mom, older brother, and stepfather in Ängelholm.

Good grades in middle school, less good in high school.

Did judo, played the flute. Her father died in a car crash when she was fifteen, which, according to her mother, caused her to lose her way. She lost interest in her studies, stopped playing music. Started partying more.

After graduating she worked as a waitress at a nightclub in Helsingborg and as a substitute teacher at her old middle school. Seemed to be looking for some kind of direction in life.

Then one day at the end of September she didn't come home after a day's work at the school.

Her last trace was an online ticket that she bought for a regional bus the same night. It was unclear, however, if she ever got on the bus, since the ticket was never scanned. The bus driver thought it was possible he had seen her on board, but he wasn't sure. She was reported as missing, her family traveled around looking for her, started a Facebook group, put up posters. But nothing helped.

After a few weeks the trail went cold, at least where the police were concerned. Julia was an adult, and there was no proof that she had been a victim of any crime.

She was just gone.

At the very bottom of the page is a picture of Julia and a description.

She has long blond hair and blue eyes. Bears more than a passing resemblance to Smilla Holst, but Julia Collin's eyes have a graver look about them.

When she left work at the school that September afternoon four years ago, she was wearing blue jeans, a white jacket, and a red backpack.

The last two words make Asker react.

Red backpack.

She replays Ulf Krook's account in her head. Cuts out the pieces that match.

A blond woman running . . .

. . . even a red backpack on her back . . .

. . . you could see the terror in her face . . .

The female figure being chased through the forest was Julia Collin.

No wonder that light bulb went on in Bengt Sandgren's mind.

He must have reacted just like she did to the figures representing Smilla and Malik.

She quickly skims through the rest of the missing people on the list.

Her eyes almost immediately latch on to the word *graffiti*.

The word appears in the description of Tor Nilsson, twenty-seven years of age. A classic loose cannon. Problems at school, fights with teachers, minor drugs, heavier drugs, various crimes, the whole same old story. His police record contains several points relating to vandalism and graffiti, and he has also been missing for just over a year. Which means in both timing and activity he fits the profile of the figure spray-painting the word *urbex* in the model.

Asker leans back, tries to gather her thoughts.

A girl with a red backpack, a graffiti artist, a young couple taking a selfie. What they all have in common is the fact that they are missing.

That they disappeared without the slightest trace.

Only to then turn up again as teeny tiny plastic figures in a railway model.

Why?

She has already touched on the answer.

Because someone wants to create their own narrative. Wants to show off what they did. What they got away with.

THE MOUNTAIN KING

For a while he contented himself with animals. First cats, and then, when he became braver, dogs and occasionally wild animals, too.

He would capture them and bring them deep into his mountain, lock them in one of the small rooms and make them his own. Would watch his spoils for hours on end through the hatch in the door. Learned things—important things.

Such as the fact that you could supply them with food and water, but that eventually, as the weeks passed, they would die anyway.

Would stop eating and drinking, stop jumping up and down as soon as he slammed the hatch shut, but instead curl up in a far corner until they died. The wilder the animal, the faster the process would be.

It took some time before he understood why. That the animals were reacting in the same way as the butterflies. That every living being had a point at which it finally gave up.

At which it realized there was no longer any hope.

He was a young man when he got his first, real catch.

One night, he arrived at his mountain to find an old Volvo parked in the turning circle. The padlock was broken, and the gate to the mountain was open.

His blood ran cold as ice. He thought that someone else had taken over Uncle Johan's work, that his secret refuge was now lost forever. But then he heard voices from inside, saw the flickering glow of a campfire over on the loading bay and decided to go inside.

The intruders turned out to be two young men. Hard eyes, brawny bodies. They smelled of spirits and cigarette smoke. The car was stolen, the kids were on the run. At first they were hostile, thinking he would run off and report them. Threatened to beat him senseless. But after a while they calmed down. Realized he wasn't the type to snitch.

Besides, he was his new self. Pleasant, accommodating. Even offered to help both the fugitives.

They had heard about the mountain somewhere and decided to find it, the elder of the two explained. Because he'd always liked abandoned places, ever since he was a kid. Abandoned plots, disused factories, barred-up houses. But this mountain was a whole different ball game.

They had already found weird things in some of the rooms, the younger of the two said.

Jars, knickknacks, underwear.

He just nodded silently as they described their invasion; forced a smile, pretended it wasn't his work that they had witnessed, his treasures that they had defiled.

The older of the two was the one who called the shots. He was the bigger and the stronger, the one with the most evil in his eyes. The younger, skinnier one mostly just went along with it, and did as he was told.

On the way there they had broken into a house, stolen some food and booze. When he found them, their party was already in full swing, and pretty soon the men were both stuffed and drunk. Started talking shit. Calling him an inbred hick, all manner of other things. He let them do it, laughed along, took fake swigs from the bottle while waiting them out.

Eventually they fell asleep by the fire, using their jackets as pillows.

He sat there for a while, observing them. They thought they were safe here. That he was harmless.

That was a mistake.

When he was sure both men were asleep, he took a heavy concrete block and stood wide-legged over the older of the two.

For a moment he stood there with the concrete block raised straight above his head. Searched for the voice that would tell him it was wrong.

But he found none.

All he felt was wrath that they had violated his sanctuary. That they hadn't understood what a sacred place they were in. Nor who they were in fact dealing with.

The concrete block crushed the man's head with a wet crack, almost like a carton of eggs when it hits the ground.

The other fugitive was so plastered he didn't wake up. Not until hours later, when he found himself in a pitch-black room behind a locked steel door. Only then did he start to scream, cry, pound.

It was seven days before the hope left him.

Nine before he died.

Fifteen before they were both rendered as two small plastic figures, which he placed, with their car, in the model railway.

Showing off his deed just as he had done with Marie's dog. Demonstrating how far his power extended.

And who he really was.

ASKER

Asker is standing outside the closed door to Attila's office. The light on the wall is shining an angry red. She takes a deep breath, then gives a firm knock and turns the handle. Locked.

The light, if possible, shines an even deeper red.

She knocks again, harder this time, more determined.

"It's Leo Asker," she says, loud enough to be heard through the door.

She spots a movement out of the corner of her eye. Virgilsson has poked his head out of his office. Slides back again, cautiously, though she's sure the little man is still watching her.

The door opens.

Attila is standing in the doorway. Strangely enough, even though they are roughly the same height, he feels much bigger than her.

The man peers at her intently. Then takes a step to one side.

"Come in."

He takes a seat behind his desk, signals at her to close the door behind her and sit down opposite.

"Plenty of curious ears on this corridor," he adds.

His room is meticulously tidy. Color-coordinated files behind him. Two bonsai trees in the window, so perfect and identical that at first Asker mistakes them for plastic plants.

"So, what can I do for Detective Inspector Asker?" His gaze is both jokey and watchful.

"I need access to Bengt Sandgren's IT account. His work inbox, documents, contacts, everything. I've contacted IT, but apparently the wait time is several weeks. So I'm wondering if you can help me."

Attila raises his eyebrows.

"And why, if I may ask, would you need to access Sandgren's account?"

Asker has anticipated this question. Has prepared an answer that isn't untrue.

"Because he was midway through an investigation and I'm missing some key information."

Attila gives her a skeptical look.

"An investigation? Bengt?"

Asker shrugs.

"Yeah, I'm pretty much as surprised as you are."

Attila goes on studying her gloomily for a few seconds, then smiles.

"The man must really have been keeping that to himself. No wonder . . ."

"It isn't?" Asker raises an eyebrow. "Why not?"

The question appears to take Attila by surprise.

He takes another good look at her. Fights her heterochrome gaze without getting very far. The corner of his mouth twitches.

"Well, I suppose the simple answer would be that no one down here can be trusted. This is where careers come to fizzle out, or die, whichever your euphemism of preference. There's no way out of this place, so everyone does what they can to get something out of it."

"How do you mean?"

Her question appears to both irritate and amuse him.

"What I mean is that down here there are no rules. Take Rosen, for example. She's in love with a journalist at *Sydsvenskan*. Takes whatever chance she can to call him up with a juicy tip, just to get a little flattery or the odd boozy lunch in return. When in actual fact the man's gay, the whole world knows."

He sniggers, seems to be picking up steam.

"Zafer, as I'm sure you've noticed, is pretty much as insane as he is deaf. He's been working on that same report for over four years now. And Virgilsson, the little toad, is bent through and through. Struts around with his key chain, pretending to be important. Barters services and perks like a man in the clink."

"And you?" she asks. "What's your deal?"

"I keep myself to myself," he says. "Calmer that way."

"OK." Asker pats the armrests. "Then I'll let you get back to it. How soon can I have Sandgren's log-in?"

He casts a glance at his watch. A diving watch the size of a hockey puck.

"I need a code from IT, but they're probably gone for the day. First thing tomorrow at the earliest."

He studies her again. His eyes narrow beneath his bushy eyebrows. There's something he wants to say.

"Asker, that's a pretty unusual surname."

He nods as though to confirm his own conclusion, which saves Asker from having to reply. She's had a hunch about this since their encounter in the kitchen.

"Back when I was working in the field for the secret police, we ran an investigation into a Per Asker." Attila lets the name hang in the air, as though expecting a reaction.

He gets none.

"He was a smart guy," he goes on. "A reservist and engineer, head of development at some munitions company. A real Einstein, according to his manager. But for some reason this Per Asker got into a dispute with his employer. Something about some patents he thought he had the right to. Asker got the sack, sued his employer and lost. Around the same time his wife left him, and apparently it all got to his head. I mean, genius and insanity are very often bedfellows."

He taps his index finger against his temple a few times.

Asker still says nothing.

"So this Per Asker moved out of Malmö and up into Skåne's primeval forest," he goes on. "Bought himself a piece of land that he named 'the Farm.' Became a doomsday prophet, or prepper or whatever those lunatics are called nowadays. Built bunkers, grew his own vegetables, ran different training drills in preparation for the apocalypse. A year or so after Per lost his final appeal, there was a mysterious explosion at a research facility belonging to his former employer. No one was hurt, but the blast cost them millions.

"They were afraid that Per had become a Swedish Unabomber—that's why the secret police got involved. But spying on him was hard as fuck."

"Oh really?" Asker says.

"Yeah, this Per was one paranoid psycho. He assumed he was

always being watched or tapped, and besides, the terrain wasn't exactly primed for your usual stakeout. So me and another colleague who also had military experience holed ourselves up in the forest. Sat out there for days at a stretch, monitoring the Farm through binoculars."

He smiles inwardly.

"I've don't think I've ever been so badly bitten in all my life. The mosquitoes up there in the forests are the size of wasps."

He looks at her as though she knows exactly what he's talking about, which she does. Still, she doesn't let on.

"Anyway. The investigation into the explosion turned up nothing. In the end my managers were satisfied that, stark raving mad as Per Asker was, he wasn't a danger. At least not to society at large, so we left him in peace. A few years later he blew himself up. Lost a hand and an eye, I seem to recall, and ended up in the loony bin."

The man pauses, as though waiting for Asker to say something.

"Cool story," she says with a nod.

"Right?" he agrees with another crooked smile. "I was watching that farm for a whole summer. Saw most of what went on. And there's one thing I couldn't ever quite forget."

"What's that?" she asks, although she has an inkling of the answer.

"Per Asker had a daughter. The girl grew up with his whole paranoid lifestyle. All those insane exercises and gimmicks. She was his life's project, and Per honed her till she was sharp as a razor. Taught her shooting, close combat, driving, you name it."

He chuckles to himself.

"Once when I was gathering intel I could have sworn that girl turned around and looked me straight in the eye, right through my binoculars, even though I was rolled up in a camouflage net, six hundred feet away. It was like she could see me, even though I was completely invisible. I'll never forget that look."

He smacks his lips in admiration.

"Fact is, I've often wondered what became of her. Did she manage to shake off her upbringing or become just as nuts as her old man?"

He goes quiet, appears to be waiting for an answer.

"Thanks for that little anecdote," Asker says, slowly getting to her feet. "Let me know when you've got Sandgren's log-in for me."

She adds a cool smile before turning slowly and heading for the door.

Shoves her hands into her trouser pockets so he won't see them shaking.

SEVENTEEN YEARS EARLIER

The chairs outside the headmaster's office are rock-hard. That's surely no coincidence. Waiting here is supposed to be uncomfortable, unpleasant. Nothing anyone should take lightly.

Leo is sitting with her eyes closed, the tears burning behind her eyelids.

Her father is inside.

Every now and then she catches the odd word between him and the headmaster.

"Violence . . . indefensible . . . abuse . . ."

She knows that she will have to pay for this. That Per is already weighing up which punishment is most fitting for the incident in the school bathroom.

Which benefits are to be taken away, which chores she will be forced to do and for how long.

Not because she hurt them, mind, but because she has forced him to come here.

Forced him to leave the Farm, his safe space, and step out among the sheep.

Betrayed him.

The sobs bubble up in her chest. She gulps a few times, to push them back down.

When she opens her eyes, Martin is sitting beside her. His sweater is still wet, but he has nevertheless managed to regain some of his dignity.

She doesn't know how long he has been sitting there, or what he has heard.

He says nothing. Just sits there quietly beside her.

On the other side of the door, it is now Per's turn to talk.

A muffled, collected voice that she can just about make out.

She knows that tone. Knows that Per is at his most dangerous when he sounds calm and reasonable. An irritating tear falls from her eyelashes, and she wipes it quickly away.

Martin clears his throat.

"He's pretty unique, your dad," he says.

She doesn't reply.

"I actually met him once, in the hardware store. He was buying an axe, a tarp, and a whole fucking basket of ammunition, and all I could think was 'God, please don't let it be me he's planning to murder.'"

Asker snorts. She doesn't know why. Something about Martin's voice, or the way he talks about Per, or just the joke in itself.

Whichever it is, her reaction appears to encourage him.

"I mean, we're talking huge serial killer vibes. My knees were rattling so hard you could hear them. Picture two maracas . . ."

Asker snorts again. For some reason she can't help it.

Martin gets up off the chair.

"Here, look." He wobbles his knees while pacing back and forth in the corridor.

She is laughing out loud now. The tears are still falling, but she doesn't care.

Martin goes on pacing up and down the corridor.

"Oh no! I'm shitting myself! Prepper Per's coming to kill me . . ."

The name makes her laugh so much she can hardly breathe.

"Prepper Per," she gasps between volleys of giggles. "That's brilliant!"

Martin stands on his tiptoes and raises his elbows to shoulder-height, so he looks like a scarecrow. Lowers his head and glares ominously.

"Look at me, I'm Prepper Per. I live in a bunker and scare the shit out of everyone. The end of the world is nigh!"

A sound makes him turn around.

The door to the headmaster's office is open. Per is standing in the doorway.

Flannel shirt, combat trousers, boots. A straight mouth and sunken eyes that, combined with his receding hairline and bent, sharp nose, make him look like a bird of prey. The gaze that always feels like it's boring through your head.

Martin straightens up.

She can see that he is afraid, which isn't unusual. Her father has that effect on most people. All of Martin's instincts should be screaming at him to get away as fast as possible.

And yet he just stands there. Meets Per's laser eyes.

"I j-just wanted to say . . ." He clears his throat, pluckily raises his chin. ". . . that Leo saved me. That I think she was amazing."

Per stares at him a few more seconds. Then snorts and mutters something before nodding at her to come with him.

On the way to the exit she glances back over her shoulder.

Martin is still standing there. His knees faintly shaking.

But he raises one hand and waves at her.

In the car, Per says nothing for several minutes. Just stares straight ahead as he drives them home. Appears to be deep in thought.

"Unacceptable," he mumbles, so quietly that it's barely audible.

She doesn't reply, just looks down.

Assumes that it's her behavior that he is referring to.

But after another long silence, she starts to wonder whether he is actually thinking about something else. How much had he caught of Martin's imitation? Did he hear their laughter; could he tell that it was aimed at him?

She is afraid of Per, as always.

Still, there is something to his voice, something she has never heard before.

Something that she could make out in those five short syllables.

Astonishment. Perhaps even a touch of—uncertainty.

He starts to talk now, sounds himself again.

Reels off all the punishments that he has devised, all the tasks she will have to do to regain his trust.

But for once she only half listens.

Prepper Per, she thinks, and sees Martin Hill before her again.

Can't help but smile.

SMILLA

The red light comes on, and, unlike the previous times, Smilla is ready. Has already leapt out of bed at the sound of the hatch rattling at the bottom of the door, and is ready and waiting when whoever is outside hits the light switch.

She bangs on the steel door with her fists, cries as loudly as she can.

"Hello? Hello? Can you hear me?"

No reply, only the faint scrape of a shoe sole against a floor.

She pounds again.

"Say something, damn it!"

But everything is silent. No trace of her kidnapper, beyond the food tray on the floor just inside the hatch.

So much for her attempt to establish personal contact. As her instructor at hostage school warned, it's impossible to humanize yourself and spark empathy when no one communicates with you.

Luckily she has a plan B.

Today's menu is the same as usual. A juice carton, a few dry hunks of bread, and a paper plate with some sort of cold creamed vegetables that she has to scoop up with her fingers. Despite being starving, Smilla waits to eat.

She has around three minutes before the light goes out again, and she wants to make the most of that time. Try to find something else that can help her get out of here. Information, some sort of tools, even a makeshift weapon.

She has already studied the door and hatch through which the food tray came. Where the door handle should be there is only a round metal plate. The hatch opens inward and is just tall enough for the food tray to fit through. From the door it is three steps back to the bed. The red light extends that far, lights up the mattress, blanket, and pillow, and beyond.

The room is rectangular, as she has already figured out.

Ten feet wide, fifteen feet long, more or less. Concrete walls, ceiling, and floor, all painted gray. On one of the walls opposite her bed there is a metal ventilation grille, around twenty by twenty inches.

She pokes her fingers inside, tries to coax it off the wall, even though she already knows it's fixed firmly in place.

Otherwise the room is empty.

But on the floor in one corner she finds a crack that she hadn't spotted before.

She kneels down, follows it with her fingers all the way to the wall.

The concrete scratches at her fingertips, but a chunk slowly gives way.

Just as the red light goes off, she manages to extract a sharp wedge, just big enough to hold in her hands.

ASKER

The time is approaching six-thirty on Thursday evening, and the street-lights have already been on a while. The mist is rolling in from the Öresund Strait, it climbs up onto the docks, creeping in slowly across the streets until everything is hazy.

Lissander and Partners' spacious offices occupy one floor of a turn-of-the-century building right next to Malmö's Stortorget.

High ceilings, herringbone floors, modern art, and Danish design furniture. The light fixtures alone cost more than what a detective inspector earns in a whole year.

The glass entry doors are unlocked, the reception desk unmanned. Chatter and music can be heard from over in the conference room. Rod Stewart doing his best American crooner impression.

Asker briefly considers sneaking back out.

Before she can make up her mind, Camille comes out of the conference room.

Her little sister is, as usual, perfect. Skin, hair, makeup, clothes—all meticulously planned and executed.

A younger copy of their mother, only much less terrifying.

"Leo, there you are! Junot will be so happy!"

She takes Asker's arm and practically drags her into the conference room.

There are fifteen or so people in there, all office employees, all so alike in dress, appearance, and behavior that Asker struggles to tell them apart. Not that she has ever taken pains to try.

Champagne fizzes in the glasses; on the table lie trays with a few leftover canapés.

Junot lights up when he catches sight of her. Works his way through the crowd to give her a hug.

"Thank you for coming," he whispers in her ear. "You really didn't have to."

"Of course I have to be here for your name day," she replies. "Though I prefer when it happens in summer."

"Me too," he laughs. "But don't say that to Isabel."

Her mother appears. Not out of nowhere—that never happens. If Isabel Lissander is in a room, then everyone knows it.

"Leo, so nice that you could come."

"Hello, Mother."

"There are still some canapés and champagne left."

Her mother gestures at the table with a perfectly manicured hand.

Asker realizes she never ate any lunch. She sweeps up a glass while wolfing down a salmon canapé. It's phenomenal, of course. Since she can't find any plates, she eats two more on the spot.

When she turns back to Junot and her mother, they have been joined by Camille and Fredric.

"Hi, Leo!" Fredric says with that daft smile of his that for some inexplicable reason she once found charming.

Her mouth is full of canapés, so she just nods in response.

"Fredric's working on a big assignment," her sister says.

"A corporate merger, nothing special," he says with feigned modesty. "But there'll be a good commission in it for the firm. How's your work going, Leo?"

Camille squeezes his arm subtly and gives him a reproving sideglance. Clearly everyone knows that she has been given the boot. Naturally Isabel maintains the façade, simply gives her champagne glass a little swirl.

"All good!" Asker says once she has finished chewing. "I've been seconded to a new role that has actually brought with it a few surprises."

"Ah, great," says Fredric, before exchanging a relieved smile with his wife.

They stand in complete silence for five excruciating seconds, which is three more than Camille can bear.

"The girls are in my office," she says. "I've given them free rein with the iPads."

Asker drains her champagne glass.

"Then I'll pop in and say hello."

Camille's office is farthest from the entrance. Light colors, birch, Marimekko patterns.

The girls are sitting on the sofa, both completely absorbed by their iPads, but they're overjoyed when Asker steps in. Grab at her neck and pull her down onto the sofa between them. Fiddle with her hands and hair while babbling on about at least three things at once, in that way that only six-year-olds can. Asker tries to keep up, but it's almost impossible.

Eventually the tablets start beckoning to them again, and after watching with the girls for a little while, Asker carefully extricates herself from hands, arms, and legs and sneaks out into the hall.

The next-door office belongs to her mother. The door is ajar, only the desk lamp is on. Asker has been here many times over the years, and can never help but poke her head inside.

The room is still imposing. Luxurious rugs, floor-to-ceiling bookshelves. On one side of the room a solid oak desk with provenance from at least two different legal institutions; on the other an Arne Jacobsen sofa suite in dark, patinated leather. Between the tall windows a bar trolley that would probably be well enough stocked to keep Churchill in good spirits.

But what is perhaps the best thing about her mother's office is that she has her own en suite, hidden behind a secret door in the wall paneling. Perfect for touching up one's makeup, or for those who don't appreciate sharing bathrooms with others. The latter being one of the few things that Asker and her mother have in common.

She sneaks inside and locks the door. Unbuttons her trousers and sits down on the toilet. She despises this entire place. Not that she really knows why. Junot, Camille, Fredric, and everyone else at the office aren't bad people.

They're just squares. Boring. Like everyone else she knows or has ever known, with perhaps one exception: Martin Hill.

Her phone buzzes in her trouser pocket.

Here's the link to the hidden camera and your log-in.

Best, Daniel Nygård.

She opens the website and taps in the details. After a little crunching, a live image of the model appears.

The room lies in darkness, but the glow of an emergency exit sign is enough to give her an overview. The camera is roughly in the middle of one of the long sides of the room. The model is too big and too close for the camera to be able to capture everything; of the room with the wintry landscape only the doorway can be seen. The main entrance and emergency exit are clearly visible, however, so she assumes that Nygård simply chose to prioritize these.

Smart. She would have done the same.

Asker adjusts the settings slightly, notes that the camera is on a twenty-four-hour recording loop. Fires off a *Thanks for your help* to Nygård, then puts away her phone and stands up.

She is just about to flush when she hears someone open the door to the office. The click of high heels on wooden floors, then silence when they reach the rug by the desk. After that, Isabel's voice.

"There. Now we can talk."

A brief silence, which means she is on the phone.

"I see," says Isabel. "And where was it parked?"

Asker's ears prick up. Clearly they are discussing a car. But Isabel has her job voice on, which means it can't be about some measly parking ticket. Asker's gut feeling is willing to bet that she is discussing the Holst case.

"And you don't know how it got there or how long it's been there?" her mother goes on. A longer silence while the person on the other end of the line explains something. Asker leans as close to the door as she dares.

"Ah, that's unfortunate," her mother goes on. "Does that mean you're reevaluating your theory around who could have abducted Smilla?"

Asker's heart skips a beat. Her gut instinct was right.

Another silence as Hellman—it's most likely him on the line—says something.

"I understand," her mother responds. "I'll inform the family straightaway. Thank you for calling."

She ends the call.

Asker barely dares breathe. They have found Malik's car—that much she has grasped. But there's something else, too.

Out in the office, her mother has made another call.

"Tomas, it's Isabel Lissander, I've just had a call from Jonas Hellman. The police have found Malik Mansur's car. It was parked outside a disused factory on the outskirts of Malmö. But I'm afraid that isn't all . . ."

A short silence before Isabel continues.

"Malik was in the passenger seat," she says gravely. "He's been dead for days."

ASKER

Forensics has set up tents over the car and the cracked asphalt around it, to shelter the crime scene from the misting rain. Shone bright lights inside them in order to do their work, which means every now and then they appear as shadow figures on the tents' sides.

The cordon in place is exemplary. An area of three hundred by three hundred feet, the far side of which follows a rusty old fence that guards the silhouette of a dilapidated industrial building.

A few law enforcement officers in rain gear are keeping an eye on the rain-drenched journalists who are trying to broadcast live to their respective audiences, with only large golf umbrellas to shelter them.

Asker has parked slightly farther back, and has now taken position in one of the dense copses of birch trees that surround the parking lot.

When she made her excuses and left the name-day party, she imagined she might have the chance to cozy up to Forensics, examine the car, and take a look at the body. But Hellman and his crew are still on the scene, and as a result she can't show her face.

She watches him through binoculars.

Sees him speaking to Forensics, but the distance is too great and the light too poor for her to be able to tell what he is saying. His body language, however, is easier to read. His movements are short, staccato. He looks tense.

No wonder. Smilla Holst is still missing, and his prime suspect is dead. His entire investigation upended.

Hellman gathers his team in a circle. Eskil is there, a few others besides.

Colleagues who just a few days ago were *her* team.

Will they start to question him now, as they would definitely have questioned her, had she been the one to put them in this predicament?

Start exchanging meaningful looks, raise their eyebrows slightly, hint that they've had a different theory all along?

There is nothing to suggest that. Their circle shrinks, as though they are speaking in hushed voices. Closing ranks around their leader.

Then Hellman turns and starts walking toward the cordon tape. Eskil trundles after him, holding a large umbrella over his boss's head.

Hellman cuts a cool figure, there's no denying that. Black trench coat and a turtleneck. A police badge on a lanyard around his neck, giving the air of a TV cop.

The journalists immediately flock to him, obscuring most of her view.

Asker gets out her phone and pulls up one of the news sites.

After just a minute or so Hellman appears in a live feed. She keeps the sound on while watching him through her binoculars.

"As you know, a car that was deemed of interest in the Holst investigation was found on this site a few hours ago," he begins. "In the car the remains of the car's owner, Smilla Holst's former boyfriend, were also found. His family have been informed, and the car will very shortly be taken in for forensic investigation. Beyond this we have no further comment to make, other than to say that the investigation into Smilla Holst's disappearance continues at full capacity. Thank you!"

Hellman ignores the questions being called out, turns his back, and returns to the Forensics tent and his colleagues. As he does, a large tow truck enters the parking lot. Asker lowers her binoculars.

She won't get any chance to inspect the car, as hoped. At least not here.

The rain is falling more heavily. She has no reason to hang around, so she turns and starts walking through the bushes with light, well-trained steps.

But then she stops dead. Looks up.

That creeping feeling is back.

The same feeling she felt earlier that day, when she noticed the van in her rearview mirror.

Slowly she turns around.

In the parking lot the journalists and photographers are jumping into their cars and vans, taking shelter from the rain. They are chatting loudly, slamming doors.

Seemingly oblivious to the world around them.

Beyond the cars' headlights and the spotlights over by the crime scene, the entire industrial site is cloaked in darkness. Not even the odd streetlight is on. She holds up her binoculars, points them at the clump of trees on the other side of the parking lot.

Everything is dark and still. Not the slightest movement or glint of light to suggest that anyone is there.

Still, she can't shake the feeling that she is being watched.

THE MOUNTAIN KING

He called in the tip-off about the car from a prepaid phone. Destroyed the SIM card and the phone and then, like a patient huntsman, lay in wait in the darkness, taking the second-best viewpoint.

The first police car turns up after only ten minutes.

After that everything happens quickly. Cordons, Forensics, that arrogant cop who appeared on the TV and in the papers.

He studies them through his powerful night-vision binoculars. Watches their every move, sees their every facial expression.

They are baffled, just as he expected. Don't quite understand what's going on, other than the obvious.

That the owner of the car is dead.

But they don't know why, don't realize that he is out there in the darkness, watching them.

That none of what is happening is by chance, not even the site on which they stand.

Still, they aren't what he is most interested in.

The reason why he has taken this kind of risk.

He could have done away with the car in a safer way. A way that ensured it was never found again, just like the two fugitives' busted-up Volvo.

But that would have meant passing up this opportunity.

The journalists have gathered by the cordon, and the arrogant cop walks down to them. Is surely trying to avoid conceding that they have come up against an unexpected snag in the police investigation. That they don't have the slightest clue what's going on, or who it is they are hunting.

For he is invisible.

A monster.

He runs his binoculars along the fence. Over to the copse on the other side of the parking lot, where the best viewpoint is.

The light is so dim that nothing is visible with the naked eye, but for the night-vision binoculars that poses no problem.

His heart starts to pound.

She came, just as he'd hoped.

Took his bait. Chose the spot that he had left for her.

He zooms in on her face. His binoculars only show her in a green tint, but even so he can intuit her magical eyes.

She is completely preoccupied with the crime scene, monitors it through both her binoculars and her cellphone. Not the slightest suspicion that the one being watched is in fact her.

He is excited now.

His breaths are short, his mouth dry.

"Leonore Asker," he whispers to himself.

Tastes the syllables one by one.

He hasn't felt like this in years. Not since he saw the girl with the red backpack step off the bus and realized that she was something very special. That he had to have her, whatever the risk.

She is an observer, just like him. Someone who stands on the outside, looking in. One who is never truly let in because she, like him, is different.

"Leonore Asker," he whispers again.

She understands him. Knows what it is he wants to show through the model.

Realizes who he is.

What he is.

He watches her through his binoculars for several minutes. Follows every little movement in fascination, the same way he once admired a beautiful butterfly in a glass jar.

When she turns off her phone and appears to be leaving, he is disappointed.

But then she stops and slowly turns around.

He zooms in on her face. Licks his lips.

And suddenly something astonishing happens.

Something momentous.

Leonore Asker stares back at him. Holds up her own binoculars and sees him, straight through the darkness, even though he is invisible.

Even though he is the hunter and she the prey.

"Magical eyes," he mumbles.

For one short, breathtaking second he feels something he hasn't felt in a very long time. Not since he was a teenager.

Fear.

Then violent desire.

HILL

Hill is at the pub with a few friends when the news flash pops up on his phone.

One of two missing Malmö youths found dead.

He excuses himself and finds a more isolated spot to watch the video clip.

A police officer in a turtleneck and trench coat, with a badge dangling around his neck, curtly explains that they have found the car and that the owner, Smilla's ex-boyfriend, is deceased.

He goes cold. It can't be anyone but MM. He searches for more information, without much success.

MM is dead, and his girlfriend, Smilla, still missing.

What terrible news!

His good mood, which had been just starting to return, has now gone with the wind. He makes up an excuse to his friends and heads home.

MM being dead just feels so unreal. Hill had seen him just days ago, and he had seemed perfectly normal then. At least he thought so.

Or was there some kind of signal, something that he missed, a suggestion that MM was in trouble?

Was there anything that Hill could have done?

As soon as he gets home, he watches the clip again, this time on his computer. The cop in the turtleneck looks determined. The camera pans across two illuminated tents behind a police cordon. Behind that, a rusty wire fence and a dark, derelict building that Hill seems to recognize.

He toggles back, pauses the image. Zooms in and out a few times to make sure he is really seeing what he thinks he is.

The building in the background is the old abandoned factory that he and Sofie visited just a few days before.

"How weird," he mumbles to himself.

FRIDAY

ASKER

Asker goes home, takes a hot shower, and changes into some dry clothes. Eats a takeout in front of a midnight whodunnit while trying to unwind.

But it's hard. Her mind is racing.

She thinks of Malik's mother, Hana, how she made his bed, trying to bring some shred of order to the chaos in her head.

Hana has first had to learn that her son was missing, only to then see him singled out as a suspected kidnapper. And now he is dead.

She must be devastated.

And Smilla is still missing. There is a risk that soon her body will be found, too. Two devastated families.

Meanwhile, Hellman's main line of inquiry has been rocked to its core. He is shaky. Potentially vulnerable.

The question is what she should do about it.

If she should do anything about it at all.

On the one hand, her most tactical move would obviously be to keep her head low. Hope that Hellman's investigation implodes on its own.

On the other hand, she can't deny that Bengt Sandgren was on to something. Julia Collin and Tor Nilsson have, like Smilla and Malik, both disappeared without a trace only to reappear as miniature figures in the same railway model. And, besides Sandgren, she is the only one who is aware of that connection.

Whatever Bengt Sandgren managed to dig up besides what she already knows will bring her one step closer to finding Smilla's kidnapper, and hopefully also give her the chance to send Hellman back to Stockholm with his tail between his legs.

If there is anything more to dig up, that is.

At some point after midnight she dozes off on the sofa; then she wakes up again just after two, with a stiff neck and a dry mouth.

She knows from experience that she won't be able to get back to sleep.

Might as well get something done. She gets dressed, backs the electric car out of the garage, and drives into the night. A gale has started to kick up. The gusts coming off of the fields make the wheel jerk.

Bengt Sandgren has his own room in intensive care. There is a bandage around his head, his face is dappled with the bluish-yellow remnants of old bruises, and his eyes are closed. Across his nose and cheeks stretches an intricate network of small broken blood vessels, the mark of many years of alcohol abuse.

The intubation tube supplying Sandgren's lungs with air coils across the blanket like a fat caterpillar, as his rib cage slowly rises and falls. In one corner a screen monitors his faint vital signs.

Asker doesn't really know quite what she'd hoped to gain from this visit. Clearly Sandgren can't give her any of the answers she is looking for.

But the feeling that he was closer to solving the mystery than she had previously thought won't go away, especially not after being followed by that dark van.

And now Malik Mansur is dead.

But some of the questions she has can be answered, at least. Such as the circumstances surrounding Sandgren's fall.

She catches a passing duty doctor in the corridor. A woman of her own age, with tired eyes. Asker shows her police ID and explains the reason for her visit.

"Bengt Sandgren?" the doctor asks. "Oh yes, I was actually working when he came in. A heart attack and skull injuries from a fall. A neighbor had found him, apparently, so the paramedics said."

"They did?"

The doctor nods.

"He'd come over to borrow something. Saw Sandgren lying at the bottom of the stairs through the window in the hall and called an ambulance—at least that's what I was told. It took a while for the paramedics to realize that Sandgren had had a heart attack and not just fallen. Luckily they spotted that he was taking heart medication and put two and two together. So Sandgren was in many ways lucky in his misfortune. Had the neighbor turned up any later, he wouldn't have made it."

"Did he have any belongings on him?"

"If he did, they'd be in the locker in his room. I can ask the nurse to open it for you."

The locker turns out to contain only a pill bottle for heart medication and Sandgren's wallet.

"No house keys?" Asker asks the nurse.

"No, his emergency contact picked them up, I think."

"Emergency contact?"

"Virgilsson, I think he was called. He pops by every now and then to visit. He's the one who brought the flowers."

She points at a wilted little bouquet in the window.

Asker thanks the nurse and stands there for a while by Sandgren's bed.

His pulse is even. The air carries on pumping rhythmically through the intubation tube.

Outside the window the night is imperceptibly turning toward early morning.

She thinks of Malik Mansur again. Of Smilla.

Of the figures in the model railway.

"What were you on to, Sandgren?" she mumbles to herself. "How far did you get?"

Obviously she gets no response.

SMILLA

The small concrete wedge isn't where she left it, just next to her bed.
After a few minutes spent crawling around on the floor, she finds it right next to the wall, as though someone has accidentally kicked it.

The discovery fills her with a strange sense of triumph. For the first time she has outsmarted her faceless kidnapper.

Learned something about him without him realizing.

What she had believed to be a nightmare has turned out to be completely true. Not her imagination or a delusion.

The moved piece of concrete is proof.

Her kidnapper drugs her food, and then sneaks into her room when she is out cold. Even perches on her bed.

He doesn't touch her, at least not under her clothes. She has rigged them so that she would be able to tell.

But she is pretty sure that he has been stroking her hair.

Which in turn means he gets close enough for her to be able to hurt him.

All it would take is for her to dare.

She clenches her hand around the sharp concrete wedge. Does a few quick jabs in the darkness.

A sound makes her stop dead.

A faint voice from the side of the room.

"Hello?" the voice whispers. "Is anyone there?"

Smilla cautiously moves in the direction of the sound. Her heart is pounding violently.

"Hello?" she hears the faint female voice speak again.

The sound is coming from the ventilation grille on the wall. Smilla leans as close to it as she can.

"Hello," she whispers.

"Who are you?" The voice sounds frightened now.

"I'm Smilla. Who are you?"

The room falls silent for a few seconds.

"Julia," the voice eventually replies. "My name is Julia."

ASKER

By just before six a.m. Asker is back at police HQ. The first thing she does is try to sneak into the Forensics garage to take a closer look at Malik's car.

This is a high-priority case, and the technicians have surely been working all night. If she times it just right she can slip in at the shift changeover and pretend she still belongs to Serious Crime. That's her plan, at least.

But the card reader at the entrance to the garage merely beeps dismissively at her pass. Someone has restricted her access rights. Hellman, obviously. Once again he is one step ahead.

Unless someone warned him, that is. Told him that giving her the boot wouldn't be enough; that he would also have to make sure she was kept well away from the investigation. Take every measure necessary to ensure that.

The only person who could be that ruthless is her own mother.

Frustrated, Asker returns to her office. Shuts the door to the desolate, depressing corridor that represents her exile.

She flicks impatiently through Rosen's pile of missing people. Tries to find leads that can link more of the figures from the model. But that doesn't prove as easy as it was with Julia Collin and Tor Nilsson. Several of the young men could conceivably be the hitchhiker with the headphones, and she can't find anyone who's a clear match for the two burglars in the beat-up Volvo that Krook mentioned.

Her computer dings. An email from Attila. No subject, not even any greeting. Has he arrived in the office without her noticing? Or was he already here when she got in?

Use this link to access Sandgren's IT account.

She clicks on the link, follows a few on-screen prompts, and suddenly she is logged in as Bengt Sandgren.

His work inbox feels like a logical place to start.

The inbox is chock-full; Sandgren doesn't appear to have cared about keeping it clean.

Most of it is useless. Newsletters, internal memos, forwarded emails, spam.

She switches to his browser and combs through his history.

Sandgren appears to have used the internet primarily for reading the news. But under his favorites he has bookmarked a link to a newspaper article about unusual hobbies.

In the article, two young men whose faces are half-obscured by hoodies talk about their interest in urban exploration. Referred to by only their first names, they vividly describe the thrill of exploring abandoned buildings and places.

"*Kinda like being an explorer and burglar in one. Only without stealing or breaking anything. That's against the UE code,*" says one man, who calls himself John. The other calls himself Tor, and John makes digs at him because he occasionally does break the rules. When the journalist asks him to elaborate, Tor replies that he is a graffiti artist and sometimes can't resist the temptation to paint or tag the places he has visited, which apparently isn't the done thing among upstanding urban explorers.

The man has to be Tor Nilsson, especially since a little later on in the feature he mentions that he has had his fair share of run-ins with the law, but isn't afraid of doing time.

"*The cops don't care about break-ins in abandoned buildings,*" he says, which is, to be fair, an entirely correct assessment.

A fact box at the end of the article provides a list of further reading for those who want to find out more about urban exploration.

The first book on the list is *Forgotten Places and Their Stories* by Martin Hill.

She returns to Sandgren's inbox and searches for the title. Sure enough, she finds an order confirmation and receipt, dated straight after when Lilja claimed to have let Sandgren know about the figure painting graffiti.

Asker leans back in the chair and recaps the timeline for herself.

Roughly two years ago, Sandgren, much to his astonishment, finds a figure representing his long-missing goddaughter Julia Collin in the model railway.

He interviews the then president, Ulf Krook, and learns that a number of mysterious figures have been inserted into the model over the years. He asks Rosen to compile a list of missing people with a link to the area, and also makes sure that she regularly updates the list.

Sandgren goes on sniffing around the model, which bothers Krook, who tells him where to go. Their cooperation, to the extent that there was any, comes to an abrupt end.

So when Lilja replaces Krook as president, Sandgren gets in touch and asks him to let him know if any new figures turn up in the model. Which they do.

A young man spraying the world *urbex*.

Sandgren suspects that the figure represents graffiti artist Tor Nilsson, who according to Rosen's list was reported missing just weeks before the figure appeared.

Based on the word the figure is spraying, Sandgren starts looking into the subject.

He finds a newspaper article on urban exploration in which a certain Tor is interviewed, thereby hardening his suspicions. In the article he also stumbles across Martin Hill's book, which appears to be something of an urban exploration bible.

Sandgren orders and reads the book, and at some point also obtains Martin Hill's phone number, clearly with the intention of contacting him.

Maybe he even did?

She should call Martin and find out. That would be the logical next step.

Still, she hesitates.

It has been sixteen years since they last saw each other. What can she say?

That she is investigating a possible link between missing people and plastic figures in a model railway? That she shares that conclusion with Bengt Sandgren, a drunk cop who's now in a coma following a heart attack?

And by the way, Martin, old buddy old pal, did Bengt ever happen to get in touch, and if so what did he say?

She scrolls on through the emails and learns that it wasn't only his inbox that her predecessor neglected. Sandgren rarely sent any emails, either. The few times he did, they were mostly just one-liners asking for a phone number so he could give the recipient a call. Sandgren doesn't appear to have liked digital communication.

But she does find an email that interests her.

It is from an Ulrika Collin, Julia Collin's mother, and was sent only a month ago.

> *Dear Bengt,*
>
> *Losing Julia is a wound that will never heal.*
>
> *But after four years we have slowly started the process of at least trying to move forward. I hope that one day you can do the same.*
>
> *Until then, please refrain from contacting me, Robert, or Julia's brother again.*
>
> *Best wishes,*
> *Ulrika*

Asker reads the email twice. There is something doubly sad about it. She still can't get a handle on Sandgren.

According to both Krook and Lilja he was all but obsessed with the case. So much so that Julia's family asked him to refrain from contacting them. But almost nothing in his office has anything to do with the case. Where is the pile of database searches that Rosen compiled for him, or the memos he surely must have kept?

She opens the documents folder on his computer. All it contains is an ancient record of the minutes from a police billiard club meeting years ago.

Which only makes what she finds in the image library all the more interesting. It contains three photos, all from the model railway.

They all depict a plastic figure spraying the word *urbex* on what appears to be a brown box. The figure is wearing a blue hooded jacket, baseball cap, and paint-spattered jeans. In one hand he is holding a can of spray paint, in the other a black bag. As with the models of Smilla and MM, the details are eerily precise.

The man is even looking fearfully over one shoulder, as though afraid of being caught.

But where is that figure now?

And where are the ones of Julia Collin and her mysterious, featureless pursuer? It's possible that Sandgren may have kept them and the rest of the case documents at home.

If what the nurse said was true and Virgilsson has the key, she could go there and look for them.

Still, something about that idea rubs.

Sandgren appeared to have slept in this office in the days leading up to his heart attack. Either didn't want to—or couldn't be bothered—to go home, even though he lives little more than half an hour away.

That behavior doesn't seem to suggest that he would keep the documents relating to the investigation that so occupied his mind at home. Unless he had a relapse, that is. Gave up on the investigation, kicked back on the sofa, and drifted off into an alcoholic haze. She transfers the images to her phone.

Gets up in frustration and walks over to the window.

The lights are on in the incident room up in Serious Crime. Someone is moving in the window.

She grabs Sandgren's binoculars and adjusts the focus.

After just a few seconds she spots Jonas Hellman. He is speaking to someone farther back in the room. Judging by the previous night's black turtleneck and the bags under his eyes, he has been here all night.

Asker understands.

Hellman's reputation of supercop is at risk. And if he doesn't find Smilla Holst, his chances of nabbing Rodic's job are basically non-existent.

Which in turn means that if she, using Sandgren's secret investigation, can track down the real kidnapper, she will have a good chance at reinstating herself.

Maybe even getting revenge.

In which case she needs to follow any leads that she has, no matter how uncomfortable they make her, or what doors they may open.

Asker goes back to the desk.

She picks up the Post-it containing Hill's phone number and dials it on her phone. Forces herself to press the call button.

Realizes only when she hears his sleepy voice on the line that it's only just after 6:30 a.m.

"Hello . . . ?"

His voice sounds exactly the same, and at the same time it's clearly different. Deeper, more grown-up. It belongs to someone else.

She already regrets calling, and for a brief second considers hanging up. But she needs answers.

"Hello, this is Leo Asker," she says. Purses her lips around the words.

Sixteen years of silence pass, though in reality it's just a few seconds. She squirms, once again regrets calling.

"Leo," he eventually says. "It's . . . been a while."

Asker's brain is caught in a strange space between the present and the past, which makes it hard for her to speak.

"So what have you woken me up for?" he asks. His voice sounds curious, but also guarded.

"I . . ."

She pulls herself together.

"I'm a detective," she says with what she hopes is a professional tone. "I'm working on an investigation. I think one of my colleagues has been in touch with you. Bengt Sandgren? I thought I'd see if you have any time to meet."

A sleepy female voice pipes up in the background.

Thanks to Google she knows that Martin has no wife or children. Though of course that doesn't mean he's single.

Not that that would matter anyway.

"If you have time, that is?" she adds.

"Of course," he replies. "When did you have in mind?"

She shuts her eyes for a second. Her brain is still refusing to co-operate.

"As soon as possible. Preferably today."

The woman's voice again. A rustling on the line.

"I'm about to go to work," he says. "But around four would work. I'm in Lund these days."

Asker is on the verge of saying that she knows.

"I can come to you," she says instead. "If you know of a place with good coffee."

"The patisserie on Klostergatan is one of my favorite spots."

"Great, then I'll see you there at four."

Another few seconds' silence, as though they both have more to say but neither knows where to begin.

"Well, see you later then," Asker ends the call.

"Bye, Leo."

She sits there with the phone in her hand.

Should she really have opened this door?

She quickly waves that thought away.

Fact is, she had already waited far too long.

SMILLA

The tears are burning behind Smilla's eyelids, and she has to swallow a few times to stop herself from letting out a sob.

There is someone else down here, in the room next door. She isn't alone in the darkness anymore.

"Have you been here long?" she whispers toward the air vent.

"I think so," Julia replies. "But I've lost count of the days. They all just run into one. He moves me sometimes when I'm sleeping. He did it yesterday, I think."

"He?"

"The Mountain King."

"The Mountain King?"

"Yeah." Julia yawns. "That's what he calls himself."

Smilla's mind is whirring. There is so much she wants to know.

"H-how did you get here?"

"He chased me . . ." Another yawn. "Sorry, I'm just so sleepy."

"He puts things in the food," says Smilla. "Drugs."

"Yeah . . ." Julia's voice is even fainter.

"What does he want from us? Why are we here?" Smilla asks.

Julia whispers something that she doesn't catch.

"I can't hear you," Smilla says as loudly as she dares. "Why are we here?"

"Because we're his," Julia whispers. "He owns us."

Her voice falls silent.

"Julia," Smilla whispers. "Julia, are you there?"

But she gets no reply.

ASKER

Asker gives Virgilsson's door a brisk knock and steps straight in.

She has been waiting for him. Heard the faint squeak of his Ecco soles as he loped in just after seven a.m. Hasn't even given him the chance to take off his coat or turn on the radio.

"Good morning!" she says. "I need help with something."

Strictly speaking, that statement isn't entirely accurate. In actual fact she needs two favors from him, but she starts with the most pressing.

The little man looks caught off guard, just as she hoped.

"Of course, do take a seat."

He takes off his coat, scarf, and flat cap and hangs them on an old-fashioned coat stand in the corner of the room. Adjusts his comb-over with one hand before sitting down at his desk. As usual he is wearing a sweater vest, shirt, and tie.

"So how can I be of assistance?" he asks.

Asker gets straight to the point.

"I need to take a look at a car in Forensics. Without anyone finding out I've been there."

"I see." He drums his fingertips against each other. Starts with his little fingers and continues in a rolling movement until he reaches his thumbs, then starts again.

"That wouldn't happen to be the car that was found yesterday evening? The one that was linked to the Holst case?"

Virgilsson goes on drumming his fingers, apparently expecting no reply.

"Tricky," he says. "Very tricky."

"But not impossible," Asker notes.

Virgilsson gives a crafty smile.

"Few things are impossible. Not even those that break half a dozen rules. It all comes down to motivation."

"What do you want in return?"

He holds up his hands defensively.

"Oh no, I wasn't suggesting anything of the sort—"

"That was exactly what you were suggesting," Asker says, cutting him off. "Tell me what you want, I don't have time for charades."

Virgilsson is smart enough to know when it's time to change tack.

"Well, seeing as you asked. See that wall there?" He points at the wall behind her, where a painting hook gapes emptily.

"There used to be a beautiful oil painting there that I, for a variety of reasons, was forced to part with. Unfortunate . . ."

He clicks his tongue and shakes his head at the same time.

"But I happen to know that there is a most suitable replacement. An early Bruno Liljefors."

"Where?" Asker asks.

"Down in Property. It was seized as part of a financial tangle. It'll be months, perhaps years before it goes to trial, and until then . . ."

He gestures at the wall once again.

"Until then you want to *borrow* the painting," she says, only just resisting the urge to use air quotes.

"Precisely," he smiles. "The chance to feast my eyes on a Liljefors would truly brighten up my long working days."

Asker takes a deep breath. Officially she of course shouldn't go along with this sort of back-scratching. But the Department of Lost Souls plays by its own rules—as she is realizing more and more by the day.

"I'll see what I can do," she says grudgingly.

"Excellent!" The little man lights up. "I'm glad we understand one another. Give me half an hour and I'll make a few calls. I have a fraternity brother up in Forensics who can probably be of assistance in your matter."

ASKER

At just after eight a.m. Asker and Virgilsson are standing outside the same locked door that Asker tried to enter earlier that morning. Virgilsson is holding a white cake box in his hands.

"*Smörgåstårta*," he whispers. "You can pay me back later." He knocks on the door, which is immediately opened by a boxy man with a well-groomed beard.

Asker has met him before, he's one of the section heads in Forensics.

"Brother Wendel," says Virgilsson, greeting him with a strange handshake, which Asker assumes must be some sort of secret salutation from their old-man's order.

"Brother Virgilsson," Wendel replies. He pokes his head out into the corridor and looks around watchfully.

"Come in. Quick," he whispers.

A short corridor with a few doors leads them to a dedicated garage. Closest in stand two technicians' vehicles, and beyond them, in a corner behind some plastic curtains, Asker spots the hood of Malik Mansur's black Golf.

"We're just having breakfast," says Wendel, pointing at a door a couple feet away.

He takes the box from Virgilsson.

"With this I can stretch the break to fifteen minutes," he says to Asker. "But no more. And if anyone catches you it's your problem, OK?"

Wendel disappears into the break room, and Virgilsson sneaks out the same way they came in, leaving her on her own.

She turns on the timer function on her watch. Gives herself thirteen minutes to be on the safe side, then slips through the opening in the plastic curtains.

The doors, trunk, and hood of the Golf are open. On the workbench beside it lies a system camera and clipboard with the technicians' notes.

She quickly flicks through them. The night shift has already lifted prints and clothing fibers from the car, but they have not yet removed anything else, other than the body.

Asker turns on the camera. Swiftly scrolls through the images until she finds the ones taken on-site the night before.

Malik is sitting in the front passenger seat, held up by the seatbelt.

He is wearing the same clothes as in the selfie. Though he is long dead he still looks terror-stricken. His face is white, his eyes wide.

His chin has dropped, leaving his mouth slightly open. His hands are clenched.

Asker scrolls to the close-ups.

Malik has grazes on both palms. Those, along with the white marks on his trouser knees and jacket sleeves, suggest he fell forward onto a rough, dusty surface. Beyond that there appear to be no injuries to the body.

She glances at the timer.

Ten minutes left. High time she took a look at the car itself. She snaps on a pair of rubber gloves from a paper box on the counter.

The interior is clean, smells of leather upholstery and car perfume.

The passenger seat where Malik was sitting has been moved as far back as possible, and little wonder. Granted, Malik isn't a tall guy, but moving a lifeless body is harder than one might think. Not to mention cramming it into a car seat. Whoever did it must have needed all the space they could get.

She crouches down, turns on the flashlight on her phone and shines it on the mat on the floor.

More white dust. She dips her index finger in the dust and rubs it against her thumb. Cement, which means Malik's fall happened indoors.

Asker takes a few more pictures on her phone, then walks around the car.

The trunk is empty, except for a promotional umbrella.

On the mat and the fluffy lining she spots more cement dust.

The body must have been transported in the trunk.

But then why not leave it there?

Why go to all the effort of shoving it in the passenger seat, thereby risking discovery?

The answer isn't particularly hard to deduce: because it was important to the perpetrator that Malik be found just so.

The driver's seat is somewhere in the middle position, which suggests that whoever sat in it last was roughly her own height.

Normally she would have confirmed that by comparing the angle of the seat with that of the rearview mirror. But the latter is missing completely. Appears to have been wrenched from the fixing.

Strange.

Another look at the timer. Seven minutes left.

The glove compartment, like the other storage compartments, contains nothing of interest.

The mat under the driver's seat is full of clumps of mud and other traces of cement dust. It calls Ulf Krook's muddy yard to mind. Ulf was wearing Wellies when they met, his stepson, Finn Olofsson, boots. Both with thick soles that could easily trail this sort of mud clump around.

She is just about to check the backseat when a sound makes her stiffen.

A door opening, followed by the sound of voices.

Asker squats behind the car and peers cautiously toward the gap in the plastic curtains.

The voices approach. The first person she sees is Wendel.

The forensic technician looks agitated. He and his colleagues should have been eating their savory sandwich cake for at least another five minutes. Through the slit she spots the clear cause of this interruption.

Jonas Hellman, with his usual arrogant swagger, and diagonally behind him the conceited little ass-licker Eskil.

"Why aren't you finished yet?" Hellman asks.

Wendel stops. Mumbles cagily that they have taken photos, lifted prints, and done plenty more besides, while anxiously looking toward the curtains and the car.

"Got any hits?" Eskil asks authoritatively. The question is idiotic, but clearly he feels he has to say something.

"No, obviously if we did we would call you straightaway," Wendel replies with yet another glance in Asker's direction.

"And where are the images?"

"We're working on them . . ."

Asker sinks down as low as she can. If the men come to fetch the camera, then she's a goner. Cornered. Behind her there is only a concrete wall, and she has nowhere to hide. Almost nowhere, at least.

She hears the scrape of shoe soles and realizes she has to do something. In one furtive movement she rounds the car and slips into the trunk. Lowers the lid and shuts it behind her as quietly as she can. The next second she hears the sound of the curtains being parted.

"The camera's here," she hears Wendel say. "You'll have the pictures in five."

"We should have had them long ago," Eskil barks, clearly assuming the role of Hellman's bulldog. "You should have finished everything off, instead of sitting there stuffing your faces with *smörgåstårta*."

Wendel mutters something inaudible in response.

The three men circle the car. Stop just outside the trunk.

"No traces of blood?" Hellman asks.

"No," Wendel replies. "The night shift did a superficial exam of the body before it went to autopsy. There were no visible wounds, at least none that could have caused the victim's death. The medical examiner will have to puzzle that one out. How did you find the car, by the way? That isn't in the report."

Asker pricks her ears.

"An anonymous tip," says Hellman. "A prepaid phone. Probably the kidnappers themselves."

The car rocks, as though one of the men has jumped inside.

"No rearview mirror," Eskil notes from the driver's seat.

"Yes, we'd noticed," Wendel replies dryly. "By the way, here are the victim's belongings. Wallet, watch, and keys. We've already sent the phone off for data extraction."

"Anything else?" Hellman asks.

"Not just yet," Wendel replies. "But we'll go through the entire car again right away. Turn it inside out."

Asker hardly dares breathe. She can smell Eskil's aftershave from the front seat. Wendel and Hellman are standing just behind the car.

All it would take is for one of them to pop open the trunk and Hellman would have everything he needs to get her fired. Caught like a rat in a trap.

Suddenly an alarm starts to sound.

"For fuck's sake." The car sways again as Eskil steps out.

"Fire alarm," Wendel says. "We have to leave the premises."

His voice sounds relieved.

The alarm goes on shrieking. Is accompanied by the sound of footsteps.

"Let us know as soon as you find anything. No more coffee breaks," says Eskil.

The plastic curtain rustles again.

". . . results from the autopsy tomorrow" are the last words Asker hears over the alarm. After that, the sound of the door shutting again.

She exhales slowly. Forces herself to lie there another thirty seconds, just in case.

The trunk can't be opened from the inside. Instead she manages to fold down a section of the backseat and worm her way out. She peers warily through one of the rear windows.

The fire alarm is still ringing, but the garage appears to be deserted.

She climbs out of the car and cautiously stands up straight. Folds the seat back into its original position.

As she does, a small object that had been hidden in the joint between the seat back and the seat pops out. It is white, barely three-quarters of an inch tall.

Asker stiffens.

She knows exactly what she is looking at.

A featureless little plastic figure on a scale of 1:87.

HILL

Hill and Sofie are eating breakfast at his new dining table. She's the one who made him buy it. She has long complained that his apartment, with its mismatched IKEA furniture and random flea-market bargains, mostly resembles a student den. That it isn't befitting of a university lecturer, not to mention a best-selling writer.

So a few months ago he drove out to the fancy furniture boutique and bought a white table and matching chairs.

As soon as he got them home, he realized they weren't at all his style, and he still eats most of his meals on his comfortably indented sofa, as always.

But Sofie was satisfied, at least.

Said that he would just have to hold any important social events in his kitchen from then on, with a no-access policy to the rest of the apartment.

She is in Malmö until Sunday, and has spent more nights than normal at his place. He likes it, likes her, has occasionally allowed himself to fantasize about how life might look if she got divorced and moved back home.

But he has never raised the subject.

As usual, Sofie is in a hurry to leave, to go to a meeting that she is already running late for. She finishes getting dressed and doing her makeup while eating.

"Oh, by the way. I checked with an old colleague at the prosecution authority. That Bengt Sandgren heads up the Department of Lost Souls."

"Huh?"

"Yeah, I'm afraid that's what it's called," she says with a disgruntled frown. "A bunch of HR nightmares who've been shunted off to the basement, where they can't do any damage. So whatever it is Sandgren's working on, I don't think it'll help either Tor or us. But I've got to get going. I'll call you later."

She checks her makeup one last time, gives him a quick kiss, and hurries off before he even has a chance to finish his coffee.

Normally this type of hasty departure would leave Hill feeling a little down, even if he usually doesn't quite want to admit it.

Today, however, he welcomes the chance to be alone with his thoughts. Did this morning really begin with a wake-up call from Leo Asker? It feels as though it was all a dream.

But the phone call is there in his calls log, along with her number. It's real, which makes him both happy and nervous.

He was thinking about her not so long ago, and then she calls right out of the blue. Suggests getting a coffee, just like that, to talk about the very same Bengt Sandgren whom Sofie has just written off.

Leo Asker the detective—he finds that extremely difficult to imagine.

Their conversation adds to the sense of unreality that has been trailing him the past few days. The sense that something is happening around him that he doesn't fully understand.

He browses the morning papers. The discovery of the car dominates the news. There is also a picture of Smilla Holst, with the headline:

MISSING FOR ONE WEEK, BOYFRIEND FOUND DEAD.

Luckily there is no picture of poor MM, at least.

The initial shock has settled, but the thought of his star pupil being dead is deeply saddening.

Hill skims through the article, which contains nothing he didn't already read online the night before. He is ashamed to have even entertained the idea that MM might have kidnapped his own girlfriend. Instead he should have trusted his gut. The same instinct that is telling him that Mya knows more about the case than she is letting on.

His eyes linger on the newspaper image of MM's car. Behind it the factory building that he visited just days ago.

Yet another strange coincidence.

The plastic figure he found in the factory basement is still in his trouser pocket. He pulls it out, spins it around while studying it minutely.

The feeling that it means something is getting all the stronger. But he still doesn't know what.

ASKER

When Asker gets back to the department, she makes straight for Virgilsson's office. The little man is sitting at his desk, his reading glasses perched on the tip of his nose. The radio is playing classical music as though nothing has happened.

"Thanks for the help," she says.

He lifts his glasses up onto his forehead.

"Did it all go well?" he asks.

"Yeah, but it was a close shave. Great thinking with the fire alarm."

A short pause, after which he cracks a smile.

"Sometimes one must improvise."

She smiles back, but his brief hesitation has given him away.

He had no idea what she was talking about, but had no qualms about taking the credit for saving her. It makes what comes next easier.

"I stopped by Property," she says truthfully. "Spoke to their manager and said we needed to borrow that Liljefors painting for an investigation into art forgeries. But apparently they've introduced new procedures down there. Any loans or transfers of that nature need to be approved by the commissioner."

She shrugs in resignation.

"Sorry, I really did try."

Virgilsson studies her thoroughly. Lowers his glasses to the tip of his nose.

"Oh, well, that is very disappointing," he remarks dryly.

"I know. But perhaps there's something else I can do for you?"

"Perhaps." Virgilsson frowns in dissatisfaction.

Asker quickly changes the subject, to the other favor she needs from him.

"Well, there was actually something I wanted to ask you about, about Sandgren."

"Ah?" Virgilsson lifts his glasses back up onto his forehead.

"Well, as you know I've tidied up his office. But there are a few documents missing."

"Have you tried his computer? IT should be able to help you with his log-in details."

"Oh yes, I've got those," she says, without mentioning who it was who actually helped her.

"But I still can't find what I'm looking for. So I'm wondering if Bengt might have taken it home?" She throws in a smile for good measure.

"Perhaps." Virgilsson gives a slow nod, but unfortunately doesn't take the bait as hoped. So she raises the stakes.

"So I wanted to see if you might have access to his house keys?"

Virgilsson sits in silence for a few seconds. His eyes flit toward his desk drawers. Then he lowers his reading glasses again and shakes his head curtly.

"I'm afraid not," he says. His face is expressionless, his voice neutral. "I wish I could help. But if there isn't anything else, then I have some things to be getting on with."

HILL

Hill's Friday lecture is normally his personal favorite. But today he struggles to get himself going. Ban himself from glancing at the front row, where MM usually sits.

After a slightly shaky introduction, he eventually manages to find some sort of flow that builds as he goes on.

Today he is showing images from an abandoned hospital in the former GDR. He discusses at length how nature has changed its architecture. Created new forms and functions that the original architect could never have imagined.

The debates tend to get both heated and intense. The majority of the students don't like the decay. Prefer when buildings are whole, clean, and peopled. A completely normal way of thinking.

But a small clique see what he himself sees. The beauty of the cracked, the crumbling, the abandoned.

Besides, this particular hospital has a good backstory. For many years it served as a closed psychiatric facility housing some of the country's most dangerous criminals. But since the GDR was a socialist model society, neither the hospital nor its patients officially existed. They lived and died in silence behind its walls, and were buried in unmarked graves in an out-of-the-way area of the hospital's large grounds.

Once the students have heard its eerie story, they see the ruins with new eyes, which is of course the whole point of the lecture.

"Architecture is influenced by many things," Hill summarizes. "Both visible and invisible. And to fully appreciate it we must keep all of our senses open. Sometimes even our sixth sense."

He concludes with a smile and a semi-bow. Is rewarded with long applause, as usual, and for a split second finds his eyes drifting back toward the front row. But he checks himself.

Just as he is about to unlock the door to his office he hears a voice.

"Martin."

He turns around. It's Mya.

She is wearing the same military jacket and beanie as before.

"I just wanted to say thanks for a great lecture," she says. "I was at the back. Hope that's OK? I'm not enrolled in the course, but I thought MM would have liked me to be there. He loved your Friday lectures."

Hill nods. "No problem, that's a nice thought."

"It's so awful, all of it." Her eyes start to glint.

"How well did you know each other?" he asks.

"We . . . dated for a while. He took me on a couple of UE explores."

"Then what happened?"

Mya shrugs, but doesn't manage to seem quite so unflappable as she is probably trying to.

"Nothing much. It just ended. He wasn't completely over his ex. And I wasn't looking for anything serious, anyway, so . . ."

She shrugs again.

"You were in love with him," Hill notes.

Mya looks down.

"Do you want to come in?" Hill gestures to his door, but she shakes her head.

"I've got to go, my ride will be here soon."

"Your cousin?"

She doesn't reply.

"See you around, Martin." She raises her hand in a wave that reminds him of the one she did in the van the other night. Then turns around and walks off down the corridor.

Hill stands and watches her go. He still can't shake the feeling that there is something else that Mya wants to tell him.

Something that she is working up the courage to do.

Once again he is struck by her similarities to the Leo Asker he once knew.

That blend of strength and vulnerability.

He wonders if Leo still has it.

SEVENTEEN YEARS EARLIER

Leo is lying on the bed in the trailer that serves as her bedroom. In reality it's more of a house on wheels than a trailer. Built to stand still, not to be towed down the roads.

She is reading a book she borrowed from the library and that she has hidden between the covers of one of the books that Prepper Per deems more suitable reading.

She worked her way through the chores she was given as punishment for the incident in the school bathroom, and since school is out for the summer he let her have some time to herself.

She hears the ringtone that indicates that someone has rung the doorbell down by the main gate. Followed by a long silence as Per speaks over the intercom and checks the camera. She thinks that he has gone to open the gate, that it's some goods delivery or one of his odd associates.

Instead Per opens the door to her trailer. Doesn't knock, since the Farm and everything on it is his property.

But today something is different. Per has a furrowed brow.

"You appear to have a . . . visitor," he says with a tone that implies surprise.

Then he turns away with no explanation, as though he needs a moment to himself.

She puts the book down. Her heart has started to beat a little harder.

The main gate is six hundred feet away, so she takes her bike. The gravel path crackles under its tires. It has rained recently, and the air is humid but mild. Butterflies flutter between the nettle flowers along the sides of the track.

Martin can be seen from afar against the verdant, early summer forest. He is hunched over his handlebars, looks breathless and ashen, as usual. His backpack is on his back.

"Hi!" he says when she stops on her side of the fence.

Bats away a pushy fly.

"Hi . . ."

She's unsure what he wants, has never had any visitors before.

"I thought I'd see if you wanted to go for a ride?" he asks.

"Where?"

"Just around." He shrugs, but gives a big smile. "It's the summer holidays. Does it matter where?"

"No." She glances at the camera on the gatepost.

"Do you have to ask . . . ?" He lowers his voice, rolls his eyes in the direction of the camera.

"Prepper Per?" she replies. Copies Martin's shrug. "Who cares!"

She unlocks the metal gate and shuffles her bike through.

Then she's off.

Out.

ASKER

Whoever kidnapped Smilla and murdered Malik is the same person who placed their figures in the model railway, Asker is sure of it. It is also at least plausible that the same perpetrator is behind other disappearances. But she can't be as sure of that until she has more links between the figures and the missing people. Had Asker still been department head up in Serious Crime, she would have opened a wide-reaching investigation into all of it. Set one team to work looking into what might have happened to graffiti artist Tor Nilsson, another into the disappearance of Julia Collin, and tasked a third with trying to link the other model figures to missing people.

But sadly she no longer has those kind of resources, and the team she currently presides over has its limitations.

Granted, Rosen has been surprisingly helpful with her database searches, but Asker still can't shake the suspicion that she was the one who went through her things and leaked the Holst case to her friend at *Sydsvenskan*. Hence for obvious reasons Asker can't let Rosen in on her suspicions.

And Virgilsson just lied to her face about the fire alarm as well as the keys to Sandgren's house, so he can't be trusted.

Which leaves the rancorous Attila, who seems far too interested in her own past for comfort, and Enok Zafer, who seems to be a few sandwiches short of a picnic.

Her conclusion isn't particularly sophisticated: she must do it all on her own, which means taking one thing at a time.

Julia Collin feels like the top priority right now, not least because it was her case that both tipped Sandgren over the edge and snapped him back out of his torpor.

Julia's mother has agreed to meet her this afternoon, so she gets the shabby old Volvo out of the police garage and heads out of town on the E6.

The motorway is full of traffic, as usual. An almost unending train of large trucks from the Continent rolling northward, with only a couple feet to separate them. Every now and then an impatient trucker heaves himself out into the next lane to overtake, which slows down the rest of the traffic, making the speed irritatingly erratic.

At least the weather is better today—to begin with, in any case. The sun peeps out every now and again, partly obscured by the clouds on the other side of Glumslöv's hills.

The drive gives her some time to ponder the moral dilemma she is facing.

Should she share her findings with Hellman? Explain to him what the plastic figure that Forensics will by now have found in Malik's car means? Help him to solve the case?

The thought doesn't appeal.

Still, Smilla Holst might well be alive, which means she can't let Serious Crime go on working blind.

It would feel much easier for her to reach out to Rodic, who also happens to be Hellman's manager, at least on paper. But if Asker is to take this information to them, she will first have to link the cases in a way that not even Hellman can question. Because that is of course precisely what he will do.

Jonas Hellman has already used his sway to get her kicked off the case and transferred. Has even managed to turn her own mother against her.

So it would be naïve, to say the least, to hope that he will take any information she gives him with an open mind—even if it comes to him through Rodic.

Which means she will have to keep flying solo, at least for a little longer.

She looks at the clock.

Her meeting with Martin Hill is just a few hours away. The thought makes her both nervous and expectant. It probably explains why she is so keen to keep busy. Why she chose to drive all the way up to Ängelholm instead of making do with interviewing Julia's mother over the phone.

As usual, the traffic thins out a lot after Helsingborg. The landscape remains open: fields, wind farms, small villages. On the horizon she spots the dark, raised silhouette of Hallandsåsen. The formation resembles a giant lying on its side. It's a description that she read somewhere, but she thinks it hits the mark.

When she stops the car outside the Collin family's house on the outskirts of Ängelholm, she receives a push notification on her phone that she needs to update the software for the hidden camera in the model railway club. She does as it suggests, then pulls up the live feed from the model.

The lights are on in the large room. On one side of the shot two men are tinkering with something. She recognizes Kjell Lilja from his posture and receding hairline. The other man also looks familiar. She tries to zoom in as far as she can.

It's the goateed man of few words—Finn Olofsson, Ulf Krook's stepson and right-hand man. Logically, therefore, Finn and Kjell Lilja should be enemies. But the two men's body language seems relaxed, and they appear to be helping each other with some type of build.

She watches them for a minute. The feed has no sound, and they are too far from the camera for her to be able to read their lips. Perhaps she should talk to the alarm technician about installing some more cameras, even a microphone?

She adds the task to her mental to-do list before opening the car door.

Ulrika Collin lives in a detached white-brick house straight out of the aspirational seventies. The Venetian blinds are shut, even though the sun isn't shining. The car outside is a typical middle-manager Volvo.

A few kids have set up a hockey goal on the street. They pause their game and glare at her as she crosses their rink.

Asker rings the doorbell. A dog starts yapping inside.

The door is opened by a woman in her fifties.

Her hair is already gray, her gaze mournful.

"Ulrika Collin," she introduces herself while grabbing the yappy dog, a little fluff ball who growls and bares its teeth.

"Come in! You aren't afraid of dogs, are you? Dido just wants to say hello."

She puts down the little dog, who goes on acting as though it is much more dangerous than it is. Asker ignores her, just like she did the blind mutt at Madame Rind's house.

The house smells of reed diffusers. On a table stands a photo of a young woman in a graduation hat. She is blond and quite petite, with lively blue eyes. In front of the photograph stands a lit candle.

"Yes, here we have my Julia," says her mother. "We haven't given up hope, but at the same time you have to be realistic. It's been four years . . ." She purses her lips for a few seconds.

"Take a seat and I'll fetch some coffee," she says, pointing at the sofa in the living room.

"So you said on the phone that you've taken over from Bengt Sandgren?" the woman asks once they have sat down and the little dog has jumped up onto her lap.

"Yes, that's right. Or taken over perhaps isn't the right way to put it. I'm tying up a few loose ends that Bengt left. It was a very sudden departure."

"Yes, his colleague called me and told me about the heart attack," says Ulrika. "A woman, I don't remember the name."

"Could it have been Rosén?"

"That's the one. I've wondered whether we should go and visit Bengt, but . . ." She throws her arm out in a gesture that is clearly supposed to fill in the blanks.

"If I understand correctly, things were a little tense between you?"

Ulrika sighs heavily, thoughtfully strokes her dog's back.

"Bengt and Karl-Johan, my first husband, were close friends. They served in the UN together many years ago, and for a while we spent a lot of time together. Perhaps you know that Bengt was Julia's godfather?"

Asker nods.

"When Karl-Johan died of cancer, Bengt was very supportive. He visited often, took Julia and her big brother Sebastian to the cinema. Even invited me out to dinner a few times . . ."

Another flap of the hand.

"But I knew that he drank, just like Karl-Johan. I didn't want to go through that again. So I turned him down as kindly as I could. When I met Robert, Bengt visited less and less, and in the end we lost contact."

She takes a sip of coffee.

"When Julia went missing, I called him. He came straightaway, even though he was pretty burned out. He spoke to the officers who were investigating. Traveled around searching for her in his free time, both in the evenings and on weekends."

The little dog looks up as though she has heard something. Jumps down off the sofa and runs into the hall.

"She does that sometimes. Dido was Julia's dog, I like to think that she's looking for her."

Ulrika shakes her head sadly.

"But time passed and nothing happened, and in the end the investigation was closed," she goes on. "Bengt stopped showing up. I think he was ashamed he couldn't solve it. Sunk even deeper into the bottle. But then around two years ago he got in touch again."

Just after the Julia figure was found in the model, Asker notes to herself.

"He turned up here one night and said he believed Julia had been kidnapped. That she was still alive. At first we were overjoyed, of course. But he got nowhere with it. And whenever we asked him about it, he would say he was about to crack it wide open, that he just needed a little more time. In the end you just don't have it in you to be tossed back and forth between hope and despair all the time."

The dog looks up again. Pricks up her ears, as though she really has heard a sound this time.

"In the end we spoke to a few other officers," Julia's mother goes on. "They told us Bengt wasn't who he made himself out to be. That he was in some sort of rejects' squad and didn't work on proper cases. So I asked him as kindly as I could to stop troubling us and let us grieve in peace."

Asker nods. It all fits with her own timeline.

The dog runs into the hall yet again, but this time they hear the sound of the front door opening.

"Hi, Dido," says a voice.

A wiry man appears in the hall. He is between fifty and sixty, wearing a shirt with a taxi company logo on it. His hair is combed back, the color at least one shade too dark to be natural. A signet ring, chains around his wrist and neck.

"This is Robert, my husband," Ulrika says.

"Robban," the man introduces himself to Asker and sits down beside his wife.

"I've told her about Bengt Sandgren," Ulrika explains.

"OK, good." The man doesn't look happy to have the police paying a visit.

"As I explained to your wife," Asker begins, "I'm just trying to tie up a few loose ends that he left. Julia's case is one of them."

She studies Robert on the sly. His body language, the way he drapes his arm protectively around his wife's shoulder. The suspicion in his eyes.

"So," she says, getting ready to steer this conversation toward what most interests her. "Obviously I've read the report into Julia's disappearance. As I understand it, there was some indication that she took a bus."

"To our summer cottage." Ulrika nods. "She would sometimes go there when she wanted to get away from it all."

"How so?"

Ulrika and her husband exchange anxious glances.

"Well, you know how teenagers can be. Sometimes they want to rebel. Julia's big brother was the same. Or almost, at least. Sometimes Julia would take the bus to the summer cottage without telling us. Spend a night or two there. She had her own key."

Asker intuits what is lurking between the lines, can read it in their eyes.

"Did you fight a lot?" she asks, as though the fights have already been mentioned.

"No . . ."

Ulrika suddenly bursts into tears and buries her head in her husband's shoulder. Robert rubs her back comfortingly, and the little dog jumps up onto the sofa and tries to squeeze in between them.

"Julia was an incredibly gifted girl," says Robert, unexpectedly softly. "Of course we fought sometimes, as I think every family does. But she had the whole world at her feet."

Asker nods. Waits for Ulrika to compose herself a little before going on.

"And this summer cottage," she says. "Where exactly is it?"

"We don't have it anymore," Ulrika whispers. "We sold it last year. It was too hard . . ." She sobs again.

"By Åsljunga Lake," her husband steps in. "The police searched it."

"And the bus that Julia would have taken, how close to the cottage does it stop?"

Ulrika takes a shaky breath.

"Y-you have to walk a few miles, but there's a shortcut through the forest. Julia's taken it a thousand times."

Asker sits quietly for a few seconds.

So Julia would have had to take a route through a forest, just like the female figure being chased in the railway model. What's more, Åsljunga Lake is only half an hour or so from Hässleholm.

No wonder Sandgren leapt to life when he saw the figures in the model.

She takes out her phone, shows them an image of the faceless little model that she found in Malik's car.

"Have you come across one of these anywhere? In Julia's things, or perhaps at the summer cottage?"

"No, I don't think so." Robert shakes his head while looking at his wife.

She doesn't look quite so sure.

"Have you seen this figure before, Ulrika?" Asker asks again.

"I mean . . ." The woman gasps.

She looks at her husband, who suddenly appears slightly concerned.

"The thing is, when we were clearing out the cottage, I did find a little plastic man in one of the flower boxes out on the deck. I remember it because I thought it belonged to Sebastian's model railway that he kept down in the basement in this house, and I couldn't understand how it might have ended up there."

"What did you do with it?" Asker asks.

Ulrika shrugs.

"Threw it away, I suppose. I didn't exactly attach any particular importance to it."

Asker casts a sly glance at Robert. He is fidgeting—either out of concern for his wife, or for something else.

"Why do you ask?" says Ulrika. "Do you think the figure has something to do with Julia's disappearance?"

"Possibly," Asker says vaguely.

She can't tell the couple about her and Sandgren's theory without risking them running with it.

"As far as I can tell, Sandgren conducted a very thorough investigation into Julia's disappearance," she adds. "But I'm afraid I can't find any trace of it in his files, so I don't know how far he got. We'll just have to hope Bengt wakes up, so I can ask him personally. But in any case, I won't trouble you any further."

She gets to her feet.

"Thank you both for your time. I'll be in touch if anything else comes up."

When she is halfway out of the room, she stops. Turns around and looks at the dog, who has nestled herself between the couple on the sofa and is now licking Ulrika's hand.

The question is clearly ridiculous, but, with a sudden thought of Madame Rind's blind mutt, she simply has to ask.

"Dido wouldn't happen to be a papillon, would she?" she asks, then regrets it immediately.

Robert shakes his head.

"No, she's a Yorkshire terrier. Why?"

"No particular reason, just out of curiosity," Asker mumbles.

So much for the spirit world.

Out on the street, the hockey game is still going. Pauses once again when she crosses their improvised rink.

Asker stops short. There are four kids playing, three boys and one girl, all around fourteen years old.

"Shouldn't you be in school?" Asker asks.

"Home study day," says the girl, almost a little sassily.

"Did any of you know Julia Collin?"

The question is mostly an impulse, but it seems to hit home. The four of them look at one another for a little too long, before the same girl speaks.

"Why are you asking?"

Asker shows them her police ID. The kids look at one another again.

"She was my babysitter when I was little," says the girl. "Our parents know each other. Her big brother and my eldest brother went to school together."

"What was she like?"

The girl looks impassive, but somehow Asker doesn't buy it.

"Nice."

"Nice?"

"Yeah."

There is something that she isn't saying, Asker is pretty sure of it. But kids and young people are hard to read.

"And her big brother, do you know him, too?" she tries.

"No. He's moved."

The girl turns away, indicating to one of the boys to pass the ball to her, as though signaling that the conversation is over.

A movement from out of the corner of Asker's eye makes her cautiously turn her head.

Someone is peering through the slats in the blinds in one of the windows of Julia's house.

The eyes follow her closely as she walks slowly back to her car, and don't let up until she has started to drive away.

SMILLA

"Julia," Smilla whispers, gently tapping the concrete wedge against the air vent. "Julia, can you hear me?"

No response.

She is probably still sleeping soundly, drugged up to the eyeballs.

Julia must have been here a long time. At least long enough to have given their mysterious kidnapper a name.

The Mountain King.

What does that mean? It sounds familiar, like something out of the folktales she read as a child.

But who—or what—is he?

Until now she has assumed this whole thing was an "average" kidnapping, one of those she learned about in hostage school. That whoever brought her here wanted to extract money from her father or grandfather.

But speaking to Julia has sent that theory up in smoke.

The Mountain King isn't after money; he is driven by something else.

He owns us, Julia had whispered.

We're his.

Smilla slides down to the floor below the air vent. But despite the desperate situation, she feels stronger than she has in a long time.

Because at least she isn't alone.

"Julia?" she tries again. But she still gets no reply.

Her hand squeezes the pointed concrete wedge.

She needs a plan.

ASKER

The caravan of trucks is less closely packed heading south, and on the drive home Asker makes the old Volvo work a little harder. When her speed is nearing eighty miles per hour, the steering wheel starts vibrating so forcefully that she struggles to keep hold of it.

She decreases her speed and tries to gather her thoughts following her meeting with Julia's family. Clearly they are grieving the loss of their daughter. Grief can manifest in many different ways, as Asker knows from experience. Still, something niggles. And the kids on the street definitely reinforced that impression.

She calls Rosen, gives her Robban's full name and address and asks her to do a few searches.

"How soon do you need it?" the woman asks apprehensively.

It's almost three-thirty on a Friday afternoon, and Rosen is probably already packed up and ready to go for the weekend.

"Straightaway," says Asker. "There's still some time before five, so I'm sure you can fit it in."

"Of c-course," Rosen mumbles. "I'll email you as soon as I'm finished. By the way, what is it you're working on?"

The question is sneaked in, almost in passing. Asker ignores it.

"One more thing," she says. "I need the cell number of a Sebastian Collin. He should be in his late twenties. Ideally right now."

"Certainly." The clatter of a keyboard is heard.

"There's only one Sebastian Collin, he lives in Stockholm. I'll send you the number right now."

"Thanks!"

The call ends, and the number follows hot on its heels. Asker immediately dials it, but Julia's brother doesn't pick up, so she leaves a message asking him to call her back.

She has just hung up when her phone starts ringing, an unidentified number.

"Asker," she says as she answers, half expecting it to be Sebastian Collin.

"Hi, Leo, this is Jakob Tell, Hässleholm Police."

"Oh, hi."

"This a bad time?"

"Not at all, I'm just on my way from an interview."

"A new lead on our railway model?"

Asker doesn't reply.

"Anything I can help you with, Tell?" she asks instead.

"Perhaps."

She can almost hear him smiling down the line.

"I'm on my way down to Malmö. Am borrowing a colleague's pad by Drottningtorget for a few days. So I thought I'd see if you fancied getting a beer, a bite to eat, maybe?"

Asker hesitates.

Tell is both good-looking and pleasant. In normal circumstances she would at least consider saying yes. But she gets the feeling that there's something more to his question than just a simple date.

"I'm afraid I can't tonight," she says.

"Tomorrow then?"

"Nor tomorrow, sorry."

"Have you got a boyfriend?" he asks bluntly. "If you do, you can just say so."

In a matter of seconds he has gone from vaguely interesting to bullish.

"Look, I've got to go now," she replies.

"Wait . . ."

She ends the call. Puts her phone on silent, in case Tell is the sort of person who can't tell when a no is a no.

She parks the Volvo in the police garage. As expected, she has already received a text message from Jakob Tell.

Sorry if I was too full-on. Hope we can keep in touch. Best, Jakob.

He ends with a few emojis that are probably supposed to excuse his overstep. Make her see that it was basically all a joke, really, that he's a cool guy with a sense of humor who just happens to get a little intense from time to time. Asker deletes the message without replying.

Once she's back in the building, she goes straight to the department to put the car key back in the locker, then hurries out again. Resists the urge to knock on Rosen's door and check if she's finished with the searches, since she's already late to her meeting with Martin Hill.

During the short train journey from Malmö to Lund, Asker notices that she is nervous.

She and Martin haven't seen each other in sixteen years. Literally half their lives. They are completely different people from who they once were. She tries to persuade herself that her meeting with Martin is strictly professional. A neutral coffee to find out what he and Sandgren discussed. Then again, she has dropped off her work car just in case there's talk of a glass of wine, and that would neither be professional nor neutral.

Even she can see that her thoughts are going round in circles.

She is five minutes early when she arrives, but Martin is already there.

"Leo Asker," he says with a soft smile. "Long time no see."

For a few seconds they stand facing each other, both equally unsure how to greet the other. End up in an awkward hug.

"Take a seat and I'll get some coffees."

The café he has chosen is cozy. Bookshelves, well-worn armchairs, the smells of freshly baked goods and nice coffee. Big windows give out onto Klostergatan, where a green city bus is inching its way along the street. She sits down at a table in one corner.

Martin returns bearing coffee and croissants.

"The best in Lund," he assures her. "A little different from those chocolate-ball sandwiches that we'd get at the youth center. Remember those?"

"Who could forget?"

"Or Maggan who worked there," he adds. "The one with the wart."

Asker smirks at the memory. Hill does the same, and the tension between them eases slightly.

She can't get over how grown-up Martin has become. Or how attractive.

A knitted blazer with a shirt and tie, loosened slightly at the collar. His skin is a rich umber, not ashen like it was when he was a teen. But his dark eyes are the same as she remembers them: engaged, lively, charming.

"So, are you going to start with a recap of the last sixteen years, or shall I?" he asks after taking a sip of coffee.

"You first," she says.

"OK, but buckle up because it's quite some ride."

He holds his hands up, as though miming a TV screen.

"As you may remember, we moved to Umeå because my parents took over a local bar up there. But we only stuck it out two years. Dad was constantly freezing, even indoors. And I didn't like it either. Cold plus heart condition isn't a winning combo. So after that it was Stockholm, and an English pub in Södermalm. Once I was nineteen and had finished growing, the doctors thought it was time to repair my broken pump."

He gives his chest a gentle knock.

"One mechanical valve later and I could live a completely normal life. Eat, exercise, get cold, party, catch up on everything I'd missed, which I definitely did. And then some. The one small hitch is that I have to take blood thinners for the rest of my life, but that's a price I'm happy to pay."

His smile is almost as contagious as Asker remembers it. She feels her nervousness trickling away, thinks she notes roughly the same reaction in him.

"I studied to be an architect, but pretty soon realized that designing new buildings and all that wasn't really my bag," he goes on. "I was, as you know, more interested in the ruins, in the forgotten places and all their exciting phenomena. So I did a PhD on the subject . . ."

"And wrote a best-selling book," Asker jumps in. "And became a poster boy for urban exploration."

"Well, I did say I had a fair bit to cover," he laughs. "And eventually I got a job at the architecture school here in Lund. I've been here three years now. Love it!"

She is waiting for him to say something about his civil status. Mention that partner or girlfriend whose voice she heard in the background when she called him that morning. Instead he takes a huge bite of his croissant and chews it in delight, as though it's the best thing he's eaten in a long time.

"So that's my sixteen years," he says with his mouth full. "Your turn."

Asker doesn't know where to begin.

Hill detects her uncertainty. His face turns serious.

"I heard about the Farm. That things spiraled."

Asker has predicted the conversation might go this way, so she has come prepared.

"Per was sloppy with some explosives during a drill," she says. "They went off, both of us got injured."

"Shit!" Hill winces, as though the words themselves hurt him.

"Per got committed," Asker continues. "Straight to the psych ward, without passing go. I moved in with my mom in Malmö. Can safely say it made for a very different life after the Farm."

She is able to keep her voice surprisingly neutral, as though the story is in fact someone else's. A sixteen-year-old girl who no longer exists, which is true, in a way.

"As soon as I turned eighteen, I moved into my own place," she goes on. "Lived with a guy called Fredric for a while."

She doesn't know why she mentions this rather personal detail, especially after he skirted around the subject. But something about Martin has always made him easy to talk to.

"But I got bored," she quickly adds. "Moved to the States, studied law, worked, traveled. By the time I came home, Fredric was engaged to my little sister, Camille. They're married now and have kids, both work at my mom's law firm, which makes our family get-togethers nice and awkward."

"Eesh," Hill smirks. "Sister-swapping, the scandal!"

Asker smiles, too. Genuinely can't help it. There is something very familiar about this entire conversation.

"OK," he says. "So the love triangle explains why you don't work for your mom. But how did you become a cop?"

She shrugs.

"The lawyer life didn't suit me, I'd already realized that when I was in the States. I did a course on criminal psychology over there, and an internship at a homicide division in Philadelphia, which I liked. As soon as I got back to Sweden, I entered police college. I've been a detective for almost five years now."

Hill shakes his head. Adds a frown that reads as both skeptical and impressed.

"Damn, I'd never have guessed. Leo Asker, a cop . . ."

She chuckles.

"You're not the only one. Mom thinks I'm throwing away the law degree she paid for."

"And your father?" The question slips out; it's clear that he already regrets it.

"Per and I aren't in contact," she replies tersely. "As far as I know he's back on the Farm. Lying low in his bunker, I suppose, waiting for the apocalypse."

She clears her throat. This topic makes her bristle, and as nice as it is to see Martin Hill—really nice, even—she isn't here for a stroll down memory lane.

High time to get down to her real business.

"The reason why I wanted to meet you is actually work-related," she says, noticing herself shifting into her work voice. "As I mentioned, your name and book turned up among my predecessor Bengt Sandgren's papers."

Hill sits quietly for a few seconds, appears slightly disappointed at the hasty change of subject.

"Yes," he says, nodding. "Bengt Sandgren called me a few weeks ago. He'd read my book and had a few questions about urban exploration. Who does it, what places they visit, how they communicate with each other, that sort of stuff."

"Did he say why?"

"He was working on some sort of investigation. But he didn't want to say what it was about. Was pretty vague generally."

"OK."

Asker chews her upper lip. She had hoped for something more, a lead that she could build on, or at least something to back up her theory.

He notes her disappointment.

"But he mentioned an urban explorer I know who's missing. A graffiti artist."

"Tor Nilsson," says Asker.

Hill raises his eyebrows.

"As usual you're one step ahead, Leo."

He studies her closely. Even though many years have passed, she recognizes the look on his face. The slightly furrowed brow, the right eyebrow that creeps up a bit above the other. The gaze that, unlike most people's, doesn't flounder in Asker's heterochrome eyes.

She knows that his mind is racing, that any second now he'll come out with something she doesn't expect. A chain of thought and conclusion that only Martin Hill could reach. She finds herself waiting with bated breath.

"My turn to throw a few names into the ring," he says thoughtfully. "Malik Mansur and his missing girlfriend, Smilla Holst. It's her you're looking for, isn't it?"

Asker tries to hide her shock, but doesn't quite succeed.

For one short, dizzying moment she is sixteen again. Back in the Shadowlands.

And for once she likes that feeling.

HILL

Conveniently enough, the café is right next door to a restaurant that is one of Hill's favorites. Décor, food, and wines that call to mind a French bistro. A cozy atmosphere, a good bar.

He knows the staff and manages to wrangle them a table by the window, even though it's turning toward evening on a Friday night and the place is filling up.

Over wine he tells her about Tor's disappearance, and how he and Sofie are still looking for him. For some reason he leaves out the fact that they are in a sort-of relationship. Presumably because Sofie is married, but he isn't quite sure if that's the whole truth.

So he swiftly changes the subject to his star student.

"MM was always nagging me to write another book. He offered to take me out to some new, exciting sites," he summarizes. "I liked him. Had a tough time believing he could have kidnapped Smilla. But the police seemed so sure . . ."

He falls quiet, sips his wine. Glances at Leo over the brim of his glass.

She is at once both the same old Asker and not, he notes. Some of her traits are exactly the same as before.

Those different-colored eyes that feel like they bore straight into his head, those eyes that he could never tire of. That slanting little smile, both amused and sad.

But she is no longer a calf-like sixteen-year-old, but a grown woman. A detective, no less, on a case.

He tries to remind himself of that. But it isn't always so easy.

"Do you know if Malik hung out with anyone else in UE circles?" she asks.

"I'm sure he did. He once introduced me to a girl called Mya, but I don't even know her surname."

He tops up their wineglasses. Skips over the detail that Mya reminds him of Leo. That that might be why he wants to make sure she doesn't get hurt. To avoid making the same mistake again.

"Has anyone from the police interviewed you, or your colleagues?"

He shakes his head.

"No, the only cop I've seen is the one who's all over the media. Do the two of you work together?"

"Something like that," she says. "There are a lot of people involved."

She takes a glug of wine, as though to close the subject.

Just like back in the café, when they were talking about Prepper Per and the accident on the Farm, she feels slightly slippery.

As though there's something she doesn't want to say, or can't.

Grown-up Martin Hill of course realizes he can't expect Leo to divulge all her secrets after two coffees and a couple of glasses of wine, especially not when they are work-related. But the sixteen-year-old within him who was once head over heels for her feels a little hurt nonetheless.

He wants to ask questions, try to get her to open up. Re-establish their connection.

He tops up their wineglasses again, so eagerly that he splashes a drop.

"It's really great to see you, Leo," he says, and grown-up Hill hears how stupid it sounds the very second the words leave his lips.

She was the one who set up this meeting, he reminds himself. Because she had questions for him from work. If he really wanted to have a reunion, he's had plenty of years to arrange one.

But he hasn't, because he's still ashamed.

He searches for something else to say, something that might interest her.

"Oh, by the way," he says. "That industrial site where MM's car was found. Sofie and I were there just a few days ago. We found signs that Tor had been there."

To his delight, she looks interested.

"What kind of signs?"

"A painting of his on a wall. And then a few of his tags, and . . ."

He hesitates, but then decides to throw in everything he knows, no matter how strange it might sound.

". . . and I also found a strange little plastic guy."

He indicates its size with his fingers. Regrets even mentioning it, until he sees the look on her face.

She gets out her phone and pulls up a picture.

"One of these?"

The image she shows him depicts a white, unpainted plastic figure that he knows all too well.

Hill nods eagerly.

"Just like it. I've got it in my kitchen drawer back at home."

A brief silence.

"That wasn't a coincidence, was it?" he asks.

"No," she replies. "There was an identical figure in Malik's car. And elsewhere besides."

"But why?"

She says nothing for a few seconds. Appears to hesitate, but then a certain decisiveness pulls at her mouth.

She pulls up another picture. A different plastic figure, this time painted in painstaking detail, spray-painting the word *urbex* onto a brown box.

Asker zooms in on the figure.

Hill flinches.

"That looks like Tor," he says. "And that brown box looks like the rusty oil tank in the basement of the factory where I found the plastic guy."

Asker puts her phone away. Seems to think for a few seconds. As though pondering what he has just said, and how much she can tell him in return.

"It's all tied to a giant model railway," she says slowly.

"Someone is inserting figures into it that shouldn't be there. Figures that both Bengt Sandgren and I believe represent people who have been reported missing."

Hill listens attentively while she tells him about the phone call she got from Lilja and all the discoveries that she has made since, right up to the plastic figure that Julia Collin's mother found at their summer cottage.

"Four people," he summarizes. "Tor, Julia, Smilla, and MM. All of them have turned up in the model, and in their place are left small white plastic figures, almost like a calling card."

"That's our theory," she confirms. "There are also a few other figures I haven't yet managed to link to any disappearances, so there may be more."

Hill shakes his head.

"What the hell?"

"Yeah, I know what you mean," Asker agrees. "And not an easy sell to my police superiors, I might add. So for the time being I'm working on it on my own."

"I'd be happy to help," he says, a little too quickly. Hears how idiotic he sounds.

But then he sees her smile. That smile that he has thought about for so many years.

"Thanks, I appreciate it. And it's not out of the question that we might need your expertise. Sandgren seemed to think so, since he called you."

They sit quietly for a few seconds. Look at each other, as though trying to deduce the answer to the same question.

Hill is the one who asks it.

"So what now?" he asks.

Asker takes a sip of wine, slowly, as though to give herself time to think.

"I've rigged a hidden camera by the model in case any new figures appear," she eventually says. "And tomorrow I thought I'd search Bengt Sandgren's house for more leads."

"Alone?"

She tilts her head to one side.

"Do you think I can't handle it?" She looks offended, but they are both a little tipsy and Hill can't quite tell if she is joking.

"I think you can handle anything," he says.

They look at each other in silence for a few seconds. Not in an unpleasant way; quite the reverse. Even though so much time has passed, it doesn't feel that way.

She smiles again, and it might be the wine or the light in the restaurant, but for a few seconds she looks exactly the way he remembers her.

Smart, strong, vulnerable.

Wonderful.

"What's that?" he asks.

Her left cuff has worked its way up her arm, revealing a black letter on the inside of her wrist.

She pulls it back down automatically, then looks at him for a few seconds.

Unbuttons the cuff and rolls up her sleeve.

There is a word there, black letters inscribed over scarred skin.

"Resilience," he reads.

"I had it done to cover the scar from the explosion," she says. "Mom wanted me to have cosmetic surgery, but this felt better."

"May I?" he asks, reaching his hand out toward her arm. Doesn't actually know why. Only that it's something he has to do.

She pulls up her shirtsleeve a little more in response.

Hill traces the letters with his fingertips. Feels the scar tissue beneath. Her skin is warm. Makes his fingers tingle.

He looks up and looks her in the eye. That two-tone gaze he has dreamt of so many times. There is so much he wants to say to her. So much he has thought about over the years.

But before he can open his mouth, she gives a start, pulls her arm away, and rolls down her sleeve.

"I think it's time to call it a night," she says.

They walk over to the taxi stand in the square. The atmosphere has changed, become more reserved. As though each of them feels that they have exposed a little too much to the other.

"You can keep me updated, I guess," he says. "Who knows, more things might come up that I can help with."

"Sure," she says, but her tone is neutral. Doesn't actually make any promises.

They stand there facing each other for a few seconds. Each wondering whether to hug, and both trying to read the answer in the other.

Before they figure it out, the moment has passed.

"Well, good night, then," says Hill.

"Good night, Martin," she replies with a soft smile.

He hears her give an area and street name to the taxi driver.

Then she's gone.

SIXTEEN YEARS EARLIER

It's early September. He and Leo have been friends for just over a year now, but it feels like longer. As though they have actually known each other all their lives.

They have just started tenth grade, and are in one of his favorite places. An abandoned barn he found on one of his very first expeditions in the area. To his delight, Leo seems to like the place almost as much as him.

Part of the barn's roof is missing, and if you lie on your back on its old gray floorboards, you can see the clouds languidly floating across the late-summer sky.

Enormous white ships always chasing an elusive horizon.

"One year left until high school," she says dreamily.

He knows that her father is getting worse. That he forces her to get up in the middle of the night to do disaster training. Barely leaves the Farm unless he has to. Prepper Per is convinced that Judgment Day is approaching, and prefers for her not to go out at all.

"Once we start high school, he won't have any choice," she says.

She has repeated these words so many times it has almost become a mantra.

"Per thinks the police are after us again," she goes on. "He's more paranoid than usual. He normally gets like this when winter's coming. It's something about the darkness, I think. He took pills for a while, but stopped long ago."

He says something in agreement, keeps his eyes on the restless clouds.

He should tell her about the papers he saw on their kitchen table back at home. The thing his parents discuss in low voices when they think he's asleep. Why they leave the room to talk on the phone.

He has seen the signs before. Knows what they mean.

Instead he goes on staring at the sky.

His parents are like two of those clouds.

Always restless, always on their way somewhere, without ever really arriving.

Should he say something to Leo?

Tell her what he thinks is coming?

He glances at her out of the corner of his eyes.

She goes on talking about high school, about everything they're going to do once they finally get out of here.

And maybe that will happen.

Maybe his parents will change their minds, decide to stay here a little longer.

He hopes so. For his own sake.

But mainly for hers.

SMILLA

Smilla has been lying awake a long time. Several hours, though it's hard to know for sure.

She has been waiting, preparing.

Julia has given her courage. Put a name to the silent horror that is holding them captive. Made her dare.

The sharp concrete wedge is cutting into her hand, but she still doesn't want to loosen her grip, for fear of losing it.

The wedge is her advantage. Her trump card.

A faint click is heard, as the hatch in the door opens.

After that the scrape of him removing the food tray. Inspecting it in silence, to make sure that she has eaten and drunk.

In actual fact she poured it all down the latrine. Perhaps he can somehow tell that just by looking at the tray? See that she's lying there wide awake, and decide not to enter?

Smilla has the impression that she can hear her own heartbeats echoing between the walls.

Another click, louder this time. An unfamiliar sound that must be the lock. Then a faint draft as the door opens.

Smilla shuts her eyes. Forces herself to take slow breaths to complete the illusion.

She detects steps. Can feel the air in the room change as he approaches.

The Mountain King.

Having a name for him helps, strangely enough.

He stops sharply by the bed. Stands there watching her, completely quiet and still. She can hear his breaths, smell him.

Resin, oil, moss, and then something else.

Something more animal.

She squeezes her eyes shut, forces herself to lie completely still.

His clothes swish faintly. She can feel his hand even before he touches her. Stifles a gasp just in time.

He caresses her hair slowly, moves his hand to her temple, her cheek.

Her pulse is racing, but she manages to stay still.

His hand stops at her chin. Stays there a second or two.

Then goes back up to her hair.

Now!

Smilla opens her eyes.

The room is still dark, but she thinks she can see him regardless.

An immense shadow towering over her.

She grabs his hand with her left. Swings her right hand with the sharp concrete wedge toward the area where she thinks his face ought to be. Her fist hits metal, as though he is wearing some sort of visor over his face.

She hears him grunt, feels him pull his hand back while reeling backward.

Smilla throws her legs over the edge of the bed and dashes toward the door.

As she had hoped, it is open.

The corridor outside is pitch-black, but she finds a wall with her right hand and follows it, moving her feet as quickly as she dares. Her fingers brush against the concrete, her breaths are short, and her heart is threatening to burst out of her chest.

In the darkness behind her she hears footsteps.

She goes on following the wall. Spots a light. A red indicator light from some sort of electric appliance.

The footsteps behind her are getting closer, will soon have caught up with her.

She lets go of the wall, aims for the red light, and runs as fast as she can. In school she was always the fastest runner, could even beat most of the guys. The distance increases. She hears him roaring with rage. The sound echoes between the walls, makes the hairs on her arms stand on end.

Now she sees something else, beyond the red light. A sliver of white light from a cracked door. She throws her last caution to the wind and sprints toward it.

Reaches out her hands to throw open the door.

She is only a couple feet away when someone tackles her hard from the side.

She loses balance, hits the ground so heavily that the wind is knocked out of her.

The next second he is on her with all his weight.

She struggles wildly, kicks and waves her arms in every direction. But he is too strong. He locks her legs down with his and takes hold of her arms. As he does so a rag is pressed to her face. A sharp smell makes her nose sting, and then the room starts to spin.

"Hold her down!" she hears a voice whisper as she tumbles back into the darkness.

SATURDAY

ASKER

Asker is woken by a headache. It is after nine, and she hasn't slept this long in years. She needs to pee, her breath tastes of wine, and her tongue feels sticky against the roof of her mouth.

It's all Martin Hill's fault. He kept pouring out the wine like there was no tomorrow. He seems to love life—probably because for so many years he was forced to run on empty. He's easy to talk to, too. Far too easy.

For a while she let herself get carried away. Told him too much about her investigation, about herself. Cracked a door she should have kept shut. A stupid move, obviously.

She needs to clear her head, so she pulls on her running gear and heads out for a run. Follows the path by the lake that leads to the golf course.

Her feet are heavy, her body sluggish.

She stops on the other side of the lake to stretch and catch her breath. From here she can see the yellow and red tree crowns around the house, and its panoramic windows.

She tries to recall if she blabbed about her living situation to Martin Hill, too. That she doesn't have any real home but is just a house-sitter? After a little thought she decides that she kept that much to herself, at least. Always something.

After her run she takes a long shower, tries to rinse away any thought of Martin and instead focus on the new information she has dug up on the case.

The small, unpainted figures of the kind that she found in Malik's car, which appeared in the wake of both Julia's and Tor's disappearances.

Which definitely links the three cases.

As she explained to Hill, it isn't an easy theory to sell, neither to Rodic nor to anyone else. Still far too easy to dismiss as unhinged fantasies.

Which is why she needs proof. Needs Sandgren's memos and, ideally, the model figures representing Julia and Tor, too.

Since they aren't in his office, the most reasonable assumption is that they are all stored at home.

And she knows that Virgilsson has a key, probably in the office drawer that his eyes were drawn to when he lied about it.

The Lost Souls almost certainly never work on a Saturday, which means she can investigate the matter in peace and quiet.

But first she has another task to tick off the list.

She calls Daniel Nygård, the alarm technician, who picks up immediately even though it's a Saturday.

"Hello," he says. "Isn't the camera working?"

"Oh no, it is," she replies. "But I need another one so I can see the entire model. Ideally one that records audio, too."

There is silence on the line for a few seconds.

"I mean, I'm not sure . . ." She hears him scratching his beard. "Obviously I want to help the police. But like I said, I feel uneasy about spying on my clients like this. Even *one* camera was borderline."

Asker suppresses a sigh. Her hangover is still knocking against her temples, and she doesn't have the time for wilful civilians.

"I need another camera on-site, preferably today," she says sharply. "If you don't want to help, then I'll find someone else. It's no more complicated than that. There are plenty of other security firms around. But the more people who are involved, the bigger the risk of it getting back to your clients."

Another few seconds' silence.

"OK," Nygård sighs. "I'll see what I can put together. I'll let you know."

She takes the electric car into Malmö. Stops off at a hardware store before parking down in the underground police garage. Officially it's against the rules to park a private car there, but it's a Saturday, and besides, she's already gotten the boot once this week.

As expected, her department is completely deserted.

She hangs her jacket up in Sandgren's office and walks back to Virgilsson's door. Locked, unsurprisingly. She tries using her own office key, but it doesn't fit. On to plan B.

She calls security, explains who she is and that she needs to fetch something from Virgilsson's office. After a few minutes a security guard appears with a master key.

But the door refuses to unlock.

"Strange," he says. "This is the right one."

"Try it in my door," she suggests.

The key works without an issue. And in another two doors, besides.

Virgilsson must have changed his lock. Not that that surprises her, either. The little man seems particularly cautious with his secrets.

She thanks the guard for his help and sends him on his way.

Then she moves on to plan C, because obviously she has one.

She returns to Sandgren's office. Fetches the long, supple metal ruler that she bought at the hardware store and jimmies open the window.

The atrium is dim and still as she climbs out.

Virgilsson's office is the farthest away from her own, so she is forced to sneak past all the windows in the department to get there.

Once there, she inserts the ruler into the slit and looks over her shoulder.

The lights in the offices above her are all off, with the exception of way up in Serious Crime. But their focus is most likely on other things.

She wiggles the ruler cautiously. The damp and grime make the window stick, and it takes some coaxing to jimmy it, but even so, it isn't all that much harder than forcing a car door.

Virgilsson's pedantic office feels even stranger when he isn't in it. The Persian rug, the oil painting of the sailboats. Above the bookshelf a bronze sculpture that she hadn't noticed before, of a horse. The office chair has a seat cover made of wooden beads, the kind one used to see in taxis.

Asker tries to touch as little as possible.

She opens the desk drawer that Virgilsson's eyes were drawn to when she mentioned Sandgren's house keys.

In the drawer there are a dozen or so different compartments, all containing different keys or bunches of keys, neatly labeled with small colored tags.

Bengt S is written on one of them. There are three keys in the bunch. Two of them appear to belong to an external door; the third looks like his office key.

A sound makes her look up. A faint thud from the corridor.

Is there somebody there?

She shoves the keys in her pocket and shuts the drawer. Then quickly climbs back out into the atrium and shoves the window shut behind her. Crouching, she sneaks back along the wall toward her own office, and is almost there when the window in front of her suddenly opens.

Asker instinctively jumps back.

A head pokes out of the window. Thick spectacles, straggly gray hair around a bald dome. Enok Zafer.

"What the blazes are you up to, Asker?" he asks.

She has no good answer.

He holds out his hand toward her.

"Come in, quick, before someone sees you," he says, glancing anxiously at the windows above.

She takes his hand and lets him help her inside.

"People think we're mad enough down here as it is," he mumbles while shutting the window and letting down the blinds. "What were you doing in Virgilsson's office?"

She considers lying, but there's no point.

"I was looking for a key."

"What?" He adjusts the hearing aids on his temple tips.

"I was looking for Bengt Sandgren's key," she says a little louder.

"To his office?"

"No, I've already got that. I've taken over Bengt's office."

Zafer snorts irritably.

"Obviously I know that. People think that just because I'm deaf I'm blind, too. I meant his other office, of course."

"Other office?"

"Yes, the one at the end." He waves his hand in the direction of the corridor. "Next to yours. I used to use it as a storeroom. But Bengt said he needed it. Not that he's my manager, really, I answer directly to . . ."

"The director of technology," Asker fills in.

"Precisely!" Zafer nods happily. "I have an important report due on Monday. Stressful, too. The missus is in a huff because I've got to be in all weekend."

Asker has an idea about how to get rid of Zafer so that she can check out this other office.

"If you want, I can talk to the director of technology. Ask them to give you an extension?" Asker suggested, knowing full well that no one was expecting Zafer's report.

Zafer's eyes narrow.

"Why would he agree to that?"

"I can say you're doing an important job for me."

"Tracing phones?" He lights up.

"Can you do that?" she asks.

"Naturally." He gestures at a corner of his office in which three computer screens form a semicircle. "It's been a while, mind, but all I need is a number."

"Good," says Asker. "We'll say that you're helping me to trace a phone, and I'll arrange for an extension on the report so that you can enjoy your weekend with the missus. Oh, and one more thing . . ."

"Yes?" Zafer leans in excitedly.

"Let's not mention to Virgilsson that I sneaked in through his office window, OK?"

HILL

Hill dreams about the Farm. The barbed-wire fence, spotlights, and gates. Barracks, trailers, and shacks. A cross between a prison and a military camp—an impression amplified by the obstacle course, shooting range, and motley fleet of odd vehicles. And, of course, by Leo's father.

Per Asker is wiry to the point of emaciated. His face almost always emotionless. His eyes vigilant, always assessing, unearthing.

Ruthless.

"Are you trying to take my little girl from me?" he hisses.

Per's eyes bore into his. Go deeper, into his brain.

"*Resilience*," a woman's voice whispers in his ear. "Don't let him see that you're scared."

But it's hard. Per Asker is the most terrifying man he has ever faced. He squeezes his eyes shut, tries to remember this is only a dream.

He is woken by his phone. It buzzes angrily around on the bedside table, while the text *unknown number* flashes up on the screen.

"Martin Hill," he says drowsily.

"It's Mya. From the architecture school."

Suddenly he is wide awake.

"Hi, Mya."

"I wanted to thank you for yesterday. It was nice to talk to someone."

She goes quiet, and when she speaks again, her voice has lowered another notch.

"But there's also something I need to tell you."

"Yes?" Hill has sensed this. He presses the phone to his ear, to make sure he doesn't miss anything.

Mya takes a deep breath. A gruff man's voice suddenly pipes up in the background.

"I have to go," she says quickly. "I'll call you."

Before Hill can say anything, the line goes dead.

ASKER

Asker is standing in front of the door at the end of the corridor. Storeroom, the sign outside claims. But if what Zafer said is true, then it isn't that at all.

From her pocket she fishes out the bunch of keys she swiped from Virgilsson's desk, tries out the one that resembles an office key. It turns.

The room she enters is pitch-black and has a musty smell.

She shuts the door behind her and turns on the light. Can't help but gasp.

The contrast between this room and Sandgren's normal bomb site of an office is like night and day.

On one wall hang images of eerie abandoned buildings and disused industrial sites. On the other, a large map of the railway model catches her attention. Sandgren has made markings indicating where some of the figures were placed. Julia's figure was found in a forest clearing, Tor Nilsson's in a back garden. Each marked with a cross.

The placement of the other figures is indicated with circles and question marks, probably because no one remembers exactly where the car thieves and hitchhiker were found.

She studies the map, finds the spot where Malik and Smilla were placed but can see no clear link between their position and that of the other figures. Besides, the selfie was taken and posted before their phones were turned off near Gårdstånga, quite some distance from any of the locations in the model railway. And the industrial site where Hill found that plastic figure next to Tor Nilsson's tag is even farther away. The same goes for Julia Collin's summer cottage up in Åsljunga.

All in all, the placement of the figures therefore doesn't seem to correspond to sites of significance in reality. The only clear link she can find is that all of the figures were inserted at the front of the model, where they ran a much greater risk of being found than if they were hidden at the back or in the artificial forests.

"He wanted them to be found," Asker mutters to herself.

She moves on to the third wall. It is dotted with passport photos topped with neat name tags. She takes a few steps back.

Kjell Lilja, Ulf Krook, and his stepson Finn Olofsson she recognizes. Julia Collin and her parents, too. She also spots a mugshot of a flaxen-haired young man—graffiti artist Tor Nilsson—which must have been taken one of the times he was arrested for vandalism.

But there are also photos and names of three other youths whose appearance and names are new to Asker. *The Hitchhiker*, Sandgren has written under one. *The Burglars* under the other two.

She goes on exploring the windowless room.

By the fourth wall stand a folding table and chair. On one side of the table two small model installations make her heart start to pound. She has seen them before in Sandgren's image bank, but this is different.

The first is a plastic figure of a young man spraying the word *urbex* on the side of a rust-colored oil tank.

The other is of a young woman with a red backpack who is running. Behind her is a white, faceless figure of the same type that she found in Malik's car.

Asker picks up the Julia figure and studies it up close.

Despite the figure being only three-quarters of an inch tall, the terror can easily be read in her body language and facial expression.

As Lilja said, it must take a very skilled, steady hand to achieve that level of detail, not to mention the right kind of equipment.

She puts the figure back down.

Beside it on the table sits an electronic typewriter, and beside that a thick case file.

the mountain king, reads the front of the file. For some reason all lowercase.

She pulls out the folding chair and takes a seat. Then opens the file and starts to read.

Sandgren's investigation is exemplarily concise and to the point. An old-school police investigation without watchwords or strings of reservations and counterpoints. Barely even any technical evidence to speak of.

Only facts and indications that, when they fit like a glove, build a solid chain of events.

Nevertheless, his investigation, combined with her own observations, offers a sort of timeline of Sandgren's own journey.

As she thought, it all begins four years ago, with Julia's disappearance. Sandgren, an experienced homicide detective who, according to Julia's mother, is already burned out, throws himself into the case. He contacts Julia's friends and family members. Speaks to teachers and old classmates, the officers who are officially responsible for the investigation. Writes up the whole ream of interviews and memos that Asker now skims.

His obsession can almost be read between the lines, but roughly six months after Julia's disappearance the work comes to an abrupt end.

She knows why. Sandgren has plowed straight through the wall that had so long been looming on the horizon. He is written off work, and not long thereafter is transferred down here, to the Department of Lost Souls.

The investigation goes on a long hiatus while Sandgren spends one-and-a-half years at the department shrouded in an alcohol haze and what she guesses is a heavy dose of self-contempt.

Then suddenly Julia's figure turns up in the railway model, a whole two years after her disappearance. Sandgren comes back to life and reopens his old investigation. He learns that this isn't the first time that unwanted figures have appeared in the model, and tries to link these to reported disappearances, too.

Asker flicks on in curiosity.

The first victims that Sandgren identifies are two young men who escaped from a young offender institution in Blekinge fourteen years ago.

Through some impressive policework, Sandgren has linked both men to a beaten-up Volvo that was stolen on the night of their escape. One of the fugitives had been incarcerated for, among other things, setting fire to abandoned buildings in the area around where he grew up. According to the staff Sandgren interviewed at the institution, some loose chatter among the other inmates suggested that the two had talked about heading to Skåne to check out some sort of abandoned military facility built deep within a mountain. *A mindblowing mountain*, as someone had called it.

Sandgren has, just like Prepper Per before him, drawn the correct conclusion that secret mountain facilities and underground bunkers are best hid beneath the Fennoscandian Shield, i.e. the northern parts of inland Skåne.

After making contact with the Swedish Fortifications Agency, and overcoming various hurdles to get around the old Cold War classified stamps, Sandgren finally manages to get hold of the blueprints of different defunct bases, all in the area around Hässleholm.

The blueprints are included at the very back of the file, as appendices. Sandgren has scribbled keywords on some of them, circled and underlined them, but doesn't seem to have pieced together which base it was that the fugitives were interested in.

Asker makes a memo to self to show the blueprints and notes to Martin Hill. This is exactly his thing.

The hitchhiker with the headphones turns out to have a similar background.

Liam Kuznicki, a twenty-four-year-old from Stockholm who has been missing eight years, which roughly matches the time when his figure appeared in the model.

According to his family, Liam was restless and often hitchhiked around Sweden, searching for exhilarating sights outside the usual tourist traps. They also confirm that he often wore headphones.

The last anyone heard of him was a phone call he made from a train between Stockholm and Copenhagen, in which he claimed to be on his way to the latter.

But one of the stops along that line is Hässleholm, which, with everything else, is enough circumstantial evidence for Sandgren to pin Kuznicki down as the hitchhiker.

Asker can't find any glaring holes in this theory.

She reads on.

Sandgren spends the next year investigating Ulf Krook and the other members of the model railway club.

Asker finds Ulf Krook's and Finn Olofsson's criminal records, which match the information that her mildly pushy colleague Jakob Tell gave her. A few minor offenses, none of which are violent.

Which makes the next document all the more interesting. The language and layout are so different that it takes Asker a few seconds to realize what she is looking at.

An investigation from Helsingør Police in Denmark, dated six years ago.

She scans the pages.

According to that investigation, Finn Olofsson was arrested on the outskirts of Helsingør. The complainant, a female prostitute from Romania, claimed that Olofsson picked her up in his truck just outside Copenhagen and subsequently held her captive for two days in the sleeper cabin of the truck, without assaulting her.

Olofsson denied the crime and claimed he gave the woman a lift at her own request. Otherwise he had little to say for himself.

After a few days in the police lockup Finn Olofsson was released, and by the time the case came to trial a year later the complainant had disappeared. Helsingør Police suspected that the woman had returned to Romania. They made one obligatory, unsuccessful attempt to contact her, after which the case was written off and ended up in the archive.

Checking Danish police records was a smart move. Something Asker herself might have thought of. Sandgren isn't remotely the hapless wreck that many want to present him as—this entire room is proof of that.

She goes on turning the pages.

After learning about the Helsingør investigation, Sandgren goes to Finn Olofsson's house to question him about it.

But the latter is uncooperative, to say the least.

Told me to go fuck myself, Sandgren states in his memo.

The timeline all fits with what Ulf Krook said about Sandgren. Only in Ulf's account he was the one who told Sandgren where to shove it, not Finn.

After a while I got sick of it and told him to go fuck himself. Said that if he went on driving round these parts poking his nose into other people's business it could end badly.

To be precise.

Perhaps both of them were mad at Sandgren, either that or Ulf wanted to seem tough in front of her. Or the third possible explanation, which is that he was trying to keep his stepson out of it.

Protect him.

She goes on leafing through the file. There is another short pause in Sandgren's investigation, but then Ulf gets booted out of his post as president by Kjell Lilja and shortly thereafter, last winter, another figure turns up in the model. This time of graffiti artist Tor Nilsson, who additionally turns out to have a personal connection to Martin Hill, whom Sandgren calls to ask some questions about the world of urban exploration.

As it happens, the transcript of their conversation is the last document in the investigation file. The very day after they spoke, Sandgren suffers a heart attack and falls down his own flight of stairs, bringing the investigation to an abrupt end. Just over a week later, Malik and Smilla go missing.

Asker leans back, links her hands behind her head while studying the pictures on the wall.

So Sandgren identified five victims, and she has added another two.

Seven missing people in all, of which at least one—Malik Mansur—is dead.

But in all likelihood more.

Which in turn means that Sandgren was on the trail of a serial killer.

A very unusual one, who can't resist showing off what he's done.

Inserting his own ugly little narrative into the otherwise so perfect railway model.

A snake in paradise.

Or a monster, to cite Ulf Krook.

She looks at the photographs of Ulf and his stepson, which are right at the top.

It's clear who Sandgren's prime suspects are.

If not for the heart attack, the case might have already been solved.

Not a hand laid on Malik or Smilla.

Perhaps it's just an unlucky coincidence that Sandgren happened to have a heart attack when he did. But all detectives hate coincidences, which in turn paves the way for another explanation.

She thinks back to what Ulf said to Sandgren.

. . . *if he went on driving round these parts poking his nose into other people's business it could end badly.*

Did Sandgren get too close?

Did he feel in danger—and if so was that why he was sleeping at the office?

Could his heart attack have actually been something else?

There is only one way of finding out. By doing what she has already set out to do.

Go to Sandgren's house.

SMILLA

Smilla hears the rattle of the breakfast tray. Smells the scents of toast and coffee. In just a few seconds her mother will knock at her door.

"Good morning, my love," she will say while setting the tray down before her on the bed. The sunlight will flood in through the windows, warming her up as she sits there.

Safe.

All of that will happen in just a few seconds.

If only she doesn't wake up.

But it's like every good dream. The very second you become aware that you're dreaming, try to string it out a little longer, the dream immediately starts to dissolve.

She wakes up with a pounding headache. Her nose and mouth are stinging, and a nausea hangs in her throat.

But the worst of all of it is still the darkness.

That same compact darkness as before.

That same bed, pillow, and blanket.

She is back in her cell.

Did she even leave it, or was her escape attempt just a dream, too?

Is anything real?

The tears break through, and she cries inconsolably. Wraps her arms around her knees and rolls back and forth in bed. Back and forth, until she can't bring herself to cry anymore.

She has lost all hope.

"Smilla!" she hears a voice whisper. "Smilla, are you there?"

She doesn't reply. Perhaps Julia is also just a part of the dream.

A figment of her imagination.

"Smilla!"

Julia's voice is stronger than before. Sounds less tired and confused. "Smilla, answer me!"

She sits up on the edge of the bed, but her legs refuse to stand.

"I'm here," she says aloud. Doesn't bother to whisper anymore.

"Oh, I'm glad," Julia sighs. "I heard cries, someone running. Do you know what happened?"

"I tried to get out," she replies. "Almost made it, but . . ."

Her mind clears slightly. Crystallizes.

". . . someone tackled me to the ground."

Slowly the memory comes back. A hissing, ugly voice.

Hold her down!

Hold her down.

Like a request, an order.

"There were two of them," she says slowly. "The Mountain King isn't alone."

HILL

Hill lay in bed for a while after his phone call with Mya, then ate a late breakfast, and tried to drown out his thoughts by reading the Saturday paper. He has considered calling Leo several times, but each time wavers with his thumb hovering over the call sign.

So he spends way too long composing a text message. Starts with *Thanks for yesterday, good to see you again*, but then gets stuck.

He searches for a suitable emoji, but doesn't find one that fits. Which emoji says: *I've been in love with you since I was fourteen and it was fantastic to see you.*

None, of course.

For the briefest of moments the night before, when he touched her scar, it felt as though their connection was back. As though they were Martin and Leo again, and not the polite, grown-up versions of themselves that they were playing.

Then she ended it all. Pulled back.

He so desperately wants to try to reach her again, but sensed that clingy text messages might not be the way to go.

But there might be another way.

He suspects that Mya knows more about MM than she lets on. That that was what her cryptic phone call earlier was about. Maybe he can coax more out of her. Find someone who can take Leo's investigation forward. Show her that he can help.

An appealing thought.

He gets dressed, makes the bed, and pulls up the blinds in the bedroom. Stands there with the cord in his hands. An autumn storm is brewing. The sky is leaden, the trees in Lundagård Park swaying their crowns in the wind.

On the roof opposite sits a bird of prey. It has caught a pigeon, which is still alive. The smaller bird is desperately flapping one wing, trying to break free from the grip of death. But with every movement it makes, the predator's powerful claws sink deeper into its breast. Turn its feathers shiny and rust-red.

The pigeon's movements grow weaker, until they finally stop.

The predator stabs it a few times with its beak, as though to make sure it is dead. Then turns its head and stares straight at Hill.

A sign—Nana Hill would have been sure of it.

Birds were important in the old religions. And blood.

An omen, she would have said.

Or perhaps simply: a warning.

He has had this feeling before. One December afternoon, many years ago.

The feeling that something terrible is about to happen.

Hill lets go of the cord, and the blind drops down again with a thud.

When he opens it again the birds are gone.

SIXTEEN YEARS EARLIER

It's early December now, and the winter darkness has descended.

They are standing outside school, and even though it's not even four o'clock the streetlights are on.

"Moving," she says. "Where?"

"To Umeå."

"When?"

"After Christmas."

He tries to make it sound as though it's no big deal, really. Has put this moment off as long as he possibly can. But now he has to tell her.

"My parents have been given the chance to take over a restaurant up there. The pub contract is almost up, and they think it's time to move."

"Right . . ."

She makes that face he knows so well. Purses her lips so that her mouth won't betray her feelings.

He tries to come up with something to say.

Something that will explain to her that the one-and-a-half years that have passed since he loaned her that screwdriver have been the best of his life.

That her friendship means everything to him.

That she means everything to him.

But he's fifteen years old, and even though he usually has the gift of the gab, the words fail him now.

Or perhaps the courage.

"But we were going to go to high school next year," she says. "Get out of here together."

Her tone is more factual than disappointed.

He knows why.

Knows that, in Prepper Per's world, disappointment is always waiting around the corner. That on some level she has already prepared herself for this.

Expected it.

In some way that makes it all so much worse.

That she has been expecting him to let her down. And that she was right.

"But obviously we'll keep in touch," he says with hard-fought breeziness. "I'll write letters and all that. Maybe he'll let you get your own phone soon. Then we can call every day."

"Maybe," she says guardedly. Absentmindedly picks at a scab on her elbow. For a few seconds she looks so fragile and exposed that he just wants to throw his arms around her.

Until he realizes that she is simply avoiding eye contact. Remembers that she hasn't actually mentioned her father in weeks, which is unusual. And not a good sign.

That's the moment when it hits him.

At least that's what he will claim afterward.

Mull over in the years that follow.

The realization that Prepper Per will never let her go.

And that he should warn her.

Do something.

Anything at all that might have in some way prevented what later came to pass.

But he doesn't do anything.

And it has plagued him ever since.

ASKER

Bengt Sandgren's house lies in one of Malmö's small suburban satellite towns. Not the well-to-do postal codes south or north of the city where IT millionaires, financiers, and retired sportspeople have driven up the house prices with their giant pads, but inland, where the homes are more unassuming.

Fiberboard façades, aboveground pools, corrugated iron.

Straggly poplars and cheerless cedar hedges to provide some shelter from the wind.

Sandgren's diminutive two-storey house probably dates back to the fifties. It would certainly have been a fine house once upon a time, but the signs of age are clearly visible now: bricks peeking out in spots where the rendering has come loose; sagging rain gutters; paint flaking around the windows. There is even a mark on the façade from where a house number must have hung many years before.

Asker parks outside. Something about the house feels familiar, but she can't quite put her finger on what.

She steps out, walks up the drive. Weeds have sprung up between the paving stones, and clover and moss have taken over the lawn.

A rusty old sundial adds to the impression that time has long since left this place behind. From the half-dead elm at the back of the house a flock of rooks glare down at her suspiciously. Beat their wings in warning, in the same way their cousins did outside Madame Rind's house.

The front door has two locks. Above them sits a sticker from an alarm firm. Both that and the top lock look new.

The door is locked, so someone must have come and locked up the house after the ambulance took Sandgren away. Virgilsson, presumably.

Asker still can't get her head around why the little man lied to her about the spare key and also completely withheld the fact that Bengt Sandgren had an extra office at the end of the corridor. Was he trying to protect Sandgren?

Or is it simply that Virgilsson does nothing that doesn't benefit him personally?

She stops below the front steps while pondering the alarm.

The vast majority of alarms for detached houses have a four-digit code. Purely mathematically, that means ten thousand different possibilities. Yet the most common code is 1234, closely followed by 1111 and 0000, and then double combos like 1122 or keyboard runs like 2580.

It was Prepper Per who taught her that. It was part of his lecture on how predictable people are, and he had precisely eight entry points to the topic. Which, ironically, made him just as predictable as the people he despised.

It dawned on her not long after Martin first called him Prepper Per.

As though that ridiculous name set off something in her head.

She shakes these thoughts away, gets back to the alarm.

The alarm system is new, and Sandgren lives alone and was concerned about his safety. So he wouldn't have chosen some predictable code. He would have opted for a code that was personal, one that worked only for him.

In which case it's most likely that he would have gone for one of three options:

His own birthday, but even that feels too easy and unsafe.

The last four numbers of his government personal identity number, which, granted, is one level up, but is still quite possible for a stranger to get hold of.

His badge number, which would have been her first guess for any other police officer's house. But she is convinced that Sandgren would have gone one step further. By this point the Julia Collin case was basically the only thing keeping him going. An obsession he just couldn't kick.

Which makes one possible combination of numbers slightly more likely than the rest.

She unlocks the door using the keys on the bunch. The alarm starts beeping as soon as she opens the door.

Thirty seconds, maybe forty, before the sirens kick off and the security firm responds.

The keypad is fitted on the wall to the right and looks completely new.

Asker enters four numbers.

1402. The fourteenth of February, Julia Collin's birthday.

The beeping stops sharply.

She looks around the hallway.

At the bottom of the stairs lie a few empty pieces of plastic packaging that the paramedics must have dropped in their efforts to revive him. She steps over them and continues on inside.

The house is stuffy, smells of stale cigarette smoke. A living room, bathroom, hallway, and kitchen on the ground floor. Despite the musty air everything seems clean and tidy, with the exception of a half-empty cup of coffee on the kitchen counter.

She walks slowly up the stairs. It is carpeted, which absorbs the sound of her footsteps. Upstairs there is a TV room, a bedroom, and another bathroom. An overturned club chair lies right at the top of the staircase.

She stops right next to it, looks down at the remnants of the paramedics' work.

It isn't hard to picture the scene.

Sandgren has a heart attack up here in the TV room.

He tries to steady himself on the chair, tips it over and loses his balance. He falls down the stairs.

If his neighbor hadn't turned up in the nick of time, it would have been game over.

She goes on, into the bedroom. The bed is made. In the wardrobe hang a few short-sleeved shirts, a couple of cardigans, and an unfashionable suit.

On the chest of drawers stands an image of a younger Sandgren and another man, both in UN uniforms. Beside that is Julia Collin's graduation photo. Asker assumes that the man standing next to Sandgren is Julia's deceased father.

On the bedside table she finds an entire battery of pill bottles.

Judging by the labels, Sandgren was being treated for high blood pressure, fatty liver, high cholesterol, and angina.

That he would have a heart attack is hardly shocking. Nor is the fact that he is still in a coma. It's a miracle he isn't already dead.

She returns to the little TV room and stops next to the overturned chair again.

The fall scenario seems completely reasonable.

At the same time, she knows that Sandgren slept at the office at least some nights, and as she has already noted, the new lock and alarm suggest that he had started to worry for his own safety.

And then there is that coffee cup down in the kitchen. Now she has had a little time to digest it.

The cup is half-full and is on the middle of the counter, as though Sandgren put it down for some reason. But if he had finished drinking, he would surely have poured it down the sink, just a couple inches away.

Perhaps he felt sudden chest pains? Went up to the bedroom to fetch his medicine? That's certainly plausible.

Either that, or something else attracted his attention.

She looks at the chair. It looks heavy. Four deep depressions in the carpet a little ways off testify to that.

But something about those marks doesn't feel right.

She measures the distance with her feet. Does it twice, to be on the safe side.

But the result is the same. The distance between the depressions in the carpet and the overturned chair is too great.

The chair couldn't have ended up where it did had Sandgren stumbled, leaned against the backrest, and toppled it over.

Someone had to have moved the chair. Placed it there to make it look like Sandgren lost his balance and fell down the stairs.

Built a little scene, just like in the railway model.

Or Malik's car.

She crouches down and examines the armchair. Sticks her hand into the joint between the seat and the backrest. Something is lodged in there, just like in the car.

She knows what it is before she can pull it out.

An uncanny, featureless little plastic figure.

She was right. The perpetrator was here, in Sandgren's house. Knocked him down the stairs and left him there for dead.

She takes the figure with her and walks slowly back down the stairs.

The fall would certainly have been enough to trigger a heart attack in someone as unwell as Sandgren. Either that, or the shock of standing face-to-face with an intruder in one's own home. An intruder one suspects to be a serial killer.

She holds up the figure before her. It's exactly the same as the one that she found in Malik's car and the one Sandgren found in the model. A featureless man with his arms outstretched, as though trying to catch something.

The Mountain King. That's what Sandgren called the case. But why? Where did he get that name? It calls to mind the stories of old lore; the mythical *Bergakungen* who would lure humans into its mountain lair, from which they would never return.

So a mountain king who presides over life and death. Is that what the figures are all about? Not just a calling card but a message.

That his victims are pawns. Insignificant, replaceable.

At the king's pleasure.

Outside, the rooks suddenly take off with loud warning cries. Prompt a familiar tingling at the back of her neck.

Something—or someone—has come too close. Made the birds take flight.

Asker spins around, sees a flash of movement through the frosted glass in the hallway window.

She leaps at the door, but has to fumble with the lock, losing a crucial few seconds. Then she flies down the front steps and out into the small lane, her hand on her police firearm. There is nothing there, but in the distance she hears the sound of a powerful engine roaring to life. She runs toward the sound, rounds the corner onto a larger street, only to see the back of a dark van disappearing at high speed.

Her own car is too far away; there's no point trying to take chase.

"Shit!" she spits angrily into the gutter.

The person with the van has been watching her again. But how long? And why didn't she notice that she was being followed?

She walks slowly back to Sandgren's house. The rooks are circling overhead, waiting for the right moment to return to their tree.

Asker stands and watches them for a few seconds, then looks back at Sandgren's little house.

When she sees the house from this angle she remembers exactly where she has seen it before.

THE MOUNTAIN KING

He is tracking her movements. Knows that she is close now. Closer to him than anyone has ever come, even that tired old cop.

She has been in the house, realized what happened there, seen what he left behind. Perhaps even realized that he took one thing and left something else, just as he always does.

Sandgren realized in the end.

Realized who he was.

A monster.

And all too soon he will be forced to show the world what he has done.

She knows that.

Is waiting for him with her magical eyes.

Waiting for his next move.

He has never felt so alive.

ASKER

"Level six," the elevator voice informs her, almost haughtily.

Asker hasn't been up in Serious Crime since Tuesday. Funnily enough it feels like much longer than that.

As though those days have already changed her workplace.

Even though it's a Saturday, they appear to be working at full tilt. There are people everywhere, both familiar and unfamiliar faces.

She heads toward Rodic's office, Sandgren's case file under her arm. Holds her head up high, avoids meeting any of the unfriendly glances aimed her way.

Notes in passing that her nameplate has been taped over, and that someone else has taken over her office.

Clearly word that she is there spreads fast, as Eskil intercepts her six feet from Rodic's door.

"Are you lost?" he sneers. "Only homicide detectives work up here."

Standing this close, the heady scent combo of his hand cream and aftershave is almost nauseating.

"I have a meeting with Rodic," Asker replies curtly.

"What about?" He nods at the file under her arm.

"About a murder investigation that's apparently going to shit because the team working on it are morons."

Eskil's face darkens beneath his fake tan. He purses his lips to a dash.

The door behind him opens.

"Come in, Leo," says Rodic.

Eskil gives Asker an angry look and slinks off down the corridor. Probably straight to his master to report back.

Rodic closes the office door behind them and twizzles the blinds so no one can see in.

"So, what was it you wanted to speak about that was so urgent?"

she says once they have both sat down. "You were very cryptic on the phone."

"The Holst case," says Asker. "It's no average kidnapping, but something else entirely."

She hands over the file. Rodic raises her eyebrows, opens it slowly. "Go on."

Asker has used the drive back from Sandgren's house to plan exactly what she wants to say and how.

"It all started when I got a call from a model railway club."

She quickly outlines how she chanced across the model figures depicting Malik and Smilla, and how that led her to Sandgren's secret investigation and her meetings with Lilja, Krook, and his stepson Finn Olofsson. She even gives away the fact that she knows that a little white model figure was found in Malik's car, and explains why it was placed there.

Finally, she holds up her phone and shows Rodic the images that she took through the basement window of Ulf Krook's workshop.

"See that model house on the table?" she asks.

Rodic leans in. Asker swipes up another image that she took just a little while ago on Sandgren's street.

"The model is a copy of Bengt Sandgren's house. The perpetrator has been there, and it's likely that he knocked Sandgren down the stairs because he was on to him. At some point he is planning to put the house in the railway model to show off what he's done. That's how he operates."

Rodic leafs through the file.

"And what do you suggest we do next?" she asks with a neutral voice.

"Search Ulf Krook's house," says Asker. "I can guarantee that the models were made in his workshop. There's a chance we'll find Smilla in the house, too, or at least something that will lead us to her."

Rodic studies her in silence. Drums her fingers against the table in thought.

Asker has done her best, laid out everything she has. For one brief moment she tries to persuade herself that that's enough. But something about Rodic's drawn-out finger-drumming says otherwise.

"I'm going to do you one last favor, Leo," she says while shutting the file containing Sandgren's investigation. "And that is to pretend that this conversation never happened. That you never told me you've been running a parallel investigation, digging around in the evidence for a case you're no longer working on, without authorization, or that you've adopted the alcohol-fueled delusions of a severely ill colleague."

She taps on the file a few times.

"In return . . ."

Rodic holds up her hand to stop Asker from protesting.

"In return, Leo, you are going to take that elevator down to the Resources Unit and quietly sit out a few months down there. The commissioner hasn't forgotten you, and new opportunities will come up, so long as you just lay low and in no way get in the way of Jonas Hellman. Is that understood?"

Asker studies Rodic. She knows that her and Sandgren's hypothesis may seem far-fetched, but they have evidence, or at the very least strong indications, connections. Things that can't simply be waved off. Unless, that is, Rodic and Hellman have a better lead to go on. One that fits the hypothesis that they were already working to.

"Someone's been in touch," she concludes. "Someone's demanded a ransom."

Rodic doesn't reply.

"When?"

Rodic is silent for another few seconds.

"This morning," she says eventually. "A USB-stick with a video file was delivered to *Sydsvenskan*."

"Can I get a look at it?"

Rodic shakes her head.

"Of course not, Leo. But if it puts your mind at rest, I can tell you we're getting close. Stockholm's best data guys are working to trace the source."

She slides the case file back over to Asker with a pitying smile.

"Like I said. Elevator down, sit it out quietly, don't make waves, OK?"

But Asker isn't prepared to give in just yet.

"Surely you can at least tell me how Malik Mansur died?"

It's a long shot. Asker doesn't even know if the autopsy is complete. But her former manager pities her, and Asker intends to milk that for all it's worth just to get a crumb of new information.

Rodic looks at her. Appears to be bargaining with herself.

"Sudden cardiac arrest," she says. "Apparently it can happen in young people, too, when under extreme stress. He hasn't been ruled out as a suspect. His co-conspirators may have dumped him to throw us off."

Asker can't hold it in.

"That's bullshit! Is that the hypothesis Hellman's working to? If so you're in trouble. And Smilla Holst, too—"

Rodic holds up her hand once again to cut her off. With the other she shoves the case file another half inch toward the edge of her desk.

"We've got the situation under control. Now go home and open a bottle of wine, Leo. And forget about anything to do with the Holst case and Jonas Hellman."

ASKER

Asker is seething. Before the meeting she had given herself around a 40 percent chance of bringing Rodic on-side, but the ransom message has blown that out of the water. Hellman has a new lead, one that fits his previous theory to a tee, thereby rendering everything she had to show irrelevant.

But the meeting wasn't a complete waste of time, she reassures herself. She has filled in a few smaller pieces of the puzzle. Malik's cause of death; the video and ransom message that Rodic doesn't want her to see.

As soon as she has shut her office door behind her, she pulls up Rosen's number.

She answers after two rings. Sounds nervous, as usual.

"Hello?"

"It's Leo. I need your help with something. You know someone at *Sydsvenskan*, don't you?"

"Yes . . ."

"They've received a video relating to the Holst case. I need a copy. In exchange I could see myself offering certain intel, off the record. You can act as intermediary."

The line goes quiet for a few seconds.

"It'll win you some brownie points with your journalist," Asker adds.

Another few seconds' silence.

"I'll see what I can do," Rosen eventually replies, with a slightly firmer voice. "I'll let you know soon."

"Thank you!" says Asker.

Straight after she hangs up, Asker receives a text message.

The new camera is in place. Best, Daniel Nygård

She opens the surveillance app. The new camera has been fitted on a wall perpendicular to the first. With both in place, she now has a view of at least two-thirds of the model.

The room is almost entirely black—once again, only the light of the emergency exit sign makes anything visible at all.

She plays with the settings for a while, increases the output from the microphone on the new camera. Has just managed to pick up the faint electric hum that she assumes is coming from one or more of the transformers, when the picture suddenly drops out. The sound is still there, but the screen is black. Perhaps it is something to do with her settings. She switches back to the first camera, which is still working exactly as it's supposed to.

She tries restarting the app, but the image feed from the new camera is still black. She swears inwardly, considers calling Nygård straightaway. But she has already squeezed the poor guy pretty hard, so might do better to wait an hour or so in case the camera comes back to life.

Her phone buzzes. A message from Rosen.

The message contains a link to an anonymous Dropbox folder with a single video file. She clicks on the file and the media player starts up.

The clip is dramatic.

Two people in ski masks on two chairs. Behind them a black screen. Their voices are distorted, sound like something out of a horror film.

"This is a message to Jonas Hellman," one of them says. "We've got Smilla Holst. Ten mil in Bitcoin and we'll release her unharmed."

"And don't you try to trace us, Jonas," says the other. "We're way too smart for you. Now be a good little piggy and do as we say, and everything will be fine. The payment details are on the USB stick. You have forty-eight hours."

The video ends.

Asker watches it two more times. Zooms in on the faces obscured by the black fabric, tries to analyze their movements.

They are two young men, she determines, around twenty-five. When the first figures appeared in the railway model, they would only have been in their early teens, if that.

In addition, even with the voice distortion it is possible to make out that both speak with a Rosengård accent, not the Göinge dialect they should theoretically have had if they had any connection to the model.

If Smilla is still alive, she has been missing over a week.

Holding someone hostage for that long requires planning and endurance. And access to somewhere far from prying eyes and ears.

In other words, a pretty high degree of professionalism, which this clip hardly radiates.

She watches it a fourth time to be quite sure, but her conclusion remains the same. These two mugs have nothing to do with the railway model, the figures, or the previous disappearances, and can therefore have nothing to do with Smilla Holst's kidnapping. It's all a scam. A bad prank or some idiots out for a quick buck.

Should she say as much to Rodic? Hardly.

Rodic has chosen to bet on Jonas Hellman's hypothesis.

Right now Asker can do no more than wait. If she's right, then the perpetrator, kidnapper, Mountain King, or whatever his name is will put Sandgren's house in the model. Probably soon.

And when he does, she will be ready.

She thinks about what Rodic told her about Malik's cause of death.

Sudden cardiac arrest, she said. According to Google, the most common causes of that among young people are various forms of heart conditions, a lack of oxygen, poisoning, and chest trauma. But Rodic expressly mentioned extreme stress as a cause.

Asker expands the search with those two words.

The first reliable source that appears in the results list is an article from a scientific magazine that bears the title "Can You Really Die of Fright?"

According to the author it is entirely possible, if the adrenaline rush triggered by the fear is great enough to upset the heart's rhythm.

She pictures the images she saw of Malik in the passenger seat of the car.

That terror-stricken expression, the clenched fists.

Was he scared to death?

ASKER

The darkness lies thick over the house and grounds in which Asker lives. The wind has picked up, it tears the autumn leaves from their trees, casts them against the panorama windows in a rustling deluge, like butterfly wings in a jar.

Asker had planned to go for another run to take the edge off her frustration, but given the wind she does an intense workout in the house's well-equipped gym instead. Heavy weights, chest, shoulders, biceps. But the thoughts just won't let up.

She is close to the solution—might even have cracked it already if she had the resources she normally has access to in Serious Crime.

On the other hand, her progress is largely thanks to a strange case that landed on her lap because of her new role in the Resources Unit, not to mention the unorthodox assistance she has gained from a few lost police souls.

And then Martin Hill, on the edge of it all. He seems just as curious about the case as she is.

She considers calling him and telling him what she found in Sandgren's office and house, maybe even sharing the new information she has managed to wheedle out. He did ask her to keep him in the loop, after all. Even offered to help out.

Normally that would be a breach of confidentiality, but Rodic has made it abundantly clear that Asker is not conducting an investigation.

So she can speak to whoever she wants.

In the end she decides to hold off calling him, anyway. It's a Saturday night, and Hill and his girlfriend must surely have plans, which she doesn't intend to interrupt.

She spends a long, scalding-hot time in the steam shower. Enjoys the feeling of the warm water against her skin. Prepper Per rarely let her take hot showers, and never for more than three minutes. Emphasized, as always, the importance of steeling both body and mind. Any sort of creature comfort was a source of weakness.

He would die if he saw her now, in a steam shower in a luxury pad. An appealing thought—in the same way that she likes the thought of him still hiding out deep down in his mountain. Eating preserved foods and listening to the radio, living as uncomfortably as he possibly can, while waiting for an end of days that, annoyingly, he will probably never see.

After her shower she changes into a sweatshirt and tracksuit bottoms.

She heats up a pasta meal in the microwave and eats it at the kitchen island, while opening the surveillance app again. The image from the new camera is still black, but the microphone seems to be working, as before. A faint rattle can be heard.

She switches to the old camera. The hall is still lit by the emergency exit sign alone. At least that's what she thinks at first glance.

But after a few seconds she spots another source of illumination.

A faint, yellow light making its way around the model. Slowly coiling from left to right, almost like a snake.

Asker zooms in as far as she can, increases the audio output from the other camera's microphone to the max. After a few seconds she realizes what she is seeing.

A lone train is running through the model. It has small headlights pointing forward, and lights on inside the carriages. The rest of the model, like the room, is dark and still. The only thing moving is that lone train, which rattles along through the artificial forests, over bridges and past farms, houses, and villages. Passes hundreds of small figures that Asker can't see in the darkness. But she knows that they are there.

Silent, watchful; almost waiting for something.

Or someone.

The train weaves closer to the camera, then gradually slows, until it comes to a stop almost at the front of the frame.

Without warning, the lights on the platform come on.

The train has arrived at Hässleholm Station.

"End of the line," says a scratchy, recorded loudspeaker voice, which almost makes Asker jump. "Please alight here. This train terminates here."

After which the lights go out and everything goes dark and still again.

At that moment Asker's doorbell rings.

HILL

Hill is spending Saturday night with a few friends. Starts at the bar at the Grand Hôtel, then moves on to Mat & Destillat opposite Lundagård Park.

The company is great, the food and wine the same, and he should be in high spirits. The heart and soul of the party, as he usually is.

But tonight he is subdued, pensive.

"How are you doing?" one of his friends asks.

"Just a little tired," he says. A lie, or a half lie, at least.

He can't stop thinking about MM, Smilla, and Tor.

About the other people who have disappeared without a trace over the years, replaced by eerie little model figures. At least if Leo is to be believed.

It all sounds so unreal, like a twisted fairy tale—especially as he sits here in a warm restaurant, his belly full of food and wine.

But even when he found that little plastic figure in the abandoned factory, he was struck by an uneasy feeling. That was why he broke the urban explorers code and took it with him. As though even then he had sensed its importance. Nana Hill would have been proud.

So where does Mya fit into all of this? And why hasn't she called back, as promised? He should tell Leo about the call. But he had planned to wait until he had something more concrete to offer. Until he was sure that whatever Mya has to say relates to the case.

But tonight he feels differently. As though he wants to reach out to Leo, at any cost.

He gets out his phone to text her. But just like before, he struggles to find the words.

He is struck by a sudden impulse, one that is overwhelmingly strong.

"I'm afraid I've got to go," he says and gets up.

He pulls on his jacket, waves at the restaurant owner on his way out.

There is a taxi standing just outside the door, as there often is.

He jumps in, gives the driver the street name and area that he heard her say the night before. Explains that he doesn't know the house number, so they may have to go slowly when they get there.

On the way he stares at the phone in his hand. Weighs up whether to call and give her some warning.

Leo isn't the type who likes surprises. Still, she was the one who dug out his phone number after sixteen years and woke him up with a call out of the blue. So it's his turn to surprise her. He puts his phone away and leans his head back in the seat.

Realizes only after a while that he's actually quite tipsy.

The taxi passes through a quiet neighborhood, continues on past fields and clumps of trees. The wind is blowing hard, makes the car sway every now and then.

"There are only two houses on this road," says the driver, pulling to a stop by a turning marked by two mailboxes. "What was the surname?"

"Asker," he says.

The driver looks at the mailboxes. There is a c/o tag on one of them.

"Asker," he reads, relieved. "It's the big house at the end."

He turns off down a tree-lined drive, passing a small cottage on their way to the large detached house.

When they are about three hundred feet away, Hill sees that there is someone crossing the front yard.

The silhouette of a tall man in a coat striding confidently toward the front door. With the wind and darkness he doesn't seem to have noticed their approach.

"Stop," Hill says to the driver. "Cut the headlights, please."

They pull up there at the side of the road, and Hill watches as the man walks up the front steps and rings the doorbell. It opens after just a few seconds.

Hill spots Asker in the doorway. She is wearing a sweatshirt and tracksuit bottoms, doesn't appear to be expecting company at all. Still, after a brief pause she lets the man inside.

Hill feels like an idiot. He shouldn't have crept up on her like this. Did he really expect her to be alone on a Saturday night? Sitting at home waiting for him?

The fault is his and his alone.

Still, he is angry at her, too, which is of course entirely irrational. Not to mention unfair.

"Change of plans," he says to the driver. "We're going into Malmö instead. We can drive."

He takes out his phone again.

Sofie picks up after two rings.

"I was just thinking about you," she says, a smile in her voice. "Feel like coming over?"

"Absolutely," he says. "As it happens, I'm already on my way."

ASKER

The doorbell rings again, and Asker peers through the narrow pane of glass by the door.

Jakob Tell is standing outside. Under his flapping coat he is wearing a blazer and shirt, the top few buttons undone. Appears to be on his way to, or perhaps more likely from, the pub.

"Hey!" he says with a confident smile when she opens the door.

"Hi," Asker replies in surprise.

"Nice digs!" His smile widens. "Aren't you going to invite me in? It's blowing a fucking gale out here."

She looks over his shoulder. A taxi is standing a little way down the drive, which must be how he got here.

"How do you know where I live?"

"Ah, that wasn't so hard to track down. I am a cop, after all." He raises his eyebrows suggestively. "You aren't going to leave a colleague to freeze on your front step, are you?"

Asker takes a few steps back to let him into the front hall. The taxi in the distance turns around and pulls off.

"So," he says. "I wanted to apologize for yesterday. I was a little abrupt on the phone, I'd had a bad day."

He throws out his hands.

"Just didn't want you to get the wrong impression, that's all."

"So that's why you came all the way out here?"

"Something like that." He smiles again, starts to take off his coat. "How about a drink?"

"No thanks," she says.

"Come on, don't be silly," he says, hanging his coat up with a movement so self-assured that you would think he lived there. "I've come a long way, and I'm parched."

"Well, you'll have to go a bit further."

He stops short and stares at her. His beaming smile has shifted almost imperceptibly.

"Come on, Asker. We both know why I'm here." His pungent aftershave doesn't hide the whiff of alcohol on his breath. "You were flirting with me at the station the other day."

"I'm afraid you must have misunderstood."

"Oh quit it!" he snorts. "Do you think I don't know what you're like. Tease a little, play hard to get."

He takes a step toward her.

"Come on, Asker," he says again. "Let's have a drink and see where it leads."

She doesn't back away. Simply tilts her head to one side, as usual. He is athletic, around six feet in height, and has been drinking. In normal circumstances a not too sophisticated opponent, who could be taken by surprise.

But Tell is a cop, which means he is a trained fighter. Looks almost like he would welcome the chance to grapple with her.

Besides, the hallway offers little room to maneuver and few possible weapons. And on top of that she, unlike him, isn't wearing any shoes, only slippery socks. A fight can quickly escalate, so it's best to try alternative routes where possible.

"I'm going to have to ask you to leave now, Jakob," she says with as much composure as she can muster.

"Give it a rest, Leo." Tell takes another step toward her. His smile has turned into something else. Something uglier.

"We both know you want it."

His eyes glint darkly, and for a second he appears to be hunching up. Curves his back like a predator preparing to pounce.

Asker breathes in. Slowly clenches her fists.

Throat, neck, eyes, crotch. She will have to meet at least one of these targets, preferably more.

Hard, decisively. And definitely before he is on her.

The jangle of the doorbell comes so out of the blue that both of them jump.

Someone appears in the little windowpane.

"Hello? Leo!"

It's her neighbor, the grandpa with the dog.

This interruption makes Tell straighten up. His ugly facial expression is gone, and all of a sudden he looks human again.

The man turns the door handle and steps into the hall. He is wearing a raincoat and a sou'wester hat, even though it isn't raining.

"Leo, oh, good," he gasps anxiously. "Sessan has run away. I was wondering if you could help me look for her."

Tell tears his coat off the hanger, mutters something angrily, and shoves his way through the door. Only then does the old man seem to notice him.

"Was I interrupting?" he asks.

"Not at all," says Asker with a quiet exhale. "Just let me fetch my jacket and flashlight and I'll help you."

After just over an hour searching in the gale, Asker and her neighbor eventually find Sessan trembling under a bush. The old man then insists on inviting Asker in for a hot toddy to warm her up. To her own surprise, she accepts.

She learns that her neighbor is called Lars, that he is a retired librarian and a widower of a few years. That he collects both coins and stamps.

And that he is most definitely more pleasant company than Jakob Tell.

It is only just before midnight, when she is back in her hallway, that Asker has a proper chance to think back over it all.

What would have happened had Lars not turned up? Impossible to say.

But there is one thing that she is sure of. Jakob Tell behaved as though he had been in similar situations before.

As though he is used to getting exactly what he wants.

It's easy enough to file him away under *obnoxious letch/potential date-rapist*. Not even the police are immune to that kind of swine.

But what if it was more than that?

When they first met, she had found Tell pleasant, but now, in hindsight, it strikes her that he did ask a number of odd questions.

He seemed to know a lot about Ulf Krook's private life and associates, and was a little too interested in getting the scoop on her case.

She gets into bed and opens the surveillance app on her phone again. In the live feed everything is dark and still.

She pulls up the recorded material and toggles back to the sequence with the train. It starts all by itself, without anyone appearing on camera. Perhaps the train can be controlled remotely, or even runs on a timer.

She follows the train's meandering route through the model. Sees it stop at the front of the picture and the lights on the platform come on, imagines the eerie announcement over the loudspeaker that she heard through the other camera. After which all the lights go out, and everything falls into darkness.

She closes the app and puts her phone on her bedside table. Falls back onto the pillow and stares up at the ceiling.

Seconds after that whole inexplicable, sinister sequence, Jakob Tell shows up on her doorstep.

Was it just a coincidence, or is there another explanation?

A much nastier one.

SMILLA

"Do you think he'll ever let us out of here?" Smilla whispers at the air vent.

"No," Julia replies. "He's told me I'll get to go home, but I'm still here."

"So you've spoken to him?"

"He's talked to me through the door a few times. Like, *Soon you'll be able to go home, Julia.* But I think they're lies to stop me from losing hope."

"Yet you still haven't lost it."

"No . . ."

Silence.

"For a while there was a guy here. In your room. His name was Tor. He was there for a while, then he vanished. I always thought he was released. That's why I haven't stopped hoping."

"How long ago was that?"

"I don't know. It's impossible to keep track of time."

Smilla tries to collect her thoughts. So she and Julia aren't the only ones who have been locked up down here. She has a nasty feeling that Julia is wrong, that Tor wasn't released at all. But she doesn't want to say that. Couldn't take away Julia's last glimmer of hope.

"But what does he want from us?" she asks. "Why is he keeping us here?"

"I . . ."

Silence.

"I think he gets a kick out of it. Out of keeping us prisoner. Controlling us."

"That's sick."

"Yeah . . ."

More silence.

"But the other one?" Smilla asks. "His helper. Do you know anything about him?"

"No. Are you really sure he exists?"

"One hundred percent. The Mountain King was after me, but someone else tackled me from the side. And then said *Hold her down*."

More silence, longer this time.

"Julia, are you there?" she asks anxiously.

"I'm here."

"Good." Smilla exhales. "We have to come up with a new plan. A new way of getting us out of here, both of us."

SUNDAY

ASKER

Asker is woken by her phone. It's a quarter past eight, and for a few seconds she hopes it's Martin Hill.

Instead it's Kjell Lilja's number.

"It's happened again," he puffs down the line. "We came in and found it just five minutes ago. This time it's an entire house. I'll send you a picture of it straightaway."

She knows which one it is even before the image of the small two-storey house with the flaking plaster appears on her screen.

"Don't touch anything," she says. "I'm on my way!"

She hangs up and opens the surveillance app. The new camera is still dead, but the old one works. She pulls up the recording again. Finds the sequence with the ghost train and then fast-forwards.

At 2:20 a.m. there is a movement. A light that flickers on and then approaches. A dark silhouette wearing a bright headlamp.

She tries to pause and find a frame where she can make out more details. But the figure is standing directly opposite the camera, the headlamp creating a constant flare.

All she can make out is a hooded jacket.

After less than a minute it's all over. The figure turns around and vanishes, just as suddenly as he appeared.

On the way out he turns off the headlamp and stalks past the spot where the new camera is.

Asker swears out loud.

If the camera had been working, then in all likelihood she would have a headshot of her mysterious perpetrator.

She phones Daniel Nygård and explains the problem, as she should have done the day before. Makes an effort to be a little more diplomatic than in their last call. Luckily the technician doesn't seem to have taken it badly.

"OK, that's weird," he says. "That camera model is usually pretty reliable. But it could be something to do with the network."

"Doesn't the camera have a local backup memory, too, in case of network failures? I know from other investigations that a number of models have that."

"Uh, yeah, possibly," he confirms. "But I'd need to pick up the camera and take it back to my workshop to check the backup. I can pass by as soon as the club premises are empty. I just hope that isn't too late, since I'm busy tonight."

"OK, great," she says, trying not to sound too impatient. She ends the call.

Slings on some clothes and downs an espresso.

On her way out she has an idea.

She calls Martin Hill.

He answers after just two rings. Sounds like he has just woken up. "Hello?"

"It's your favorite alarm," she say exaggeratedly breezily, without quite knowing why. "Get your clothes on, we're going to Hässleholm. Sandgren's house has turned up in the model. Thought you might want to see it up close. I'll come by your place and pick you up."

A short silence. For a few seconds she is convinced he's going to say no. Tell her that he has plans, that he's not interested, after which she'll hear that woman's voice in the background yet again.

"OK," he says instead. "I'll come. But I'm in Malmö."

He gives her an address in the middle of town.

"OK," she confirms. "I can be there in half an hour."

A weary autumn sun is slowly heaving its way into the sky when Asker pulls out of the garage. The trees along the drive have lost their vibrant colors, most of the leaves blown away in the previous night's gales.

The furrows in the fields have lost their shiny luster, grown dull and grayish from the wind.

As she makes her way to the address Hill gave her, Asker calls Rosen.

Unlike Hill, she appears to have been awake awhile.

"I need your search skills again," says Asker. "This time regarding a colleague. A Jakob Tell in Hässleholm. I want to know everything about him. Especially the kind of stuff that the normal databases won't turn up. Complaints, HR inquiries, that kind of thing."

"I see," Rosen says with her usual, slightly anxious tone.

"I need it today," Asker adds.

"Ah, that'll be difficult. Some of those records still haven't been digitized. I'll have to go into the office. And it *is* a Sunday . . ."

"Obviously you'll get overtime," Asker says.

Rosen is still hesitant.

Asker braces herself. She has been contemplating this move ever since Rodic sent her packing.

"You can give your friend at *Sydsvenskan* the following: A source with links to the police investigation into Smilla Holst's disappearance claims they are on the wrong track. That they've gone all-in on a dead-end theory and now don't dare to back out."

"OK," Rosen gasps. "I'll head in straightaway. Should be done by this afternoon."

"Good, I'll stop by a little later."

"Oh, by the way. Did you get the data I sourced on the other man? The Robert from Ängelholm who's married to Julia's mother? I put it in your pigeonhole."

Asker had almost forgotten that she had asked Rosen about that.

"Thanks, I'll pick that up, too."

ASKER

Hill is waiting for her on the pavement outside the entrance to one of Malmö's nicer apartment buildings.

His jacket is open, even though it's only 43 or 44 degrees. No gloves or hat. Apparently he doesn't feel at all as cold as she does.

He jumps in and gives her a drowsy hello. Doesn't explain whose address he slept at, which he obviously isn't obliged to do, either.

She quickly recaps what Lilja just told her, then hands over her phone so he can watch the clip from the hidden camera.

"Shit, you can hardly see anything," he notes. "And the other camera didn't work?"

"No, or at least not via the network. But there's a chance there may be a local recording. The alarm guy's going to check it."

The car falls silent. A sort of angular silence, as though both are trying to find their way back to the mood of the other night, but without really succeeding.

"So, what did you get up to yesterday?" Hill asks.

"Nothing much. Helped my oddball neighbor look for his missing dog."

Hill gives her a long look, as though he can tell she has left something out.

"You?" Asker says, in a tone that's supposed to sound just interested enough.

"Dinner with friends," he replies. "By the way, you never told me what you found in Sandgren's house."

Asker tells him that story, too. Starts with how she found his secret office, and the discoveries she made there. The map, the photos, the figures, the case file with the title *the mountain king*.

Then she goes on to Sandgren's house, how she got past the alarm thanks to Julia Collin's birthday, tells him about the overturned armchair and its secret and, finally, her mysterious pursuer in the van.

Hill sits quietly for a while after she has finished.

"Wow," he says. "So you think Sandgren got too close. That whoever did this tried to murder him."

"It all points that way," Asker nods. "The fact that Sandgren's house then turned up in the model has to be the final proof. Whoever is doing this seems to have a need to show off what he's done. Even if that involves risks. That's why he is inserting the figures where they are easy to spot."

"So this guy is abducting people and swapping them with small figures. Putting them in a fairy-tale landscape where they tell his story, time and again," Hill summarizes.

"Until someone stops him."

Hill sits quietly for a few seconds.

"Why do you think he was there yesterday? At Sandgren's house?"

Asker has had some time to ponder that, too.

"There are a few possible reasons," she says. "Either he forgot something. Or regretted leaving the model figure there and planned to take it back. Or . . ."

". . . he's watching you," Hill fills in. "Wants to make sure you don't get as close as Sandgren did."

Asker doesn't reply, but Hill can piece together the rest himself.

"Which means you need to be fucking careful from now on, Leo," he says quietly. "Especially if you, like Sandgren, are working on this investigation all on your own."

"But I'm not," she says with a sideways smile. "Am I?" Hill smiles, too. The atmosphere in the car lifts a little.

"Which reminds me, there was actually something I wanted to ask you to take a look at. In my bag there are a few old blueprints that Sandgren got from the Swedish Fortifications Agency. Thought it might be more your area of expertise."

She points her thumb at her bag on the backseat, and after a little twisting Hill pulls out the papers.

"Hmm," he says while scanning the bundle of drawings. "Most of it looks like disused Cold War bases. The kind of places that urban explorers typically like to visit. I've been to a couple of them myself."

"Clearly Sandgren thought they were significant," she says. "He had to really badger the authorities to get them. But it doesn't really look like they led anywhere. All I can see are sporadic notes that I don't really understand."

Hill goes on leafing through them, hums to himself.

"Cave rain," he says.

"What?"

He holds up one of the sheets.

"Sandgren has written *cave rain* here along the edge. A rare phenomenon where the humidity in a cave or something similar is very high and the air is forced upward, giving the impression of rain. I've never seen it before, only heard of it."

He frowns.

"Actually, MM did mention cave rain once. Said that it would make a perfect chapter for my next book. That he knew someone who knew a place."

"Did he say who or where?"

Hill shakes his head.

"No. Most urban explorers are very secretive about their favorite sites. And like I said, cave rain is very rare. It could have been all talk. MM did like to talk himself up."

Hill smiles faintly at the memory.

"Anything else?" she asks.

He keeps flicking through.

"No, or at least nothing that stands out. But the blueprints do explain why Sandgren called me to ask questions. Clearly he was interested in UE sites. And given that Tor, MM, and Smilla all counted it as a hobby, he was probably on the right track."

"In Sandgren's case file it said that the car thieves had talked about a 'mind-blowing' mountain they wanted to check out in Skåne. And that the hitchhiker was fascinated by exhilarating sites."

"Well, cave rain is a pretty mind-blowing sight." Hill nods. "An urban explorer's dream."

"So our man could have been using the cave rain as bait?"

"Maybe. I know quite a few people who would take it. MM definitely would have."

Asker thinks for a while.

"So that could be where he and Smilla were heading when they disappeared. The 'new adventure' she mentioned in her Instagram post."

"Absolutely," he agrees.

Asker continues in the same train of thought.

"Do you think someone could keep someone captive in a place like that, too? I'm thinking of Smilla."

"Maybe," Hill replies. "But a place that has cave rain would have to be cold and damp. No one would last all that long there. Besides, these disused facilities have neither electricity nor water, so it would be pretty tricky."

"OK."

Asker casts Hill a quick glance. Calling him was a long shot.

Not to mention against the rules.

But she doesn't regret it.

When they arrive at the model railway club, they find twenty or so people waiting outside.

"We're open to the public today," explains a stressed Kjell Lilja as he greets them. "And we'd rather not cancel. Entry and ticket sales are a big part of our revenue, so I've asked them to wait a little. Blamed a technical issue."

Lilja gives Hill a questioning look, as though he has only just noticed him.

"This is my partner, Hill," Asker explains. "We work together."

Out of the corner of her eye she sees Martin try to suppress a smile.

"Ah," Lilja replies. "Then come in, I'll show you!"

He leads them in through the door and into the main hall.

They stop by the plastic screen in front of Hässleholm Station.

She casts a sly glance at Martin. He has never seen the model in real life, and, just like her, he seems floored by its size and richness of detail.

"Over here!"

Lilja ushers them through. Leads them to the as yet incomplete section, where Smilla's and Malik's figures were previously found.

"And there you have it!"

He points at a house on the edge of the model. It looks eerily like Sandgren's little two-storey detached house. The flaking plaster, the ailing gutters, even the mark left by the absent number sign on the façade.

And perhaps even more than that.

Asker leans in, shines her cellphone through one of the windows. By the foot of the staircase lies a little figure on his back.

She stands up, nods at Hill to take a look himself.

"Sandgren," he mumbles. Leans in even farther. Then points at one of the first-floor windows.

"Look."

Asker peers in through the little windowpane.

Another figure is standing at the top of the stairs.

An unpainted male figure without features, his arms outstretched as though he has just pushed Sandgren.

"He couldn't resist boasting," Asker mumbles while taking photos with her phone.

"Aha, so our guests from Malmö have graced us with their presence yet again."

The voice makes Asker and Hill turn around.

It's Ulf Krook and, diagonally behind him, his taciturn stepson Finn Olofsson.

"What are you doing here, Ulf?" Lilja hisses.

"I'm still a member," Ulf sneers. "Rumor had it a whole unwanted house had turned up in the model, so curiosity got the better of me. Wanted to see it with my own eyes. And run into Asker here, of course."

He winks at her.

"But you've brought a new face with you." The man turns to Hill. "You don't look like a pig."

"Nor do you," Hill replies.

Ulf glares at him for a few seconds. Then snorts and turns to the model.

"Ah, so this is what the fuss is all about."

He leans in over Sandgren's house. Smacks his lips.

"Nice work! Pretty damn profesh!"

Asker doesn't mention the fact that she saw the model house in his basement workshop.

Instead she studies both Ulf's and his stepson's facial expressions.

Ulf looks both excited and intrigued; his eyes are twinkling, his tongue roams over his yellow teeth.

Finn Olofsson is quiet, as usual. Studies her more than the model.

She saw him and Lilja on the surveillance camera just a few days ago. They seemed to be making small talk, didn't look remotely hostile. Now they don't so much as look each other's way.

"Feast your eyes on this, Finn!" says Ulf. "Nice job, innit?"

He waves his stepson in. Finn glances at the house.

"Yup," he says, which is the first word Asker has heard him utter.

"Finn's the best modelmaker in the club," says Ulf. "Maybe the whole country. Helluva touch he's got—isn't that so, Lilja? You wouldn't get by without him."

The headmaster looks away, as though he didn't hear the comment.

"Do you use the workshop in Ulf's house?" she asks Finn.

"Obviously," Krook interrupts with an irritated nod. "I've got the best workshop in all of northern Skåne."

He glares at her, his eyes narrow.

"Though of course all my kids have access to it," he says, as though realizing that he has said too much. "Me, I've got a whole pack of kids and stepkids, and all of them come and go in the house as they like. Everyone knows where the key's hidden."

He smirks again and looks relieved, as though he has fixed some sort of mistake. Asker and Hill exchange a brief glance. She sees that he has noticed the same thing.

She pulls on some disposable gloves and takes a folded paper bag out of a jacket pocket. Then, with extreme care, she starts transferring the house into it.

Lilja, Finn Olofsson, and Ulf Krook edge away a couple feet. Hill goes with them.

"So, what do you say, Finn?" Asker hears him ask. "Who do you think built that house? In your expert opinion, I mean?"

Out of the corner of her eye she sees Finn stare at Hill for a few seconds. Then he smiles in amusement, as though he likes how he is being addressed.

"Someone who is very meticulous," he says with an unexpectedly soft voice. "Someone who doesn't let go of his builds until every last detail is exactly how he wants them."

"Do you know who that might be?" Hill asks.

Finn exchanges glances with Ulf, and then Lilja.

Then slowly shakes his head.

"No idea," he says.

Asker straightens up. Holds up the paper bag containing the model house.

"You can let the visitors in now," she says.

Before leaving the club premises they do a lap of the model so that Hill can take a closer look. He is even more engrossed now that the train has started moving, the cars and the other movable parts, too.

Gradually a surprising number of visitors trickle in.

"I thought model railways were a thing of the past," says Hill. "It feels like something my dad did when he was a kid. Or my granddad."

"That's what I first thought, too," Asker replies. "But there's something captivating about it all. A fairy-tale landscape, just like we spoke about in the car."

"One filled with stories, no less," Hill adds. "If you just stop and take a closer look."

"That's exactly how Lilja explained it to me," Asker says and nods. "Little scenes that come to life in the second a train passes."

They stand there for another minute or two. The train goes on traveling here and there. The cars and the busses, too. Even cranes, tractors, cyclists.

All in precise, synchronized movements where nothing ever falls out of line.

The rattle of the tracks mixes with the momentary sound effects. Platform announcements, car horns, children laughing and playing, accordion music.

The longer they stand there, the harder it is for Hill to tear his eyes from it all. There is something about the model that appeals to him. Evokes childhood, innocence. Security.

A perfect world, down to the last detail.

"He loves this model," Hill mutters, just as much to himself as to Asker. "But he hates it even more."

ASKER

When they are leaving the premises, a thin veil of cloud has overtaken the sun, lending the light a sepia tone.

Over by a hot dog stand, Asker sees yet another familiar face.

Clearly Jakob Tell has returned to Hässleholm after his night's escapades.

He is dressed differently, in a fleece jacket and dungarees, and is chatting to Ulf Krook. Their conversation looks relaxed. Not like that of a police officer and an old troublemaker, but more like that of two neighbors.

Finn Olofsson, however, is nowhere to be seen.

The two men turn to look at Asker.

Krook's face still bears an amused curiosity, while Tell's is openly unfriendly. Clearly his version of the previous night's events isn't at all the same as hers. He twists his head, says something about her to Krook that she can't read, but if his facial expression is anything to go by it isn't anything flattering. Which also suggests he and Krook know each other pretty well.

She ignores them, goes on walking back to the car with Hill, the paper bag in her hand. Tell goes on glaring at them.

Watches them until they leave the parking lot.

"So, now you've not only seen the model but also met both prime suspects," she says as they head back south. "What do you think?"

"It was obvious Ulf felt he had to explain that many people other than Finn have access to his workshop," Hill replies. "And hearing Finn talk about the model-maker almost admiringly was pretty grim."

"As if he was talking about himself."

"Maybe."

Hill looks pensive.

"But there are a few other things I was wondering about our perpetrator."

"OK, go on."

"Well, why does he only sometimes put himself in the model? He's done it now with Sandgren's house and Julia Collin, but not the car thieves, hitchhiker, or Tor."

"Or Smilla and Malik," Asker adds.

"Exactly. What do you think that means? Why did he want to show himself in those scenes, specifically?"

Asker frowns. This thought has also occurred to her in passing, and Hill makes a good point.

"I couldn't say," she says. "Maybe those instances were particularly important?"

"I think so, too," Hill agrees. "I mean, Sandgren was his adversary. So I guess it's not so strange that he would want to show off that he had won. But Julia . . ."

"There's another thing that's different about Julia," says Asker. "The other figures turned up a few days or a couple of months, max, after they disappeared. The car thieves, the hitchhiker, Tor, Smilla and Malik. Even Sandgren's house, which must have taken a lot of time to build, turned up after only a few weeks. But Julia's figure only showed up in the model two years after she went missing. Why did he wait so long with her?"

Hill looks through the side window. Appears to be searching for an answer.

"Maybe because she, too, was extra important in some way, like Sandgren," he says hesitantly.

"Yeah, you may be right there. But how?"

Neither of them has any good answer to that question.

"So what's the next step?" Hill asks.

"I'm going to try to convince someone in Forensics to search the model for fingerprints or DNA," she says. "And once the club's closed for the day, the alarm guy is going to try to extract a recording from the other camera. With any luck we'll have a shot of him."

Hill sits quietly for a while.

"I have another avenue I thought I might try. Mya, the friend of MM's who I mentioned before. She called me yesterday and said she had something she wanted to tell me. But she got interrupted in the middle of the conversation. I got the impression it might have something to do with MM's death."

"What made you think that?"

"A hunch, mostly. They dated for a while, and she's also into urban exploration."

Asker mulls it over.

An urban explorer friend who also dated MM is a decent lead, not least given their new theory about the cave rain as bait.

Now she's doubly glad she contacted Martin Hill.

"What's Mya's surname?"

"I don't know. She isn't enrolled in the course."

"And what did she say, exactly?"

"That she and MM went on some UE expeditions together. That she was in love with him, that's basically it. But I get the feeling she knows more than she's letting on. And that I might just be able to get her to open up."

"Would you like me to be there?"

"No," he says, perhaps a little too fast. "Mya's shy," he adds. "I'm pretty sure she doesn't trust the police."

"OK. Well I guess you can start by getting her full name so I can look her up."

Asker stops at an intersection. One of the signs bears the name of a familiar place. Both of them notice it.

"How far is it from here to . . ."

Hill leaves the rest of the sentence hanging in the air, but Asker hears it all the same. *To the Shadowlands, to the Farm, to Prepper Per, to the past.*

"Not all that far. Fifty, sixty miles."

"And you've never been back there, not even out of curiosity?"

"No!" she says. "There's nothing to be curious about. Per's insane, that's as much dirt as there is."

Silence. The atmosphere has shifted again.

"I've always felt bad about what happened," Hill says. "The accident, the explosion . . ."

He takes a deep breath before going on.

"I should have raised the alarm. I mean, I'd been on the Farm, I'd met your dad, I knew what you were going through. That he was only getting worse. But I just upped and left. Left you."

He looks away.

"You were a teenager," she says quietly. "There were plenty of adults around who didn't do a thing. School, social services, the police, my mom. What could you have done?"

"At the very least I could have reached out afterward. Found out how you were doing, sent a letter. I mean, we were best friends . . ."

"Well," she says with a shrug, "I suppose it still wouldn't have made a difference. The accident would have happened anyway. And after that it was just one massive shit show, what with the social services, Mom, everything else."

She goes quiet, stares straight ahead down the road.

"Would you like to talk about it?" Hill asks after a pause. "What happened that night. The accident, the explosion, the scar . . ."

"No," she says sharply. Sounds cold, though she doesn't mean to.

"OK," Hill turns to face the side window. Tries to look unaffected, but she can read his disappointment.

She has never told anyone about what happened that night. Not the police, not social services, not her mother. Always claimed she didn't remember what happened before the explosion. But that isn't true. She remembers every detail. Every last one is seared into her memory.

She looks straight down the road.

The spruce forest lining the verge is a silent, bluey-green wall that sucks up the daylight.

The Shadowlands.

A place she never wants to go back to, be that in real life or in her mind.

Not even with Martin Hill.

FIFTEEN YEARS EARLIER

An early August night. It's just after two a.m., which she knows because that's almost always when Per's emergency drills start. When the brain has just transitioned to deep sleep and it's hardest to wake up. He has been preparing this exercise for a while.

The tension between them has been building all summer, charged with crackling, sharp ions, like the impending thunderstorm on the breeze.

Has made the air on the Farm heavy, hard to breathe. Harder than normal.

She is sixteen years old. In two weeks she will be moving into the city to start high school. Will leave the Farm, get out into the world.

Leave him.

And there is nothing that he can do to stop her.

At least that's what she tells herself.

The alarm goes off and she rolls out of bed. Starts the timer on her watch. Thirty seconds to put on her clothes and boots, grab her backpack and make for the trailer door.

It's locked from the outside, not for the first time, and the windows are barricaded shut.

She looks at her watch. Almost one minute has passed, four left.

If she can get down to the boat in five minutes, there will be a surprise waiting for her.

If she is late, she will have two weeks of punishments to look forward to. She has no intention of giving him that satisfaction. Nor of showing up to her first day of high school with cuts on her knuckles and knees.

Never!

She slides down the evacuation hatch at the bottom of her wardrobe. Pushes her backpack in front of her as she worms her way through the passage that runs under the belly of the van.

The alarm is still sounding over the Farm, mixes with the sweep of the spotlights lining the barbed wire fence.

Her heart is pounding, she works her knees and elbows to get through the passage.

Two minutes.

She's out now, sprinting. Takes a shortcut over the obstacle course and shooting range, slides open a hatch and crawls through one of the secret tunnels under the fence. Pulls herself up on the other side and, despite the black of the night, manages to find the trail that will lead her down to the lake and the boat.

She tries to lift her feet, anticipate where he will have laid trip wires. Even so, that usually doesn't help. Prepper Per is an expert at mines and explosives. At any moment she will feel a tug on one foot, followed by an explosion, one close enough to lash her skin with dirt and gravel, send shock waves rippling through her chest.

With each new drill he rigs them a little closer to the trail. So close that her ears ring for days afterward.

But nothing happens, which surprises her.

Could it be that she has cleared the trip wires?

If so, it would be a first.

She goes on running through the forest. Moves with light, quiet steps. Listens out for him, even though that's usually pointless.

Normally he moves soundlessly. But this time something is different. Somewhere behind her a twig snaps. Then another one.

He's hurrying, being careless.

But why? She gets a feeling at the nape of her neck.

Something isn't right.

She stops short, tries to gather her thoughts. The night-vision goggles he uses show the world in green tints. But they also have an infrared lamp that can be turned on for extra assistance. The lamp transforms warm objects, such as her body, into light silhouettes that appear particularly clearly when in motion.

But the infrared rays have only a couple inches' range, and they don't give him X-ray vision. If she sits very still behind a dense object, it will greatly lessen the chance of her being seen.

Asker deviates from the trail. Fifteen or thirty feet into the forest stand a few boulders, and she squeezes in between them. The rugged surface retains the sun's heat, which makes her even harder to detect.

She purses her lips around her breaths. Tries to force down her pulse.

The feeling that something is wrong is growing all the stronger.

Thunder grumbles threateningly in the distance. As though it can already sense what is coming and is trying to warn her.

The air thickens, changes scent.

Electricity. Danger.

Steps are heard on the trail. Fast, stressed.

He stops dead. She can hear the faint beep of him turning on the infrared lamp. Knows he must be scanning the terrain with his night-vision goggles, searching for her.

Beyond that, all is silent. No wind, no birds of the night.

As if the entire forest is holding its breath before the discharge.

A deathly silence.

It's why she is certain of what she hears next. Is still certain, even fifteen years later.

The most devastating sound she has ever heard him make.

A sob.

And that's when she realizes what it is that Per has planned. What kind of surprise is waiting for her down by the boat.

And that he is never, ever going to let her go.

ASKER

Asker drops Hill off outside his apartment in Lund. They agree to call each other later, and then she heads back to Malmö.

She parks down in the police garage, as usual. Sees a couple of colleagues from Serious Crime float past in a brand-new dark, unmarked car. Neither of them acknowledge her, though they must have seen her clearly.

Evidently Hellman and his gang are working flat out to identify the young men from the ransom video.

The corridor down on level minus one is as grim as ever. Even so, Asker is in a better mood than usual.

She has a lead. Wrong, *she and Martin* have a lead, and that little correction might just be what makes all the difference.

For the first time in a very long time she has an ally, someone she trusts, someone who gets her.

Two brown internal envelopes are lying in her pigeonhole. Both are from Rosen. She takes them into her office.

The first contains data on Robert Mattson, Julia Collin's stepdad. It all starts unremarkably. A couple of speeding fines on his record, a bankrupt construction firm to his name. However, all of his debts have been settled with the Swedish Enforcement Agency, and for the past few years Robert has been running a taxi company with five employees. Once divorced before he married Julia's mother, Ulrika. Two children from a previous marriage, of whom he had joint custody.

A normal researcher would have been satisfied with that. Would say that nothing about Robert Mattson stood out, or gave any reason to do more digging.

But Rosen wasn't satisfied. She has left no stone unturned, has checked the general enforcement database and its intelligence records, withdrawn reports, memos from social services.

And slowly another picture emerges.

First, an anonymous tip-off to the police that alleges that Robert has been violent toward both Julia and her mother. Shortly thereafter social services record the same information.

Both investigate independently. The police investigation is soon laid to rest, after interviews with Ulrika and Robert, who both strongly deny everything.

Julia, however, doesn't appear to have given a statement.

Social services are more thorough. In addition to the parents they speak to Julia, who initially confirms the allegations, but then does a U-turn and denies them, too. Robert's ex-wife is also interviewed, and she rejects the suggestion that Robert could have been violent.

A later memo reveals that Julia was in contact with social services once more, and that she intimated that life at home wasn't exactly rosy. The case worker even made a note of the fact that Julia was afraid of Robert.

But before any measures can be taken, Julia turns eighteen, and the social services interest wanes in the same way as the police's.

In short, there are more important, urgent cases to focus on. And, beyond a retracted witness statement and some vague insinuations, they have no proof of any crime.

Still, it helps to give a clearer picture of the Collin family.

The glances that Ulrika and Robert exchanged.

A credible reason why Julia might run off to the summer cottage every now and then.

Asker opens the other envelope.

This one contains Rosen's research into their colleague Jakob Tell, and she has been even more industrious than Asker had dared hope.

Tell got decent grades in police college and is well regarded by his managers and colleagues. Obviously no criminal record to speak of. Thorough, ambitious, and sociable are words that come up repeatedly when describing him.

However, Rosen has also managed to unearth an old internal investigation that brings another side of Tell to light.

The complainant was a female colleague who had had a brief relationship with him.

According to her, Tell was controlling from the very start of their relationship. He didn't like her spending time with her friends, wanted to know who she was meeting and where. When she eventually ended the relationship, he turned up outside her house in the middle of the night. Even flashed his siren lights, told her he was watching her. The complainant also claimed that on a few occasions during their relationship he had locked her in a room and refused to let her out.

Tell denied everything, obviously. It was his word against hers, but the allegations were considered so credible that a note was nevertheless added to Tell's record in the police HR database. As a result, he has been denied several other jobs that he has applied for in the force, including in Serious Crime. Has been forced to stay in the local force and slowly work his way up that way.

Asker leans back in her chair. Rosen has done an outstanding job. Better than many of her colleagues up in Serious Crime.

She has only to open *Sydsvenskan*'s homepage to see that the nervous woman has also found the time to speak to her journalist contact. *Source with links to the police investigation into Smilla Holst's disappearance claims they are on the wrong track.*

She knows for a fact that her mother doesn't miss a single word written in *Sydsvenskan*, so Hellman probably has his hands full right now trying to convince Isabel that it's all just claptrap and that he has everything under control.

The thought is strangely appealing.

But the satisfaction soon fades, edged out by her thoughts on the case.

She still can't quite get over the events of the previous night. That Jakob Tell rang her doorbell just seconds after the ghost train stopped. And then turned up today at the model, looking pretty at home, as though he knew everything and everyone.

She flicks through the data on Tell again.

At the back, Rosen has listed his next of kin.

Tell is noted as single, which means he is neither married nor officially lives with a partner. The Swedish Tax Agency's data confirms that no marriages or partnerships have ever been registered.

She reads on.

A father long since out of the picture, a mother who moved up north to Norrland.

Tell, however, has several half siblings through his mother's second husband.

The name makes Asker gasp.

Ulf Krook.

Jakob Tell is Ulf Krook's stepson.

SMILLA

"Smilla, are you there?"

"I'm here!"

"Remember Tor, the one I mentioned? The one who was here before you?"

"Yes."

"He never got out of here, did he?"

Smilla thinks for a few seconds. Contemplates the best way to answer.

"Maybe," she says.

"I don't think so," Julia replies. "The Mountain King never lets anyone go. Tor's dead. He died down here."

She sobs.

"I've been so lonely . . ."

"But you aren't alone anymore," says Smilla. "And we're going to get out of here, together. Soon! I promise."

ASKER

Asker sits in the office for a while, trying to get her head around how Jakob Tell fits into the picture.

Clearly he is manipulative. Can be charming one minute and a piece of work the next. Plus he has a dark past that suggests a problematic attitude to both relationships and breakups.

And since Ulf Krook is his stepfather, he probably also has access to the old jerry-built house of horrors, and to the workshop where she saw Sandgren's house.

Tell claimed he hadn't been in touch with Sandgren, but of course that could have been a lie. If Tell is the culprit, and Sandgren turned up asking questions about the model and missing people, Tell would have immediately known to keep an eye on his police colleague.

Take action if he got too close.

Has he done the same thing with her? Followed her, found her home address, made sure to turn up when she was alone?

This is all wholly plausible, which means she has a new prime suspect.

She locks up the office, stops by Forensics, and rings the bell. Tries to convince the technician who answers to examine the model of Sandgren's house for possible prints and DNA.

Not that Asker thinks they'll find any. If Jakob Tell really is their man, he will know better than to leave a trace. Still, obviously she has to try.

"We're at capacity," the technician says. "What case does this involve?"

"The Holst kidnapping," she replies, entirely truthfully.

The technician gives her a questioning look. Then shrugs.

"OK, in that case I'll take it. The Holst case is priority number one."

"Thanks!"

The police garage is quiet and empty. She sets her course for the corner where she parked the car. Almost immediately she feels a tingling at the nape of her neck.

Quiet footsteps are heard; two people behind her.

Asker carries on walking toward her car, neither speeding up nor looking around.

More footsteps now, diagonally to her left. Quieter, but still audible.

Another person trying to cut her off, in the belief that they have surprise on their side.

Time to turn the tables. She stops suddenly and spins around.

Two men straight in front of her.

Her third pursuer remains hidden in the shadows.

"What do you want?" she says.

The men take a few steps closer. Their faces come into the light.

One is Eskil, the other a colleague of the heavyweight variety, who makes Eskil look even shorter than he is.

The heavyweight's name is Jim, and he is one of Serious Crime's new arrivals. Has a bull's neck and walks with his arms out. Likes lifting weights and watching MMA clips on his phone. That's pretty much all she knows about him.

"What the fuck do you think you're playing at, Asker?" Eskil hisses.

"What?"

"You're leaking to the press, running around talking shit about us to Rodic."

Asker calculates their distance. Her car is thirty feet away. She would make it, if it weren't for the third person, who has now maneuvered around her, cutting off her escape route. Which means she needs to buy time to come up with a new plan.

"Ah," she says, as annoyingly as she can. "So your master's sent you to give me a stern talking to. Doesn't that make you nervous?"

"Why should it?" asks Eskil.

"Well, because if Hellman thinks I'm such a big fucking threat to his investigation that he's sending his lapdog and a gorilla after me, clearly he must be worried about something. Maybe he doesn't believe his own theory anymore."

The men throw sideways glances at each other.

"Hellman's scared I'm going to solve the case before him, it's as simple as that. And that's why you're here. Whether he gave you the order or not, the idea still came from the top."

She slowly shifts sideways, to give herself more space to maneuver from the third person.

"Bullshit," Eskil sneers. "Jonas knows exactly what he's doing. This case is going to be over tomorrow."

Asker tilts her head to one side.

"Well if that's true, then what are you doing down here with me?" she asks. "If it's all such a dead fucking cert, I mean. Or is there something that Jonas isn't telling you?"

"Shut your trap!" Jim yelps.

He takes one step toward her, flips out a hairy index finger.

"You better watch your fucking step, Asker. Watch it!"

"Or what? Pray tell."

She looks back and forth between Jim and Eskil. Tries to figure out their weak points, gauge the easiest, most pain-free way for her to wriggle out of this fox trap.

The third person is now somewhere behind her. Could be on her back at any second.

"You've always been a bitch," Eskil splutters. "Act like you're so much fucking smarter and better than the rest of us."

"In your case that isn't so hard, Eskil," she says. "The average fifteen-year-old writes better reports than you."

"Shut it!" Jim shouts again, since apparently that's his job.

A faint scrape of shoes behind her back tells her that the third person has moved into position and is ready to ambush her. The same conclusion can be deduced based on Eskil's and Jim's scornful smiles. The attack will come from behind, and is meant to take her by surprise. The same tactics the bullies used to use in school.

She warily tenses her body, fights the urge to turn her head. Another faint scraping sound just a few feet behind her back.

Now!

Asker takes a quick step to the left while spinning in the opposite direction, and throws her right elbow up over her shoulder.

Her strike is almost a bull's-eye. It lands on the nose and not the chin as intended, but still, the effect is immediate.

She hears the man's nose crack, his teeth clap together.

Then a short groan as his knees buckle and he lands like a sack of bricks between two of the parked cars.

One down, two to go. But the blow has also wiped out any possible misgivings the other two men might have had.

Jim is already heading toward her, his head lowered like a bull's.

He must weigh two hundred and twenty pounds, maybe more, and she has limited room to maneuver. Behind him stands Eskil, who may be smaller, but is still a decent opponent.

The odds are stacked against her.

Suddenly a sharp voice cuts through the garage.

"So what's going on here then?"

Jim stops short, just out of reach. Both he and Eskil turn around.

A sinewy older man with closely cropped hair is standing behind them with his hands in his pockets. It's Attila.

"Stay out of this, old man!" Eskil snarls. "This has nothing to do with you. Jog on."

Attila raises one eyebrow. "And what if I don't?"

Jim has changed his target. Steps over to Attila, towers over him. His face is red, his fists clenched. A vein thrums in his temple.

"Really want to find out?" he grunts.

Attila doesn't budge.

The man behind Asker scrambles to his feet while clutching at his nose, which is bleeding heavily. He groans loudly in pain.

She makes a fake lunge at the bleeding man. He jumps back between a pair of cars in fright, then turns tail and runs.

She should really make the most of this moment to escape, too. But part of her is fascinated by the show.

Eskil has started to look concerned. His eyes flit between Attila, Jim, and Asker. It's clear that whatever his plan was, it has seriously derailed.

But Jim doesn't seem to have twigged. He takes another step toward Attila, who calmly stands there with his hands in his pockets.

"Didn't you hear, Grandpa?" Jim snarls again. "Get out of here!"

He fires a giant fist straight out at Attila's chest.

A mistake, Asker realizes long before Jim.

Attila's movements are so fast you can hardly see them.

A swing of the hand, a step to one side, a sharp kick to the back of the knee, and suddenly Jim is on his knees with Attila behind him, squeezing his neck in an unbreakable lock.

Jim tugs at Attila's arms while gasping for breath, but it's no use. After just a few seconds his brain is starved of oxygen and shuts the whole body down. His face turns gray, his limbs floppy.

Attila releases his hold and lowers Jim carefully, almost gently, down to the blacktop. Then gets to his feet and brushes the dirt from one of his trouser legs.

Eskil stands there unmoving. His face is white, in both rage and fear.

"You've got two choices," Attila says quietly. "Your friend will come to in thirty seconds. Either you can help him get to his feet and scamper with your tails between your legs. Or . . ."

". . . you'll kick the shit out of me," says Eskil. "Yeah, I get it."

Attila shakes his head. "Not me."

He points at Asker.

Eskil glares at her. Clenches his fists a few times, as though weighing up whether to throw down the gauntlet. Asker tilts her head to one side. Gives him her two-toned look and raises him with a smug smile, as though she has already started planning how to hurt him.

Which she has. In detail.

Eskil seems to catch on.

The uncertainty comes creeping onto his face. He looks around for the third man, then down at the snoring Jim.

Comes to the obvious conclusion that his whole plan is shot to shit and that he has no choice. Eskil opens his hands, lowers his shoulders.

"You can both go to hell," he mutters.

Eskil bends down and helps Jim to his feet. Wraps one of his arms around his shoulders and staggers off with him toward the nearest exit. A door slams heavily shut, then everything goes quiet.

Attila stands there opposite her.

"Thanks!" says Asker.

"No problem," he says.

"The fire alarm, the other day in Forensics. That was you, too, wasn't it?"

"Perhaps."

"I thought you just kept yourself to yourself," she says.

Attila gives a hint of a smile and shrugs.

Then turns around and calmly walks away.

HILL

In theory Hill has plans with a couple of friends. Their Sunday movie outings are one of his favorite rituals. But against his usual principles he cancels.

Instead he takes a walk to try to collect his thoughts.

After the day's excursion his head is full of concerns.

And the conversation he and Leo had in the car worries him.

If their perpetrator attacked Sandgren in his home because he got too close, what would prevent him from doing the same to Leo? All of the men around the model—Kjell Lilja, Ulf Krook, and Finn Olofsson—could hardly tear their eyes off her. Finn is clearly the oddest of the three. Was he talking about himself when he described the model-maker? It felt almost that way.

Leo calls just as he is getting in the door.

"Are you home?"

"Just got in," he confirms.

"I've found something. A new person of interest in the investigation."

She tells him about Jakob Tell. How she met him at the police station, and how he tried to ask her out. How he turned up at her place without warning the previous night and tried to force himself on her, and then showed up again today at the club.

Strangely enough, this new information makes Hill feel a little relieved. So the man he saw outside Leo's house was Jakob Tell, not some secret boyfriend she hasn't told him about.

All the same . . .

"How did he know where you live?"

"He didn't say."

Hill takes a deep breath.

"I actually crossed paths with him. Or, rather, saw his back."

"What?"

Hill tells his side of the story.

"So it was your taxi I saw," says Asker. "I thought it was his. Did you pass another taxi on the way? One that was leaving my place?"

"No."

"Are you sure?"

"One hundred percent. I mean, it's a small street. I'd have remembered if another car passed."

Asker goes silent for a few seconds.

"So how did he get to my place? And where did he go after my neighbor showed up?"

"No idea. Maybe he had a car that he parked somewhere else."

"Doubtful. He reeked of booze, seemed a little drunk. Though of course he might have driven regardless."

"Or someone gave him a lift. Someone who parked a little out of the way and then waited for him."

This thought worries Hill. Asker, however, already seems to have taken the line of reasoning further.

"A police officer can travel anywhere, at any time of day or night," she says. "Stop people, make them get into cars, like the hitchhiker or Julia. Maybe even arrest them, like Tor. And he'll know if someone starts digging around in the case."

"Like Sandgren."

"Exactly."

The line goes quiet again.

"So how do we prove it?"

"I've left the model house with Forensics. Tell will be well aware of how to avoid leaving prints and DNA, mind you, but all it takes is one stray hair."

She sounds dubious, as though she doesn't hold out much hope herself.

"And then we have the pictures from the hidden camera," she goes on.

"Have you got them?"

"No, I just got a text from Nygård, the alarm guy. Apparently Lilja and the gang were still there working on something until a little while ago. But Nygård was busy tonight and couldn't get there straightaway, so we'll have to wait till tomorrow."

"OK." Hill tries to organize his thoughts, somehow. However

strange it may sound, and despite the—mildly put—unpleasant circumstances, he is enjoying this conversation. The fact that he and Leo share a secret, just like they used to do.

"Have you heard anything from that girl? Mya?"

"No," he says. "Not since yesterday. And she calls from a private number. But I have the feeling she'll get in touch again. I'll try to find out what she knows."

"Good. If you want, I can ask a colleague to trace the private number she's calling from. He loves that sort of stuff."

"That might be a good idea," he replies. "At least if she doesn't get in touch soon. But I don't think we should push her."

The line goes quiet.

"On another note, why were you at my place last night?" she asks, with a softer tone of voice.

He has no good response. After a few seconds she catches on and lets it slide.

"I'll call you tomorrow," she says, ending the call. Possibly even with a smile in her voice.

Hill opens a bottle of wine, mindlessly flicks through some TV, and dozes off on the sofa. The rain is drumming against the windows. Reminds him of the rattle of a model railway.

He dreams of an enormous fairy-tale landscape where the sun always shines, where trains wind their way through happy scenes.

One of the houses resembles Asker's. He can see her in the upstairs window. Or, more accurately, a figure that represents her.

Painted in such detail that you can even make out her different-colored eyes, which would be near-impossible to notice in anything but a dream.

But by the trees near the house another figure flashes past. An unpainted one, who, despite lacking any facial expression, appears to be watching her.

A train approaches on the tracks. The second it passes the entire scene comes to life.

The trees sway in the wind, a little dog runs along the road.

The featureless figure moves among the trees. Then the train is gone and everything falls still again. Awaits the moment when another train will bring it all to life.

Every time it happens, the featureless figure edges ever closer to Asker's house. But she doesn't seem to spot it. Even though she is standing in the window facing out, she is looking in the wrong direction.

Hill tries to scream at her to turn. Warn her of the approaching danger. But she doesn't hear.

He is woken by his phone's ringtone. A call from a private number.

"Hello?" he says drowsily.

"It's Mya." Her voice is quiet, almost a whisper. "I'm on the train. I need your help."

Hill sits up.

"Which train?"

"To Lund. We're arriving in fifteen minutes. A bunch of stuff happened, so I cut and run. But I think someone's after me."

He gets to his feet.

"I'm on my way," he says. "I'll meet you on the platform!"

When he steps out onto the street, the rain is even heavier. Makes the autumn darkness feel even deeper.

He opens his umbrella and jogs down toward the station. The rainwater splashes onto his shoes and trousers.

The station is in the very center of Lund. Streets and buildings line the tracks, with a sheltered overpass at one end of the station. The train arrives just as Hill makes it to the platform.

The doors open and twenty or so passengers step off.

Mya is one of the last. She has swapped her beanie hat for a cap that she has pulled down over her forehead and covered with the hood of her jacket. The young woman walks straight toward Hill with brisk steps, looks over her shoulder a few times. She is carrying a black sports bag on her shoulder.

"Come on," she says through clenched teeth and takes his arm. "Anyone could see us!"

She pulls him along up the overpass steps, constantly looking over her shoulder.

"What's going on?" Hill asks.

"Not now." She stops and peers down at the main road.

A few cars are slowly creeping along on the street, their windshield wipers struggling in the rain.

"Fuck!" Mya murmurs. She takes Hill's hand and pulls him over to the steps on the far side of the overpass. At the bottom of the steps, the wind catches hold of the umbrella and the rain hits them square in the face. The water is freezing, makes the eyes sting.

"Come on!" Mya starts running, heads for a cluster of apartment blocks.

Hill tries to keep the umbrella over them, but after a hundred and fifty feet of running he gives up and puts it down.

Mya runs diagonally across a well-lit inner courtyard and out onto another street. Hill stamps in a big puddle, sending water up over his ankle.

Ahead of them, a woman with a little poodle disappears through a door.

Mya catches the door just before it shuts, pulls Hill into the hallway, and shuts the door behind them.

Stares out nervously at the street, where the headlights of a vehicle are approaching. Presses up against the wall, signals at Hill to do the same.

The vehicle crawls past slowly. They stand there while the water drips off their clothes.

Mya is still holding Hill's hand. Clutches it so tightly it almost hurts, until the car disappears out of sight.

The street outside is empty. The rain continues to pound against the asphalt.

"I think it's high time you explained what all this is about," says Hill.

Mya lets go of his hand.

"Soon," she says. "But not here!"

ASKER

As always whenever she has trouble sleeping, Asker gets out her backpack.

Unpacks, checks and repacks the contents. This usually calms her down.

But not tonight.

There is a serial killer out there. Someone with six people's lives on his conscience. Maybe more.

And she is certain that she has met him.

That he was here in her house, in her front hall.

The question from before is back.

What would have happened if her neighbor hadn't showed up?

A good question, and one which she luckily has no answer for.

She has checked all the locks, activated the house's state-of-the-art burglar alarm. From the TV in her bedroom she can track all the camera feeds that monitor the entrances to the house. Besides the escalating rain and gales, everything is calm. Nothing is moving that shouldn't be.

How Jakob Tell got here is one of the questions she just can't let go of. And how could he get away, just as quickly and unnoticed?

Did he park farther away and drive drunk, or did he have someone else to drop him off and pick him up? A helper, as Hill suggested.

On top of that, she still hasn't quite digested the scene in the police garage. She rubs her elbow. It is sore and a little swollen.

Did Hellman know that Eskil and his two henchmen were planning to attack her? Could it even have been his idea?

Probably not. At least not expressly.

One of Hellman's talents is the ability to nurture a group culture in which that kind of command never needs to be explicit. He simply leaves Eskil and the others to interpret what he wants them to do, thereby raising himself above the dirtiest tasks. A leader whose hands and conscience are always sparklingly clean, and whose loyal hangers-on work hard to ensure things remain that way.

She herself has been one of Hellman's sect, knows where blind, misdirected loyalty can lead. Now she is a renegade, a traitor who is to be treated as such. Who deserves a good beating in a dark garage.

So why is Attila sneaking around and helping her? Might it have something to do with what he revealed he knows about Prepper Per and the Farm?

There is one other thing on her mind.

Eskil blurted out that everything would be over tomorrow.

It can only reasonably mean one thing. Hellman and his team have managed to trace the people who sent the ransom video and are planning a raid.

She still doesn't believe that the video is connected to Smilla's kidnapping, but of course she could be wrong.

Every statement must bear up to questioning. Only once you have asked "why?" three times will you be starting to get near the truth.

That was one of Prepper Per's favorite quotes, one he would use to point out the importance of always questioning what others accept as truth.

Ironic, since he himself didn't tolerate being questioned for a single fucking second. Still, that doesn't mean his approach is wrong. At least not when used within reason.

She tries it out on her hypothesis.

Question: Why would someone record a video, demand a ransom, and threaten the police if they haven't kidnapped Smilla?

Answer: To make money and/or screw around with the police and the Holst family.

So then: Why take that kind of risk?

Answer: Because they think the result is worth the risk.

So then: Why would they think that?

Answer: Because they don't fully understand the risks. They don't realize that the police are going to hunt them down with every conceivable resource, and that their chances of success are minimal. Or because the result—the ransom fee, or seeing the police and the Holst family humiliated—is still worth it.

So then: Who would believe that?

Answer: Someone who is inclined to take risks, who isn't well versed in how the police work, who puts feelings before logic, who thinks that they are smart, invincible.

In short: someone young.

Add to that the information she inferred from the video—that the would-be kidnappers are two men who are too young to have been behind the first figures in the model, and also don't speak the right dialect—and her theory passes the test.

The ransom video is much more likely to be fake than real.

And tomorrow Hellman will be gambling all his resources and credibility on a red herring.

She wishes she could be there to see it happen.

To watch on as his investigation implodes. See the look in his eyes when he realizes that he is wrong and she is right.

She checks the camera feeds again. The wind and rain outside are picking up. Gathering force.

Perhaps it's because she has recently let Prepper Per back into her head, but for one brief moment she is back in that summer night all those years ago. Can feel the tension slowly building up ahead of the inevitable discharge. At some point she will tell Martin what really happened there that night. He deserves to know.

But not yet.

She opens her backpack and empties the contents onto her bed again.

HILL

Hill and Mya are sitting at his overly expensive designer table. He has made some tea while Mya changed into some less wet clothes from her sports bag.

He is wet, too, but is too taken up with everything going on around him to care about that.

He would prefer to press her for answers immediately, but he sees that that would be a bad idea.

Mya is still worried. Insists on keeping the lights off, and checks the street below from the window every two minutes, while nervously dragging on her e-cigarette.

"So," he says. "Can you please explain to me what all this is about?"

Mya takes a sip of tea, unnaturally slowly, as though trying to buy herself time to think.

"I met MM on an UE web forum this summer," she says slowly. "We both loved your book, that's what got us talking. He told me he was in your course and that you were his idol. So we met up for a coffee and one thing led to another. He'd just been dumped by Smilla. She'd gone off to Paris to study. MM was pretty beat up about it all, so obviously I knew I was a rebound."

She takes a drag on her e-cigarette. Blows out a cloud of berry-scented vapor.

"But that didn't bother me. I wasn't looking for anything serious, as least not to begin with. MM and I went on a few explores together. There's something so hot about sex in ruins. Primitive in a way. Decadent."

She gives Hill a long look, as though to see his reaction.

He tries to look unfazed. Hide how impatient he is to hear the rest of the story. To piece it together with what he and Leo already know.

"Anyway. We kept hooking up, and after a while I got a bit more involved than I meant to. And I saw that MM was starting to patch things up with his ex."

She takes another drag. Hill tries to contain himself. Let her tell her story without interrupting her with questions.

"I . . ." She sighs, as though the next part is going to be more difficult. ". . . I've got a cousin who's into UE, too. He knows a couple of really special sites that basically no one else knows. Never posts any pictures, doesn't boast on any forums. I told him about my mess with MM. He offered to take him to one of his secret spots. I don't actually know why I agreed. I guess I thought it might somehow make MM like me more. You know, *see what I can do for you that Smilla can't*, that kind of vibe."

Mya makes an ironic hand gesture.

"Clinginess isn't a turn-on, I know," she goes on. "So anyway, my cousin and MM got in touch. I went out with them the first time, but then I got sick and they went out a couple of times without me. After that it was like I was cut out of their UE stuff, just like that. And on top of that MM started avoiding me because Smilla was coming home. I was fucking angry at him."

Mya laughs sadly.

"And then suddenly he and Smilla were gone. I asked my cousin if he knew anything, but he said he hadn't talked to MM in a long time, which I was sure wasn't true. I'd happened to see them WhatsApping each other just a few days before. So I started to twig that something was up. My cousin's . . ."

She pauses, searching for the right word.

". . . a little weird. Paranoid, you could almost say. I thought it was more that he was very careful about his secrets. That he didn't want other urban explorers running around his spots. But when I kept on asking him about MM he got angry. Or . . ."

She takes yet another deep drag.

". . . fucking lost it is probably a better description. Told me I should stop poking my fucking nose in it. That I should forget MM and get rid of everything that had anything to do with him. He also started keeping tabs on me. I live in a cottage owned by his stepdad, which makes things even more complicated."

Hill nods patiently, battling the urge to interrupt her.

"And then when MM was found dead . . ."

She purses her lips, glances at the window for what must be the tenth time.

"I got paranoid. Got it into my head that my phone was bugged and all that. Hardly dared leave the house."

She goes quiet. Turns off her e-cigarette with the press of a button and starts spinning it on the table.

Hill tries to wait her out, but his eagerness is getting the better of him. This horrible story fits with what he and Leo have unearthed, and he has so many questions. The first is clear.

"What's your cousin's name?" he tries, with as much coolness as he can muster.

Mya looks down at the table without replying. Goes on playing with her e-cigarette.

Hill waits, but she purses her lips again, this time so tightly that they go white. His patience is about to crack. But the slightest little misstep will probably make Mya fly off the handle and disappear again.

He forces himself to sound calm when he asks the next question.

"So what happened tonight?"

"My cousin heard me when I last called you. He's been suspicious ever since. Put a tracking app on my phone, has banned me from going anywhere without telling him. It's been almost like living in a prison."

She flicks the e-cigarette so that it spins a few times.

"So I decided to get out of there. I've got a new phone, so I left my old one in the cottage and cycled to the train. But I felt so damn jittery. Got it into my head that he knew I was planning to do a runner. That he was following me in his car."

She casts another anxious glance at the window.

"And what's your plan? Where were you planning to go?"

She shrugs.

"I've got a friend in Stockholm. Planned to take the train there tomorrow. He doesn't know her, so I can lie low there. But I need somewhere to stay the night."

She looks at him pleadingly.

"No problem," he says. "You can take my bed, I'll go on the sofa."

"Thanks." She sighs in relief. She has let her guard down a little now, and since he is doing her a favor he feels brave enough to ask slightly more probing questions.

He takes the unpainted plastic figure from his kitchen drawer and sets it down in front of her.

"Have you ever seen one of these?"

She flinches.

"My cousin's stepdad has a hobby workshop in his basement. It's full of these. Why do you ask?"

She tilts her head to one side, in almost the same way that Leo often does.

"Because an identical one was found in MM's car, and in a few other places where people have disappeared."

The color drains from Mya's skin.

Hill decides to get straight to the point.

"And I think your cousin's behind it," he says, leaning in.

"I think he's luring urban explorers into his den and murdering them. Leaving a little plastic figure as his calling card. I think he's the one who murdered MM, and he might be holding Smilla hostage, too."

He leaves out the part about the model railway for now; partly because he doesn't want to give away too much, and partly because it sounds so macabre.

Mya claps her hand to her mouth and stares at him, her face chalky-white and her eyes wide.

She leaps to her feet without warning.

Hill is afraid she's about to bolt for the front door, considers running after her for a second or two. Instead Mya disappears into the bathroom and slams the door shut behind her.

He can hear her retching, then the sounds of her turning on the tap and flushing the toilet.

He tries to gather his thoughts. Was it really such a good idea to tell Mya all of that?

Scare her in that way?

Perhaps not.

He wonders whether to call Leo, but it's the middle of the night and he doesn't want to lose this precarious bond he has with Mya.

If Leo found out what Mya just said, she would immediately jump in the car, drive over here, and try to extract the name of Mya's cousin from her, which he is convinced is entirely the wrong tactic.

He needs to take a step back, try to build confidence. Show that he can be trusted.

Only then will he get the name.

After around five minutes, Mya comes back into the kitchen.

The color in her face has returned, but she still looks shaken.

"Are you OK?" he asks.

She sits down. Her hands are shaking slightly, she links her fingers to stop them.

"My cousin likes scaring people," she says quietly. "Has ever since he was a kid, I think."

She takes a shuddering breath.

"This one time he snuck into my cottage when I was sleeping. When I woke up, he was sitting on a chair in my bedroom, wearing some sort of night-vision goggles. And now, after what you just said . . ."

She reaches into one of her jacket pockets, pulls out a little object, and places it on the table.

Hill gasps. It is a small, unpainted plastic figure with no facial expression, identical to the one that he has.

"I found it in my underwear drawer this morning," she says, her voice trembling. "It wasn't there yesterday, I'm sure of it. He wanted to show me he'd been there, that he's watching me." She sniffs.

Hill stares at the two identical figures on the table.

"Here's what we're going to do," he says. "It's late, let's get some sleep. Tomorrow you'll tell all of this to my friend Leo Asker. She's a police officer."

Mya makes a horrified grimace.

"Not the police," she whispers. "He'll find out it was me. Please, anything but the police."

"Just take it easy," Hill says. "Leo will know what to do. He won't find out it was you."

"Are you sure?"

Hill nods.

Mya looks at him, as though trying to figure out whether he's trying to trick her. Then she casts a furtive glance at the plastic figures.

Hill sweeps them up and puts them in the kitchen drawer.

"You're safe here," he says with emphasis. "And tomorrow it'll all feel better."

MONDAY

ASKER

Asker leaves the house long before dawn. Checks the electric car's rear-view mirror every thirty seconds to make sure no one is trailing her.

This time she steers clear of the police garage. Instead parks on one of the side streets where she can make a quick getaway.

She has stocked up the car with binoculars, water, and a couple of protein bars. But she needs a few more things.

She collects her firearm and one of the two portable police radios that the Resources Unit has at its disposal. Then gives a loud knock on Enok Zafer's door. Just as she hoped, he's in early.

"I need help with something," she says. "Can you make this radio belong to a different department than ours? So that I can hear their group communications?"

The man peers at her over his glasses.

"Oh yes," he says. "Which department did you have in mind?"

"Serious Crime," she says.

Zafer gives her a long look, then takes a step to one side and throws out his arms.

"Come on in, it only takes a few minutes. And thanks for the help with the report. The director of technology hasn't been in touch."

"Great," says Asker. Almost feels a little bad for having tricked him.

SMILLA

Smilla wakes up with a strange feeling in her bones.

She has neither eaten nor drunk anything in a long time for fear of being drugged, and at first she thinks it's the hunger that is making her sick.

But gradually, as she lies there still in the darkness trying to gather her thoughts, she realizes that it's something else that she can feel.

A sort of tension in the air.

Of course, it could just be her imagination. Wishful thinking, pure fantasy.

But the feeling refuses to go away, instead gets only stronger.

Something big is on its way. She sneaks out of bed and heads over to the vent.

"Julia," she whispers. "Julia, are you there? I think something's happening!"

HILL

Hill dreams again, the same dream as the night before.

The model railway, those perfect small scenes brought to life by the train. Leo's house, the featureless figure creeping ever closer through the trees.

But something has changed. It is no longer Leo standing in the window of the big house, but Mya.

"He calls himself the Mountain King," a voice whispers in his ear. "He takes one thing and exchanges it for another. And he's getting closer."

He wakes up on the sofa. Tries to get back to sleep, but it's impossible.

He gets up. Peers out of the window. The street looks just as calm as usual.

He opens the curtains. Turns on the light above the kitchen countertop and drinks a glass of water.

The bedroom door is slightly ajar, which it wasn't when they went to bed. He walks over silently and peers through the crack to make sure that Mya is still there.

The room is dark, but enough light is seeping in from the kitchen for him to be able to see that she is lying in bed.

Her eyes are shut, her breaths slow, as though she is sleeping soundly.

He studies her for a few seconds while his eyes adjust to the darkness.

Without her heavy makeup and wary gaze, she looks even more vulnerable.

She stirs slightly in her sleep. He steps back quickly, so that she won't wake up and see him. Then goes back to the kitchen.

It is six a.m., so he puts on a cup of tea and flicks through the morning papers. Wonders again whether he should call Leo.

Decides that he has to at least wait until Mya is awake, so she doesn't think he's trying to trick her. Besides, he wants to have something concrete to share. To confirm who Mya's cousin is.

Just before seven, he hears her sneak into the bathroom.

He sets the table for breakfast. Bread, toppings, juice, yogurt. Even starts slicing some cucumber for open sandwiches.

Meanwhile he tries to decide on a tactic for the rest of their conversation.

Mya appears in the doorway. She looks more relaxed than the previous day.

"There's heart medicine in your bathroom cabinet," she says. "Are you sick?"

Hill raises his eyebrows.

"I didn't mean to pry," she says. "Thought you might have a spare toothbrush in there. You seemed like the type."

Hill buys the explanation.

"I've got a mechanical heart valve," he says. "Have to take blood thinners so it doesn't get blocked."

"Blood thinners. You should be careful with that then!"

She gestures at the knife he is holding in his hand.

"Naturally," Hill replies and deliberately gives the cucumber a violent chop, which brings a smile to her face.

The mood between them has lightened, he notes. As though a good night's sleep in a safe place has made her less paranoid.

That or she has simply decided to trust him.

This conclusion gives him a dose of courage.

He waits until she has had a little food, then gets straight to the point.

"Your cousin," he says.

She stiffens, her eyes go watchful again.

"Yeah . . ."

"Would you tell me his name?"

She shakes her head slowly.

"If *I* say a name then?"

It's not exactly a watertight approach, but he can't think of anything better.

Mya hesitates.

"Jakob Tell," he says slowly. "Works as a policeman in Hässle-holm."

She gulps. Gives him a long look that is both scared and curious. "H-how did you know?"

"Leo found out that Tell is Ulf Krook's stepson. The rest I pieced together myself. Ulf has a model workshop in his basement, and you rent your cottage from him."

Mya sits quietly for a long time. Then nods slowly.

"Jakob's a sick fuck," she mumbles. "I don't get how they let him become a cop."

Hill thinks about how Tell tried to force himself into Leo's house. The featureless, threatening figure in the dream who is drawing ever nearer to her house.

"So how can we prove that Jakob has something to do with MM and Smilla's disappearance?" he asks.

Mya goes quiet again. Immediately looks remorseful, as though she has said far too much.

"Don't know," she says bluntly. Her eyes are shifty, yesterday's fear is back.

"Can you think of anything that links him to MM? You mentioned something about some WhatsApp messages."

Mya bites her lip.

"He uses an alias on those things. Calls himself Berg. But I'm sure he's deleted all of that long ago. He's not stupid enough to use anything that can be traced."

"But you've seen them together at least . . ."

Mya interrupts.

"I'm not testifying against him, you can forget about that."

She looks at the clock.

"I've got to go now. The train for Stockholm leaves in half an hour."

"But you can't just leave," Hill protests. "We have to make sure Jakob gets put away."

Mya shrugs. Then stands up.

"Not my problem. I can see exactly where this is all headed. You want to push me into testifying against Jakob. But he's a cop, he'll find out straightaway. Besides, it's my word against his."

She puts her teacup in the sink and walks toward the front door. Hill goes after her.

"Please, stay a little longer. Can't we talk about this?"

Mya shakes her head.

"He's too smart. You haven't got a chance."

She starts tying up her boots.

"And in any case, it's not my problem. It's the police who should put a stop to Jakob, not me."

She stands up, picks up her sports bag.

Hill tries to think of something to say. If he doesn't stop her, in just a few seconds she'll be gone.

"Please, stay a little longer," he tries. "I'll call Leo, we can talk this through."

Mya pulls on her jacket. Her face has hardened, as though she was expecting him to betray her. Was prepared for it.

Just like Leo. The very thought of her gives him a stab in the gut.

"Thanks for letting me crash here. Bye!"

She turns around and puts her hand on the door handle. Her jacket still has wet patches over the shoulders from the rain. Suddenly Hill has a thought. The words he read in Sandgren's blueprints.

"The cave rain," he says. "Was that where he was taking MM?" It's a wild guess, a last-ditch clutch at straws. But it's the best he has.

Mya stiffens, then slowly turns to face him. Her face has gone pale.

"H-how the fuck do you know about the cave rain?"

"MM told me about it," says Hill, which is partly true. He's been given a chance, a little opening that he might just be able to coax further if he just treads carefully.

"Have you been there?" she asks. "In the mountain?"

"No," he says. "Not yet," he adds, since he senses that it's important. "But I've seen the plans."

A white lie. The word was scribbled over several different plans, and he doesn't know which one it referred to. But Mya doesn't need to know that. What matters is that she doesn't leave.

Mya gives a pained sigh.

"You see . . . The mountain is his secret place. I've only been there once. It's creepy as fuck."

"Did Jakob take MM there?" he asks again.

She licks her lips nervously.

"I don't know. Maybe."

"Can we go there?" Hill asks. "See if there are any traces of him?"

Mya goes even paler.

"No way. Not a chance in hell!"

She looks over her shoulder, as though considering whether to make a run for it. Hill touches her arm.

"There might be something there," he says gingerly. "Some kind of proof that can link Jakob to MM. Or lead us to Smilla. What if she's still alive, Mya?"

Mya squirms. He can see the thoughts churning in her head.

"We can go there right now," he says. "I'll ask Leo to check that Jakob's at work. I'm sure she'll want to come with us."

"No," Mya says firmly. "It's dangerous."

"Not if we make sure that Jakob's at work! Then we can search the place uninterrupted. And if we find anything, Leo will arrest him. You won't have to be a witness, and Jakob will get put away. You'll be safe."

He gives as gentle a smile as he can muster. Touches her arm again.

"And I'll be right there with you."

Mya purses her lips, looks around shiftily. Clearly what she most wants to do is get out of there.

But his social superpowers gradually overcome her resistance.

"Think of Smilla," he says once more.

Mya sighs again. Throws up her hands as though she gives in.

"OK," she says. "But we have to be completely sure that Jakob can't show up."

ASKER

Asker is sitting at the ready when the cars drive through the gates. Three unmarked cars from Serious Crime. Two police vans carrying tactical firearms units. Over the police radio that Zafer has fiddled with she can hear them discussing the operation.

"One of the suspects was there last night," says an officer who is already on-site. "He left at around twenty-two hundred hours. We expect someone to arrive at the premises within the next hour."

The convoy makes their way out of town, with Asker following them at a distance.

After around fifteen minutes of weaving down small streets, they arrive at a meeting point on the outskirts of an industrial estate.

Asker parks a ways off. Looks on through binoculars as the tactical units unload bags of equipment. Heavy protective vests, automatic weapons, helmets fitted with cameras. Clearly they are preparing for every eventuality. And why not? Hellman and his team are expecting a run-in with violent kidnappers.

She sees him speaking to the operation commander and the two unit leaders. They are studying something that she guesses is a map of a building, agreeing on a plan of attack.

Reluctantly she admits to herself that she's a little anxious. What if he's right after all? If he finds Smilla, becomes a hero, lands Rodic's job as chief of Serious Crime.

She shakes off the thought.

"A car is approaching," says one of the surveillance team. "Linking you up to the video feed."

Asker swears inwardly. She would have given almost anything to be able to watch the video feed, but as it is she will just have to content herself with the audio.

"A Mazda, the same as yesterday. Three people in the car," says the officer. "It's pulled to a stop in front of the premises."

"Copy," Hellman acknowledges. "Confirm as soon as you can that it's the suspects."

"A woman has stepped out of the car," the voice continues. "She's looking around. Seems nervous."

"Do you think she's spotted you?"

"No, we're in the building diagonally opposite. We've put tinted solar film on the windows so they can't see in. But she's nervous. The two others are still in the car. You should now be able to see the video feed."

"Yes, we've got it, but there's a slight lag, so go on describing what you see."

The radio goes silent for a few seconds. Asker listens on tenterhooks.

"OK, two men have stepped out of the car," the voice says. "They are nervous, too. Constantly looking around. The woman has lit a cigarette. Now another car is approaching. A dark Volvo that we haven't seen before."

Another silence.

"Now the Volvo has driven past. The suspects watched it for a long time and appear to be discussing it. It looked a little like an unmarked police car, so that may be why."

The radio crackles. Then the surveillance officer's voice returns.

"It looks like there's a quarrel. The woman's waving her arms in frustration. Now she's moved to one side, is still smoking. One of the men has unlocked the doors and entered. The other is still outside, waiting for the woman."

"OK," says Hellman. "Then let's prepare for entry. Let's aim to strike at ten-thirty."

Asker looks at the clock. That's over an hour from now. Although she knows they want to give themselves time to ensure there's no risk of Smilla coming to any harm, she sighs. Why not just get it done?

She sinks down in her seat, goes on watching Hellman and his team through the binoculars. A cup of coffee wouldn't have gone unappreciated.

Her phone rings. Hill's number.

"Hi, Martin," she answers.

"Hi," he says with a quiet yet eager voice. "Mya's here at my place. She's showering now, so she can't hear us."

He quickly recounts Mya's story.

"It's just as we thought. Tell has a secret place that he uses as bait. Supposedly there *is* cave rain there, just like Sandgren scribbled on the plans. If we're lucky, there'll be some kind of evidence there that can tie Tell to MM, Smilla, or one of the others."

The radio sounds, but then goes quiet again.

"Mya can show us how to get there," Hill goes on. "How soon can you be here?"

Asker bites her lip.

There is still over an hour to go until the raid. If she leaves now, she'll miss everything.

"I'm just in the middle of something," she says. "Can we hold off? Just a few hours?"

"I don't think so," Hill replies. "If we drag this out, I'm afraid Mya will get cold feet. She's terrified of Tell, has already talked about getting out of here."

"Shit!" Asker hisses. She can see Hellman swaggering around down there. Confident, arrogant, surrounded by admirers.

They all betrayed her, sided with him.

Her colleagues, her boss, her own mother.

Soon they are going to find out just how wrong that decision was.

She wants to be there, wants to see it happen. Deserves that much.

"We can go on our own," says Hill. "I can borrow a friend's car."

"No way!" says Asker. "What if Tell turns up?"

"You can check that he's at work. If we're sure about that, then we aren't in any danger."

The police radio crackles to life once again; the heat is rising ahead of the raid.

"Just a quick look!" says Hill. "We have to take this chance."

More radio chatter now; clearly they are starting to prepare.

"OK," she says reluctantly. "I'll make a few calls. Don't do anything until I've confirmed that Tell is at the office in Hässleholm. Find out where the place is and then wait for me, and I'll be there as soon as I can, OK?"

"Got it, Chief," Hill says with a smile in his voice. "And don't worry, we won't take any unnecessary risks."

HILL

Despite his promise, Hill doesn't dare wait for Asker to call back before setting off. Mya is anxious and fidgety, from time to time still looks like she might do a runner at any second.

He fetches his friend's car, picks up Mya, and heads north as fast as he can, counting on the fact that Asker will call them along the way.

They don't talk so much. Mya is mostly fiddling with her phone.

Hill tests out the car radio, flicks past a few channels before finding anything worth listening to.

The landscape north of Lund is marked by rolling hills. Fields and wind farms that give way to broad-leaved woodland around Ringsjön Lake. The sky is overcast.

Gradually the conifers take over. Replace the autumnal colors with bluey-green shades. Deep shadows that creep in ever closer around the road.

The text message from Asker arrives after about half an hour, when they are just north of Hörby.

Tell has management training today until 4 pm. I've double-checked and he's definitely there. A colleague on-site will let me know if Tell leaves the station. I reckon I'll be finished here in an hour or so.

Hill reads the message aloud to Mya. She just gives a grim nod.

"It's not so far now, is it?" he asks, mostly to get the conversation going. "To the mountain."

"Not particularly," she says. Goes on fiddling with her phone.

"When were you there last?" he asks.

"A year or so ago, I think. Maybe longer."

"How did he find the place, anyway?"

She looks up.

"I don't really know. I think he found it when he was a kid. But the entrance was sealed with concrete, so it's been empty a long time. The bottom's full of water."

She goes quiet, looks through the window.

They go on in silence for a while.

"Martin," she says eventually. "When all this is over. Would you like to go on a date with me?"

The question throws him. Her tone, too. Grave, exposed.

He can't come up with any better response than to try to laugh it off.

"Aren't I a little old for you?"

She doesn't reply, just goes on looking out the window.

"Turn here," she says after another five minutes, pointing toward a side road.

After a while she points out a second, and a third.

With every turning the roads get smaller and narrower.

Eventually they reach a logging road that's barely more than two wheel tracks with a strip of grass down the middle, full of potholes filled with brown water. The forest curves in on both sides. Extends green fingers that sweep against the sides of the car in warning.

The logging road ends at a little turning circle.

"Here!" she says tensely. "We'll have to walk a little way from here."

ASKER

Down at the meeting point the tension is ramping up. Asker's former colleagues from Serious Crime are pacing around nervously, while the tactical units have donned their protective vests and helmets and await the order to get on the move.

The surveillance team go on providing updates over the radio.

"All three suspects are in the building. Still no sign of the hostage."

Hellman is talking to the operation commander. Both men have steely looks on their faces. Through the binoculars Asker sees them shake hands; they seem to have made some kind of decision.

Seconds later the tactical units start loading up their vehicles.

Her phone starts to ring. Not Hill, as expected, but a private number.

"Hello, my name's Sebastian Collin. You left me a voicemail?"

It takes Asker a few seconds to place the name. Julia's big brother.

"Yes, that's right, thank you for calling back."

"No problem. Sorry it's taken a while, I was out of the country. I'm assuming this is about Julia."

"It is," says Asker.

Down at the meeting point, the units start to pull off.

"I've spoken to your mother and to Robert."

"Right." It may just be her imagination, but his tone sounds curt, perhaps even suspicious. Asker decides to get straight to the point.

"After my visit I came across an anonymous police tip-off and a social services inquiry into Robert. He was accused of violence toward both your mother and Julia."

The line goes silent for a few seconds. Down at the meeting point Hellman and his team are also jumping into their cars.

"I'm guessing my mom told you about the amazing Julia," Sebastian says. "Good grades, a bright future, and all that."

"Something along those lines, yes," Asker confirms.

He sighs.

"My mom talks about Julia like she was a saint. Refuses to say anything against her. But the fact is . . ."

He pauses, as though the words are painful to say.

"The fact is, my sister was a complicated person."

"In what way?"

"Julia idolized our father. She took his death very hard, and never accepted Mom remarrying. She was the one who made those complaints. Robert has never been violent toward either her or our mother, I can promise you."

Asker frowns.

"So you mean to say she lied to social services and the police, just to create problems for Ulrika's new husband?"

"Julia hated Robert," he replies. "I mean really *hated* him. But my mom won't let anyone say a peep about that. Not even Robert, who was the one in the firing line. I'm guessing you haven't heard the babysitting stories, either."

"No," says Asker. "Or, I know she babysat some of the neighbors' kids."

"She did. When she was fifteen, sixteen. But that came to an abrupt end when a bunch of the kids started getting nightmares. Turns out Julia would tell them scary stories and then lock them in a dark room to scare the shit out of them. Threatened to beat them up if they told on her."

"Why are you telling me this?"

"Because I'm sick of pretending Julia was a fucking saint. She was smart and funny, but she was also manipulative and could even be downright cruel. But no one ever wants to talk about that side of her, especially not since she disappeared."

The last cars at the meeting point start pulling away, and Asker is keen to follow them.

"I'm sorry, but I'm afraid I have to go. Thank you for calling," she says to Julia's big brother as she pulls out.

"No problem. I hope it's helpful," Sebastian says.

"Of course," says Asker, more out of habit than conviction.

She ends the call and follows Hellman's team at a suitable distance. Her heart has started to pound all the harder.

HILL

Mya leads Hill up a long slope. The spruce forest is dense, interrupted only now and then by dashes of yellow from young birches. The ground is slippery with dead leaves, and he slips a few times. Is slightly out of breath when they reach the top.

They are farther from civilization than he initially expected, and he wishes he had brought his trusty UE backpack with him. But it's far too late to turn back now.

"Almost there," says Mya, pointing at a dense thicket flanked by large boulders.

They round the thicket and find themselves standing before a low concrete bunker with big wire cages filled with rubble instead of windows. Hill has seen similar constructions before. Knows that the bunker itself is a kind of enormous air filter that is often a feature of military bases.

"This is the top entrance," says Mya. "At the bottom there's a big gateway that leads straight into the rock, but like I said, it's sealed with concrete, so this is the only way in."

She rounds the bunker. Part of the wall is in fact a concrete blast door that is slightly ajar. Reveals a dark, one-and-a-half-foot-wide opening.

Mya looks around nervously.

"The door's open. It isn't usually."

Hill stops, gets out his phone to call Leo.

Bad reception, which is hardly surprising.

He walks over to the gap in the door. Humid air is streaming out of it. If there is a tunnel at the bottom, as Mya claims, and this is the upper air inlet, the conditions could very well be perfect for cave rain.

"What time is it?" she asks, and he takes out his phone again.

"Almost ten-thirty. We've got plenty of time."

"OK." She appears to take heart. "Shall we go inside?"

Hill hesitates, looks around. He promised Asker to wait until she arrived.

He should go back to the car, find a place where he can call her and let her know where he is. But he hasn't told Mya about that part of the plan yet. And if he does, she might change her mind. Tell is at work, and he has to admit that the prospect of seeing cave rain does appeal. It's almost calling out to him.

When he turns his head back to the bunker, he sees Mya slip in through the opening. After another few seconds' hesitation, he follows.

The space inside is small. Thirty square feet at most. Floor, walls, and ceiling in rock and concrete. In the middle of the floor there is a round hole, the frame of an in-built steel caged ladder sticking out of it. A faint waft of air from below brings with it a dark, damp smell of rock.

Hill pulls his flashlights out of his jacket pocket and hands her one of them. Then bends over and shines his flashlight down the ladder. It continues deep down into the rock, appears to pass a number of chambers on the way.

Mya has already started climbing.

Hill follows. Checks each rung before putting his full weight on it, to minimize the risk of cutting himself. The rungs are galvanized, but in some spots the rust has eaten into them regardless, leaving the surface speckled with brown.

As he descends, he sweeps his flashlight over the rock walls.

No graffiti, he notes. That means few outsiders can have been here since the base was closed down. Time has almost stood still here for what must have been fifty years, perhaps even more.

The thought is fascinating, which makes his mechanical heart work harder, as usual.

Mya goes on climbing down, into the darkness.

The third room they pass through is bigger than the ones above.

Hill glances up over his shoulder. They must be fifty feet down in the mountain now. He can physically feel it. As though all the thousands of tons of rock above them make the air thicker, more loaded. He loves that feeling.

By the time they are down in the fourth room, Hill has figured out the pattern.

Each room is a copy of the one above, only enlarged. The higher you go the smaller the room; the same is true of the hole around the ladder.

The contracting size of both the rooms and the holes toward the bunker creates a draft through the mountain, like an enormous chimney.

The air swelling up from the heart of the mountain gets damper the farther they descend.

There might actually be cave rain here.

"Come on!" Mya says anxiously.

In the fourth room the steel ladder comes to an abrupt end. It appears to have been cut with an angle grinder. An easy and not all too uncommon trick for preventing access, not unlike removing the handles from a door.

Instead, someone has replaced it with an ordinary portable metal ladder, which leads them down the last stretch and into a space with an opening on one wall.

Hill estimates they must be at least a hundred feet down now. Maybe even more.

The air is so humid that his skin is wet.

Mya takes the lead again. Shines the flashlight at the opening that is in fact a passage.

"This way."

The passage slopes downward, the pebbles in the crushed stone flooring bounce around their feet.

They enter at one end of an enormous cavern.

It must be three hundred feet long and fifty feet wide, and at its far end stands an enormous stone gateway. The water trickles down one of the monumental walls, turning most of the floor into a pool. Immediately in front of Hill lies a railway track, which is gradually submerged by the water as it travels toward the gateway, before eventually disappearing completely under the surface.

Along the right-hand side of the track runs a sixty-foot-long loading bay, here and there dotted with what look like the marks of an open fire. Two rusty-brown steel doors up on the bay appear to lead deeper into the mountain, toward new rooms.

Hill sweeps his flashlight up at the ceiling. The draft from the giant chimney they have descended through is so strong that it sucks up the moist air along the ground. Forms small, but fully visible droplets of water in the flashlight beam.

"Cave rain," he mumbles, awestruck.

It is more beautiful than he imagined. The droplets of moisture glitter in the light, hover, almost weightless, in the air, like tiny, glistening crystals.

He snaps a few shots on his cell. Wishes he had brought a real camera with him that would have done the phenomenon more justice. MM was right. This place could definitely feature in a new book.

Mya has stopped and is waiting for him, but she is clearly struggling to keep still.

"Come on, I don't want to be here any longer than I have to. This way. There's another area."

She pulls him along toward the steel door on the left of the loading bay.

It's heavy, the hinges creak dimly before giving way.

The door turns out to be one of two identical doors one after the other, creating an airlock of sorts.

A faint puff of air hits them when they open the second door. The air on the other side of the airlock is much less humid, it smells of iron and something else raw and musty that Hill can't quite put his finger on.

On the other side of the doors he finds a sixty-foot-long corridor with painted green doors along both sides. At the end of the corridor shines a red light that suggests, surprisingly enough, that there is still functioning electricity in the base.

The contrast with the great cavern is striking. Hill snaps another few shots on his cell.

Mya gestures at him to go first.

He runs his flashlight over the concrete floor. After just a couple feet he sees that the corridor doesn't end at the light, but rather takes a sharp right and continues deeper into the darkness.

He stops, listens. Mya does the same.

It's dead silent in here. No dripping water, like out in the cave.

A sort of mute silence, broken only by their breath and the faint but fully audible click of Hill's mechanical heart.

He continues, steps up to the first door.

Like the corridor, it looks surprisingly normal to be situated deep within a mountain. A green door with flaking paint. The metal underneath hasn't rusted, as the humidity here is much lower than in the rest of the mountain. The door handle has a fifties style, no lock, seal, or any kind of warning sign. Nothing that in any way suggests danger.

A normal door.

And yet it is as though a little alarm bell has started ringing in Hill's head.

At first faintly, then louder and louder as he approaches the door.

It merges with the ever-faster pounding of his mechanical heart.

Until now this mountain has mainly inspired fascination within him. That same curiosity and eagerness that he always feels around abandoned places.

Not to mention his awe at the beautiful cave rain.

But those feelings are suddenly gone, replaced by something else, something amplified by the red light glaring at them from the corner of the corridor.

An unpleasant inkling that he shouldn't be in this place; that he shouldn't open this door.

Nana Hill would have told him to follow his instincts. Turn around, take Mya with him, go back to the ladder, and climb up it as fast as they can, no looking back. Get far away from this dark place.

But before he can finish the thought, Mya presses the door handle and opens the door.

Hill looks inside. The room is perhaps eighty square feet. The walls are lined with shelves, which in turn are filled with glass jars in meticulous rows.

Hundreds of jars of different sizes, with small holes in the lids.

Hill has never seen anything like it. He shines his flashlight over the jars in fascination. They all contain the same thing. Only the size of the bodies and the faded color of their paper-thin wings distinguish one from the next.

At the bottom of each jar lies a lone, dead butterfly.

"What the hell is this?" he gasps and turns around to Mya.

But the corridor behind him is silent and black.

ASKER

For some reason the raid has been delayed, but it is due to take place any minute.

With the help of an obliging security guard, Asker has managed to access a nearby rooftop where she can watch what is going on through her binoculars, without being detected herself.

The building that Hellman and his gang are interested in is a single-storey property on the edge of the industrial estate. On the front an entry door and two windows, at the back a freight container and loading bay with an industrial sliding door. The sun-bleached sign outside claims that the tenant is an import firm. In actual fact the place looks boarded up.

Asker holds her binoculars to her eyes. The car that the surveillance team mentioned is still out front. At the back of the building, one tactical unit is creeping cautiously toward the loading bay. One of the officers appears to be arming something on the sliding door.

"Alpha 2 is in place," the unit leader informs them.

"Good," the commander acknowledges. "Alpha 1, proceed."

Now one of the police vans comes rolling down the street. The unit is standing on footrests along the sides of the van, holding on to the roof rack with one hand, their automatic weapons with the other. Asker's heart beats even faster.

When it reaches the parked car, the driver slams on the brakes and the unit surges toward the entrance.

"Alpha 2, proceed!" the leader commands.

A brief clap is heard as the lock on the sliding door is blown off. The door opens and Alpha 2 storms the premises from the back.

As this happens, plainclothes policemen arrive with their weapons drawn, covering all four of the building's walls in case anyone attempts to make a getaway.

Asker hunches up slightly, doesn't want to be seen or, even worse, taken for a co-conspirator.

She hears loud cries, followed by a bang and a flash of light that must be from the distraction grenades that the tactical units love.

More cries, then the radio crackles into life.

"Alpha 1, premises secured," one of the unit leaders announces. "We have three detained."

"And the hostage?" she hears Hellman ask. "Have we found her?"

"We're looking for her now."

Asker's phone starts to ring. Without taking her eyes from the binoculars, she holds her phone to her ear. Assumes that it's Hill.

"Are you there? Where is it?"

"Uh," says a self-conscious voice that definitely doesn't belong to Hill. "This is Granqvist, Hässleholm Police."

"Ah," says Asker, still not tearing her eyes away.

"Look, I just passed the conference room upstairs, and apparently Tell went home a little while ago. Apparently something urgent. He must have snuck out the back door, since I didn't see him leave."

Asker's blood runs cold. She lowers the binoculars.

"How long ago?" she asks.

"I don't know, it could even be as much as an hour, I think," the man says sheepishly. "Sorry!"

He ends the call abruptly.

"Shit!" she hisses to herself. The chill builds within her.

Quickly she dials Martin's number.

"Pick up, pick up, pick up," she mumbles.

The phone clicks.

"Hi, this is Martin Hill, I'm afraid I can't take your call . . ."

She hangs up, tries again.

But the result is the same.

Martin Hill cannot be reached.

HILL

"Mya!" Hill cries.

His voice bounces off the corridor's concrete walls.

"Mya!"

He shines the flashlight around. A few short seconds ago she was behind him. Now she has been swallowed up by the darkness.

Has she got cold feet? Been struck by the same violent apprehensions as him? But then why not say something?

He shines his flashlight down the corridor, but, just like before, it reveals only smooth walls, a row of green doors, and a dusty floor.

Around the corner, beyond the red eye of light, the darkness closes in on everything tightly.

No Mya.

Hill feels the hairs on the back of his neck rise toward his collar.

His heart valve is now a drumroll.

"Mya," he tries again. His voice falters.

He has visited many similar buildings before. Military bunkers, inoperative factories, hospitals, abandoned cabins. Some of them pretty creepy. But none of them have scared him as much as this place does now.

He shines his flashlight around the room again. A macabre collection of dead butterflies.

And yet this is only what is lurking behind the first of the corridor's green doors. What is behind the others?

Who is waiting in the darkness around the corner?

The drumroll from his valve rattles against his chest.

His Nana Hill instinct finally takes over.

He turns around and walks, faster and faster, toward the doors they came in through. Quickly shuts both doors behind him and goes back out into the grotto. The beam from his flashlight wanders over the walls, bringing up ghostly shadows in every direction. The cave rain is no longer beautiful; instead it looks cold, unpleasant.

A sound makes him instinctively look over his shoulder.

He stumbles on a rock, throws his hands up, and manages to land on his knees, but the flashlight flies out of his grip. Lands with a splash in the pool that covers most of the cave's floor.

He leaps after the flashlight, plunges his hands into the ice-cold water, and grabs hold of it again. Luckily it is still shining. His hands and knees are still in one piece, too. No sign of bleeding, and that at least is a relief.

A stone clatters down the cave walls and lands in the water just a couple feet away. The sound brings him back to his feet.

He starts running. The flashlight flickers a few times, but is still shining. He races through the passage, up into the room with the ladder at the base of the shaft. In just a few seconds he'll be on his way out of here. On his way back up to the light.

But as he nears the spot below the opening in the ceiling, he sees that something is wrong.

The portable metal ladder is gone.

His flashlight flickers again.

Then cuts out abruptly.

ASKER

Asker has tried to call Martin at least ten times. Sent him three mes-sages to tell him that wherever he is, he has to get out of there. Now, right away, before Jakob Tell arrives.

But his phone is still going straight to voicemail and her texts are going unanswered. Not the slightest confirmation that he has gotten her warning. She has even called Enok Zafer. Asked him to trace Hill's and Tell's cellphones and get in touch as soon as he has found their positions.

But what to do until then?

Hellman and his gang are on their way toward the building that the tactical units have now secured. She hears them chattering excitedly over the radio. Taking their victory for granted.

She would dearly love to run in there, too.

Witness the moment when Hellman realizes he's wrong. Realizes that the investigation he elbowed her out of has completely derailed, and that he has no fucking clue where Smilla Holst is, or who might be behind her disappearance.

Look him in the eyes as he picks up the phone and calls Isabel to explain that everything has gone to shit and she backed the wrong horse.

Asker looks through the binoculars again. Hellman's car rounds the corner with screeching tires.

He is in the front seat; she sees the arrogant smirk on his face.

And somewhere else, Jakob Tell is on his way to Martin Hill and Mya's whereabouts.

May already be there.

"Fuck, fuck, fuck!"

She lowers the binoculars. Then turns and runs for the stairs.

HILL

Hill's phone may have no reception down here in the mountain, but at least it offers some light.

He empties the batteries from his flashlight and dries them off on his sweater while trying to gather his thoughts.

Someone must have removed the ladder—it's the only plausible explanation. Stranded him down here in the darkness.

The sound of a fifteen-foot metal ladder scraping against a concrete rim should have echoed loudly through the cave, but he didn't hear a peep. So the ladder must have been pulled up while he and Mya were in the corridor on the other side of the two insulation doors.

But if Mya didn't get out using the ladder, then where has she gone? And how can he get out of here himself?

He tries putting the batteries back in the flashlight and pressing the button.

Nothing happens.

The dread from before is still lingering at the back of his neck. The feeling that someone—or something—is lying in wait for him in the darkness, ready to leap on him at any moment.

He holds up his phone. The little flashlight offers only a couple feet of LED light, which is at least enough for him to confirm that he is alone in the room, which quiets his heart just a bit.

He needs a plan to get himself out of here. First of all, he must take stock of his resources. He feels around in the pockets of his jacket and jeans. Besides his cellphone and busted flashlight, he has a penknife, a few coins, two receipts, and a couple of the rectangular sleeve adapters that he brought on the expedition with Sofie and forgot to put back in his backpack. Plus his wallet, a pair of gloves, and the keys to the car he borrowed.

Water is no problem, but the cold and humidity will soon be. His jacket sleeves, knees, and shoes are wet after his hunt for the fallen flashlight, the cave rain has left the rest of his clothes and hair damp, and he is already shivering faintly from both cold and fear.

He is stuck deep down here in this mountain, a place that no one has visited in years.

No one but the serial killer Jakob Tell and Mya, who has now vanished without a trace.

So how can he get out?

The hole in the ceiling is too high for him to reach.

Mya claimed that the stone gateway in the cavern was sealed with concrete, and in order to reach it and check if that's true, he would have to wade through the ice-cold water.

Which leaves only that sinister corridor.

The air in there is dry, and he felt a puff of air when they opened the second door. So it must have its own supply of fresh air. Perhaps even an exit?

With just under 50 percent battery left on his phone and feeling ever colder, he can't take too long to decide.

He gets to his feet, shines his phone flashlight up at the hole in the ceiling one last time. But he has no other option.

The corridor is his only chance.

Cautiously he returns to the cave. The faint light of his phone bounces off the large surface of water and the droplets of moisture in the air. All he can hear is the drip of water. A few short minutes ago he found this place so beautiful, but now it only makes him all the more unsettled.

He walks through the second of the doors. The draft of air hits him again. Rock, iron, and that third scent that he can't identify.

The red eye is still lit. Stares maliciously at him from the end of the corridor. He tries to stay calm.

There is an exit somewhere, he has to convince himself of that.

Suppress every other feeling, ignore the hundreds of jars of dead butterflies and the thought of what sort of person could have put them there.

He walks up to the next door. With any luck this one will be his way out of here.

His route away from the red eye, and the turning where the corridor plunges into darkness.

The door is unlocked.

Inside is another room, this one also filled with shelves.

No jars this time, but small wooden drawers instead.

Hill can't help but peer inside them.

They are full of trinkets.

Cheap jewelry, stone ornaments, underwear, tie clips, scrunchies, makeup accessories, foreign coins, even a rearview mirror.

He remembers Mya calling this place creepy as fuck, which is one almighty understatement.

On one of the shelves stand row upon row of small, unpainted plastic figures without facial features. All identical to the figure he himself found. He shudders. But he has to go on. Somewhere there's an exit.

An answer to where Mya has gone.

He reaches the third door. This one is slightly different from the others, he notes. Has a bolt on the outside, among other things.

His sense of unease swells even more than before.

Makes his heart valve start pattering once again.

But he has no choice—has to find the exit if there is one.

So he puts his hand on the bolt.

HELLMAN

Detective Superintendent Jonas Hellman is out of the car almost before it has stopped.

He bounds up the front steps to the building in two great strides. Behind him follows his right-hand man Eskil and the rest of the team, all with tense, expectant faces.

Inside the door is a small reception area filled with debris, collapsed boxes, and various clutter left behind when the previous tenant moved out.

The double doors to the warehouse are wide open. An officer in full riot gear is standing in the doorway. Takes one step to the side and waves them through.

The warehouse space covers roughly three hundred square feet. There are no windows, and only half of the fluorescent tubes in the ceiling work. They just about muster enough light to illuminate a few empty shelves, a pile of pallets, and a heap of sacks filled with random scraps.

The room is heaving with tactical officers. Three people are lying chest-down on the concrete floor with their hands cuffed behind their backs.

Eskil walks over to them.

"They're our suspects," he confirms, stating the obvious.

Eskil might not be the sharpest officer in Malmö, but he's a loyal foot soldier. Hellman had noticed that even before he was assigned the Holst case.

One of the ones who never betrayed him, not even when Leo Asker stabbed him in the back and got him exiled. But now his revenge is complete. Leo has wound up down in the basement among the loons and HR nightmares. Her attempts to undermine him with her own theories have also failed, and now he is within reach of cracking the Holst case. Of pinching the post of chief of Serious Crime from under her nose, while also making powerful allies among Malmö's elite. That one of the most important of them also happens to be Leo's own mother makes the revenge all the more sweet. The only thing that could make it better would be if Leo were here to witness his triumph with her own eyes.

"Have you found Smilla?" he asks the commander, who comes to locate him.

"Not yet, but there's a locked security door at one end of the premises. We waited to break it open until you were on-site."

"Excellent!"

Hellman turns to the suspects. Two men and one woman, all around twenty-five years of age.

"Which one of you has the key?" he asks authoritatively.

One of the men writhes around on the floor.

"Is it you?"

The man raises his head. He is bleeding from a gash in his cheek.

"Don't know what you're on about," he says. "We haven't done anything."

The others look away, don't appear to agree on that point.

Hellman walks over to the woman. Pokes her with the toe of his shoe.

"The key," he says. "Tell me who has it and we'll get you on your feet and out of those cuffs."

"Him!" The woman nods at the man who just spoke.

The latter spews out a harangue of swear words and insults, but abruptly falls silent when Eskil puts his knee over his neck and starts emptying his pockets.

"Here!" Eskil holds up a bunch of keys triumphantly.

"Help her up," says Hellman to a couple of the riot police. "But the cuffs stay on."

He nods at the commander.

"Show me the door!"

They walk over to the darkest corner of the building. Round a forklift charger with a big, red warning light.

Yet another riot officer is keeping guard outside the security door. An automatic weapon hangs from a strap around his chest.

"Look out for rats. Some of the rubbish bags have food in them." The riot officer points at a pile of rubbish bags a couple feet away.

Hellman's pulse is pounding all the harder. The moment has arrived now. His triumph is close.

He signals to Eskil to open the door. Holds his breath as the key is put in the lock.

The riot officer raises his automatic weapon.

SMILLA

She is woken by a voice, she is certain of it.

Or even more than one?

Julia might have known, but she hasn't replied to her in a long time. Is asleep, presumably. Julia doesn't seem to care that their food is full of sleeping pills and that the Mountain King is lurking in the dark. Perhaps because all this time in captivity has dulled it all.

The only thing Smilla knows with certainty is that the tension she felt in the air earlier has risen. The feeling that something is coming is now so strong it's almost tangible.

She gets to her feet, walks over to the door, puts her ear up to it.

She hears something.

A faint scratch.

She presses her ear even closer to the door.

There is someone out there.

She takes a few terrified steps back.

The door opens without warning. A white light hits her.

Burns her eyes, forces her to throw her hands in front of her face.

She backs away. Cries out—in pain, in fear.

"Smilla?" says a soft voice. "Smilla, it's OK."

HELLMAN

Jonas Hellman is still holding his breath when the security door opens.

The darkness within is compact, but diffuses as soon as the riot officer activates the light on his weapon.

The room is perhaps twenty square feet. Contains a camera tripod and the black fabric background that appeared in the ransom video.

Nothing else.

A shudder runs through Hellman's belly. The sort of sinking feeling you get from standing on the edge of a precipice.

"Are there any other rooms?" he asks the operation commander. "Any other locked spaces?"

He hears the tension in his own voice, but is powerless to do anything about it. The commander shakes his head.

"We've combed the whole building. This was the only space we couldn't search straightaway."

Hellman bites his lip. The eyes of his team, of basically every police officer on-site, are burning at the back of his neck.

He strides back over to the three detainees, grabs the arm of the young woman who has been allowed to take a seat on a stack of pallets.

"Where's Smilla?" he hisses.

"How the fuck should I know?" she says. "We don't know her. Only her boyfriend."

"Malik Mansur?"

The woman nods.

"MM's a good guy. It was fucking shitty of you to accuse him. And then he got murdered. So we thought you could pay damages."

Hellman can feel the inside of his temples starting to boil.

The sinking feeling intensifies.

"If you've hidden her somewhere and aren't telling us . . . ," he hisses. "If anything happens to her—"

"But I've already told you." The woman cuts him off with a crooked grin. "We don't have her. We've never had her, don't you get it?"

Hellman tries to gather his thoughts.

"You . . ." He gulps. "You faked that you had her?"

"Exactly," the woman says with a nod. "We planned to share the money with MM's family, I swear."

Hellman pinches the bridge of his nose.

In a matter of seconds the rug has been pulled out from under him, revealing a pit that threatens to swallow his entire career. Decimate everything he has worked so hard for, for years.

There is only one thing he can do. One single way to save face.

He straightens up, makes an effort to seem unperturbed.

"Write them up and we'll meet you back at the station," he says to the commander, with as much composure as he can muster. Then he walks calmly back out of the premises while getting out his phone.

"Isabel," he says with hard-fought assurance when the woman answers. "Jonas Hellman here. We've detained the people behind the ransom video. Unfortunately it turned out to be a hoax. But it goes without saying that we have allowed for every eventuality and have been exploring another lead in parallel, which we will now—"

Isabel Lissander says something sharp that Hellman only half hears. Instead he presses the mute button and waves Eskil over.

"Get me someone who knows what the fuck Leo Asker is working on," he barks. "I want to know what she's done, who she's met, and where she is. Everything! Now!"

HILL

"Smilla," Hill says again, as calmly as he can.

The young woman looks panic-stricken, covers her eyes with the back of her hand.

He moves the light away from her face.

"My name's Martin Hill, I'm here to help you."

She lowers her arms, stares at him incredulously.

Smilla is pale, her eyes swollen, her body unnaturally thin. But her gaze is alert, and after just a few seconds she appears to take in what he is saying.

"Martin Hill? MM's teacher?"

"The very same," he says.

A sound from the corridor makes Hill whip around.

He raises his phone light, takes a step toward the door.

But he doesn't make it in time to stop the door from slamming shut in his face.

The bolt clatters outside.

They are locked in.

ASKER

Asker is speeding north as fast as she dares.

Hill's phone is off, and all Zafer could get was the rough area he was in when it last had a signal.

As already suspected, the area turned out to be in the Hässleholm region.

Jakob Tell's phone is also off, and hasn't been on since just after he left the police station in Hässleholm, which is a bad sign. The good news is that at that point he was driving eastward, so not in Hill's direction. But that could obviously have changed.

What she wants to do is call the duty commissioner and have all available units sent out to find and arrest Tell. But she still has no concrete proof that he is the Mountain King, and in a case as strange as this, circumstantial evidence and gut instinct won't cut it.

She thinks of what Martin said about Tell's secret den.

Sandgren had written the words *cave rain* on some of his drawings, so he must have been on his way to pinpointing where it was.

Perhaps that was why Tell decided to get him out of the way? What would he then do to Hill if he were to catch him snooping around that very place?

She could go back to HQ. Try to narrow down which base is most likely.

But she doesn't have time for guessing games.

There might be another way of reaching Tell, a more immediate way.

She calls Daniel Nygård. Has to try a few times before the technician picks up.

"Have you got the broken camera from the model?" she asks before he can even get out a greeting.

"No, not yet. I thought I'd get it later today."

"I need you to do it now. I'm on my way to you."

The line goes silent for a few seconds.

"I mean, I'm on another job. And like I explained, I don't know if we'll be able to extract anything."

"It's urgent," she says. "Life-and-death, in fact."

She hears him sigh.

"OK, I'll finish off here and get going straightaway."

"Thanks! See you!" She ends the call.

It's a long shot, she knows, but if Nygård can get a screen grab of Tell holding Sandgren's model house, she will have the evidence she needs to get a warrant for his arrest.

She pulls out to overtake impulsively, and when an oncoming car appears, she only just manages to heave the car back into the other lane in time.

Forces herself to take her foot off the pedal just a little.

Hill isn't alone, she tells herself. He's with Mya.

He could call any second and let her know that they are safe. That the danger is over.

Meanwhile, she also can't help but wonder how things went for Jonas Hellman and his dramatic raid.

The radio on the passenger seat has gone almost dead silent, and the few sentences exchanged are mostly about various personnel transfers.

No whoops of joy, no mention of Smilla.

Which is no wonder.

Smilla's fate is linked to that of the other missing people.

Of Julia Collin.

She thinks back to the phone call she had with Julia's brother earlier. He gave an entirely different picture of Julia than what her mother had. And she still has no good answer to the interesting question that Hill posed about Julia:

Why did it take a full two years for Julia to appear in the model?

What was so special about her?

Her phone puts an end to her ruminations.

It isn't Hill, as hoped, but Virgilsson.

"Are you on your way into the office?" he asks. "There's a matter I should like to discuss."

She wonders if he has noticed that she stole Sandgren's keys from his desk drawer. If Zafer blabbed. But she doesn't care.

"I'm out on a case," she says, "won't be back in the office till tomorrow."

"I see—where?" he asks, in a tone that is probably supposed to convey only polite interest. But something tells her that isn't the case.

"Why do you ask?" she asks.

"Oh, no particular reason," he says, and now she knows that he's lying. "I saw that one of the portable radios wasn't in the charger, so I was a little puzzled, that's all. It wasn't signed out, and as you know I *am* responsible for the inventory . . ."

He pauses, as though to give her another chance to satisfy his curiosity.

"As I said, I'm out on a case," she replies curtly. "So that's why I have a radio. If there isn't anything else . . ."

"No, no," he says placatingly. "We can discuss it tomorrow. Bye for now!"

Asker stares at the phone. In the few days that she has known Virgilsson, he has never done anything that wasn't motivated by his own self-interest.

So why is he suddenly so interested in what she is working on and where she is?

HILL

Hill shines his phone flashlight at the door. Where the handle should be lies only a flat metal plate.

He swears loudly. How the fuck could he have been so stupid as to just trot into the room? Or, more accurately, cell.

In his defense, he was only trying to calm Smilla.

He points his light at the ground so as not to dazzle her.

"We . . ." He clears his throat. ". . . seem to be locked in."

Smilla doesn't reply. Her eyes have glazed over, and Hill can see why. She has been sitting here in complete darkness for over a week. Then a minute ago got to experience the briefest glimmer of hope, only for it to be torn out from under her. That sort of thing can easily break someone. Prepper Per would do the same thing to Leo. Over and over again, until she learned to stop hoping.

"It's OK," he says and touches Smilla's arm. "We just need a plan. Tell me everything you know. How you got here, what you've seen and heard, everything, OK?"

She nods slowly.

"We'll figure this out," he says. "You aren't alone anymore."

That last sentence seems to strike a nerve. Smilla seems to pull herself together.

"What do you know about who's holding you captive?"

"Not so much. Only that he calls himself the Mountain King. And that he doesn't act alone."

"He doesn't?"

"No."

Smilla tells him about the time she almost escaped. That she almost made it to the door below the red light, only to be tackled by someone. That the Mountain King spoke to the other person.

"How do you know what he calls himself?" Hill asks.

"There's another girl in the other room. Julia. She told me."

"Julia Collin?" he gasps.

"Maybe," Smilla replies. "Do you know her?"

"She's been missing for four years," Hill replies. "Everyone thinks she's dead."

"But she isn't."

Smilla places her mouth by the vent.

"Julia," she whispers. "Julia, are you there?"

No reply.

"Julia!"

"Yeeeah," says a feeble voice. "What's going on?"

"There's someone here, someone who came to save us. But we're locked in together."

"Oh . . ." Her voice sounds slurred, Hill notes.

"Hi, Julia, my name's Martin. I'm trying to understand who it is who's holding you captive."

"The Mountain King," Julia whispers.

"Yes, I know that. But Smilla thinks he has a helper. What do you know about that?"

"Nothing. I've never seen anyone but him."

"But you've seen him?"

"Yes, or almost . . ."

Her voice has grown weaker.

"I'm so tired," says Julia. "Do you think . . ." It sounds as though she sobs. "Do you think we'll ever get out of here?"

ASKER

Asker parks outside the premises of the model train club. There is another car there, and it isn't Daniel Nygård's pickup, but a BMW estate.

She pops inside the club. The lights are on, and on the model a few trains are traveling around the tracks.

"Hello?" she says. "Anyone in?"

Kjell Lilja peers out in surprise from around a corner.

"Oh," he says. "Is that you?"

A young man appears behind him. He looks like a younger version of Lilja, has long, greasy hair and is wearing a denim jacket with a fleece lining.

"This is my son Oliver," says Lilja. "He's been away. Came home today. Oliver, this is Detective Inspector Asker."

"Hi," says Asker.

Oliver Lilja doesn't reply, instead avoids eye contact.

She thinks about what both Krook and Tell have said about Oliver Lilja. A petty crook with the usual mix of minor drugs, burglaries, and driving offenses to his CV. That this journey that he has just returned from is in fact a stay in a young offender institution.

"I was actually looking for Daniel Nygård," she says. "Had a few questions about the alarm."

Lilja shakes his head.

"We haven't seen him. But Oliver and I just got here."

"OK."

Asker wonders if Daniel has already been able to get the camera, or if he's still on the way. Considers calling him.

"So how is the investigation going? Do you know anything more about that model house?" Lilja asks.

Oliver tilts his head to one side, immediately appears to be listening with interest.

"We're working on it," Asker says evasively.

She wants to call Nygård straightaway. But Lilja appears to know everyone around these parts, so perhaps he can help her with something.

"Actually, there was something I wanted to ask you," she says. "I ran into another one of Ulf's stepsons here the other day, Jakob Tell from Hässleholm Police. Do you know him?" She tries to sound relaxed, as though the question doesn't remotely concern a would-be serial killer.

Lilja grimaces.

"Oh yes, Jakob's sister teaches at my school, so our paths cross every now and then."

"What do you know about him?"

"How do you mean?" Lilja asks, unexpectedly cagey.

Asker fights the urge to grab the headmaster by the collar and shove him up against the wall. Instead she tries out a new tactic.

"Fact is, he asked me out," she says with what she hopes is a soft smile. "I haven't decided whether to say yes."

"Ah." Lilja's caginess vanishes.

He sucks in air through his teeth, as though weighing up what to say next.

"Jakob Tell loves women," he says. "So much so that he will quite happily see several at the same time, without a care as to whether they're married or not. And some women do like a man in uniform—"

He cuts himself off.

"But each to their own, of course," he concludes, as though glossing over what he just said.

Asker thinks. Tell's phone indicated that he was on his way east, not toward Hill. It could be that he simply turned it off for a discreet rendezvous. But she doesn't dare take that for granted. She has to find Hill, has to prove that Tell is the Mountain King before they run into each other.

Her phone vibrates. A message from Daniel Nygård.

I've got the camera. Have taken it to my workshop to try to extract the material. Will be in touch if I find anything.

Asker looks up. Lilja and his son are staring at her curiously.

"I'll let you get back to it," she says with hard-fought calm. "Just one last question. Where would I find Daniel Nygård's workshop?"

HILL

Hill has spent the last half hour scouring the room they are trapped inside with the flashlight on his cellphone. Julia has gone quiet again, but Smilla has told him everything she has experienced in her ten days down here in the mountain. He hasn't told her about MM, partly because she hasn't asked him straight-out, and partly because he doesn't want to distress her now when she needs her wits about her.

Once he has finished his checks, his battery has only 10 percent left. But he thinks he may have found something that just might work.

The door is their only chance.

Since it doesn't have a handle, it is impossible to open, and besides, there is a bolt on the outside.

But the bolt is small, and it's fairly high up. The doorpost that it is mounted on is also seventy years old.

If they can somehow turn the door handle until the latch retracts, and at the same time give the door a good knock, they might just be able to get it open.

He explains the plan to Smilla and asks her to hold the phone while he pulls out the few tools they have at their disposal.

First he uses the penknife to unscrew the metal plate covering the door mechanism. Beneath it he can see the spindle that drives the latch, but it's too short for him to get hold of.

Luckily he has a few of the sleeve adapters that he used to open the doors on the old industrial site a few days ago.

He pushes one of the adapters onto the spindle. Makes sure not to push it in all the way, then feeds the penknife a half inch into the rectangular hole. He tries to turn his makeshift handle, and after a few unsuccessful attempts, the spindle turns, pulling with it the latch. However, after just a second, the penknife slips and the latch snaps back in.

"Here, Smilla, you'll have to hold it in place!"

He puts his phone down on the floor and shows her the right positioning and hold.

"You turn it, and I'll try to knock open the door," he says. "But you'll have to turn it just before, because if the latch is still in when I hit the door I could break my shoulder."

"OK," she says. "No problem."

Despite having been down here in the darkness for over a week, she is impressively determined. Ready to take on the task at hand.

"Good!"

Hill steps a few paces back. Does a practice run in slow motion. Tries to remember how high on the door the little bolt was and figure out how to land the most force just there.

"Ready?" he asks Smilla.

She nods in concentration.

"OK, then let's go. On the count of three turn as much as you can. Here goes!"

"One . . . two . . ."

Hill braces himself.

"Three!"

HELLMAN

Hellman is in the car, blue lights flashing, and has started heading north.

He brought only Eskil with him for company, since he's the only one loyal enough for this task.

The control center is feeding them the coordinates of the GPS in Asker's police radio. It gives her location accurate to a matter of feet.

They have Virgilsson to thank for that tip.

The cunning little man had no qualms about selling out his own boss, so long as the price was right. A kind of irony of fate, since Asker once double-crossed Hellman in a similar way.

"How far are we?" he asks Eskil.

"About an hour to her last position. But she appears to be on the move again."

"Which way?"

"Northwest."

Hellman puts his foot down as much as he dares.

There is only one way out, one single solution to his problem.

They have to find Leo Asker and take over her investigation, as fast as they can.

Be that through threats, bribery, or promises—whatever it takes.

Anything is better than failure, after all.

HILL

The impact of the door is so heavy that it knocks the wind right out of Hill. For a split second he thinks they mistimed it, and that the clink he heard was the crack of his shoulder. But then he feels the door give way.

It opens half an inch and then just hangs. One or more of the screws holding the bolt in place still clinging on, grasping at the aged metal. Hill totters backward, gasping for breath.

"Watch out," says Smilla. She takes a step back and gives the door a good kick with the sole of her foot. It moves another half inch. Smilla kicks again and again, and suddenly the screws give way and the door opens up.

"Come on, let's find an exit," Hill whispers.

"Julia," says Smilla. "We have to get her out, too!"

They run to the next door along. It is identical to the door they just forced, but with one crucial difference.

There is no bolt.

Smilla opens the door.

"Julia," she whispers into the darkness. "Julia, do you hear me?"

No response.

Hill steps inside the room, cautiously shines his phone flashlight around.

"Julia?" Smilla repeats.

The room looks identical to the one they just left. A bed with a blanket and a pillow, on the other side a latrine. But there are another few objects inside. A stool is placed right next to the air vent.

On the floor between the stool's legs lies a tiny plastic bottle. Hill bends down and picks it up. Reads the label.

"No," he mumbles.

The room lurches, and he feels sick.

Suddenly he understands how it all fits.

The evil he felt in the corridor, Mya's mysterious disappearance, the Mountain King's secret helper.

He should have seen it long ago. But he was too caught up in playing the hero. Trying to protect Mya the way he failed to protect Leo.

"What is it?" Smilla asks.

Hill holds up the bottle between his thumb and index finger. The room still won't stop rocking.

E-liquid, it says on the label. *Forest fruits flavor.*

"Vape liquid," he says, subdued.

"Where's Julia?" Smilla asks.

Hill gives a heavy sigh.

"Not Julia," he says. "Her name's Mya."

ASKER

Daniel Nygård's workshop appears to be next to his home. It stands at the foot of a large peak that is swathed in spruce trees, and when Asker looks at her map she realizes that, as the crow flies, it isn't particularly far from Ulf Krook's grim house of horrors.

Nygård's property, however, is in much better shape. A red house with white trims, a freestanding double garage in the same colors, and a third building that is connected to the main house on one side.

NYGÅRD'S ALARMS AND SECURITY, reads a sign above the door.

The company pickup is parked just outside. She parks her car next to it. Has hardly stepped out of it before the door opens and Nygård appears.

He is wearing dungarees and a flannel shirt. His beard is just as bushy as she remembers it.

"Ah, you came here," he says. "I told you I'd be in touch if I found anything."

"Yes, but I was in the area. And as I said, it's urgent."

A dog barks at the forest's edge.

"Yours?" Asker asks, turning around.

"Nope," says Nygård. "The neighbor's mutt. I'm allergic to dogs. Can't go near them."

He shows her into his workshop. The room smells faintly of rubber and electronics. Reminds her of Enok Zafer's office.

The walls are lined with tools in arrow-straight rows. Underneath them a workbench that hasn't the least trace of scraps or dust. At one end of the room stands a desk with two connected desktop screens.

"I've got the kit over here."

He gestures toward the desk, where there lies something that resembles a little matchbox with a wire sticking out of it.

"I was just going to connect the camera and see if I could breathe some life into it," he says. "Cross your fingers."

He fiddles with a few wires, opens a program on one screen.

Mutters something and scratches his beard while tapping on the keyboard.

Suddenly the muffled sound of a phone ringing cuts through the air. Not a cellphone, but the old-fashioned trill of a landline, coming from inside the main house.

Nygård looks up, his brow furrowed in concern, as though the sound disturbs him.

The phone goes on ringing. Stops mid-ring. Daniel appears to go on listening in the direction of the house, as though expecting something.

Then a woman's voice calls his name.

"Excuse me," he says. "I'll be right back."

He opens a door that leads into the main house and disappears.

This interruption stresses out Asker even more. Hill still hasn't called, and she has no idea where Tell is.

Now she is starting to get really worried.

HILL

Hill and Smilla walk toward the red light at the end of the corridor. The strange smell that Hill noticed before is stronger here. Wet earth, iron, compost.

"This was where I ran when I tried to escape," says Smilla. "The door was ajar and I was almost there when someone tackled me. Do you think it could have been Mya?"

Hill nods, clenches his teeth. He is still shaken by the realization.

He thought it was his combined social superpowers and persuasive skills that made Mya bring him here. In actual fact she was the one who manipulated him.

Who lured him here, either because she realized he knew about the cave rain, or because that was her plan right from the very start.

Presumably it was also Mya who locked the door behind them, before she sneaked into the other room to pretend to be Julia Collin.

But why?

That question will have to wait until they are out of here.

"Here." Smilla points at the door next to the red lamp.

It is different from the others. Besides the fact that it's gray, it is also newer, heavier.

Hill feels it. Locked, with a real deadlock this time, not a bolt. He holds his hand up to the hinge. Feels a faint draft of air.

This door is an exit, but without tools he can't get past it.

He looks to the right. The corridor continues beyond the range of the faint cell light. Perhaps there's something they can use behind one of the closed doors.

"Martin!" says Smilla. "Shine here."

She points at the red light, and he aims his phone there. The red light is part of a modern electrical cabinet, which seems completely incongruous with the rest of the base. Next to the cabinet hangs an old-fashioned phone.

"We can call for help!" Smilla whispers.

Hill lifts the receiver. There is a dial tone. He is about to laugh out loud with relief. His heart pounding, he dials Asker's number.

It rings.

One, two, three, four. He is already thinking about what he will say.

How he will explain where he and Smilla are.

A click is heard on the line. It stops ringing.

Silence.

"Leo?" he says.

No response.

"Hello? Leo?"

Still nothing.

The line is silent, only the buzz of the wires and the faint tick of Hill's mechanical heart can be heard.

Still, he is sure that there is someone on the other end of the line.

Someone who is listening carefully.

Someone who now knows that he and Smilla are no longer locked in.

ASKER

It has now been five minutes since the phone rang, and Daniel Nygård still hasn't reappeared. Why is he taking so long?

She needs the pictures, ASAP.

With every minute that passes that she can't link Tell to the train model, the chances of him crossing paths with Hill and Mya increase.

She paces around the workshop, trying to control her impatience. Admires, in spite of her restlessness, the perfect order of the place.

Prepper Per strove for this kind of symmetry. And he managed to achieve it, at least to begin with. But as the chaos took over his mind, it became all the harder for him to maintain order.

To maintain control.

She walks over to the window and looks out across the yard. Dusk is approaching. The shadows on the edge of the forest beyond the garage have started to grow heavier.

The barking has stopped.

In the window stands a glass jar. A knickknack from some online gift store. A plastic insect lies at the bottom of the jar, and when you press a button it comes to life.

She presses it. The insect, which, when its wings unfold turns out to be a butterfly, flies up and flutters around the jar. Its wings beat against the glass, and even though the butterfly isn't real, the sounds and flapping of its wings are so anxiety-inducing that she immediately has to turn it off again.

The butterfly plunges back to the bottom of the jar, where it lies still.

Asker snorts.

Who would buy such a thing? Who would want to experience an artificial version of a beautiful butterfly's desperate attempts to regain its freedom? To listen to the unpleasant beating of its wings?

Papillon mécanique reads the label on the lid, which, if her high-school French doesn't deceive her, means "mechanical butterfly."

"Papillon," she mumbles to herself. Something stirs in her head. Madame Rind's voice pipes up.

Keep your eyes out for a papillon.

She puts the jar back down on the windowsill and walks over to the computer that Nygård was tapping away at before he disappeared into the house.

A notification window is open on the screen.

Files deleted.

"What the fuck!"

She walks over to the door to the house and cracks it slightly.

"Hello!" she calls.

No response.

As she stands there on the threshold, out of nowhere that strange premonition returns. The same feeling she woke up with exactly one week ago. A sense of foreboding, of danger.

"Hello!" she says again.

All is still; a strange, oppressive silence.

She steps into the house, walks through a side entrance, past a washing machine and laundry hangers. Beyond that a kitchen.

IKEA cabinets, laminate flooring. The faint aromas of coffee and something fruity. On the kitchen counter stand two colorful mugs with names on them. Beside them a car key and a clicker for a garage door.

"Hello?" she says a third time. "Daniel?"

Everything is still silent.

The kitchen leads to a living room. A sofa, TV, a few bookshelves with an assortment of paperback thrillers.

On the wall hangs an old-fashioned phone, without a number dial or buttons. It reminds her of the one linked up to the intercom at the Farm.

The receiver is dangling on its cord, almost touching the floor.

She turns around, is about to hurry back into the kitchen when an object on the wall catches her attention.

A framed photograph containing a number of familiar faces. She takes a few steps closer.

Ulf Krook is in the middle of the photo. He is wearing a T-shirt that says *Dad*, which is such a crisp white that he must have only just put it on.

Why would Daniel Nygård have a picture of Ulf?

Around Ulf stand a dozen or so men and women, all in their early thirties and up. Finn Olofsson she recognizes straightaway, as she does Jakob Tell.

But farther out to the right stands a tall man with a beard.

It's Daniel Nygård. Next to him, with her arm around his waist, is a slight young woman in an army jacket. After scouring her memory for a few seconds, Asker realizes that it is the same woman she spotted in Ulf Krook's forest.

Only now does Asker notice the text at the bottom of the image. *Family dinner*, it reads, followed by a date from the previous year.

She flinches. Feels her pulse start to race.

Daniel Nygård must be another one of Ulf Krook's sons or stepsons.

But who is the young woman at his side?

Filled with foreboding, she quickly returns to the kitchen, on the search for some clue as to who lives here with Nygård.

The name mugs are sitting on the middle of the counter. They look as though they were bought in the same sort of knickknack store that sells mechanical butterflies.

Daniel, the blue one says.

The other mug is still half-full with tepid coffee. She turns it around. The mug is bright red and has three letters on the front.

Mya.

She gasps. Her whole body goes ice-cold, her thoughts run wild. Calculating connections, consequences, dangers.

Nygård must have access to the basement workshop over in the house of horrors. Thanks to his role as alarm technician he has also enjoyed free access to the train model for years. And he would also know how to disconnect a burglar alarm, like the one at Sandgren's house.

Asker grabs the door clicker from the countertop, aims it at the garage door across the yard, and presses the button.

The door slowly glides open. Inside it stands a familiar dark brown van. The same van that followed her.

"Shit," Asker whispers to herself, while fumbling for her firearm.

The Mountain King isn't Jakob Tell.

But Daniel Nygård.

And the timid Mya who was leading Hill into his secret mountain lair isn't his cousin, but his girlfriend.

HILL

"Someone's coming," Smilla whispers, her eyes on the gray door. "I hear voices."

"We've got to get out of here," Hill replies.

He takes Smilla's hand and pulls her down the as yet unexplored stretch of corridor. Holds his phone flashlight in front of them as high as he can.

The battery is now down to 5 percent, and in a matter of minutes they will be fumbling around in the dark. They must find a hiding place as quickly as possible.

The air is heavier the deeper into the corridor they go. It doesn't end here, as Hill thought, but turns off to the right again, back toward the huge cave.

They stop just around the corner. Hill turns off the phone as they press up against the wall, listening intently in the darkness.

They hear the gray door open. The sound of steps. But strangely enough they don't see the light of any flashlights.

"Lock the door, let's split up," says a gruff man's voice that must belong to Jakob Tell. The Mountain King.

If Mya wasn't lying about that as well, that is. Which is quite conceivable. Maybe even probable, he realizes.

All that Hill knows with any certainty is that the Mountain King is deadly. That he will kill them as soon as he gets the chance.

"You take the cells and the collection rooms," the gruff voice commands. "I'll take the other side. We'll meet in the cave."

"OK," a familiar female voice replies.

Mya doesn't sound the slightest bit afraid anymore. Only decisive. Dangerous.

Hill cautiously pulls Smilla farther down the corridor, feeling his way along the wall until he finds a door handle. The door is unlocked, and when he opens it they are struck by a nauseating stench. But they don't have time to be choosy.

Hill carefully shuts the door behind them, turns his phone flashlight back on again and holds it up.

The room is in fact an infirmary. Curtains, stainless steel tables, five hospital beds along one wall.

On each bed lies something that looks like a big, dark sleeping bag, bearing the logo of the Swedish Armed Forces.

It takes Hill a few seconds to realize what they are.

He stops mid-step.

Body bags.

Smilla claps her hand to her mouth.

There is another door on one of the side walls, with a frosted-glass panel in the top half. Hill pulls Smilla inside.

An office, probably for the doctor. A heavy metal desk, a chair, a shelf that is empty except for a few moldy bundles of papers.

He shuts the door and signals to Smilla to get on the floor. Then turns off the flashlight again so the room is pitch-black.

They can hear doors opening out in the corridor.

One by one, as the Mountain King scans the rooms.

The sounds are getting closer.

"Get behind the desk," he whispers to Smilla.

He follows her.

The door to the infirmary opens. The Mountain King still doesn't appear to be using a flashlight.

They press their backs up against the side of the desk. Footsteps are heard, then the squeak of the office door handle slowly being pressed down.

Hill holds his breath, feels Smilla do the same. The door opens with a faint creak.

The room is so small that they can hear the Mountain King's breaths. Even smell him. An almost animalistic scent that mixes with the odor of the body bags in the infirmary.

Hill waits for the Mountain King to hear his clicking heart.

For a light to turn on, and for him to command them to come out from behind the heavy metal desk.

But none of that happens.

The Mountain King goes back into the infirmary and shuts the door behind him. Shortly thereafter the door to the corridor shuts, too.

They hear him go on opening doors.

"What the fuck was that?" Hill whispers. "Why doesn't he have a flashlight?"

"Night-vision goggles," Smilla replies. "I felt them when I hit him with the concrete wedge. I think the desk saved us."

She taps faintly on the thick metal.

"Shall we stay hidden here until they've gone?"

Hill shakes his head.

"The gray door is locked. They know we're hiding here somewhere, so sooner or later they'll come back and find us."

"So then what shall we do?"

Hill stands up and turns on his phone again. Only 2 percent battery left.

"There must be another way out. A place where they could easily evacuate patients from the infirmary."

Cautiously he sneaks back into the infirmary, with Smilla right behind him. On the back of the door hangs a yellowish map.

"Look," he says. "This level looks like an upside-down U. You were being held on one side, the phone and red light are on the middle section, and now we're on the other side. And look!"

He points at a spot at the end of the corridor that they are currently in. A green dot that indicates an exit.

"We've got to get there," he says.

Hill turns off his flashlight, carefully opens the door, and listens.

He can hear doors opening farther down the corridor, as the Mountain King works his way through the rooms, one at a time.

"When he goes into the next room, let's run past to the emergency exit," he whispers.

"OK," Smilla replies. Her voice is shaky, but also determined. Hill can't help but admire her. She has been kept captive for over a week down here in the darkness. And yet she is still standing. Prepared to fight for her life.

He knows only one other person with that kind of strength of will.

He hopes that Leo is out there somewhere, that she is looking for them.

But he can't count on that, has to focus on getting him and Smilla out of this.

They wait, listen. The sound of a door opening cuts clearly through the darkness. Then the sound of it shutting.

"Now," Hill whispers.

He turns on the flashlight, opens the door, and pulls Smilla along toward the end of the corridor.

It is at least thirty, fifty feet away, and they run as fast as they can.

A door appears in the beam from the flashlight, and Hill even has time to wonder if it's locked. If so, they will crash straight into it and be trapped like rats in a cage when the Mountain King re-emerges.

He leaps at the handle. The door opens, reveals a couple of steps, and a short tunnel.

He pulls Smilla inside, and is just about to shut the door behind them when a shot rings out. The door shakes from the impact, but Hill still manages to get it shut. Another shot hits the door, but doesn't penetrate the metal. Then a third.

Hill hands Smilla the phone and pulls out his penknife. Bends down and shoves it into the crack at the bottom of the door, then gives it a hard kick to wedge it between the door and the concrete floor. Just as he is straightening up, the door is struck by a fourth shot. Hill catches the sound of it ricocheting between the stone walls, then feels a sharp pain in one thigh.

He's been hit.

ASKER

Asker searches Nygård's house methodically. Moves quietly from room to room with her firearm drawn, as quickly as she dares. Besides the kitchen, the side entry, and the living room, the bungalow only has two bedrooms and a bathroom. No sign of either Daniel Nygård or anyone else.

Mya must have been here, too, judging by the warm coffee in her mug. It must have been she who called for Daniel when the phone started to ring.

So where have they gone? And why the hurry?

The only reasonable conclusion is that whatever has dragged them away has something to do with Martin Hill.

Outside the windows it's starting to get dark. The shadows of the spruces are extending.

There is only one access road to the plot, but the cars are still in the yard, which means it's most likely that Daniel and Mya set out on foot, straight into the dark spruce forest. In which case she has basically no chance. They must have had at least a ten-minute head start, and she doesn't even know which direction they were going in. Still, she has to try.

But just as she is about to leave the house, it strikes her.

One detail that doesn't quite fit.

She goes back to the bedrooms. The two of them are completely identical. The bed, curtains, bedspread, pillows, lamp on the bedside table—even the IKEA armchair in the corner—are all exactly the same.

But on just one of the bedroom floors lies a rag rug. What's more, it's slightly askew, which doesn't sit with the otherwise so symmetrically perfect house.

She kneels down and lifts up the rug.

Beneath it she finds a hatch in the floor. The rug is attached to the hatch in such a way that it falls down by itself when the hatch is shut. She sticks her finger inside the retracted pulley and pulls it upward, her other hand at the ready with her firearm.

The hatch glides open smoothly. Reveals a steep staircase, and lights leading beyond. Asker sticks her head in cautiously.

A tunnel.

HILL

"Hurry," Smilla cries. She is a couple feet ahead of Hill, holds the phone flashlight with her hand outstretched so that she can run as fast as possible.

He does his best to keep up. The ricochet hit him halfway up his thigh, and the trouser leg beneath it is already soaked through. Thanks to the drugs he takes, his blood is thin and his pounding heart is pumping it out at the fastest possible rate.

In just a few minutes the loss of blood will make him light-headed, and in another few he'll be unconscious.

And then there will be no more that he can do.

The passage they are running through splits off, and without a second thought Smilla swerves off to the right. A crash is heard behind them, as the door shot full of holes is kicked open. All too soon the Mountain King will be at their heels. A murderer with night vision and a gun. A superior adversary whom they can only hope to outrun. But Hill's body doesn't have so much running left in it.

Smilla opens another door, the hinge creaks rustily.

Hill is right behind her. His phone is about to die, and it takes him a second or two to realize that they should have turned left before, not right, to reach the exit they saw on the fire escape map. Instead they are now back in the big cave, through the right-hand door of the loading bay. And now it's too late to turn around.

"Shit!" Hill curses.

He slams the door behind them, tries to barricade it with a stone.

The movement makes him dizzy. Blood has started to fill his shoe.

Then his phone dies, and the darkness hits them like a sledge-hammer.

"No!" Smilla gasps.

Hill stands up straight, has to support himself against the door. He reaches into his pocket and pulls out his flashlight. Maybe it has dried out enough for them to revive it.

He presses the button. A white cone of light illuminates the room.

For a second Smilla looks relieved, but then she spots his leg.

"You're bleeding," she says. "A lot!"

"Don't worry," says Hill. "Here, I know a way out!"

He shines the flashlight ahead of them, staggers as fast as he can through the passage toward the room with the ladder.

Or, more accurately, the room without the ladder.

"I recognize this place," Smilla says. "MM and I came down this way."

Hill totters, tries to stay on his feet. He shines the torch up at the hole in the ceiling.

In the distance he hears feet kicking against a steel door.

"The ladder has to be up there," says Hill. "If you get up on my shoulders, you can pull yourself up through the hole in the ceiling and then pass it down to me."

"OK," she says. Gives him a worried look. "But have you got the strength?"

"Yes. But we have to hurry."

He kneels down and leans against the wall. Lays the flashlight on the ground.

"Now sit on my shoulders."

Smilla follows his instruction.

Hill gets to his feet. Totters, comes within a second of tumbling down, but manages to catch his balance just in time. He maneuvers himself just under the hole in the ceiling.

"Now stand up. Use the wall and ceiling for support if you need."

He is struggling to stay upright. Smilla is both light and agile, but it's still arduous.

He puts his hands around her heels to support her.

"I can't reach," she says. "I'm about a foot short."

There comes a crash as the door in the cave flies open. Then the sound of agitated voices sharing information. The Mountain King and Mya have reconvened.

In less than a minute they will be here.

"OK," says Hill. "I'll count to three and then you jump. I'll give your feet a push at the same time."

He doesn't wait for a reply.

"One, two, three." He thrusts her upward with all his might. For a brief moment he thinks that she has missed, and that both of them will tumble to the floor.

But then the weight lifts, and she disappears through the ceiling.

Hill bends down and picks up the flashlight.

"Here, catch!" he says, throwing it up to her. His legs are about to give way beneath him.

"I'll lower the ladder," she says.

Hill shakes his head. "Not worth it. Just go on."

"But I can't leave you," she says, a sob in her voice.

The sound of footsteps is getting ever closer.

"You have to," says Hill. "Unless you want to go back to that room. Hurry!"

He turns his back to her and slumps next to the wall. His body feels floppy, his eyelids heavy. The light disappears with Smilla.

He hears the steps arrive.

The Mountain King's gruff voice cuts through the darkness.

"Mya! Climb onto my shoulders," he commands. "I'll lift you up through the hole. She can't have got far."

"But what about him?" Mya asks. "You promised he'd be mine. That I'd get him instead of MM. Can't you see he's bleeding out?"

The room goes silent.

"You promised," Mya whines.

"OK," the Mountain King replies. "But first you have to get rid of Smilla. I'm sick of her as it is."

Hill hears the crunch of boots, a faint grunt from Mya.

"Are you up?" the Mountain King asks.

"Yes," Mya replies.

"Good, now get going. I've got to get back."

Hill feels the Mountain King crouch down beside him. Feels his hands groping over his wound. Then farther up, over his waist.

The Mountain King unbuckles Hill's belt and removes it. Wraps it around his thigh just over his wound, then yanks the belt so hard that Hill cries out in pain.

"You're lucky," the Mountain King whispers. "You'll last a little longer. But now I've got to leave you, I've got another prey to catch."

Hill knows instinctively who he means.

Leo, he thinks. He tries to muster the strength for some form of resistance.

But the Mountain King has already disappeared into the gloom.

SMILLA

Smilla runs through the forest, the flashlight flickering before her. Branches scratch at her face, brambles tear at her skin. The steep downhill slope and damp spread of dead leaves make it hard for her to keep her balance, and she tumbles several times.

With every fall it becomes all the harder to get back up. She has hardly eaten or drunk in days, and before that she was drugged repeatedly. Now the adrenaline is the only thing keeping her on her feet.

The tears stream down her cheeks, tears of fear, anger, and despair.

She has known Martin Hill only an hour, but in that short time he has become her security. Her savior.

And now she has abandoned him. Betrayed him.

She hears a branch snap in the forest somewhere behind her. Her panic sparks up again, releases a fresh kick of adrenaline. New strength.

The ground finally levels off, and in the flashlight she can make out the logging road where MM parked the Golf.

It feels like an eternity ago.

The thought of MM makes her feel another pang in her chest. He's dead, she's sure of it. Martin didn't want to tell her, but she could see it on his face anyway.

She swings the flashlight around, sees that MM's Golf has gone, but finds another car parked a little farther away. It must be Martin's. She tugs at the door handles.

Locked.

The key must still be in his pocket. He was too dazed with blood loss to think to give it to her.

"Fuck fuck fuck," she moans.

Another sound comes from the forest behind her.

Standing there by the car with the flashlight on, she is easy to spot, she realizes. She turns it off and puts it in her pocket. Then starts creeping as quietly as she can along the logging road.

The clouds have drifted apart, and the sky gives her enough light for her to be able to keep to the road.

She looks up at the stars.

Some part of her believed that she would never see them again.

Another sound from the forest. Closer now.

Smilla lowers her head, tries to summon her last energy reserves.

She likes running, has always been good at it.

But she has never run for her life before.

ASKER

The tunnel is professionally built, Asker notes once she is down at the bottom of the steep staircase. A series of large, steel, interlocking road-drainage pipes, installed beneath the foundations of the house. Lighting and ventilation in the ceiling. Crushed rock on the ground to let the rainwater drain.

On a post at the bottom of the staircase stands an electrical cabinet, and on a shelf below it two empty charging stations, both with the text *Night Vision* printed along the sides.

Night-vision goggles and a secret tunnel. Prepper Per would have loved this place.

She looks down the tunnel. It curves slightly to the left after around sixty feet, obscuring where it leads.

Everything is silent. The smell of damp and earth, eerily familiar.

She raises her weapon, starts moving through the tunnel with quick, fleet-footed steps, stopping every now and then to listen.

After several hundred feet the tunnel changes character. Links up to what must be an older construction of reinforced concrete that slopes downward.

There is a gentle circulation of air here, and Asker guesses that Nygård must have joined his homemade tunnel to some sort of old ventilation shaft.

She keeps moving forward. The walls have damp stains, and here and there the concrete has crumbled, letting small pools of water form. In a few spots she finds graffiti that, judging by the years on the tags, appears to have been done by conscripts doing their military service in the sixties.

After around a hundred and fifty feet of a gentle downhill slope, she reaches a gray door that looks surprisingly modern.

The door is shut, and she has just enough time to wonder what she will do if the door is locked when the light in the tunnel cuts out.

She crouches down. It could have been a timer that broke the circuit, but she doubts that.

From the end of the tunnel she hears a click, followed by a faint thud.

She presses herself against the wall; waits, listens. But everything is silent.

After a few minutes she turns on the flashlight on her phone.

The gray door that was previously shut is now wide open. Inside it shines a faint, red light.

She understands what this means.

The Mountain King knows she's coming. Is waiting for her in there, in the darkness.

Goading her.

She has been through this before. Or at least something similar.

Many years ago. In another life.

She takes a deep breath.

Turns off the flashlight and sits there quietly in the dark.

Waits.

After just a few seconds he appears in her head.

Prepper Per.

FIFTEEN YEARS EARLIER

She sits there, hidden between the boulders, and hears Prepper Per sob up on the trail. Finally understands that the father she once loved so much, the man she trusted and followed blindly, no longer exists.

All that remains is a maniac who can no longer tell chaos from reality. And who is never, ever going to let her go.

Cautiously she feels around on the floor and finds a rock. Throws it as far as she can in the direction she came from.

She is in luck. The stone flies a long way before it smacks into a tree trunk.

She hears his footsteps moving in the other direction, toward the sound.

Waits ten seconds before sneaking back up to the trail and continuing in the opposite direction, down toward the jetty.

She has at most a few minutes left. But she intends to make the most of her time. She is, after all, his daughter.

Knows how he thinks.

Even now.

When she reaches the jetty, the moon has peeped out, transforming the lake into mercury. But a thunderstorm is approaching with menacing grumbles, and all too soon the sky will be covered with dark clouds.

The boat is in its berth, and normally she would sneak out and sit on the edge of the jetty. Proudly show off to him that she passed the test. That she was a good girl.

But tonight is no normal night.

There is something in the boat. A backpack that reminds her of her own, only one size up. Has even more patches and pockets. Per only brings his backpack out on very special occasions, which strengthens her misgivings.

Three minutes later he appears on the trail. Raises his night-vision goggles to his forehead when he sees her there by the jetty.

His face is more emaciated than usual. His eyes so sunken that she can't read the look he gives her.

"*You made it,*" he says. "*Good!*"

Normally she would have reveled in that brusque praise. Basked in it for several weeks. But not tonight.

"I thought we would continue all the way this time," he says. "Take the boat to the other side."

He steps out onto the jetty, sweeps past her back, and takes a seat in the stern of the boat.

"Get in," he commands. "Move my backpack to make space." His voice is almost as harsh and expressionless as usual. Still, there is something there. A faint hint of something else. Sadness, even fear.

The thunder rumbles again. It's closer now. The moonlight is about to give way, the rain is heavy in the air.

She stands up, gets into the boat. Stops with her hands on the backpack.

"Are we really going out onto the lake?" she asks. "In the middle of a thunderstorm?"

"Don't worry," he says. "You needn't be alarmed. It'll soon be over, Leo . . ."

When he says her name his voice cracks. He stifles the sound before another sob gets out.

"Move the backpack," he says softly.

She turns around and looks at him. He is sitting at the stern. Has one hand on the tiller of the outboard motor, the other on his knee.

For one brief moonlit moment he looks like her father again.

Like the Per Asker she loved. Still loves.

Then his face contorts, transforms him back into Prepper Per.

"Move the backpack, now," he says, this time with a sharper tone. Then he shuts his eyes, as though waiting for something.

She picks up the backpack. Takes its place and sets it down on her lap.

It's heavy; she knows that the back is reinforced with Kevlar to make it bulletproof.

She sits quietly and waits.

After a few seconds he opens his eyes again. Stares at her questioningly. He looks bewildered, as though he can't comprehend what just happened.

Or, rather, what didn't happen.

Then something else happens.

The realization worms its way into his confused brain.

Takes a few seconds to convince his face of what's going on.

The realization that he, after all these years, is no longer her teacher.

Is no longer the predator.

But the prey.

"Shall we get going then, Per?" she asks, trying to keep her voice steady.

He stares at her for another few seconds.

Then nods slowly and moves his hand to the starter cord.

She wishes there were another way. That she could simply explain to him that he has to let her go.

But she knows that Prepper Per will never, ever do that.

And that she has no other choice.

The explosives he prepared for them are no longer in the backpack.

She has transferred them to the boat's motor, placed them on the outside, since she, unlike him, doesn't want them to die.

When he pulls the starter cord and the explosion comes, she is already halfway overboard.

Shielding her body and head with his bulletproof backpack.

A piece of red-hot metal plants itself in her forearm. Goes on burning into the flesh even once she is in the water.

And that isn't what pains her most.

But she is finally free.

ASKER

Asker rises gently from the floor of the tunnel. Her brain has already reviewed the situation. Assessed the risks and opportunities, just as Prepper Per once taught her.

She knows that Daniel Nygård is waiting for her down in the mountain. That he and his girlfriend both have night-vision goggles, which gives them the upper hand. At least that's what they think.

But she also knows that he won't attack her straightaway. There is a reason why the Mountain King places his victims in the railway model.

He wants to show off what he has done; point out what he has gotten away with.

It is also why he has opened the door at the end of the tunnel, turned on the red light.

To invite her in, show her who he really is. Challenge her.

Come and get me, if you dare.

She can turn around. Ignore the challenge, return to the staircase and the house. Try to raise the alarm.

But, like with Prepper Per, she knows that no help is coming. At least not in time.

Back then it was her own life that was at stake; this time it's Martin Hill's.

To save him she must defeat the Mountain King.

She fills her lungs with the tunnel's air.

Turns on her phone screen just enough to get a faint LED light and creeps up to the steel door. Beyond the first light she sees more.

A little pearl necklace of red dots in the ceiling, guiding her.

Into the mountain.

HELLMAN

"Yes, her police radio's in the front seat!" says Eskil, shining his flashlight through the window of the electric car. "What's Asker doing out here in the sticks?"

Hellman has no clue, but of course he can't let on, even though the question is a good one. He and Eskil have just arrived, but according to the GPS, Asker's car has been stationary for over an hour.

"Go ring the doorbell," he tells Eskil. "Make up an excuse, say we need to talk to her about Smilla Holst, whatever the fuck you want!"

Eskil grimaces, as though the task doesn't appeal at all. But he says nothing, and instead tramps off to the front door.

Hellman leans against Asker's car. Eskil's question is actually right on the nose. What the fuck is Asker doing here? Does it even have anything to do with Smilla Holst?

He checks his phone. A whole hoard of missed calls; some from Rodic, a few from Isabel Lissander, a few more from the colleagues left to clean up the mess of the failed bust.

He can't ignore them forever.

Eskil comes back.

"No one's in," he says with a shrug. "I've checked through the windows—diddly-squat. We must have missed her somehow."

Hellman is about to swear aloud, but gets ahold of himself just in time.

"OK," he says collectedly. "Let's take a drive around these small roads and see if we can pick up the scent again. She should be nearby. I mean, her car's still here."

He looks at Eskil, waits for the usual affirmative, along with some fawning, ill-conceived comment.

But the latter doesn't look him in the eye. Jumps into the car without a word, which can only mean one thing.

Even Eskil is losing faith. And once he does, it's all over for Hellman. They have to find Leo Asker.

And fucking soon, at that.

SMILLA

Smilla has now been running for perhaps five minutes along the dark logging road, with only the starlight to guide her. Has tripped several times on the uneven surface, turned her ankle.

She has tried to remember what she learned at hostage school about escaping. Preserve energy, keep your head cool, try to find a way to raise the alarm.

But the pain and fatigue are starting to take their toll, and all the adrenaline is making her feel sick.

Fortunately, she hasn't heard her pursuer in a long time. They must have either given up or lost her. At least that's what she hopes.

Smilla clenches her fists, tries to compel her legs to keep up the pace, but it's getting all the harder.

The vomit attack takes her by surprise, makes her stumble out onto the roadside.

Her stomach cramps, the bile stings in her throat.

When she straightens up, she realizes that she has almost reached the spot where the logging road meets a larger forest road.

This discovery gives her renewed hope.

She takes a few deep breaths and makes her reluctant feet start moving again. But she can get no more than a few steps before a figure detaches itself from the darkness ahead of her. A flashlight comes on, the beam dazzles her.

"There you are," says a voice that she knows well. Only now it no longer sounds soft, supportive, or tired, simply evil.

The light shifts away from her face.

The woman before her is her own age and doesn't look at all the way Smilla imagined her to look during their whispered conversations through the air vent.

She is wearing a military jacket and boots. Her hair is short. Around her neck hang some sort of goggles, presumably for seeing in the dark.

In one hand she is holding a flashlight, and in the other a big, shiny revolver.

Smilla's stomach contracts, in both exhaustion and fear. She puts her hands on her knees and vomits straight down between her feet.

The woman opposite her laughs.

"Wh-who . . ." Smilla wipes her mouth with her sleeve. "Who are you, really?"

The woman shrugs.

"I mean, I've told you.".

"You called yourself Julia, but Martin said your name was Mya."

The woman laughs again.

"Poor Martin. I mean, he just didn't get it."

"Get what?"

Mya clicks her tongue condescendingly.

"Oh, little miss perfect. Guess you're just as thick as Martin Hill." She smiles. "Most of what I told you is actually true. My name's Julia Collin, Daniel kidnapped me. Locked me up just like he did you and the others. Only difference was that I didn't fight. Didn't cling on to some idiotic idea of escaping or being saved. Didn't cry, beg, or plead. I just said I understood him. That we were the same."

"S-so he let you go?"

Julia shrugs.

"After a while. I moved in with him, changed how I looked, started calling myself Mya. Helped him."

"You introduced him to MM," says Smilla, with more bite than she thought she had left. "Dragged him into all of this. Did you sleep with him, too?"

"Oh come on!" Julia grimaces. "You're the one who dumped him. He was completely crushed. I'll have you know I actually liked MM, for real. If he hadn't gone running back to you as soon as you snapped your fingers, then neither you nor him would have ended up here. But he did, and the two of you were perfect for us. One for Daniel, one for me. Only it didn't go as planned. MM dropped down dead when we hunted you down in the mountain. His heart just cut out. Daniel said we'd scared him to death. That made me sad. But now I'll get Martin instead."

Smilla feels the tears burning under her eyelids, but she is too drained to be able to cry.

"Well, I guess that's all we have to say to each other, you and me," Julia says, then waves the revolver. "You can start by walking that way, into the forest."

Smilla takes a quivering breath.

So this is how it's going to end. Shot in the back, left in the forest for the foxes and badgers.

In the distance she spots a faint flash of light. A car approaching. She has an idea. A tip she remembers from hostage school.

Smilla makes another retching sound, bends over. Scoops up a handful of gravel as she does.

"For fuck's sake," Julia groans in irritation. "Surely you've already puked it all up."

Smilla spins around and throws the gravel straight at her face.

"What the . . ." Julia instinctively throws her arms over her eyes.

Smilla turns and starts sprinting along the dirt track, away from the light of the approaching car.

She hears a crack. Jumps to one side, then the other, to make herself harder to hit.

Another crack. She feels the shock wave of a bullet fizz past her ear.

"Smilla!" Julia screams.

She glances over her shoulder.

Julia is standing in the middle of the road. She is supporting the revolver hand with the one holding the flashlight, and both the light and the barrel are aimed at Smilla. Doesn't see the car approaching until it rounds the bend just behind her.

Julia spins around. Fires a shot straight at the windshield.

Then another one.

The cracks thunder through the forest.

Mix with the roar of the car's engine.

HELLMAN

Hellman and Eskil have been weaving along these roads for half an hour, and the mood in the car has gradually dropped to the freezing point. Neither of them says it straight out, but any minute now they will be forced to give up and return to Malmö with their tails between their legs.

Hellman will be forced to face the commissioner, the Holst family, and Isabel Lissander. Admit that he has bet everything on the wrong horse, and that that decision might have—if not probably—cost Smilla her life.

The realization makes Hellman put his foot down even harder on the accelerator. He skids around the curves, sends gravel clattering against the mudguards.

Eskil grips the grab handle, but says nothing.

Not until they round a bend and find someone standing in the middle of the road. A young woman who is pointing a revolver straight at them.

"What the he—" Eskil blurts out before a bullet shoots through the windshield and lops off his left ear, making him scream out in terror and pain.

The blood spurts into Hellman's face, and he instinctively slams his foot on the accelerator.

Another bullet breaks the glass, turning it milky-white.

But Hellman doesn't take his foot off the pedal.

The car's bumper hits the woman at knee height. Throws her several feet into the air like a rag doll, before she crashes to the ground on the road behind the car.

Hellman brakes. The tires hiss against the gravel and the car swings dangerously close to the shoulder, but stops just on the edge.

Eskil is bent double and is still screaming, both of his hands clapped to his wounded ear. Hellman ignores him.

He opens the door, pulls out his firearm, and runs toward the woman on the ground. Can quickly state that she no longer poses any threat.

Her arms and legs are splayed at nasty angles, but she is still alive. Her eyelids flutter, and she is groaning faintly.

Hellman kneels down beside her. With trembling hands he pulls out his cellphone. Has just come through to the duty superintendent when someone taps him on the shoulder.

He whips around in terror.

Behind him stands another young woman. She is filthy and red-eyed from crying, and has lost several pounds in weight. But Hellman would still recognize her anywhere. He has been staring at her photo for a whole week.

"My name's Smilla Holst," she says. "Julia there just tried to kill me."

THE MOUNTAIN KING

He has been waiting for this moment so long. Basically ever since he first met Leonore Asker at the model railway club.

The moment when she would eventually step into his world.

At first he was shocked when she turned up at his home. He had planned to delete the recording in peace and quiet and blame a technical error, just like when he disconnected the camera feed from the network. Go on drawing out their game, like he did with Sandgren. Watch her, let her go on believing they were allies.

But this is even better.

He has let her enter his mountain, his realm. Has turned on the faint red ceiling lights so that she will go where he wants her to go.

Now he observes her from afar through his night-vision goggles as she turns off into what he calls the hospital wing.

That's where he keeps them. His most treasured prizes.

Four of them so far, and soon even more.

Fact is, he has started to tire of Julia. She has become increasingly irrational, taken far too many risks. Has also angered him by devoting excessive time and attention to others. First to MM, and now Martin Hill.

These are unwelcome feelings, human feelings, that aren't becoming to someone like him.

He plans to let Julia have her way with Martin Hill—if he survives, that is—mainly to keep his promise. Then it will be high time to add her to the collection, too. Give himself a little peace and quiet.

In the meantime, he plans to make the most of Leonore Asker.

She has followed the ceiling lights around the corner to the hospital wing. She isn't using the flashlight on her phone, only the faint light of its screen. Probably to save battery.

This makes his advantage even greater.

He slowly starts moving in her direction. His revolver is itching against his hip, but for now it can stay in its holster.

For she can't see him. He is invisible.

ASKER

She has followed the dim red ceiling lights through the darkness. After a while she was met by a familiar scent, the sort of scent you never forget once you have smelled it.

The scent of death.

She has found her way farther down the corridor, into his most hallowed room.

The place he wanted her to see. The things he wanted her to see.

His catches.

She doesn't turn on her phone's flashlight until the door has shut behind her.

Keeps one eye closed so that it doesn't readjust to the light.

This also makes the sight inside the room easier to take.

Four beds, with as many full body bags.

The bags bear the seal of the Swedish Armed Forces, so he presumably found them here in the base. Sheathed his victims in black plastic and let nature run its course, which is clear from the yeasty smell.

The two bags farthest to the left are the flattest, which means they have been there the longest. The fugitives in the old Volvo.

The contents of the third bag are slightly greater in volume. The hitchhiker with the headphones.

Which means the fourth in all likelihood contains Hill's friend Tor Nilsson, who has lain here less than a year.

On a fifth bunk, an empty bag awaits Smilla Holst.

Or perhaps even Martin Hill.

In any case, it is an enormous relief not to find either of them here.

Part of her wants nothing more than to turn on every light and start kicking down doors to find them. Make sure that Martin is still alive, without a thought to the risks.

But, as with Prepper Per, that would be the wrong tactic. A sure-fire way to lose this duel. Instead she must be patient, crafty.

She has only minutes, if that, until the Mountain King will be on her.

She has already sensed him in the darkness.

Knows that he has seen the faint light of her screen. Seen her groping her way along the corridor, like helpless prey.

He thinks he is invisible. That he has the upper hand.

So she must prepare herself.

She must set a trap.

THE MOUNTAIN KING

He gives her five minutes in there.

Five minutes to realize his greatness.

Understand who he really is.

Someone who outwardly resembles a person.

But is in actual fact a monster.

And once she knows that, it will be time to make her his.

To own her.

He turns out the dim lights that have guided her to the right place. Moves soundlessly and effortlessly through the corridor in spite of the total absence of light, knows every inch of this mountain like the back of his hand. Would probably manage even without night vision.

He knows that there is a side entrance to the infirmary through one of the other rooms, but bides his time.

Tries to draw out this moment as long as he can.

Enjoy all its wonderful nuances.

He cautiously cracks the side entrance to the infirmary.

Sweeps his night-vision gaze around the room. The darkness is so compact that all he sees are grainy greens. But he doesn't need to see all that much. He knows this room inside out, too.

His four prizes on the beds, the fifth spot waiting for the next.

It is just as he expected.

He spots her silhouette over by the main door. She has hidden behind an overturned table with her back to him. Has her firearm pointed at the door to the corridor while silently waiting for him in the darkness. Acting like the hunter, when she is in fact the prey.

He can't help but admire her.

Leonore Asker.

Now she is his.

He owns her.

Which leaves only the final act. He cautiously pulls his revolver from its holster and turns on the infrared light on his night-vision goggles.

Moves slowly toward her back.

But something is wrong, he realizes when he is halfway there.

The infrared light should make her silhouette light. Instead it remains green and grainy. What's more, she isn't moving.

He creeps closer.

Soundlessly, invisible.

The figure behind the table isn't Leo Asker, but one of his prizes.

The graffiti artist he picked up from the disused factory last winter.

The half-rotted corpse is propped up against the table with the help of two chairs.

A smart trap, one that he was oh so close to stepping into.

As soon as he fired the weapon at the dead body, he would have no longer been invisible. She would have jumped out of her hiding place to confront him.

Just as he thought. Leonore Asker is something quite special.

Someone who understands him.

The thought makes his heart pound all the harder.

So where is her hiding place? Where is she waiting, quietly and patiently, for him to reveal himself?

He casts his night-vision goggles around the room. Immediately sees what is wrong.

Despite the body by the door, there are still four body bags on the bunks.

They are made of thick plastic, and don't let out much heat that can be picked up by his infrared light. Still, one of them is lit more than the others. Contains a warm, living body.

For one brief moment he considers saying something. Explaining to her that yes, she is smart, but that he outwitted her nonetheless.

That their little game is over and that he is the victor.

But that would be an unnecessary risk.

He raises his revolver. Aims carefully.

For a second he feels almost a little sad.

Adieu, Leonore Asker.

He squeezes three deafeningly heavy revolver shots at the middle of the body bag.

Expects a short shudder, then stillness.

Instead the heavy bullets rip through the ageing plastic, releasing a sharp stream of light that dazzles him through his night-vision goggles, forcing him to tear them off.

Suddenly he is neither soundless nor invisible.

Only confused.

He blinks in shock at the bright light, trying to understand where it is coming from.

It is a cellphone, propped up by a few old pillows, with the flashlight turned on.

The glare of the light casts long shadows across the room, where the sound of the shots is still echoing off the walls.

And for the first time in many years he is afraid.

His heart is bolting in terror, and he knows that there is only one possible hiding place left. The little office at the back, where a more patient hunter than he is awaiting her prey.

Has filled her prey with hubris. Lured it into a trap.

He spins around. Leonore Asker is standing in the office doorway, her pistol aimed at his face.

For one frozen millisecond their eyes meet, and in her heterochrome gaze he sees what choice he has.

To drop his weapon and give up.

Or go for it.

It makes no difference to her. She is the hunter, he the defeated prey.

So he chooses to go for it.

Giving up is something that humans do.

He roars into the air like the monster he is.

Raises his revolver.

ASKER

Asker fires off two bullets at the Mountain King, straight at his chest. Hits Daniel Nygård long before he can raise his heavy revolver, sending him staggering back toward the wall.

The shots echo through the infirmary, followed by the sounds of empty cartridges on concrete and the thud of a heavy body slamming into the floor.

She picks up her phone and lights up his face.

Nygård is still alive, lies slumped with his head against the wall.

His eyes are wide in terror and disbelief.

His mouth moves slightly.

She crouches down. From his chest comes a nasty wet rattle.

The bullets have gone straight through him. Punctured his lungs, heart, and arteries, as a red pool expands across the floor below him.

There is no way that he can be saved, not even had she wanted to.

"Where's Martin Hill?" she says quietly.

Nygård draws back his upper lip, exposing his teeth, as though he intends to bite her.

She doesn't move. Just stares him straight in the eye with her two-tone gaze.

Nygård shuts his mouth again. Coughs a few times. With what looks like a great effort he raises his hand and points in one direction, then collapses with a wheeze.

When he dies, Asker is already out of the room.

She finds Hill at the bottom of the ventilation shaft. He is hunched against a wall, his face gray, his trouser leg bloody, and for a few seconds she thinks that she is too late. An ice-cold chasm opens up within her, and to her own surprise she is on the verge of tears.

But then his eyelids flutter in the flashlight beam, and she realizes that there is still a faint flicker of life left somewhere deep inside.

And that she must keep it alive at all costs.

She takes his hand.

Whispers in his ear.

"Help is on the way, Martin," she says. "But you have to stay awake. Now listen carefully, because I've never told anyone what I'm about to say now."

THREE DAYS LATER

HILL

Hill wakes up in a hospital bed. Cloudy memories echo through his head of blue lights, voices shouting, the rumble of a helicopter. Leo sitting next to him, squeezing his hand. Whispering a story right into his ear.

The story of a sixteen-year-old girl running through a forest for her life. Running from a madman who can't fathom letting her go. Letting her grow up.

A story so tense and so raw that he simply has to cling on until its sorry end. Until the explosion that was intended to bind the girl and man forever in death, but which instead set her free.

And even in the state he is in, he realizes that Leo has entrusted him with something.

A fragile gift that comes with great responsibility.

But there is something else, beyond the story itself.

It is the way she told it. As though every word she whispered in his ear were a burden releasing stone by stone, from her shoulders.

Freeing her for a second time.

Perhaps that is why he managed to cling on.

In order to share that freedom with her.

He fidgets uncomfortably. His body feels incredibly weak, and his head hurts.

There is someone in a chair at his bedside. He can tell who it is by her faint snores.

"Sofie," he croaks. Swallows and tries again. But she is already awake.

Sofie rubs her eyes, gives a sideways smile.

"Sleep well?"

"So-so," he mutters. "There was a bit of a racket out there for a while."

"True, but it's starting to settle now."

"Did Smilla make it?" he asks, concerned.

Sofie nods.

"She and her parents want to meet you as soon as you feel up to it. The flowers there are from them."

She points at an enormous bouquet of flowers by his bedside table.

"They found Tor in the mountain," she says calmly. "Dead for months."

"Oh, Sofie, I'm so sorry."

"Thanks." She clears her throat. "I suppose in a way I'd already come to terms with the fact that we'd lost him. But now that we know what happened, I can at least start mourning him properly."

Sofie gives a sad smile.

He waits for a few seconds before asking the question that has been burning inside him since he woke up.

"And Leo?"

"I'm here."

She is standing in the doorway. Has tilted her head to one side in that way she does when she finds someone a little extra. Her two-toned eyes flit between him and Sofie.

Hill is struck by an intense urge to explain who Sofie is. That their relationship isn't really a relationship.

But he quickly realizes that is an exceptionally bad idea.

"So what's happening?" he says instead. "With everything."

Asker shrugs.

"The Mountain King is dead. Mya, or Julia Collin, rather, is in intensive care. Hellman saved Smilla. He's the press's sweetheart. The commissioner has named him the new chief of Serious Crime now that Rodic is moving on."

Hill's face clouds over.

"And you?"

She shrugs. Doesn't look at all as disappointed as he expected.

"The official version is that I was working under Hellman's command. The alternative would have been a long internal inquiry that was guaranteed to find me guilty of multiple instances of misconduct."

She shrugs.

"Which isn't actually too far from the truth."

Hill struggles to stay calm.

"So Hellman gets the glory of nabbing a serial killer and you get . . . what?"

"We'll see. The commissioner and Hellman want to meet me this afternoon."

"So you'll at least get something out of all this?"

Asker gives him a long look, tilts her head to one side again.

"Oh yes," she says, an unexpected warmth in her voice. "But I won't disturb the two of you anymore. I've got another visit to make. Get well soon!"

"Leo!"

She stops in the doorway.

"Thank you," he says.

"Thank *you*," she says with a slanting little smile.

"She seems nice," Sofie says once Asker has gone. "You said you were childhood friends, right?"

"Yes." Hill nods. "Something like that."

ASKER

Bengt Sandgren has been moved from intensive care to a normal hospital room. The tubes are gone, and some of the color is back in his face.

He can't speak yet; according to the doctor his throat needs time to heal from the intubation. But when Asker enters the room, he is awake. Nods faintly when she introduces herself and explains why she is there.

"The Mountain King," she says. "You cracked it. Or . . . we did it together, you could say. But I couldn't have done it without you. So I just wanted to give you this."

She walks over to his bed. Puts her hand in her pocket and pulls out a little white plastic figure.

It is unpainted, lacking in facial features.

Looks like a person, but isn't.

She takes his hand, places the figure in his palm, and gently closes his fingers around it.

Then leaves the room in silence.

It might just be her imagination. But for a brief moment she could swear she hears Sandgren chuckle.

The police commissioner's window has a view far out over Malmö's rooftops. The weather is clear, the sky over the Öresund strait a crisp autumn blue. A few seagulls soar in the wind. Their cries are heard even from the office.

". . . a token of our appreciation, Detective Inspector Asker," says the commissioner, a stiff man in late middle age. "Jonas, if you would explain . . ."

The commissioner turns to Hellman, who is sitting in the armchair next to hers.

"Well, Leo," he begins. Appears to be making an effort to seem friendly. "I suppose it's no secret that you and I have had our differences. But you are a very capable detective, and I would very much like to see you return to Serious Crime and your position as head of section."

He squeezes out a smile, which must take quite the effort.

"I believe that together we could develop this department even further. Make it even sharper."

Asker tilts her head to one side. Hellman does his best to look her in the eye, but doesn't quite succeed. Something is getting in the way, cramping his otherwise smug style.

It takes her a few seconds to identify it.

Shame. Jonas Hellman is ashamed.

He knows who really cracked the case. Which of them was right.

And that knowledge torments him.

"And what's the alternative?" she asks.

The commissioner and Hellman look at each other in shock.

"Uh . . ." The commissioner clears his throat. "I suppose that would be for you to stay in the Resources Unit until further notice. But surely you wouldn't want that?"

A few minutes later she is standing in the elevator. The camera in the ceiling stares at her blankly, as usual.

"Level minus one," comes the voice, with a hint of hesitation. As though unsure whether she really means to get off here, or just happened to hit the wrong button.

Virgilsson's door is open. Classical music is streaming from the radio.

The little man is sitting at his desk.

"Hi, Leo!" he says in greeting. "I heard you stopped in to see Bengt Sandgren at the hospital. How is he doing?"

"Better," she replies.

"I see." Virgilsson raises his eyebrows questioningly. "Do you know anything about when he's returning?"

"He isn't."

"Isn't?" Virgilsson's eyebrows hit the roof.

"No, Bengt's going to take early retirement as soon as he's discharged."

"Can he really afford to?"

"Oh yes, the commissioner gave him a generous offer."

Out of the corner of her eye she sees that Rosen's door, which was previously just cracked, is now half-open.

"So who'll be taking the helm down here?" Virgilsson asks. "After all, your placement was only . . . temporary."

Asker pulls a little frown.

"Not anymore," she says. "From now on I'm the permanent chief of the Department of Orphaned Cases and Lost Souls."

"I see," Virgilsson says again. His face is neither pleased nor displeased.

"I assume you'll let the others know," she says. "That and the fact that we're getting two new cars at the end of the week. And a decent coffee machine."

"Well how about that. What news you come bearing." The little man gives her a look of surprise. "Oh yes, of course I shall inform the others. But as it happens there was one thing I meant to ask you."

"Yes?"

"Well, I noticed that a bunch of keys was missing from my desk. Would you happen to know anything about that?"

Asker shakes her head slowly.

"No, sorry!"

She points at the wall opposite his desk, where an oil painting hangs depicting yachts at sea.

"Nice painting. A Liljefors, no? So you managed to get the commissioner to sign it off, after all?"

"Uh, yes. As it happens," he says. Clears his throat self-consciously. "Well, let me be the first to welcome you here—for real, I mean. I look forward to our continued collaboration, Detective Inspector Asker."

"Thanks," she says.

She turns her back on him and walks briskly toward her office.

Mainly so he won't see the smile on her face.

She takes a seat in Sandgren's creaky office chair. The room is still full of files, and the atrium outside is as dingy as ever.

Still, something has changed.

The office somehow doesn't feel quite so depressing as before. And her new role and colleagues are, given their feats of the past few days, perhaps not as hopeless as she originally thought.

They might even offer some interesting opportunities.

No one has any idea what we're doing down here in Resources. The bosses upstairs couldn't care less what we're working on or what rules we're following, so long as we keep a low profile and don't attract attention, as Sandgren supposedly said.

She thinks of Martin Hill again. Has often done so of late.

The relief of finally telling him what happened that summer night so long ago.

The sense of freedom.

Her thoughts are interrupted by the jangle of her office phone.

"Leo Asker," she answers, since from now on this is both her extension and her office.

Silence on the line. All that is heard is a faint scraping sound.

And then, out of nowhere, that feeling is back.

The same feeling she woke up with just over a week ago.

A sense of foreboding, of looming danger. Of a glaring, dazzling threat steaming straight toward her.

"Hello, Leo," says a deep, rasping voice that she hasn't heard in fifteen years. "It's your father."

ACKNOWLEDGMENTS

A special thanks to Emily Bestler and the team at Emily Bestler Books for this US edition.

Turn the page for an exclusive look at the
next thriller in The Leo Asker Series,

THE GLASS MAN

WINTER 2019

"What the hell was that?"

Something scrapes ominously against the bottom of the rowboat, and Elis starts to splash with the oars.

He and Nick have been rowing for almost half an hour, in more or less pitch darkness, and the sudden noise scares him.

"Shit! Did it make a hole?" he gasps, once he has managed to back up the rowboat a few feet in the black waters of the lake. His breaths rise like plumes of steam from his mouth before being consumed by the cold night air.

"No," says Nick, who is sitting at the bow. "It takes a lot to sink a plastic tub like this."

He raises his binoculars again and peers into the darkness before them.

Elis isn't satisfied with that answer.

"I told you we should have brought life jackets," he hisses. "It's the middle of winter, the water's ice-cold. There's no way we can swim back."

He points toward the stern of the boat. Far off in the darkness by the water's edge, the lights of the boy scouts' cabin where they stole the rowboat are still visible. It is one of few sources of light in the wooded hills around the lake.

"Shall we go back? Try in daylight instead?"

Just as Elis says the words the cloud cover breaks. The full moon peers out, transforming the lake's black waters into liquid glass.

"Look," Nick says excitedly. "We're nearly there. I can see the head frame and observatory."

He points at the island that looms beyond the bow. A bank of mist hovers at its shore, but the faint moonlight picks out a tall tower with a domed top just above the treetops.

Elis gives a shudder. It is probably caused by the chill in the damp air, but he can't be completely sure. A bad feeling has stalked him ever since they pushed off from the jetty at the boy scouts' cabin.

He casts a glance toward the mainland.

It's far away, all too far.

He pulls his hat up a little, wipes his forehead with his jacket sleeve. Both of them are dressed in black, with gloves, boots, and tightly rolled-up balaclavas.

Their *urbex uniforms*, as they call them.

Nick lowers the binoculars and checks his watch.

"It's almost midnight. Veer left and row along the shore, and I'll keep an eye out for more rocks," he instructs Elis. "The dock should be on the southern side."

Elis reluctantly starts to row again. The creak of the oarlocks melts into the lapping of the water.

As they round the island more details emerge from the mist. The creeping spruces along the shoreline are perched upon a spiky carpet of sharp stones that extends out into the lake, the largest crags of which rise up like the menacing teeth of beasts of prey, just yards from the boat's plastic hull.

Elis rows cautiously, only lets the stone teeth out of his sight to cast the odd glance back at the light of the boy scouts' cabin.

Nick seems to realize that he needs to lighten the mood.

"Do you think those two UFO nuts who gave us the map watch alien porn at home?" he asks over his shoulder. "Dress up as Martians for a bit of roleplay?"

Elis can't help but smirk.

"Definitely," he says. "I still don't know how you persuaded them to help us."

"Oh, that was a piece of cake," Nick laughs. "I just convinced them I believe in the whole story too—old 'Space-case' Gunnar Irving and the flying saucer, the spaceman. Then I gave them Martin Hill's book and wrote *the truth is out there* in it. They practically peed themselves they were so excited."

Elis chuckles, and the tension lifts slightly.

"There's the dock," Nick says and points.

From out of the mists a cracked concrete jetty emerges. At its very end a dented sign hangs askew, only just legible in the moonlight.

"*Risk of collapse. No trespassing,*" says Nick. "Then we've come to the right place."

They moor the boat next to a rusty ladder, pull on their backpacks and climb out. Elis turns back to the mainland.

The southern shores of the lake are mostly swathed in forest and darkness, just like the north. But on a headland directly across the water stands a large, palatial building with subdued lighting along its façade.

"How far do you think it is to Astroholm?" Elis asks.

"A third of a mile, maybe," Nick replies. "Much closer than the scouts' cabin. But there's no need to worry, the Irving family aren't looking this way. They'll be too busy scouring the skies for flying saucers."

He does an overblown gesture up at the night sky, then turns and makes for dry land.

Elis hangs back for a few seconds. He shivers again, or shudders, he can't tell. The uneasy feeling doesn't seem to want to settle.

Where the jetty meets land there stands a ramshackle hut without a door. Nick stops, unfolds a hand-drawn map, and tries to orient himself in the mist and murky light.

"This way!" he says, then walks another thirty feet along the edge of the forest. "Here it is! The old mining road!"

Two almost completely overgrown wheel tracks carve a path between the spruce trees, hardly visible for all the undergrowth. Elis and Nick wait to turn on their headlamps until they are out of sight of the water.

The fog is thicker here in the forest, making the lamplight milky.

The forest floor is blanketed with moss and fern thickets, interrupted here and there by windfalls or subsidence holes. Crooked stone teeth jut up all around, just like in the water.

"Creepy," Elis mumbles to himself, without quite knowing why. He isn't usually afraid of the dark, but something about both the island and the forest makes his skin crawl.

Nick on the other hand seems completely unperturbed. He stops and shines his headlamp on a large boulder by the road. The rock is pale and grainy, with a faint sheen.

"Rhyolite," he says with satisfaction, patting the rock. "Boulder Isle is one of the few places in all of Scandinavia where this type of rock can be found. And look at that!"

Nick points at an engraving on the rock.

"*GUS 2009*," Elis reads.

"Göinge UFO Society," Nick sneers. "Even the name is corny. But at least now we know they were telling the truth."

Nick pulls out his multi-tool and unfolds a sharp screwdriver.

URBEX 2019, he carves.

"There, now we've proved that we got at least as far as them."

They go on, following the wheel tracks. The forest sprawl extends so far over the road that on several occasions they must part the branches to pass.

In one place the road has collapsed into a three-foot hollow.

"A cave-in," Nick says. "The whole island's like Swiss cheese. The tunnels are filled with water, they can buckle at any time. Drown us like those poor guys in 1965."

He laughs, but Elis doesn't find it quite as funny. The thought of those black waters beneath his feet makes his blood run cold.

After a few hundred yards a large shape appears on the edge of their lights. A tall, rust-flecked steel gate with pendulous lichen that dangles like giant cobwebs from its mesh.

Above the gate runs a metal arch with rusted lettering.

ASTROFIELD MINE.

Beneath it, on either side of the thick chain that secures the gate, hang two signs. The first is identical to the one down on the jetty.

Risk of collapse. No trespassing!

The other sign contains a single word.

DANGER!

Nick is already at the gate, testing the chain.

"It won't budge," he says. "And I'm not so keen on climbing this tetanus pile—are you?"

He sweeps his headlamp upward. The gate and fencing on either side must be almost fifteen feet tall. At the top is a Y-shaped bracket laden with rusty barbed wire.

"But thanks to our UFO buddies we have a back door."

Nick takes another look at the map and starts walking along the fence to their left.

Elis hesitates, his eyes still locked on the gate. He has seen his fair share of warning signs in the past and has never given them a second thought. But something about this one puts him on edge.

The rust, the font, the faded yellow color. Or maybe it's just the short message.

DANGER!

He gulps instinctively.

"What the hell are you waiting for?" Nick whispers over his shoulder. "Come on!"

Elis reluctantly tears his gaze from the sign and follows him.

Soon Nick stops by a large bush that has grown through the fence. He takes one last look at the map, crouches down and crawls into the bush.

"Here it is!" He pulls a few branches aside to reveal a small sluice that runs under the fence.

The sluice is shallow and dry, and they must first shove their backpacks under it before they can follow.

"Shit," Nick puffs once they are out of the bush on the other side, brushing the soil and dead leaves from their pants. "I'm surprised those UFO chubsters managed to get through that. Though I guess it was ten years ago, so maybe they were more mobile then."

Elis isn't listening. He is too busy sweeping his headlamp around anxiously. Despite his excitement, his anxiety won't let up.

The area within the fence is populated by a different kind of vegetation. Instead of dense spruce trees, the land is scattered with self-seeded birches whose trunks have a ghostly white shimmer. In the mist beyond the birches, the mine buildings loom like big, oppressive shadows.

"Finally," Nick says excitedly. "Are you ready to travel back to 1965?"

Elis doesn't respond.

As they approach the buildings the grass underfoot increasingly gives way to bare patches of concrete and crushed stone. Eventually a yard opens up before them, flanked by two forbidding buildings.

The building on the right is twice as large as its counterpart, its gable roof and walls made of rusty corrugated sheet metal. Beneath its eaves runs a row of squat, horizontal factory windows.

Nick points his headlamp toward them.

"See, the windows are intact. And no graffiti either."

Elis knows that this is good news: it means that few—if any—others have set foot here in a very long time. Even so, he struggles to muster the right level of enthusiasm. They are currently exploring a deserted island, in the middle of a dark and icy lake, and no one knows they are here. Not to mention the fact that the whole island has been mined by waterlogged tunnels that could collapse at any second.

He checks his cellphone. Its lonely, flickering signal bar does nothing to improve his mood.

"Lousy signal, right?" says Nick. "Those UFO nuts had a theory that it might be something to do with alien interference on the radio waves. Their eyes got all twinkly just talking about it. But I asked a friend who works at one of the phone companies, and he said it's just that the lake's at the bottom of a deep crater, so it's difficult for phone signals to reach all the way down here. So much for the fucking *X Files*."

He starts walking along the factory wall. Elis stuffs his phone away and follows suit.

The moon peeps out again, and from out of the mist and darkness on the far end of the yard he sees a tall and gloomy concrete tower that soars up toward the sky.

The tower must be at least fifty feet tall. Its sides are open, allowing them to see straight through its three-story concrete frame.

"The head frame," says Nick, sweeping his flashlight over the gloomy construction. "It's where they used to hoist the minecarts up from the mine. And up there on the roof . . ."

On the flat roof of the tower, next to the hoist wheel, the dark dome they glimpsed from the water is visible once again.

"Bernhard Irving's observatory," Elis mumbles. Finally the right sense of excitement sets in, dispelling all the unease.

"Exactly," Nick says with a smile. "The spot where the giant, red-eyed creature landed."

Their footsteps crunch as they draw closer, and when Elis shines his headlamp down at the ground, he discovers that the crushed stone is mixed with shards of black glass.

Nick steps in under the head frame and takes a closer look.

"Solid stuff," he says, illuminating the six concrete columns on which the tower rests. "This'll still be standing in another hundred years."

He stops beside a moss-topped slab on the ground.

"And below that's the mineshaft. The trapdoor to the underworld."

Elis simply hums in reply, too busy searching for a way up the tower. The next story must be around twenty-five feet off the ground. A steel staircase zigzags down the left-hand side of the tower, but it ends abruptly at the second floor.

"The stairs have been cut," he says. "Just like the UFO flunkeys said."

"Good thing a cut staircase won't stop us," says Nick, giving Elis's backpack a pat. "But before we get out the rope, I have another idea. Look!"

He points his headlamp upward. A sloping footbridge links the third story of the tower to the factory building, where it meets a dormer with a wooden hatch.

"That must be where they rolled the minecarts once they'd been hoisted up. The stone crusher must be inside there, and maybe even some stairs that haven't been demolished. Much easier than hanging from a fucking rope, wouldn't you say?"

Elis can only agree. He is a good thirty pounds heavier than Nick, so is happy to avoid climbing where he can.

The door to the factory building is shut and locked. But when Elis gives the handle a tug the doorframe creaks alarmingly. They look at each other.

Nick takes off his backpack and pulls out a crowbar. It's against the rules, they both know that. Urban explorers must never force entry. But this is a special case. A once-in-a-lifetime event.

The door gives way almost immediately, flying open with a short, sharp clap as soon as Nick puts a little weight behind the crowbar.

Inside they find a vast, dark industrial hall that stinks of stone dust, oil and bird shit.

In the middle of the hall stands a large crusher that reaches almost all the way to the ceiling. A narrow staircase right beside it leads down to a closed door. Under normal circumstances that is where they would begin: go as far down into the building's underbelly as possible, to then methodically work their way up.

But tonight, the normal rules don't apply.

They turn their headlamps up toward the ceiling. Up there, supported by wooden posts, runs the footbridge they saw from the outside.

"Bingo!" Nick shines his lamp at a wooden staircase just below the wooden hatch.

A sudden noise makes them jump. Something takes flight from the top of the stairs, casts itself into the hall on flapping wings before disappearing into the darkness.

"Pigeons," Elis sighs in relief. "They get us every fucking time."

"Speak for yourself," Nick sneers. "You seem jumpier than usual tonight. Are you scared of aliens with glowing eyes?"

"Get lost," Elis mutters.

Nick climbs the creaking staircase with Elis at his heels.

The wooden hatch up in the dormer proves easy to open. The footbridge to the tower turns out to be no footbridge at all, but a fifteen-foot-long section of narrow-gauge rail track that inclines quite steeply in the direction of the tower. Between the two tracks run metal crossbars that give the whole construction the appearance of a crude ladder.

Nick places a tentative foot on the first crossbar, then bends forward, takes one track in each hand and starts to climb. Elis watches his lithe movements with envy.

"Easy peasy!" says Nick once he has reached the tower. "Your turn!"

Elis copies Nick's climbing technique, trying not to look down. Not that he's afraid of heights, but the feeling of clambering across a sixty-year-old metal construction is unsettling enough without knowing exactly how far he risks falling. Especially when the ground beneath him is a mix of rock and shattered glass. Just as he reaches the tower, the metal emits a crack that echoes between the buildings like a whip, making his heart pound a few frenzied double-beats.

Elis wipes away the sweat that has beaded on his forehead in spite of the cold. They are now on the tower's third and upper story. As expected, the rails continue to a large hole in the middle of the floor, where the cage would have been hoisted up, loaded with the full minecarts.

Nick has already rounded the hole and made his way to the steel staircase outside. Elis follows him. They are fairly high up now, thirty-five feet at least.

Above them the staircase zigzags up toward the roof. Nick's excited footsteps make the steel grating tremble. Elis hurries to keep up with him.

Upon reaching the top, they walk to the middle of the roof. To their right hangs the rusty old hoist wheel, while to their left the dark dome looms large.

"Bernhard's observatory." Nick's tone of voice is almost reverent.

"No wonder he had it built up here," says Elis, pointing over the treetops. "You can see the whole lake."

They are now above the bank of mist that has spread across the black waters. Beyond the lake the forest-lined hills rise up, equally high and steep in every direction.

"It's like standing in the middle of a funnel. And just look up! Wow!"

Through the gaps in the clouds they glimpse flashes of the full moon and the star-filled sky. From this vantage point the celestial bodies look brighter, more luminous.

"All the light pollution is blocked by the edges of the crater," says Nick. "Even the lights at Astroholm Manor are dimmed."

Elis turns to follow his gaze. The estate across the water is clearly visible, but its outdoor lighting is unusually sparing for a building of its size. He looks back at the observatory.

"Fucking hell, what a place."

"I told you it'd be worth it." Nick gives him a clap on the back. "Come on, let's see what it's like inside."

The lower section of the observatory is made of concrete, while the dome itself is topped with flaking, rust-flecked sheet metal. Before them stands a normal door.

Nick slips the crowbar into the gap in the door, as close to the lock as possible. The door creaks but doesn't give way. He puts his foot up against the wall and tries a second time, but the result is the same.

"Wait, let me try," says Elis. He puts his foot against the wall, just as Nick did, and leans back, pulling against the crowbar with all his weight. The door flies open with a muffled crack, and he falls backward.

By the time he has scrambled to his feet, Nick is already in the observatory.

"Fucking hell!" he cries. "Get a load of this!"

The inside of the dome is made of wood painted black. A platform on the floor reveals where the telescope once stood.

But that isn't what has attracted Nick's attention. Around almost the entire circumference of the dome runs a shelf brimming with strange objects: books, yellowing magazines, random coffee mugs; dark glass jars with some sort of cloudy liquid inside.

In a much creepier section of the shelf, a number of plastic heads of varying sizes are lined up on display: dolls, action figures, even the head of a mannequin. Their eye sockets gape emptily as they stare blindly out into the dark room. The back of Elis's neck starts to tingle.

"Check this out!"

Nick shines his headlamp at the ceiling.

Only now does Elis see that there are objects affixed to the inside of the dome.

Blue, brown, big, small.

Paper, plastic, glass. Cut from newspapers and magazines, scooped from toys and dolls' heads.

The tingle turns to a shudder.

The ceiling is full of eyes.

Hundreds of eyes.

"What the fuck is this . . . ?" Nick asks.

Elis doesn't reply. Another feeling has started to take root within him. It grows with every breath he takes, intensified by the eyes observing them from up above.

"Look at this."

Nick lights up a green toy alien with plumose antennae on its head. He flicks it with his finger, and the antennae start to sway.

"Shall we take it back to the UFO nuts as a thanks for the help?"

"Don't touch it," says Elis.

Nick laughs.

"Why the hell not?"

Elis has no good reply. But the feeling he has is only getting stronger.

Nick takes his camera out of his backpack and starts snapping off shots in quick succession.

The light of his bright flash bounces around the dome, reflecting off the glass, metal and plastic in the room. The eyes in the ceiling.

Flash.

Darkness.

Flash.

Darkness.

As though the eyes up in the ceiling were blinking.

Moving.

Watching them.

Elis's blood runs cold.

All of a sudden, his feeling turns to a conviction.

This is no forgotten place. No derelict ruin.

Someone owns this place. Someone who has collected important objects and carefully arranged them. Who has built themselves a small shrine inside the dome, one whose meaning Elis doesn't grasp. But he is certain of one thing.

Right now, in this place, he and Nick aren't urban explorers.

They are intruders.

He thinks back to the sign on the gate.

DANGER!

Then of the tall fence topped with barbed wire that angled both outward and in.

To all appearances intended to keep intruders out. But perhaps just as much to keep someone else inside.

"We have to go," he mumbles.

"Not until I've taken my pictures."

Nick goes on setting off flashes. He moves with such excitement that he knocks the shelf, sending one of the dark glass jars tumbling to the ground. It shatters with a loud crash.

Its contents, a liquid with a sharp alcoholic scent, spills out over the floor, carrying on it what appear to be small white balls.

Elis recoils in horror.

Eyeballs of different sizes scatter across the floor.

And they aren't from dolls or toys; these come from creatures that once lived.

Elis and Nick stand there for a few seconds, their headlamps bowed at the floor.

"What the fuuck . . ." says Nick. "Do you think those are animals' eyes?"

The excitement in his voice has disappeared, replaced by something wholly different. Uncertainty, fear.

"We have to get out of here," Elis says. "Right now."

This time Nick heeds his words.

The night sky outside is now almost entirely shrouded in cloud, the moonlight growing all the fainter. They run toward the staircase.

After a few steps a familiar sound rings out in the darkness.

The flap of wings echoing down in the factory building.

"The pigeons," says Nick. "Something must have frightened them."

They hurry to the edge of the tower, from where they can make out the open railway hatch.

The factory building is bathed in a red glow. The light moves quickly in their direction, then disappears out of sight, only to be replaced by the creak of the wooden staircase.

"Someone's coming," Nick hisses.

They turn out their headlamps and dash to the steel staircase.

"The rope," Elis says. "We can lower ourselves down from where the steps have been cut."

He races down the steps without waiting for a reply, pulling off his backpack to get out their rope and grappling hook.

The moonlight disappears completely, flooding the staircase in darkness. Elis almost misses the last step, but he grabs the railing just in time to stop himself from running straight into thin air.

He catches Nick, who is close on his heels, and gestures at him to be quiet.

The sound of groaning metal is clearly audible over their breaths.

Whip-like cracks that echo between the buildings. Someone is climbing the railway track. Someone much bigger and heavier than them.

"Hurry," Nick hisses.

Together they attach the grappling hook to the railing and sling their backpacks down. Elis grips the rope with both hands and rappels himself backward from the last step, down into the darkness. Above him he sees Nick's feet through the grating on the bottom step.

"Come on!" he whispers, but Nick doesn't move. "Come on, Nick," he repeats while lowering himself further. He feels a tug in the rope, a vibration that grows all the stronger. Heavy footsteps on the staircase.

"Nick!" he cries, but his friend appears to be frozen. He stands gazing up the staircase, as the steps come all the closer.

Elis inches his way down.

"Nick!"

He is silenced by the sight of a gigantic silhouette through the grating. It approaches slowly, a red glow hovering around its head.

Elis's heart stops. The creature is huge and black, and its eyes are red, just like in the legend. He gasps for breath.

The steps get closer.

Thud

Thud

Thud

The scream comes so unexpectedly that Elis almost wets himself, but it speeds his heart up again.

It is Nick who is screaming, howling in sheer terror.

He goes on screaming long after his lungs should be out of air.

Then suddenly the scream stops, replaced by a nasty crack.

Elis can see Nick's feet leave the step. His toes hover a few inches in the air, as though the creature has raised him up.

Something wet and warm splashes down through the metal grating. It lands on Elis's face, forcing him to blink.

It's blood.

Nick's blood.

When Elis opens his eyes he sees Nick's body fly down through the air, less than a foot away. A second later he hits the ground with a dull thud.

Elis looks up again.

The creature is staring down at him through the staircase. Its face is cloaked by darkness, and where its eyes should be he sees only two big, red orbs.

Elis is as though petrified.

The creature unfastens the grappling hook and lifts up the rope, apparently effortlessly. Holds Elis in the air for a few seconds, its red eyes fixed on him.

Then it drops the rope.

Lets him fall.

Elis lands heavily. His upper back hits a rock. The wind is knocked out of him, and he thinks he hears one of his ribs snap. But at least he hasn't landed on the shattered glass.

Nick is lying a few feet away. Elis crawls over to him and turns on his headlamp. Knows even before he has touched his soft body that his friend is dead.

Nick's face is white as chalk, his eyes bulging, and his half-severed tongue is dangling through his clenched jaws, covering his chin in blood.

Elis's stomach contracts, but he doesn't have time to puke.

Not if he wants to survive.

He can already hear footsteps up there, hear the creature lumbering up to the railway track to get back down to the factory. To find him and finish the job.

Elis scrambles to his feet, forces his legs to move. His ankles hurt, but to his surprise they carry him anyway.

His ribs feel the worse. Every breath is like a knife through his lungs. But his heart is pumping wildly, pressing the adrenaline through his body, and with that he can move in spite of the pain.

The light of his headlamp whips through the darkness as he races toward the fence. He hears the bang of the factory door being hurled open. Then footsteps over the crushed stone.

He doesn't look back, just sprints as fast as he can toward the bush. Leaps under it and crawls on all fours toward the sluice. Sharp thorns scratch at his face, tear at his knees and elbows.

His lamp finds the sluice. He presses his belly to the ground and starts wriggling under the fence.

Behind him he hears the sound of twigs snapping, and above that a faint growl, as though from an animal. Elis worms his way forward as fast as he can.

The sluice is way too narrow for the creature; he can make it.

He is almost out on the other side when a wire from the fence catches on his pants.

He rolls over onto his back and tries to prize himself free while tugging and pulling with his leg. The sharp wire digs through the fabric and into his skin.

The growl approaches, embodied in the form of a giant-like silhouette with glowing red eyes on the other side of the fence.

Elis's heart is bolting. He gives his leg one last jerk. The wire takes a clump of flesh and skin as it releases him, but Elis hardly feels it. He is through, the creature stuck on the other side.

He twists back onto his stomach and tries to scramble to his feet.

One foot finds purchase.

Just as he starts running, something grabs hold of his ankle.

Pulls him to the ground with such brute force that his headlamp flies off and lands out of reach.

Desperately he digs his fingers into the soft soil to hold on, tries to kick with his free foot.

Screams an agonizing scream.

But it's hopeless.

The creature drags him back under the fence.

Away from the light.

And into the darkness.